WATCHING FOR COMETS

Also by Jordon Greene

A Mark on My Soul

WATCHING FOR COMETS

JORDON GREENE

F/K TEEN

An imprint of Franklin/Kerr Press

Published by F/K Teen
An imprint of Franklin/Kerr Press
Kannapolis, North Carolina 28083
www.FranklinKerr.com

Edited by Christie Stratos
Cover art and design by Emir Orucevic
Interior design by Jordon Greene

"It heals to be free" poem used by permission.
Copyright © 2020 by Sabina Laura

Printed in the United States of America

FIRST EDITION

Hardcover ISBN 978-1-7354373-1-6
Paperback ISBN 978-1-7354373-0-9

Library of Congress Control Number: 2020917428

Fiction: Young Adult Contemporary
Fiction: Coming-of-Age
Fiction: LGBT/Gay

To Grace Fongemy
Without you, this book would
have never happened.

ACKNOWLEDGMENTS

I have so many people to thank for this book coming into existence, but above all I have to thank Grace Fongemy. Had it not been for you sitting down and discussing my (at the time) hole-ridden plot and brainstorming with me, this book literally would never have seen the light of day. I'm eternally grateful. Thanks, Grace!

I want to thank my mom, Kim Greene, and little sister, Kallie Greene (who you'll see more of soon), Katie Messick, Keean Sexton, David Kummer, Nicole Scott, Jeb Holt, Dominica Scudieri, Alex Blades, and Jennifer Upright in particular for their various parts in planning, writing, changing, and fine tuning this story into something real and meaningful. Thank you to Jeb Holt, Grant Turner, and Abby Breeggemann who entered my comet naming contest and are now immortalized as the comet's namesake in the story.

Christie Stratos stuck around for this book after editing my last, and I couldn't ask for a better editor. I mean, how many editors will debate which is the better looking Star Trek captain with you in their notes?

To my friends in our weekly Writer's Block authors group at the coffee shop, thank you. You all mean the world to me and have absolutely encouraged me over the past year to keep writing and telling stories. And as always, thanks to everyone at Editions – Coffee and Bookstore in Kannapolis, NC for dealing with me (and scaring me constantly) while I hang out and write. I love you all!

It hurts to let go

but it heals to be free.

\- Sabina Laura, *Moonflower*

TYLER
Tuesday, May 14

Life sucks. It fucking sucks.

That's what I tell myself over and over again while I stare at the empty pavement between the class of 2006's massive blue-gold painted rock and the open gate hailing entry to the student parking lot.

I'm waiting for Brayden, but I'm not waiting on him. Like, I can't really expect his dinged-up Nissan to come squealing around the corner. That'd be fucked.

He's dead.

I clench my fist around the steering wheel and grit my teeth.

"Why? Why?" I beat the steering wheel, trying to exorcise the anger in my chest.

Nothing works. Nothing. It just sits there balled up inside, this heavy, empty nothing, this black pit churning in the deepest chamber of my heart. I clamp my eyes closed to dam back a tear. I'm not crying. Not doing it, not today, not ever again.

I loosen my grip, let out a deep breath, and allow my arms to fall to my lap.

"Why?" I sigh again.

"Morning, bitch!"

"What the—" My body attempts a somersault in the upright belted position, and the back of my hand slaps the gear shifter with a loud thud. "Damn!" That hurt!

"Woah, Ty. Calm down." Kallie clutches her gut, her laughter muffled through the glass.

I could ki… No.

I could banish her to some massive party. That's it, that's the sinister thing to do to an introvert. One where everyone is up and dancing and moving around, and they *all* want to talk. Somewhere she'd be forced to interact with other *people*. But no, I won't. I'm not a monster, and it's not like I could make her anyway. Plus, I sort of need her. But I'll *never* tell her that.

"Kal." I swing my door open, pulling Brayden's green-and-gold UNC Charlotte hoodie taut around my stomach. It's the same one he gave me the week his acceptance letter came in the mail. Okay, he didn't technically give it to me. He let me wear it one time, and I never gave it back. Same thing.

It still smells like him.

"So, who's murder were you planning?" she asks.

I stifle the instinct to wince and turn to face her. She's pretty. Really pretty, actually. She's got this pale-skinned, stormy ocean gray-eyed, short—like five foot even short—dark-humored, I-wish-every-one-would-leave-me-alone sort of way about her. She's like e-girl with like a splash of VSCO, and oddly, it works.

But her greatest quality is that she gets me. She gets me like no one else. Brayden didn't even know me like Kallie. That's probably my fault, but whatever.

I give her my evil eye, which is not nearly up to par with hers. She shoots her own back with a timid half-grin. She's trying, and I love her for it.

"Only your murder. Actually, funny enough, it's always your murder," I tease as we mount the sidewalk and stop next to the massive painting of a blue-and-gold Indian warrior complete with headdress under the letters *WCHS* for West Caldwell High School.

The day hell came to earth, I made her promise not to treat me different, like everyone else does. The last thing I need is my BFF since I can literally remember—so like pre-pre-K—to start acting careful around fragile ol' me. I'm not a snowflake. I've been through hell, aka "conversion" therapy camp, and back before, plus I live with parents who don't get me, and I have to listen to Kallie's god-awful music all the time, and I've made it through each.

I know this is different, like really different. It's a whole other level of messed-the-hell-up. My boyfriend is dead. He's gone. But I don't need people looking at me like *that*.

I don't know half these people yet they're determined to look at me all deer-in-headlights like I'm about to fall apart, limb by limb, right here and now. You know the look, that I'm-not-sure-if-I-should-say-something-so-I'm-going-to-stare-awkwardly one. I hate it. So much!

Kallie's been my beacon of hope. Mom's been good too, but she and Dad will never really get it, and they didn't "approve" in the first place, so I don't talk to her about it. Hell, I barely talk to Kallie about it. But she treats me exactly the same as before.

She's been here for me since everything went to hell seven weeks and one day ago, the day my world literally fell apart, but she knows I'm okay. She knows I don't need all the sympathy and words. All the fake bullshit "it'll be okay" and "just be strong" sympathies. Well shit, Karen, thanks for the God-level wisdom.

"Ooh. So bitter, Tyler." She smirks.

I'd usually say something dark and snarky, but nothing hits.

I am bitter. It hits hard. Bitter at myself; bitter at Brayden for leaving; bitter at the world for taking him; bitter at my family for not accepting me; bitter at the assholes at that damned camp a few years ago; bitter at the bitch who wouldn't go at least the damn speed limit this morning; bitter at everything and anything. But what's changed?

She takes the cue and changes subjects.

"I can't wait for fourth period!" Her eyes lock on me in that anti-Kallie way, the one that beams excitement and smiles and shines rainbows. Fourth period, of course. It's her Forensics class, so this is normal. All it takes is a good serial killer or gruesome murder documentary and she's in. "We're watching *Catch Me If You Can*. You know, the one about the con-artist pilot."

She looks at me for a second like I'm supposed to know it. I purse my lips. It doesn't ring a bell.

"Seriously?"

"Seriously." I mimic her bitchy eyebrow raise and head twitch. I'm not sure if it's my mimicry or not knowing what *Catch Me If You Can* is that earns me the middle finger, but it does warm my heart a little.

"It's this movie about some dude, way back when, who was like a scam artist or something, I think." Her eyes wander upward in thought and her mouth hangs open for a moment. "You know, I'm not sure, but DiCaprio is in it, so who cares."

"Ah! Yes!" It all comes together. DiCaprio. That's all it took. But I'm still sort of confused. It doesn't sound like something they'd watch in Forensics or anything Kallie would be excited about. "Gotcha. So, like young, hot DiCaprio, or old, decent-looking DiCaprio?"

"Well first off, *rude!*" Kallie shimmies her head, something I can never get down, and I can't help but giggle a little. "DiCaprio's gorgeous, period. No question."

I wait. I know it's coming. She can't help but answer.

"Okay, fine. It's young, hot DiCaprio."

She gasps like it's exhausting to give in. This is why we'll never fall for the same guy. She typically likes older with either tons of muscles or dad bods, and I don't. It makes our guy talks interesting, but I can't right now. It still feels a little wrong to talk about guys, like it's too early.

"Good," is all I give her for her effort. I check my phone. The warning bell for first period is about to ring, so I start toward the glass entry doors.

"Well, I can't wait." She rolls her eyes at me and follows. But she stops as we pass the entrance, halting at the stairs. "Only problem is we have to watch it with this stupid machine that takes out all the *bad* words, because Jordan. So pissed. I don't hate him or anything, he's a little irritating with all his religious stuff, but can he not give us this?"

She's literally got me by the collar like I'm Jordan. I pull back, scared she might try to strangle or kiss me. She wouldn't. Well, on second thought, she would to get under my skin.

Jordan's not a bad guy, just sort of zealous. He does get on my nerves a bit, but maybe it's good he at least cares about something that much. I sure don't. Plus, it's not my class, so I don't have to worry about it.

"You'll live," I tell her and pry her hands from my t-shirt as the warning bell goes off. I give her a grin and put as much sarcasm in my voice as possible. "You can say fuck all on your own, Kal. I promise. He can't take that from you."

AIDAN

"You have to go!" Bryce hasn't stopped talking about the movie since we left the theater last night. "It's *the* best Marvel movie. No, no, no! It's *the* best movie of all time."

I roll my eyes. It's reflex with Bryce. Yeah, *Endgame* was amazing, *maybe* even epic, but the best movie of all time? Not sure about that. He just hasn't had the time to decompress after all three glorious hours of film yet. I think he's still hyped on all that caffeine he had too. He probably barely slept last night. It's a Bryce thing.

"Of all time, huh?" The are-you-on-crack look on Rhys's face is similar to mine, except his eyes are a lighter brown.

We're a diverse little group. You've got Bryce Gragg, the super pale, tall, maybe a little stereotypical, thick-rimmed glasses-wearing, nerdy white dude. Then there's Rhys Whitaker, the short, built-like-an-ox, country music-loving, varsity running-back black kid that makes Bryce look even whiter than he already is. Then there's me.

I'm what some of the school's rednecks probably consider the typical soccer-playing Mexican. I've heard worse. Plus, I'm actually Venezuelan, but I gave up correcting their asses a long time ago. Some say I still have an accent, but I don't hear it, and I'm pretty sure Bryce and Rhys have hung around long enough to miss it if it does exist. Now mi madre, yeah, you can tell she came from somewhere else, even if technically she was born in Hickory. Somehow, she managed to keep the accent from my abuelos and I didn't.

"He's a little wound up," I explain, raising my voice over the raucous auxiliary gym crowd. It's packed in here, always is in the morning. There are pockets of athletes and their girlfriends. There's us soccer boys. A few groups of both the boys' and girls' baseball teams, and some of the cheerleaders, at least the ones not in the football circles with their boyfriends. The biggest circle, obviously, is the football players led by the infamous Sean Addison and Christian Norwood. Neither of whom I'd call friends.

"Wouldn't have guessed." Rhys shrugs, and Bryce drops us a frown.

"You have to admit it was awesome." Bryce sounds desperate. His eyes plead with me. "Come on."

"I mean, yeah, it was great. The fight scenes, wow. But isn't it a little soon to call it the greatest *of all time*?" I propose, trying to keep focused on the conversation instead of the image in the back of my mind. "Maybe it needs a few more watches before we go there."

"Eh! Those fight scenes, yes!" And he starts up again. "God, when Captain Fucking America picked up Mjölnir at—"

"Woah!" I throw my hand over Bryce's over-talkative mouth. "Spoiler much?"

"Ah, yeah…" He slinks against the blue padded wall. "You have to see it, Rhys. I'm not sure how much longer I can keep all this shit to myself. Do you even know what Mjölnir is?"

"Duh." Rhys's lips purse into this weird skewed thing. "Thor's hammer. But you could have just said *Thor's hammer*. You know, like a normal person."

"But it's—"

"*Normal* person," I re-emphasize Rhys's point, cutting him off before he goes into a diatribe.

"Brayden would have understood," he comes back.

I don't say anything. I'm trying not to lock up instead.

Brayden. Yeah. Brayden would have understood. Thor was his favorite. He knew it all, inside and out. I think he liked him so much because he came from a different realm, maybe not the stars, but still. It's close to all the astronomy stuff he loved.

God do I miss him.

There are BFFs and then there was Brayden. We pretty much did everything together since second grade when he took my Batman pencil bag. He straight swiped it off my desk a few weeks after school started. I didn't realize he'd taken it at first. But even back then he was too good a guy to do that. I remember him coming back up to my desk, all scared and skittish, and giving it back. All he said was something like *I like Thor better* before running off. That much never changed, and neither did our disagreement on the coolest superhero. But somehow, we became inseparable after that.

It's still so hard to believe he's gone. I hate thinking about it, but it's so damn hard not to. I mean, he's not here. He should be here.

"So…" Rhys breaks the silence I hadn't noticed crept up.

"Sorry." I shoot my eyes to the floor and then back up, trying to rezone myself, and act like my eyes aren't getting wet.

"Sorry, A, I shouldn't have." Bryce shuffles.

I don't remember when people started calling me A, but it just sort of happened and it stuck years ago. Sometimes it sounds weird, but we just go with it.

"It's okay," I whisper.

None of them knew Brayden like I did. Hell, we didn't even know Bryce until last year. His dad's a Marine—well he was, or is, I don't know. It's all so confusing with that once a Marine, always a Marine stuff. The point is he lived near Cherry Point while his dad was enlisted but moved back to be closer to family. So Bryce transferred in last year a few weeks into my junior year and his sophomore. We adopted him quickly once we met on the soccer team. His nerdy weirdness is just close enough to my awkward weirdness to click. Rhys I've known a little longer. He's been at West as long as we have, and Brayden and I played soccer with him since freshman year. He's sort of off and on, but he's a good one.

The bell saves us from having to say more.

"I'll catch you at lunch, Bryce." I throw up a peace sign. I don't know why, it's just always been my thing. "Later, Rhys."

Their muffled *see ya later*s catch me as I mount the stairs. *Just breathe, Aidan, just breathe.* It's been almost two months, but right now it feels like Brayden's funeral was yesterday. I can see it all, clear as a high-definition movie playing in my mind, but I push the memory back because I'm not breaking down in the middle of this torrent of moving bodies on the stairs.

Just move. I quicken my pace and jog up the steps. I accidently bump into some random girl on the way and apologize without stopping. There are so many faces, yet so many names I don't know. I've seen most of them day in and day out for years, but I still don't know them. Maybe that's best, at least it won't hurt to lose them. I've only got a few more weeks until graduation, so it's a good thing.

I take the switchback to the next set of stairs. Out of the corner of my vision, my eyes catch something familiar. That hoodie, Brayden's hoodie. Well, Tyler's. I remember when Brayden got it. We'd gone down to Charlotte after we both got accepted and spent, like, two hours in the bookstore, roaming through all the cool stuff. We both came back with hoodies, bumper stickers, some t-shirts, and I even got some shot glasses. Mi madre wasn't too thrilled with the shot glasses, but eh. I managed to keep my hoodie, I don't have anyone to steal it. From how Brayden told it, he let Tyler wear his when it was really cold one day and just never asked for it back.

I want to say hey. I know he's hurting too, but we haven't really talked lately…well, for months. He sort of hates me.

TYLER

"You skipped Nazi lady's counseling again, didn't you?" Kallie clanks her tray on the table, earning her more than a few glances.

"Shh!" I wince.

Nazi lady is the junior class assistant principal and my counselor. In all fairness, she might be a little stern, but she's actually nice. She just has the supreme misfortune of having the last name Reich.

Kallie shrugs. "You did, didn't you?"

I sit down and immediately stuff a half-soggy fry in my mouth just to piss her off. She hates it when I don't answer right away, or I leave her text messages or Snaps on read for longer than like ten seconds.

So naturally, I make her wait.

"Really?"

"Of course I skipped it," I finally say.

At first, when *it* happened, they made me go to counseling every other day, but the past five weeks it's been once a week. I'm too fragile to handle it on my own, it would seem. But to hell with that, I'm good. I can handle anything this shitty life can throw at me. I don't need some adult patronizing me, and telling me how sorry they are for me, or how they understand.

'Cause no. You don't understand. You just don't.

"Figures." She nods. "That's, what, the second or third time? How many times until they come looking for you?"

I shrug. Honestly, I'm not sure. I skipped last week and the week before that, and I skipped a few early on too. The school keeps sending letters to my parents. I only know because I see the envelopes on the kitchen counter.

It's not like Mom or Dad are going to push me to go. They'd rather me see our pastor—the whole not wanting the "secular" influence from a public school counselor.

"Something like that. I just don't need anyone's sympathy. I'll have Mrs. Kropf next period to treat me like a little snowflake anyway." I can handle this shit. "All Mrs. Reich is going to do is say I'm *masking my emotions,* or *oh, that's good, keep talking it out.*"

"Well, you've got me. What more could you want? I mean, really. I'm awesome." Kallie puffs her chest.

I roll my eyes. It's time to change this conversation.

"So, movie night tomorrow? Or are you ditching me for work again like last week?" She did. She put her job above me. The nerve. I giggle inside a little. "Your job is really getting in the way of our social life."

"Us? A social life?" Kallie eyes me. "I don't think coming to my house and watching movies qualifies as a social life."

"Eh." My shoulders flinch.

Our "social life" consists almost exclusively of her, me, and Bray… I mean her and me. And the occasional forced interaction with others here at school, or with family, also usually forced.

"Well…" She leans back and squints.

Damn. Not a good sign.

"Really? Again?" I whine.

"Trina asked me to pick up Hanna's shift," Kallie explains. "Apparently she's got bronchitis."

"Shit." Just my luck.

That means two nights I have to find something else to do because I sure as hell ain't gonna sit at home and let my dad judge me. He doesn't say anything, but it's just the way he looks at me when I walk through the living room, or outside when he's feeding the chickens. Yes, we have three chickens; no, we don't have a farm.

"I'm the only person she could get to do it," Kallie says. "Maybe we can do movie night on Thursday. I don't work Thursday."

Do I work Thursday? Uh… No. I guess that'll work. I'll just have to see if Jacob can play *Overwatch* tonight instead.

"You're lucky I don't have to work, fool. We're still watching *Hill House*, right?" We've been hooked on *The Haunting of Hill House* since the first episode, but I always check. Plus, she's ditching me again tonight, so there's that too.

This show has been amazing. It's not your typical horror. Not just a bunch of brainless scares or gratuitous blood and guts, which I don't have a problem with at all, not one bit, but this, this is better. It's like this super tense, deep, mysterious, webbed drama that you can't stop watching.

"Duh, that show's creepy as hell," Kallie says. "What are we on, like episode four?"

"Sounds right." I shrug. "Netflix knows. Unless you watched some without me like some cheap street whore."

"Well first, I'm a classy whore, not a street whore," she corrects me with a prominent middle finger. "And no, I didn't. We good."

She's not a whore, I promise. If anything that would be me…well, not really…maybe. No. I've messed around with… The point is I'm not a whore.

"Well good then."

I don't know what I'd do without my best friend.

AIDAN
Tuesday, May 14

"See ya, Reed." I throw up a peace sign to my shift manager, who's literally one year my elder, and get the hell out of Food Lion.

Bagging groceries, restocking drink machines, and dealing with obnoxious people isn't my idea of fun, so the last four hours, yeah, not fun. And on top of all that, Kallie didn't work tonight, so I didn't have her here to make it at least half bearable.

I slide into my Mustang. It's older, with more nicks than I care to keep count of, but the flat black paint job makes them harder to see, and well, it goes fast. I steer onto the main road and gas it. The engine roars and my back slaps the seat. I need speed right now, and music, lots of loud, hard, *angry* music. I let off the gas and shuffle through my playlist until a good riff from Pantera comes on. The beat courses through my body and a little of the day's stress melts off my shoulders.

I have to get away. That's why I'm headed to Collettsville. I have to escape everything, even the city, if I can even call Lenoir a city. It's not exactly big, but it's huge compared to Collettsville. I'm talking no stoplights, one general store, and one elementary school, small. And that means it's quiet, and on a clear night you can see every single tiny star in the sky. I think that's why Brayden liked it so much.

I'm heading to the park. I need to walk and breathe in some clean country air. The old gang—Brayden, Bryce, Rhys, Tyler, and me—used to go out there all the time. But that feels like such a long time ago. I can't remember the last time we were all together voluntarily.

Every tree I pass on this old curvy road reminds me of it. We'd come out to the park and play soccer or tennis, sometimes badminton, and on the rare occasion American football. That was never a favorite of ours. We only played to get Rhys off our backs, and even then he'd fuss because we could never remember all the rules.

I take a left and there it is. Hard and Flossy Park, which apparently used to just be the Ruritan Park. So naturally we call it the Old Ruritan Park, because why in hell would we call it Hard and Flossy? Like, really?

I pull in and my stress kicks up a notch. Tyler's white convertible occupies the spot nearest the main baseball field.

"It's okay," I tell myself as I park. I exhale slowly and get out. He's not going to want to talk anyway, so why worry about it? Just walk and breathe.

Now it's in my head though, so I'm going to worry about it. What if he says something? But what? Chances are he'll just look at me weird and ignore me. That's what he does at school at least.

I shake off my anxiety and start down the cracked walking path. I've done this a lot lately. There's just something about taking a late-night stroll by myself. It's monumentally better than dealing with a panic attack sobbing in my bed, and mi madre isn't going to come barging in asking if I'm okay. It's peaceful, even with the single tear breaching my eye. Maybe it's something about all the games we played on these fields. Maybe it's just the way the air feels softer here. Or maybe it's because it reminds me of the nights I strolled down these same paths with Brayden when something was bugging him and we'd just talk, friend to friend.

I remember the time Brayden nearly took out Bryce's ankles playing soccer back in February. The ground was still cold and a little damp from a thunderstorm the night before, but we'd been determined to get out and play. Then there's the middle school baseball games we'd go to our freshman year at West just because we could. I think something about it made us feel older, back during that short-lived time when Brayden and I were dating. Yeah, we dated. It just wasn't for us though. We were better friends, so we kept it that way.

It feels good out here, even with clouds hanging over my mind. I take my eyes off the path and gaze up at the millions of brilliant tiny dots and sigh. He's up there somewhere. My best friend in all the world, he's up there, I know it. I wish he wasn't though. I wish he was here, alive, so I didn't have to feel like something's missing.

I know they say friends fall apart after high school, but Brayden and me? No, we were tight. We were going to the city together, we were going to play soccer at Charlotte and go to parties, probably get way too drunk, and struggle through classes, the whole college experience. But no… I wipe at my wet cheeks and swallow back the lump building in my throat.

I hear sobbing. For a moment I wonder how I missed my own crying, but it's not me. It's coming from up the path. I consider stopping and turning around, but then I remember. Tyler's here. Okay, maybe I *should* turn around. The last time we talked, he wasn't technically hateful, but it was clear he didn't like me around. I'm the last person he wants to find him crying. But what type of friend or person would I be if I turned around now? Ugh. Sometimes a big heart sucks so bad. Like why can't I be that guy that just says *fuck it* and leaves?

My feet are moving before I have time to make up my mind. I keep my steps quiet. I don't want to startle him, but I'm worried how he's going to react too. The fence lining the baseball field obscures my view as I approach, and the sobs get louder. It doesn't seem like he's trying to hide anything, I mean anyone could walk by, I'd think he knows that. I make the bend and there he is, Tyler, bent over one of the old prickly picnic tables with his head buried in his arms.

I stop. What do I say? Do I say anything? Maybe I should turn around. This is probably a real bad idea anyway. Yeah, really bad idea.

But my feet don't stop. Instead, I keep walking and trying to find the words to say.

"Tyler…" It's barely more than a whisper, but he hears me. I freeze in place.

He whips around, his hands immediately swatting at his cheeks and eyes.

"What—" But when his eyes catch *me*, he stops and his face goes cold. "What the hell do you want, Aidan?"

"I… Uh… I just heard, uh…crying." I wince, certain that's not what he wants to hear. "You okay?"

"Do I *look* okay?" Tyler throws his hands in the air. "Do I?"

"No…" I take a step back. I hate confrontation. I fight back the urge to cry, but not because he yelled at me, no. I can feel the stress and sadness inside me, the same stress I came here to let out, bubbling up. Please, no.

"Well?" His shoulders become stiff and unyielding.

"I…" But that's all I get out before the waterfall breaks the dam. I drop my eyes to the ground, like somehow that'll keep him from seeing me looking like a loser. The only time he's ever seen me cry was at the funeral, and I really wanted to keep it that way.

"What the…" I hear the words slip from Tyler's mouth, but he stops himself.

I want to throw a dose of his own meds back at him, but I don't. It's the wrong prescription. I know because I feel the same thing as I'm pretty sure he does right now.

"Are you okay?" he mumbles, but it isn't condescending.

I cough to dampen the sobs tightening my throat and shake my head.

"Brayden," I push out the name.

The look in his glassy eyes tells me he understands.

"Same." Tyler frowns. Another tear streams down his cheek and he has to push away an unruly strand of nearly black hair poking from beneath his beanie. It looks super black in the moonlight, but it's actually a rich dark brown.

"You want to talk about it?" I ask before thinking through what I just said. Do *I* want to talk about it? And with Tyler of all people? It's good though. He'll say no.

A long pause fills the space between us. Actually, I do sort of want to talk about it. And maybe it's selfish, but I don't want to for Tyler's sake—I want to for mine. I know he understands, even if it isn't in quite the same way. We both loved Brayden.

The silence is too much. I want to turn and walk away, to go anywhere, to my car, to the river just over the bank, to one of the old dirty baseball dugouts, or even one of the nasty bathrooms where I'm sure more than peeing takes place. Anywhere but standing here awkwardly waiting for a response to a question I shouldn't have asked.

"Sure." It reaches my ear as a whisper. Tyler's eyes scan the ground, like looking at me might scald his retinas.

"Oh." I'm not sure how to react. Sure? "Okay…yeah."

I stand in place a second too long and Tyler raises an eyebrow as if to say, "You coming?" I snap to and take a seat on the opposite side of the bench, careful not to slide across and receive the gift of a wooden splinter up my ass. It wouldn't be the first, we've all gotten them at one point or another. Seated, I survey the old tabletop, stained with all manners of junk, some probably less wholesome than others—

anything not to see Tyler's dampened cheeks. Sure, he doesn't care for me too much, but I hate seeing a friend like this.

"Why are you even here?" Tyler asks.

I'm not sure he intends it to sound mean, so I try not to take it that way. I tug my shoulders back trying to find the words.

"Just been a day. I needed to…get away?" My words fade off, and he doesn't attempt to step in. I squeeze my eyes shut as the pain swells. "I miss—"

"Brayden," he finishes for me.

"Yeah." I nod, and neither of us says anything for a while.

The nearest lamp is too far off to shed any light. I'm not sure what the park planners were thinking when they put picnic tables in the darkest area next to the forest and river. They apparently weren't expecting two grieving teenage boys to be here close to midnight.

A minute passes and I take my eyes off the table, staring off past Tyler, searching a clear sky. I can see every single star in the highest clarity, like the most detailed painting. And the air has the slightest nip to it.

I drop my attention back to Earth to find Tyler looking up at the stars too, a single tear etching a path down his cheek. I should say something. I should be a friend, even if he hasn't let me be one in a while. I need to be. But what do I say?

"So, you want to talk about it?" I try again.

"About what?" Tyler comes back with the slightest irritation in his voice. "About why I'm bawling? Why I'm out here all alone? How Brayden's gone? How it's my fault?"

"Woah." I throw a hand up. Kallie told me about this, how he claims it was his fault, but I thought for sure he knew better by now. "Your fault?"

"Yeah. It's my fault he's dead." His voice gets louder and his face scrunches into this angry mess. "If it hadn't been for my stupid, fucking selfish ass, he'd still be alive. He'd still be here!"

"That's not true." I try not to raise my voice, but at the same time he's got to know he can't do this. He's only hurting himself. "You didn't do this. It's not on you."

"I was the one texting him when it happened," he tells me, as if I didn't know already, like some big revelation that's supposed to make me hate him. And I'll admit I did the first week. I hated Tyler with a passion I hadn't felt in years, but that's because I needed someone to blame. But it was petty, and I left that behind. It isn't his fault, and it never was. "I'm the reason he was looking at his phone while he was driving. I'm the reason he was going too fast, why he went flying off… I was being self…"

His words fall into sobs, and his body shakes. I don't know what to do.

"It's not your fault, Ty. It's not." I know I'm not the first to try. He worries Kallie too.

What do I do? My eyes dart from one end of the table to the other as if somewhere among the splinters, cracks, and stains there's an answer written in the wood. I don't know what I'm doing, but I reach out a hand and place it on his arm. He doesn't pull back. Part of me wishes he would, because I don't know what to do next and it's awkward.

"We're all hurting, Ty," I tell him, fighting back my own torrent. Then the words just come. "I miss him so much. Every day. It's been easier lately, sort of, but even that feels bad. Nothing ever seems to *feel* okay. And today… Today's been rough. Everything makes me miss him."

"Everything. Every damn little thing." Tyler calms down just enough to agree, and the steam in his voice dampens to a whimper.

"Why?"

"Why what?" I ask.

"Why does it have to hurt so much?"

I consider it for a second and wipe at my face. I'm not the right person for this conversation. What was I thinking? *I need someone to talk to, not the other way around.*

"I don't know," I mutter. "It just…does."

I don't think he likes that answer because he huffs and drops his gaze to the table again. Why *does* it have to hurt like this? Why is it that any of this has to happen? Brayden was a good guy—no, he was the best. None of it makes any sense.

"Did he ever tell you what our last fight was over?" Tyler doesn't look up. "Well, I guess it wasn't really a fight, but…"

It comes from way out in left field, so I give him a second, but he doesn't continue, and I realize he's holding back the floodgates again.

"Uh…I'm not sure," I tell him. I know they had some fights, but they didn't really do that much. I just know Tyler had a tendency to go really quiet when they did.

"Kirk," he says.

I'm not following. My mouth hangs open a little. Maybe I should understand, but I don't. What does Kirk have to do with any of this? The guy's a freshman transfer from California. Sure, he's sort of cute, but not Tyler's or Brayden's type. He's the I'm-a-real-man-and-I-have-to-make-certain-you-know-it type, and he's also very straight. He tries to make that much clear.

"Why would you two fight over Kirk?" I say.

"I know. Stupid." He shrugs.

Yeah, sort of, but I'm not judging right now.

"He was determined Kirk was the better captain," Tyler starts up, his eyes twitching up to meet mine.

I slouch back and kick myself in the ass mentally. How could I have been so blind? Just think about who you're talking to, and who we're talking about. Two major, unabashed nerds.

"But clearly, *the* Jean Luc Picard is the best captain." Tyler looks at me expectantly, and then a laugh breaks through the sobs. The slightest amusement reaches my eyes. "He couldn't understand how a more structured command was better. Kirk was too unpredictable. But Brayden always said Kirk's Enterprise was more like a family, and that inspired loyalty. But Picard's was like that too."

"Yeah, they both did." I agree with them both actually. I'm no Star Trek buff, but I've watched most of the movies, but that's only because Brayden made me. "I think I have to agree with Brayden on this one, Ty."

"Seriously?" He cracks a small grin, moonlight reflecting off the trails of his tears. "You don't even like Star Trek."

"Not one hundred percent accurate, but eh…" I dip my head. "Brayden made me sit through enough, so I've got an idea."

I stop short of elaborating so I don't come off as the complete Trek noob I am. He knows I'm more a horror, action, and comic movie guy anyway, and they both took their Star Trek very seriously.

"It was a stupid fight. I was literally mad at him for a little." Tyler looks back up at the stars, and his eyes seem to be searching. "Who has real fights over shit like that?"

In one way I agree, but at the same time, what would be the fun in life otherwise?

"I remember when we were in…" I stop and think about it. Was it sixth or seventh grade? "I think it was seventh grade, and Brayden got that telescope for his birthday. Remember it?"

Tyler nods.

"He made me stay up *all* fucking night trying to see Jupiter," I tell him. I remember sitting in the damp grass of Brayden's backyard trying to find the huge-ass planet on his tiny telescope. "We found Mars easy, but Jupiter, nah. Come to find out right before we gave up that it wasn't even going to be visible that night."

I laugh, and I'm surprised to hear Tyler do the same.

"He loved the stars. He really wanted to see Breegge. I mean, he *saw* it," Tyler says, and his eyes slip upward again.

I do the same, as if by some miracle I could magnify the night sky a million times to see Breeggemann-Holt-Turner's Comet. It still seems like a long-ass name for a comet, but that's how they do it. I know Brayden told me why it was so long and awkward, but I can't remember the reason. Damn, I hate that I can't remember. But that's not the point. The point is it won't be visible to the naked eye for another three months.

"But he wanted to see it without a telescope, you know," Tyler continues. "With his own eyes, close, up in the mountains. He said he wanted to feel like he could reach up and touch it. We were planning to go up to Boone and watch it together."

"I know," I say. I'd only heard Brayden mention it a million times. He was obsessed with Breegge…and Ty. Then I speak before really thinking about it. "Maybe you should still go and see it. You know, in August, when it's close. For Brayden."

"You think?" he asks.

I nod. It sounds good in my head. A way to put a close to all this chaos. I might do the same thing, but on a different mountain.

"It can't hurt, right?"

TYLER

"I need a nap," Kallie huffs and drags a palm over her face in the most dramatic way.

"Same," I say.

I'm *actually* tired though, she's just whining. I couldn't sleep at all last night. Not sure why, but I'm about one hundred and fifty percent certain Kallie slept all night, she just didn't get to sleep in until 2 p.m. because it's a school day. Like, I actually have bags under my eyes my face masks aren't touching.

"Why can't school start at noon?" she asks.

But I'm still trying to figure out what happened last night. I don't let Kallie see me cry, but I sat on a bench and bawled in front of Aidan. Aidan! Of all the people in the world, *Aidan*. The boy I swear was trying to steal Brayden from me no matter how much Kallie says he wasn't. I mean, they did date before us.

And God, I talked to him about Brayden.

I mean, what was I thinking? I should have left the moment he walked up. Like, just got up and left without a word. But no, I sat there and let him see me bawling. And even worse, I told him how I felt. The thought makes me shiver.

"Ty… Tyler!" Kallie's voice hits me.

"Yeah, what?" I jerk.

"You good?" she asks as we mount the stairs to third period, Honors Biology.

It's one of those classes I'm not sure how I got into. I may be a Trek nerd, but honestly, sciency stuff isn't my forte. I'm more a history guy. Talk to me about the Revolutionary War or the Third Reich and I'm all ears. Try to carry a conversation with me about how the mitochondria does—whatever it is it does, I just remember Mrs. Kropf saying something about ATP, which makes me think of a sports car for some reason—and I might *accidentally* not hear a word you say. Sorry, Kallie…and Brayden…and pretty much everyone I know.

"Yeah." I tilt my head. "Sorry, I was just thinking about the new John Wick trailer. It looks so cool!"

I wasn't, obviously, but it's only partially a lie. It did look good! But that's all she needs. If I tell her what I'm really thinking she'd… Hell, I don't know what she'd say, but I'm pretty sure I wouldn't like it. She has a soft spot for Aidan, even if she does respect my dislike of him.

"Okay…" She drags out the word way longer than she needs to.

I roll my eyes. Act like you're confused all you want, fool, I know better. She knows something is up, but I'm not telling.

"*So*, we going to see it?" she asks.

"This weekend?" I give her the are-you-stupid look.

"Of course not. Next week, and on, like, a Tuesday night or something," she says.

That's more like it. She knows me. We hate people too much to be stuck in a packed theater over the weekend with idiots who won't shut up while the movie is playing. Those types shouldn't be allowed in the room. Just my opinion, but they shouldn't be.

"In that case, yes," I say. "I can't wait to watch Keanu Reeves kick some serious ass."

If I were to have a crush on an older guy, Keanu would be the man, or maybe Chris Evans, but definitely Keanu. On top of being ruggedly handsome, he's the most amazing action star ever.

We top the stairs and pass into the science and math wing. The walls are covered in corkboard plastered with strings of DNA and math figures with eyes and legs like we're still in elementary school. I couldn't care less about the artsy boards. I'm still questioning my life choices last night.

"Hey, you two!" Katie's adorable, yet a little too smiley, face greets us.

"Hey," I say and smile instinctively. It's hard not to around Katie, even if you don't do it often like me.

She's one of the few people other than Kallie I can deal with at West. There's something about her tiny, red-cheeked, golden-blonde self I can't be mean to or ignore, even if she is the exact opposite of me: an optimist. And believe me, I tried. I just can't ignore her like I can everyone else. Hell, sometimes she even sits with us at lunch, I just have to make Kallie behave when she does.

"I have tea," she leans in and whispers like the Cold War-era Russians might hear us. I still don't get why it's called tea, but whatever.

"Uh-huh?" I stop and grin at Kallie. Her brow raises. She hates drama but she's still somehow all about the tea. We look back and forth at each other for a few seconds before Kallie's eyes go wide over the silence.

"*And?*"

"I just got elected editor!" Katie's grin screams across her cheeks, and she starts jumping and shaking her arms.

"Of?" The question hangs in midair while Katie continues her dance. I probably should know the answer, but I don't. Maybe it's the school paper… Do we even have a school paper?

"The yearbook, of course!" she beams, shaking her head in that isn't-it-obvious, yet I'm-the-sweet-happy-Katie so not bitchy way. "I'm so flipping excited!"

"That's *so* awesome," Kallie says a little *too* sarcastically.

I throw her a glare. I guess it's a girl-to-girl thing.

"Oh my! That *is* awesome! Congrats, Katie!" I say.

"We'll have to talk later, don't want to be late for class." Kallie pulls me away, barely hiding an eye roll.

"Be nice," I tell her once we're out of earshot.

"If you weren't super fucking gay," she twitches her head and purses her lips, "I'd honestly think you had a thing for her."

"Uh, ew. No. Dicks only," I remind her.

"Mmm… Maybe a little bi?"

"No. I repeat, dicks only," I try again.

"So, what *is* going on?" Kallie asks, but I'm not following.

"What?" Does she really need more explanation about my sexuality, like we've not been friends since literally forever.

"Something's up, I know it." She eyes me down and twitches her head.

And talk about a total switch. Like, give me a moment to catch up.

"Nothing's up, I promise." Well, I lie. But am I really lying? Nothing is up, nothing more than has been since Brayden died.

"Right," she puffs, and we slip into Mrs. Kropf's room and take our seats at the back. "I know you know this, but I'm going to say it anyways. I know you're hardheaded, but if you need to talk, obviously, I'm here."

"I know." I give her a half-grin, and that's that.

AIDAN
Wednesday, May 15

It's so cold!

This lady came in an hour ago and raided the ice cream aisle of our off-brand vanilla, strawberry, and chocolates. It must be someone's birthday, but who the hell knows enough people to need that much ice cream?

I slice open another box from the stack I wheeled from the cold storage in the back room and transfer a container of strawberry. My fingers are stiff, and my arms are covered in goose bumps. Of course, I'm wearing short sleeves. This is not my normal job. Curse Tavon for calling in today. Had he not I'd be up front helping bag or something, anything else, just not freezing my ass off.

Plus, I'd prefer to be sitting at home at my tiny desk writing my "novel." Okay, maybe I should call it a story. I'll probably never finish it, like all the other "novels" I've started, and even if I do it's probably stupid and no one will want to read it, so yeah.

Still, writing about Kit's struggle against a post-apocalyptic cult under the control of the sinister Under Shepherd after the world goes to shit is so much more interesting than stocking shelves. Oh, and I finally decided on the back story for Kit's love interest last week, but I still don't know his name. I keep going between Cooper and Ben. I don't know. What I do know is they're going to have grown up in the cult but be sort of rebels. At least something like that.

I drop the last bucket of ice cream in the cooler and wheel the cart back to the stockroom. The Under Shepherd is one of my favorite bad guys. He's this cult leader, sort of like a super fundamentalist preacher, but like Jim Jones meets Mad Maxx. He's a total bad dude, but he really believes the crap he teaches and he isn't afraid to cut a guy's head off to make a point, which he has already. A few times.

"Aidan." Jesse, the six-foot-three slick-headed pole also known as my boss, calls me over. "Go back up front and help with bagging. They're getting hit hard."

"Sure," I say. You don't have to ask that twice. I let the cart roll to a stop on its own next to the cold storage and head back out to the floor.

I'm walking through the cereal aisle when Jesse's voice comes over the intercom calling "all available cashiers" to the front, which is pointless. One, there are only three cashiers here today, and two, I already see Kallie and Tina scanning away at the edge of the aisle. He could have just said *Riley to the front.*

As the rest of the registers come into view it seems even more absurd. Riley is already working a register. I roll my eyes and work my way around an old lady's buggy to take up residence at the end of Kallie's register.

"What took you so long?" she says, but her eyes scream *thank God you're here.*

"Had to fight off…" But I stop before finishing with *some homeless dude in the cereal aisle.* Mainly because I don't think the little gray-headed woman carefully placing her bread on the conveyor belt would appreciate the humor as much, and I'd really like to keep my job.

Kallie throws me a rare grin. She might not know what I was going to say, but she got the gist. I bag up the lady's groceries and work through a few more customers before the rush slows.

"You think you can handle it now?" I ask as her last customer scoots past me.

"Obviously." She smirks.

I smirk right back and start to head off, but for some reason I stop and the stupidest thing happens. I open my mouth.

"I talked to Tyler last night…" I clench my fists, begging my mouth to shut the hell up, but not before my stupid brain further inserts my foot again with amazing skill, "at the park."

"Really?" Kallie swings around and props her back against the register, a big no-no. I just hope Jesse doesn't see.

"Uh…" I stumble. Why did I tell her? "Yeah."

"Well, that little bitch. He didn't tell me you talked." Kallie wiggles her head and rolls her eyes. "So…"

"So what?" I play it off, like somehow the words that just came out of my mouth didn't just come out of my mouth.

"You talked to Ty…at the park."

I'm not sure if she's being serious, or mocking me, or maybe a little of both right now, but either would be total Kallie.

"It was nothing." I grin nervously but pull my shoulders back to show I'm still in control. I could have told anyone else and it wouldn't have been a thing, but I told Kallie. I always do though. I probably tell her more than Bryce. "Yeah, I went last night to clear my head. I was having a bad day, missing you-know-who, and it always helps."

"Sorry." Kallie skews her lips, and I can tell it's not just for show, even if she isn't great at being emotional.

"But yeah, Tyler was there too."

"What did you two talk about?" Kallie twists around to check her lane, more to make sure Jesse isn't around than a customer.

"Brayden," I say plainly. Suddenly I feel even more stupid than before.

"Makes sense." She hangs her head. "Sorry."

"It's okay. It was a good talk. I haven't talked to Ty in a while, at least without him giving me that look," I tell her. She knows the one I'm talking about. That one that says *I'm not going to tell you I don't like you, but I don't.* "We both miss him. Just felt like the right thing to do. Plus, I'd have been a complete ass to see him upset like that and just walk on."

"Yeah, that would have been a real dick move." She smacks her lips. "And that's definitely not you. You're too sweet for that. And I swear I've tried to work on him about that look. He holds on to shit though, even shit he makes up in his head. Have you talked since?"

"Oh, no." I crinkle my brow. Really, Kallie?

"You should," she suggests.

"Really?" How in hell would that be a good idea?

"Yeah. If you got him talking, maybe that's good for him *and* you." Some skater dude walks up and drops a Monster on her conveyor, the red sugar-free kind, and she snaps around, but not before giving me one last command. *"Text him."*

TYLER

"You're not working tonight, right?" I dump the wrapper for my chicken sandwich and second Monster can in the cafeteria trash can.

"I wouldn't dream of it." Kallie squints at me.

"Good. Otherwise I'd have to resort to *Overwatch* tonight, and Jacob isn't free." His band is playing at some local venue down where he lives, so they have to practice.

Jacob is my gamer friend. I've never met him in person, just through Instagram and *Overwatch*. He's one of the later casualties of my early Insta stalking campaign before I started dating Brayden.

I used to search for cute guys to follow, 'cause why not. It was a phase. Okay, a long phase.

"Is that the white-haired cutie?" Kallie asks.

"Sure." He is cute, and his hair is dyed stark white. He plays guitar in his friend's band, and I think he does backup vocals too. I think.

And no, I didn't follow him *just* because he's cute, it was at least twenty percent his love of *Overwatch*…okay, make that ten percent. We do play a lot, at least once a week on the support side. I take Moira and he takes Mercy, and we heal and wreak major havoc at the same time. And with a gamer tag like NoMercyCult02, it makes sense.

Come to think of it, I have such a nerd-ass gamer tag, TAGtheBorg. It's my initials, Tyler Alexander Gentry, and of course the Borg from Star Trek. So not creative at all, and sort of embarrassing now.

"I wouldn't want to keep you from a cute boy." Kallie tilts her head.

"I said he *won't* be on tonight. You deaf, fool?" I squint.

She throws me a middle digit as we crowd into the stairwell up to third period. "I'm, like, the only person you talk to. You need more people. Maybe text someone."

I eye her. What the hell is she talking about? It's like the normal, albeit strange and dark, Kallie disassociated from her body and I'm left with…this.

"Like who?" I ask, still withholding the fact that Aidan texted me last night. I didn't respond. Maybe I will later, but I don't know. I can't make up my mind yet. Something about him still bugs me, and telling Kallie he texted would only make things worse.

She has too much of a sweet spot for him. And I already ignored him all the way through American History today, which was awkward enough after Tuesday night.

"I don't know." Kallie's shoulders bounce. Her nearly black hair falls over her shoulder and tumbles out of view. I highly doubt she doesn't know. "Anyone."

"Except you?"

"I didn't say that." She gives me the evil eye. "You better not stop talking to me."

We pass a bulletin board with an atom mapped out in like a bazillion times zoom, electrons, protons, neutrons and all that shit, then it's Mrs. Kropf's classroom. I make a hard right and Kallie follows me down the aisle.

"Yeah, yeah." I wave at her, which riles her up.

"Listen here, little boy," she starts, and I can't stop a tight little grin as she whispers the last bit to keep it between us. "I'm just saying you need to get out, talk to people. But you better not stop talking to me for someone else. I'll cut a bitch."

I giggle as I pull out my phone and lay it on my desk. Class hasn't started yet, so I'm not in danger.

I get a lot of threats like that from Kallie. So far none have been real, but I'm just waiting for the day one is. Part of me could see her cutting some bitch's throat because I'm not giving her enough attention, a very, very small, weird part of me, but I'm like ninety-nine percent sure she's not a psychopath. But there's always that one percent hanging on.

"I know," I whisper back, and force back an image of Brayden's face that pops into my head from last Christmas, our only Christmas together. I'm not thinking about that now.

I bring my phone to life and just under a Snap notification from Mom is the text from Aidan. I didn't swipe it away earlier because I wasn't sure if I wanted to reply or not.

Like, I still can't stand him, but it was good to talk to someone else about Brayden the other night. Hell if I ever admit that to Kallie since she basically just said I should do that. It's like a rule. But if I don't respond, I'll look like a total douche too.

AIDAN: Hey! Good talking to you the other night.

I read the text again. It's simple, but was it necessary? If he'd just not, I wouldn't feel like I need to say something.

Oh hell! I type out a quick reply.

TYLER: You too.

I hit send before I have the chance to take it back. Hopefully it's short and to the point enough that he'll get the real message. That is, I'm trying to be nice but also cut this convo short, like end it.

AIDAN
Thursday, May 16

The hall is a bustle of bodies rushing to get to class, Bryce and me among them. We're off to Creative Writing.

It's one of those courses I *might* have nudged Bryce to take, and by nudge, I mean I *might* have implied he'd ruin my senior year if he didn't take it with me. I can't remember what I used as leverage or how it even made sense, but I couldn't get Brayden, Rhys, or Tyler to take it, so Bryce took the fall.

But he complains about it all the time. Now being a prime example. The others would have complained too. Of course, Tyler would have simply because I'm in the class. It was the previous semester when he started hating me after all, and I think my presence bugged him enough in second and fourth periods. Speaking of Tyler, he hasn't replied to my text.

"I'm going to fail this class, man!" Bryce stops at his locker and starts rummaging through an assortment of hoodies, comic books, dirty shirts, and maybe some snacks. I don't know how he stands it. It's a nightmare.

"How?" I tug on my backpack straps anxiously. "And hurry up."

Part of me knows Bryce is going to make us late for third period again, and I really don't want Mr. Hagan fussing again. The other part wants to check my phone to see if Ty replied, but after half the day with zilch and sitting through American History with him, it's probably a no. Plus, why the hell should I care, it's only like we were good friends for years before he thought I was going to steal his boyfriend or something. It's still so stupid.

"Calm your tits." Bryce pushes the comics aside and pulls out a bag of Skittles. "Got it. Now, what was I saying?"

"Class. You're going to fail," I remind him, rolling my eyes.

"Well that's rude." He smirks.

"Your words, not mine," I remind him.

"Ah, true." He nods and we're off again, weaving through throngs of people I don't know but I've seen every day the past four years. "I can't write. It's like no matter what I do it sounds stupid as hell. You know, like your music."

"You mother…" I stop short of saying it and allow my middle finger do the rest. Bryce is more a hip-hop and pop guy, not an admirer of the sweet riffs of the old rock gods. I'll never understand. It's almost blasphemous.

"Just say it." He grins.

I roll my eyes. I don't know why, but I just don't like it. It doesn't bother me when other people swear, I just don't. Weird, but that doesn't surprise anyone I know.

"I'm just going to act like you didn't commit blasphemy and forget it was ever said." I shake my head. "Your writing though, it's probably fine. Probably. I think it always sounds horrible to the person writing it. At least mine always does, but it's fine. At least I *think* it is."

Damn. Now I'm second-guessing everything I've written. I've always been told even the best authors doubt their work, and some of them can't even stand to hear people read their words aloud, like me. I figured it was just one of those things, and my writing was at least okay, but now? I'm not so sure.

"Or maybe your stuff sucks too," Bryce says what I'm thinking.

"Not helping," I say.

"Just serving up some realness," he says.

Ahead we veer into Mr. Hagan's room and take our seats between walls plastered in sentence diagrams, quotes from Shakespeare, a bunch of poems, and the movie posters for all three Lord of the Rings movies. These walls are where I first heard of Wilder. Her work takes up at least a quarter of the wall space, and I honestly get why, but my favorite is still the one taped up above Mr. Hagan's desk.

Sometimes all that matters

Is that you're still trying.

It's not your typical poem, not so much lyrical as it is meaningful and beautiful, and I didn't realize how important it was until Brayden passed. I can't begin to say how much I clung to those words in the weeks after. Just keep moving, just keep living, just keep trying. I still do.

Speaking of which, I still haven't heard from Tyler. Guess he still hates me, or dislikes me, I'm not really sure which. I think it's hate though. What's certain is that it's stupid and annoying. It doesn't make any sense. I was never competition. We were friends. Actually, *I'm* still his friend, whether he likes it or not.

"You're done with your story, right?" Bryce leans forward and props his elbows on the desk.

"Of course! I still have to edit though," I say. There is no way in hell I'm turning in a first draft of any story, especially one that also happens to be the final project for this class. "Only two weeks to turn them in."

"I know." Bryce rolls his eyes, which is code for him not even being close to ready.

"You want help finishing yours, don't you?" I slip out my phone. I've only got a minute to spare, so best to check now.

"Eh." He skews his face into this contortion of what might be considered confusion rather than begging for pity. Have no doubt though, he's begging for pity.

"You do." I purse my lips and laugh. "How far are you?"

"Just over halfway…" he says.

"Did you wait till this week to start or something?" I throw my hands out.

"No, it just doesn't come to me like it does you." He shrugs.

"Whatever, I'll help after school sometime," I tell him and open my phone.

In the middle of my notifications one surprises me.

TYLER: You too.

So, do I take that as he's coming around and getting over the shit he has against me since he answered, and he's just blowing smoke up my ass, or he's just being half decent? You know what? I don't care. He's going to be my friend whether he knows it or not, and whether he likes it or not. It's what Brayden wanted.

The bell rings as I type back. Here goes nothing.

AIDAN: Maybe we could hang out sometime?

TYLER

Thursday, May 16

"Break time!" Kallie yells in my ear and rolls off the bed, her bed, with *The Haunting of Hill House* still playing on the TV.

This is how it's always been. She's rarely come to my house, and honestly I'm glad now, because that's the last place I'm staying if I can get away with it. Coming here is more than just spending time with my bestie, it's like an oasis. I don't have to feel like I'm being judged the entire damn time.

"I need more Cheerwine anyway." I pause our show, slip over the other edge and head for the kitchen.

"Get me some while you're at it." She gives me no out as she disappears into the bathroom.

I do a quick one-eighty, make sure she can hear my huff for effect, and fetch her glass. She's so bossy, always has been. It's something you get used to when you're around her what amounts to basically every single day. At least she isn't cooking me another cheese sandwich with a whole stick of butter again. That was almost unbearable.

In the kitchen I fill our cups and start back to the bedroom. Kallie's and her parents' faces are scattered in frames along the walls. She's an only child, but it's still like my childhood too. This is basically where I grew up half the time.

It was either here or her grandparents', the house across the driveway. We'd spend whole days in their basement constructing elaborate blanket forts out of whatever we could find or eating all the toasted cheese sandwiches her grandma would make us. And she'd make us as many as we wanted.

"This show is getting crazier by the minute, I swear," I say when Kallie walks in and plops down beside me. "That was like sleep paralysis, but not, just in your head, right?"

"Isn't that exactly what sleep paralysis is?" Kallie wrinkles her brow.

"Uh… Not the point." I try to glaze over it. "And no one believes her, it's sort of sad."

"I'm not letting you off that easy," she grins. "That was stupid."

"Come on," I beg. Then my mind switches, like a dimly flickering bulb. "Have you seen Breegge lately?"

"Uh—" Kallie eyes me with confusion before the light behind her stormy grays goes off and she realizes what I'm talking about: the comet. It's easier than saying the Breeggemann-Holt-Turner Comet every time. I mean, that first name, it's a killer all on its own. "No."

"It's getting brighter," I tell her. A part of me feels dirty for using this to dig me out of my stupid hole. Sorry, Bray. Okay, now I feel horrible about it. But I had wanted to ask her anyway. "I mean, I haven't seen it. It's still too far away. The pictures online are just getting better."

"Well, that's what they do when they get closer." She eyes me.

"I know, it's just…" I stop. Now I totally regret bringing it up.

I'm not sure what I'm trying to say. It's just suddenly I've got this weight pulling down on my chest, and I know what his name is, but I don't want to utter it. I just want to enjoy the moment, but he isn't letting me. I mean, it isn't him, I know, it's me, but it is still.

I just…

"It's okay." She gives me that caring half-grin I rarely get from her and literally pats me on the head.

"Really?" I duck.

"What?" She sinks back.

"You're going to pat me on the head like a dog?"

"I mean, that's not what I was envisioning," she says, but there's that sly grin. "But you are sort of like a little lost puppy sometimes."

"Bitch." I roll my eyes. "I don't know what I was trying to say. Either way it won't be until August that it's closest. I think I'm still going up to Boone to see it."

"Why not look at it here?" Kallie asks. "I'm pretty sure you'll be able to see it here too. It's not a Boone-only thing."

"It's brighter up there," I tell her. "Y'all just don't get it."

Honestly, I'm not sure that's completely true. Light pollution isn't exactly a big issue out here in Collettsville where the closest business is, like, five miles away and it's this tiny country gas station. Light poles aren't exactly common.

"Uh-huh." She isn't buying it.

I can't think of what to say next.

It gets quiet and I purse my lips, trying to come up with a way to explain it without sounding like I'm obsessed. I'm not. I just need to do this. I need to do what we'd planned. A certain person, who'll remain nameless, was at least right about that.

You know what, Ty, just drop it.

"Let's—" I'm about to ask Kallie to start the show. I'd much rather focus on Nell, Luke, and Theodora's problems, but she interrupts.

"So…" Kallie stretches the word out. It's immediately obvious she has something she's been dying to say. "I hear you might have talked to Aidan."

"Huh?" My head jerks back as if the mere accusation is a blow.

But… Well, I did, and apparently, he thinks that means we're all buddy-buddy again. He did text back in less than a minute of my reply today. It seems agreeing with his "Hey! Good talking to you the other night" text wasn't the best idea I've ever had. Probably not the worst either. I did at one point think it was smart to look up porn on the family computer back in middle school and gave it a rather explicit virus. I got it cleaned up before anyone found out, but still. So yeah, not my worst mistake.

"So, you didn't?" She looks confused.

I wish I had the ability to look her in the eye and just flat-out lie. But either I'm too good a person for that, which I don't think is the answer, or I just suck at dishonesty because I can't keep a straight face. And I did make things worse all on my own by responding—*again*. I tried steering around his "hang out" question, at least. I pushed it off a little, and so far he's letting me be.

"I did. So?" I shrug and push against the dozens of pillows we have set up behind us, trying to get comfortable. "We talked at the park, that's it."

"Oh," she says matter-of-factly.

"We going to start this show back up?" I ask.

"What did you two talk about?" Kallie flips onto her side and stares me down.

"How do you even know we talked?" I huff. She's in story mode now. Yay me. "Is he going around telling people? Did he say we fucked in the woods too?"

"You fucked in the woods?" She looks shocked.

"No!" I sit up. That she would even think we did is insane. "I was being—"

"So what *did* you do?" she asks again, the flash in her eyes dimming a fraction. "And no, he isn't going around telling people you two talked. He just mentioned it to me at work last night. I basically had to pry it out of him. Don't think he even meant to tell me."

"But he did." I grimace and throw my hands in the air.

"Talking is no big deal, Ty, you're talking to me. Come on," she says. "Talking can simply mean you said hey."

"Yeah, yeah, I know. It's just—" I try, but she jumps in again.

"I know, you hate him. He was 'trying' to steal your man. He's our arch nemesis. Blah, blah, blah." Kallie goes on and on, then stops and squints at me. "*Is* he still our arch nemesis?"

"Oh my God, Kal." I swear my eyes are bulging. I can't with this girl sometimes. She's the best, but I could kill her about now. "I never said he was our arch nemesis, I—"

"And I quote, 'He's like the fucking Borg.'" Kallie throws up air quotes, and unfortunately I can't say she's misquoting me. "I'm no Star Trek buff, but you've made me sit through enough of those god-awful films *enough times* that I know the Borg are some big bad shit for old Pick-ard."

I'm not sure what's more traumatizing. The fact that she can quote something I said nearly a year ago or that she still mocks the great Captain Picard's name.

"First, fuck you. Star Trek is amazing! And second, okay." I roll my eyes and purse my lips in defeat. "I might have said it, or something like it. And it's Picard, fool, not Pick-ard. Get it right."

"Ooh, the whore's testy." Kallie smirks and shakes her shoulders before lying back on the pile of pillows. "So, what did you two talk about?"

I can't help but admire her determination, even if she's going to drive me off a cliff with it one of these days.

"It was just about Brayden. I was there before A showed up, out behind the field. You know, where those picnic tables by the playground are?" I ask.

"Yeah." She nods.

"Well, I was out there…you know…" I don't want to say crying, but that's what I was doing. I so rarely show any real emotion, and that's the last one I want to admit to.

"Crying?" she asks but doesn't stop there. "It's not a crime to say it, you know, or do it. I know your gay ass thinks it makes you less somehow, but it doesn't. I mean, you're allowed to feel. Even Tyler Alexander Gentry the Great has emotions."

"I know," I bite back. Sometimes having Alexander as a middle name sucks, especially when she uses it like that. "I was just there stargazing, but I couldn't stop crying. Aidan walked up on me like some stalker and —"

"Or he just so happened to be at the park for *the same* reason you were and was trying to be careful," she suggests. "Hmmm… Maybe. You know?"

God, I hate it when she's right and it contradicts my narrative.

"Yeah, whatever." I roll my eyes. "We just talked about Brayden. And yeah, he texted me yesterday."

I don't know why I admitted that last part. It's not like she asked.

"And you replied, right?" she asks.

"Yeah," I say, but it barely comes out. It's like it's hard to admit that I did it, that I replied back to *him*.

"Good. You should have. You two really need to make up." She pauses, looks at the ceiling, and then finds me again and starts pointing at me. "Nope, correction. *You*, just you, tu, only you, need to make up."

I roll my eyes again. Hell, she even threw in the singular bit of Spanish vocab she knows.

"It'd be great if we could all hang out again," she goes on. "He's not a bad guy, and you two *used* to be friends, you know."

"Sure," I mutter. Doubt that's going to happen, but I'm not arguing with her. I'll lose. I always lose these. "So, we watching this or not?"

"Promise me you'll at least *try* to be nice to him." She eyes me seriously.

"Is that what I have to do to keep watching the show? You know, the one we were *already* watching?" I ask.

"No." She grins. It's bad, she knows she has me. "It's what you *have* to do because you're not a *total* ass. You're only partly an ass."

"Whatever. I'll try," I tell her. And by try, I mean I'll try not to ignore his fake ass and stare all evil-like at him when I'm forced to see him. "But you're saying I'm an ass?"

"Obviously." She sticks her tongue out between her teeth. "But, like, you have to *really* try. Like hang out with us together or something."

Oh my God, she's almost bouncing. I can feel my stomach churning. She's way too excited about my pain.

"Really?" I whine. "Come on."

"Promise!" She snaps her head in this do-what-I-say-bitch sort of way and points at me with a bony finger.

"Ah!" I groan. Why me? "Fine! Just start the damn show."

A I D A N
Sunday, May 19

The words are coming easier today and I decided on a name for Kit's lover—or well, the dude that's going to be, at least. Ben. It just feels right. Kit and Ben.

It isn't exactly a love story. I guess post-apocalyptic stories can be, but not really. Hunger Games did it, sort of. And maybe this is too. Kit and Ben are going to fall in love, but the ending…well, that isn't going to be happy.

I tap the keys and send Kit tripping over a woven basket next to Ben. I laugh a little inside. It's going to be one of those cute encounters where my main guy—that's Kit—embarrasses himself right in front of the guy he's been eyeing—Ben, obviously—who hasn't shown any real interest yet. I haven't decided what happens next. I probably should plan more, but I think it gets in the way of my creative flow. At least now with my story for class done, I can focus on my real story.

Right now, I'm just glad Mamá's at work. It's just me and Genji, the cutest little tabby cat in the world. If she was here instead of serving food to Lenoir's ten-percent tip crowd, she'd be constantly checking in on me. And it wouldn't stop there. She'd see I'm writing, and as always, she'd attempt a glance over my shoulder and start reading it.

And let me tell you, I can stand a lot, but there is something about another person reading my words aloud that just gets under my skin.

I stare at the screen, but between Kit falling and thinking about Mamá being nosey, I lose focus. Instead of the screen I see a reflection of Brayden's pale brown eyes staring at me. I know he isn't there, but it doesn't stop me from turning to face my tiny clothes-littered room like he's standing in the middle of it all.

He helped me come up with the idea for this story, and he was there every step giving me advice and telling me how bad certain parts sucked. But it was never mean. It was just Brayden. Honest and sarcastic and witty. He's also the only person I ever voluntarily let read it. At least what I had done then. It's his story just as much as it is mine, and I'm going to finish it.

I miss sitting here on Monday nights after class, bouncing ideas off him while he chilled on my beanbag in the corner and tossed my soccer ball over his head. He'd wanted me to call my main character Ben, but I was determined he was a Kit instead. Guess I ended up using the name anyway.

It's so crazy. We were BFFs, best friends forever, it was us to the end. I guess sometimes forever is a lot shorter than you think it's going to be.

I let my eyes drop to the keyboard and release the air from my lungs in one slow breath. I miss him.

Stop it.

I shake my head and pull myself upright. *Just stop it. This isn't helping.*

Meow. Meow.

I check my side and Genji's staring up at me, and he keeps meowing. I pat him on the head and slide my palm down his back.

"Good Genji. Do you miss him too?" I ask. "Me too, buddy."

I close my eyes and breathe. All at once the heavy feeling in my chest jumps away and is replaced by the here and now.

"Oh no!" I'm late.

Bryce and Rhys are expecting me at the park before work. It's our Sunday thing, we just have to wait for Rhys to get out of church. I roll my eyes, it's 12:45 p.m., so *I'm* going to be the one running late today. It doesn't help any that part of me doesn't want to go. It just wants to sit here for a little longer, or maybe crawl into bed and lie there, but that's the exact opposite of what I need.

I huff and look down at myself. Dammit. Now I have to get dressed. I can't play soccer in Deadpool pajama bottoms.

TYLER

Sunday, May 19

"Bastion's around the corner!" I yell into my headset.

"Got it," Jacob's voice booms in my ears. He maneuvers D.Va's massive Meka suit around a white stone column in view of the point. Bastion's waiting for him, but Jacob deploys his defense matrix and not a bullet touches him.

I swivel my controls, swinging Moira around the wall, and throw a purple attack orb at the enemy as Jacob's defense goes down and he sends a volley of rockets into Bastion's face. The robot canon crumbles to the ground with an electronic whimper and we push our avatars forward.

"Yes!" Jacob screams. "I told you we'd be fine with a tank/support combo."

"Yeah, yeah. Whatever." I roll my eyes, but he might have something there. We are rushing the point and laying total waste to the other team.

We've been going berserk for the past two hours, but every match has been so intense it feels like minutes. I love the quick surge to the point and protecting the payload, even if half the team, especially Widow mains, doesn't know how to get their asses on the payload.

VICTORY flashes across the screen and I let out a *whoop whoop*.

"Did it again!" Jacob cheers. "Look at that board."

The game summary board comes up, and guess whose name is stamped under D.Va's likeness. Jacob's, or rather NoMercyCult02, and guess who's not. Me. I chuckle. It's no surprise. I swear I can carry the entire team as Moira, keep them from flatlining with my healing spray and orbs the whole game, get gold in healing and objective eliminations, like this round, and still not appear on the leaderboard. It's the curse of being a Moira main. We're so underappreciated.

"Well, you would have died like six times had I not been there, so you're welcome, fool," I remind him.

"I play to win," Jacob mimics D.Va's voice line, even raising the tone of his voice to sound like her.

"Stupidity is not a right," I bite back with my best high-minded Moira impersonation. I almost break up with a laugh, but I hold it in.

"Ooh," Jacob says, and I can imagine him squinting his bright green eyes down in Kannapolis, yet another place I've never been. "Nice!"

Sometimes I think we know too many of our characters' lines. Like we even have quick conversations on Snap in nothing but *Overwatch* quotes at times, especially Moira and Sym quotes because they're both such bitchy characters. They have *the best* lines.

My phone buzzes next to me on the bed. It's Kallie.

KALLIE: Would you kill me if I invited Aidan to come with tonight?

Yes flashes in my mind.

"Oh my God!" I moan.

"What's up?" Jacob asks.

"It's Kallie," I tell him. "She wants to invite Aidan to hang with us tonight."

"Aidan…" He says it slowly. I'm not sure I've mentioned the name to him before. "Hold up! Isn't he the dude you can't stand?"

Okay, maybe I've mentioned him.

"Yeah." I shrug even though he can't see me.

"Why would she do that?" Jacob asks.

"I don't know," I tell him. "She likes him. Always has."

"Hold up, weren't you friends with him at one point?"

"Sort of—"

"Yeah! Like when we first met you were." It's like a light bulb goes off, and I'm thinking how much I want to punch it out right now. "That's right, but you said he was after…you know who."

"I mean, well, I never *said* he was after Brayden, but he…uh…" I don't know why it's suddenly so hard. "I don't know, he just got in the way."

"Uh-huh," he says it with just enough doubt. "I'm pretty sure you said he was, but that's none of my business."

"Okay, enough about this," I tell him as the loading screen for the next map, Busan, goes away and I lock in Moira again. "He's not coming though."

TYLER: Uh... Yes. I would.

I hit send. She couldn't have expected more. I mean, she does know me, right?

"Come on, Ty," Jacob says as Mercy's avatar flashes onto the screen above his username. "What could it hurt? And if I remember right, he's sort of cute."

"Are you finished?" I quote Moira. Maybe that'll get him off track.

"Why do you struggle?" Jacob gives his best Symmetra impersonation.

I roll my eyes. "Oh my God! No. I mean, yes, but no. I'm not sitting around with him."

My phone vibrates again, and I let out a deep huff before checking the message, which I already know is from Kallie.

KALLIE: Please!!! ::sad emoji:: ::sad emoji::

I don't hesitate.

TYLER: NOOOOO! ::middle finger emoji::

"So he *is* cute," Jacob says, then switches to a poor Mercy impersonation. "I'll send you my consultation fee."

I shake my head and throw one last Moira line at him before the game countdown begins and we're off again.

"The state of you."

AIDAN

"God, you can tell Jesse's been on break." I put an arm over my nose to block the smell.

"Think he smokes like three cigs every break," Kallie says, and nods for me to follow to the other entrance where the smell of cigarettes isn't overwhelming. "It reeks over here."

We don't usually get to take a break at the same time, so this is a bit of a treat. Plus, it's been a busy day. I've bagged for Kal most the evening, so that helped.

"So how did your game go?" Kallie asks. "Heard you lost?"

Everyone—well, everyone I hang around, which isn't that many people—knows about our religious Sunday soccer matches. And by religious I mean we've played almost every week since freshman year. It just sounds better calling it religious with it being on a Sunday and all.

"You heard I lost?" I squint. Who the hell's she been talking to? "Bryce and James lost."

"Yeah, I didn't hear anything." She grins.

I grin back. I should have known.

Kallie bounces her shoulders and takes a seat on one of the simple black metal benches, and I settle in next to her and sip at my Monster.

"Bryce and James lost," I repeat. "Ivan got stuck at some church lunch thing, and Roberto had an early shift, so we were down two. Still a good game though, besides that face-plant James did."

"Face-plant?" Kallie asks.

"Yeah, it looked painful." I hold back a laugh. The way James popped back up and shook it off was something else. The last thing he wanted was to look like a wimp, which is stupid because it obviously hurt. "He acted like it wasn't bad. It was bad."

"Sounds like James," Kallie agrees. Something in her body language shifts, or maybe it's just her stance. "So, Ty finally mentioned you two have been *talking*."

"*Talking?* That's a stretch." I lean back against the bench just enough that my calf kicks Kallie's leg. She swats me away and I give her another playful kick. "I wouldn't call a few random texts, talking."

"That's not what I mean, but it's more than before," she says, and I can't disagree with that.

"Yeah," I say. Kallie has this look of mischief in her eyes and I can only think of one reason for that. "I'm just being friendly, that's it."

"Uh-huh." Kallie tilts her head.

"Uh yeah," I give it right back. "We miss Brayden, that's it. Can't I just be his friend?"

I know what she's thinking. Before Ty and Brayden got together I was sort of into Ty. Okay, maybe "into" isn't the right word. I definitely never got *into* him. Dammit. What I'm trying to say is I liked him, but he ended up with Brayden. And that was okay. It's what he wanted, and Brayden loved him, so that made me happy. But somewhere along the way I became like the sworn enemy, and I'm still not completely sure how.

"Of course," Kallie says. "It's still early—"

"Really?" Part of me wants to lash out, but I know she's not trying to be insensitive. It's just Kallie.

"Sorry." She gives me a half-grin. "But you two would be cute together. Right?"

"Stop it." I fail at hiding the embarrassed grin on my face.

"I'm just hoping this is the start of me *not* having to be the middle woman between your sorry asses," she says.

"I get that. But how about we stop the matchmaking?" I suggest.

"Nah." Kallie gets up and starts back toward the automatic doors.

"Come on," I groan.

"Actually, Ty's coming by after work," she says. My mind tells me I ought to rush past her so I don't hear what's next, but I wait. "We're going to grab something to eat. You two should talk then."

Before I have a chance to rebut, she turns and escapes inside, leaving me alone under the awning. It's nothing new for Ty to come by after Kallie gets off. It's just that for the past year, he's refused to acknowledge my existence when he's here. I'm not sure tonight will be any different, so I'm probably in no danger.

But part of me wants to be in danger.

TYLER

Sunday, May 19

I need my Kallie time.

Two church services in one day is enough to wear out anyone. On top of that, it's three times worse when your dad threatens that it's either church Sunday morning, Sunday night, and Wednesday, or shipping your ass back off to some internment—sorry, I mean "conversion therapy"—camp again, as if the first time worked. Talk about a total drag, and not of the good variety.

It's always the weirdest thing hearing the pastor talk up the love of God, and how we should love everyone, and then without breaking pace, jump into this long laundry list of people who should burn and rot in hell. Maybe it's just me, but I feel like there's a bit of a disconnect in there somewhere.

But I'm in safe waters now. I steer into a spot two down from Kallie's little black Kia Soul. I switch off the engine and glance at my phone as the K.Flay track that was playing goes silent. *8:54 p.m.* I've a few minutes to spare before she clocks out.

I might as well make her work a little, it's the least I can do.

Kallie is standing behind register two when I walk in with all the cheer of a basset hound. I giggle inside and walk around the other end of the registers so she doesn't see me. I know she's short, but for some reason, seeing her behind the register always hits a little different. Like she can't even see over it. Not even on her tippy toes.

At the end of her register I spy the Monster cooler and set my course. The red ones are the best, but they're out, so I settle for the white can.

"Those things will kill you, you know."

I know that voice. I roll my eyes before turning; it's become involuntary at this point. Aidan.

"Purely circumstantial," is what comes out of my mouth. Why that's what comes to mind first I have no idea, but my mouth often moves before my brain has a chance to catch up.

"Huh?"

"I'll be fine," I tell him. "Die happy, right?"

Okay, maybe not happy. I'm not sure that's a real thing—dying happy, that is.

"Ah." Aidan purses his lips. I don't think he knows what to say. But of course he opens his mouth right as I'm trying to start off to Kallie's register. "You and Kallie hanging out after work?"

"Yeah," I say, not bothering to hide my scowl or turn back around.

"Okay." Aidan does this nervous half-grin thing, nods, and walks off.

Finally.

I step around the magazine rack and drop my drink on Kallie's conveyor belt—the very opposite end, of course. I lock eyes with her. They're glaring at me. I lift one brow and blow her a kiss. She doesn't break character as the Monster moves along the belt.

"Hey!" I say as happily as I can.

"Bitch," she whispers, and her façade drops into a sarcastic smirk. "You drink these too much. And did you just blow Aidan off?"

She scans it anyway and hands it over. I pay and pop the can open immediately to take a swig.

"Not possible," I tell her, totally ignoring her question. "You're off at nine, right?"

"Thank the gods of Greece, yes," Kallie says, over the top as usual.

"I'm about to pull my eyes out. It's been so slow the last hour, but Jesse won't let me leave."

"Aw, it's so sad." I fully earn the middle digit she throws me.

Kallie pulls her hand back like lightning when a middle-aged lady in a flowered blouse and jean skirt pulls a shopping buggy into her lane. Close one. I smile, and Kallie does the same back.

"Last customer?" I whisper. She's only got a minute left.

She shows me her crossed fingers as she greets the lady, and I step to the end of the register where the baggers usually stand. I think about it for a second and take a few steps back so jean skirt lady doesn't think I work here and expect me to load up her cart.

I check my watch when jean skirt lady starts rolling out the door. *9:04 p.m.* Before I comment on the time, Kallie's already switched her light off and is abandoning her post.

"Ugh," Kallie grunts. "I'm not feeling that great. Let me go clock out. I'll be right back."

"You're…" I start, but she disappears down aisle eight and I'm talking to myself, "…sick? You better not be sick."

It's quiet up here. Kallie's right. It's not exactly hopping tonight. Guess everyone went out for dinner or home instead of hitting up the grocery store.

A few registers over, Grace — at least I think it's Grace — is waiting for someone, anyone, to come to her register. She's taller than me and every time I've seen her, she has her long brown hair up in pigtails.

Kallie says she's super hyper, but I've never really talked to her before. I remember Kallie telling me that Grace herself referred to her hyperness as "ADHD, but not quite ADHD." I'm not sure how that works.

"Hey, Grace." I chance getting her name wrong. It's better than standing here all awkward-like. At least I think it is.

"Hey," she says, her eyes darting between me and her register.

I'm not sure if she's nervous, hyped up, or both.

"How's it going?" I ask.

"I work," she says, and immediately her eyes go wide. I tilt my head as she spins around and all but runs to the end of her lane and out of sight.

Okay… That was awkward.

Not soon enough Kallie appears, and I let out a sigh of relief.

"Took you long enough," I say.

"Calm down." Kallie waves me off. "But I don't think I'm going out tonight. I'm not feeling that great."

"Wha?" I leave off the *T* and let my mouth hang. No! I don't want to go home yet.

"Sorry," she says. "My stomach's not feeling right. Taco Bell is definitely a bad idea. Like a major no-go."

"But… Come on! You don't have to eat anything, or we can go somewhere else," I say, maybe a little pouty. Like, I really don't want to go home. I've spent most of the day with my parents, and I need to just not right now. "Please! I need my Kallie time!"

"I know, obviously you need your Kallie time," she crows. "But I really don't feel good, Ty. I'm going home, taking a long bath, and getting in bed."

"Come on, be a big girl!" I try again, and I about grab onto her shoulders, but I stop myself. Maybe that's a bad idea if she's sick, as if making her hang out isn't.

"Going to Taco Bell again?" Aidan comes out of nowhere.

Usually I'd let Kallie take this conversation, she likes him better, but not now.

"No, she's being poor little sick Kallie and isn't going." I cringe inside. It sounds a lot more whiny now that I hear it come out of my mouth than before the words spilled out.

"Ah, poor Kal," Aidan says.

"Yeah, hashtag *poor Kallie*," I mock. Not stopping now.

"Maybe you two could go instead." Kallie's eyes pierce my soul, then jump to Aidan a little *too* happily. "Yes. That's *exactly* what you two should do. Aidan, you like Taco Bell."

"I—" He looks scared.

"Uh, but—" I try.

"It's perfect," Kallie interrupts us both. "Hashtag poor Kallie is going hashtag home and taking some hashtag Pepto."

"I don't—" Aidan starts, but Kallie jumps in again.

"It's settled," she says, and walks out before I can grab her, which is a good thing for her right now.

I close my eyes for a brief second, then look at Aidan and sigh. He appears just as confused as me. I mean, what the hell just happened?

"Uh…" Aidan purses his lips and squints. "Taco Bell?"

A groan escapes my lips.

"Taco Bell."

What I meant to say was, "Nah, I'm good," but no, of course that's not what comes out. Like, what the actual fuck, Tyler?

"Uh… So…" Aidan squints when I don't move.

"Oh yeah." I teeter on my feet and make for the exit. If he's coming, he better be moving. I'm not turning to check. Maybe that's my way out. Maybe he won't move quick enough and I can just leave him. But no, I can't be that fortunate. My hope is dashed when I exit the automatic sliding glass doors.

"Your car or mine?" he asks.

My first thought is *Uh, drive your own ass*, but I bite my tongue and roll my eyes while he still can't see.

"Mine," I decide.

Hell, he drives a Mustang, I should have said his. Sure, it's not a GT or a convertible or anything special, but it's still a Mustang, plus it's this cool matte black color I always liked. It's ten times nicer than mine with its unintentional dual-tone white paint. The only bright side is that if I'm driving I can end things early if I want. It's nice to have the option available.

"Cool." Aidan follows. "Just don't kill us, please."

Oh my God. We haven't even gotten in the car and he's already critiquing my driving. It never ends. Everyone has something to say about my driving.

The car is quiet on the ride there. It's a rule while I'm in the car that music is playing, but I ignore my rule this time. I want to make this uncomfortable and awkward. I don't need him wanting to do this again, plus he's not really on the same wavelength music-wise.

Inside Taco Bell I order and abandon him at the register to find a table. It's practically empty in here, so it's not hard. While he's ordering I glance at him. What am I doing here with *him*? I mean *really*?

I swore I'd never *voluntarily* talk to him again. Sure, he and Brayden were BFFs, but I don't really care. Brayden always talked about him, but the way Aidan would look at Brayden. It makes me sick.

"You forgot your cup." Aidan is suddenly standing across the table with his arm outstretched toward me, my cup in hand. "Probably need it."

He grins. The look on his tan freckled face is way too proud, and I fight back another eye roll. At least I think I do. I could be wrong, sometimes my face does its own thing.

"Thanks." I swipe the cup and fill it with Mountain Dew, because they don't have Dr. Pepper or Sprite here. Such lack of respect, I tell you.

I step away and put a lid on my cup as Aidan fills his up and the short, dumpy fella behind the counter calls out my name.

"That's you," Aidan says, like I need help recognizing my own name. Yeah, I'm about to walk right out the door, right now.

I fake grin and get my tray. Before I'm back, Aidan's name is called and he's sitting across from me.

Why me?

I unwrap my chalupa and start in on it. Aidan keeps darting his eyes around. He won't look me in the eye, and honestly, I like it. I like that even now he's nervous to be around me. A few seconds go by, and I focus on chewing. Like, this is a good chalupa, and I'm going to savor it. But at the same time, I don't know why I'm here. Oh yeah, Kallie.

"So, you still dance?" he asks.

It's not been *that* long since we last talked. *Really, fool, it might have been a year, and that's your fault.* And of course I still dance. My heart's broken, not my damn feet.

"Yeah," I blurt, and go back to trimming the top of my chalupa. The top must go first, then the bottom. It's just how it has to be.

Another long silence bears down on the table. And I think I like it. Like, silence is usually annoying, but right now, it truly is golden.

Just because we talked at the park, and I actually, only God knows why, responded to his text this last week, it doesn't mean we're all friendsy again. He should know that.

"Recorded any dance vids lately?" he asks. "I still can't see your Insta… Still blocked…"

I flinch a little. I'm not sure if he was trying for a low blow or just stating a fact, but did he have to mention it? Yeah, I blocked him on Insta… And SnapChat… And Facebook… And maybe Twitter too. Seems I forgot to block him from texting me though. Nobody's perfect, right?

"Sometimes." I shrug. It's been nearly two months since my last video, I posted it two days before Brayden died. *Don't let it get to you, Ty. Video. Focus on the video.* "Last one was to Halsey's 'Without Me'."

"Oh, I bet that's dope." He leans in. He's obviously expecting me to say more.

I raise my brow as if to say, "What?"

"Can I see it?" he asks.

I try, and fail, to hide a groan.

"Sure." I pick my phone off the table and open Instagram. It takes me a moment to find. I might, just maybe, have flooded my feed with every picture of Brayden I had on my phone over the past month. Actually, why did I not just open TikTok? Ugh. Finally, I pull it up and hand it to Aidan with the video already playing. "Here. It's not that good. I'm a little off beat in a few places."

"I'm sure it's great," he says without seeing it. I roll my eyes, he's not looking at me now anyway.

The music starts up and I can imagine myself in my head, dancing. I clench my fists. I chose that specific song, "Without Me", because Brayden and I had been fighting the week before. I've almost deleted it like a hundred times now.

"This is really good." Aidan smiles and hands my phone back. "I wish I could move like that."

"You probably could," I tell him. Hell, why not. "Just have to practice."

"No amount of practice is going to let *me* move like *that*." He points at my phone.

"Eh." I shrug. "I've watched you dance before."

"And?" He purses his lips and puts on this grin that I can't help but imitate. "Be honest."

How do I say this? It wasn't the worst I've ever witnessed, but I'm not so sure I'd call what I remember him doing last Halloween at Jaylen's place dancing either. *God, just be honest, it's not like I care if it bothers him.*

"Solid three out of ten," I tell him. Okay, maybe a four, but why get his hopes up.

"Three?" His head jerks back and his eye go wide, to the point that I can see the whites around his chocolate-brown irises. That's the one thing I can't deny about Aidan, he has really nice eyes. "Just a three?"

"I mean, like maybe a four." My head teeters. "Maybe…"

"God, I was at least hoping for a five," he whines.

"If you didn't want to know, you shouldn't have asked," I tell him bluntly.

Suddenly he busts out laughing, and now I'm the one jerking my head back. What the hell just happened?

"I'm kidding, Ty," he blurts between laughs. "I suck at dancing, like royally suck, like it's as scary as vagina."

Oh my God, he didn't just say that! But yes, he did. I fall forward laughing.

"Did you just? Seriously?" I can barely talk.

Aidan nods proudly.

"I mean, it's not a lie," he says.

"Well, yeah," I agree. "Kallie's living proof of that."

"Damn! She'd kill you for saying that." Aidan sticks his tongue out, and well, it's sort of cute, but no.

"Good thing she's sick then." I shrug.

"No." Aidan's lips go pouty. "Not my Kallie."

"Fool! You mean *my* Kallie." I let my mouth drop open for emphasis. She is *my* Kallie, not his. I'd cut a fool for less. "*My* Kallie."

"Of course." Aidan does this bow thing, and I'm not sure whether

I want to kill him or applaud him for it.

"Speaking of Kallie," I say while I pull up SnapChat. I take a picture of Aidan and show it to him. She won't believe me tomorrow otherwise. "Proof I didn't ditch you."

It's probably not what I should have said, considering the way his shoulder sort of flinches, but it comes out anyway. I turn my phone back around and type a caption at the bottom and hit send.

TYLER: Why me? I hate you. ::yellow heart::

"Are you going to do any new videos?" Aidan asks, but I'm barely listening.

It takes her less than ten seconds to respond.

KALLIE: Love you too.

I shake my head and pull up the SnapChat map. She's always checking my location, and if she doesn't know why I am wherever I am, I get creepy little stalker snaps with stuff like, "Hoe, why are you at the bowling alley without me?" and "Where you at, bitch?" when she knows full well where this bitch is.

"Hmmm," I say when the maps comes up.

"Don't know that one," Aidan says.

"Huh?" I glance up.

"I asked what video you're going to do next," he says.

"Oh, don't know," I tell him and double-check the map. "Kallie's at Cook Out."

"What? I thought she went home." Aidan leans in and I show him the Snap map. "Maybe it's not updated. It does that sometimes."

I double-check the timestamp.

"Nope, it *caught* her at Cook Out two minutes ago." I emphasize *caught* because that's exactly what it did. "That bitch."

I look up at Aidan and he eyes me all wide-eyed.

"Did she put you up to this?" I snap.

"What? No. I mean she told me you two were going out after work, but that's it. I was planning to go home and write." Aidan sits back and huffs. "I don't know what she's doing."

I let my shoulders relax and trace the bright colors on the table with my finger and eyes. For some reason I believe him. Why the hell is Kallie at Cook Out? What fathomable reason would she have to ditch me and stick me with Aidan of all people in this scary world?

I lift my eyes and settle on Aidan.

"Up for a little stalking?" I propose.

He looks down and bites at his lip.

"Maybe she just stopped and grabbed something and went home," he counters.

"That wouldn't have been two minutes ago," I point out. "Come on."

I feel like it shouldn't be that hard a decision, and honestly, I'm going to stalk on over to Cook Out either way. And just in case he forgot, he's riding with me, so, like, there's that.

"Why not," Aidan gives in. "If she gets mad, I'm blaming you."

"Fair enough." I wrap up the last half of my second chalupa. It can wait. There's treachery afoot.

"Oh, like now." Aidan stops lifting his quesadilla.

"Uh, yeah." I get up and eye him down, giving him my best what-the-fuck-are-you-waiting-for look.

"Okay." He stands and swipes his bag from the table and follows.

In the car I leave the music off, and this time it's not out of spite, no, I'm too focused on my traitor friend. Aidan says something, but it's nothing more than sounds in my head with no discernable meaning. What the hell does she think she's doing? Trying to hook me up with this asshole? Is she tired of me? What?

"She better not still be there when we get there," I say, more to myself than to Aidan.

"She probably isn't." Aidan shifts in his seat.

We speed down the highway and I slow at the traffic light where Cook Out sits off to the right. I scan the cars outside for her devious little Kia.

"You see her car?" I ask, further dragging Aidan into my mission. He's here, he's going to help.

"Uh…" It's more of a noise than a word. "Is that it, next to that green truck?"

I find the truck. It's one of those I've-got-a-tiny-dick-mobiles with the massive tires and nauseating rebel flag in the back window. It's lifted so high I'd need a stepping stool to get in. And sure enough, Kallie's Kia is parked next to it.

"That bitch," slips out.

"Ty…" Aidan sounds uncomfortable.

I don't answer as we pull into the lot and I start around the back of the restaurant, and then around front where the windows give a halfway decent view inside.

And there she is.

"Who's that?" Aidan says, just as my eyes lock on to the dude sitting across from my BFF.

"Yeah, who's that?" I blurt.

All I can make out from this distance is short brown hair and his hands waving in the air. Whoever the hell he is, he's a hands talker. Already bad news. I growl and grip the steering wheel. Who did I get ditched for?

"I can't tell, keep driving." Aidan pulls out his phone and I don't know if he's taking pictures or what, but right now, I'm on his side. Or maybe he's on mine, not sure how it's working.

"You get a picture?" I ask.

"Yep, it's—" He pinches at the screen.

"Who is it?" I interrupt him. I need to know. It's not that she can't talk to dudes. I just need to know who, and preferably before she meets them, and with my approval. Okay, maybe not my approval, but still.

"Jeremiah." Aidan sucks in his lips. "As in senior Jeremiah."

"Redneck Jeremiah?" I ask.

"What other senior Jeremiah do you know?" Aidan asks.

"Point taken." I nod and pull back onto the road before I do anything stupid, like stop and walk into Cook Out. "What's she doing here with him?"

Jeremiah's not bad. He's not like a lot of the guys at West, especially the jocks and country boys who mock me going down the hall throwing the F-slur at me. Or better yet, one of the many who've added me on SnapChat just to ask for nudes, or begged me to suck their dick and then threaten to kick my ass if I tell anyone. I don't really know him though, but at least he's not a douche that I know of. Of course, the good ol' country boy, let's go hunting clique just isn't me. Hell, he even went to the same elementary school as Kallie and me.

"So…" Aidan starts.

"I'm going to kill her," I say. "And him. It's simple. I'll drug them, then bury them both out behind Dad's chicken coop."

"Maybe a little much." Aidan sounds nervous. "I mean, you probably shouldn't bury them near your house. I don't know, at least take them to Hickory or something. Ooh! Dissolving them in acid is good too. It gets rid of most the evidence."

A grin breaks across my face and I look away from the road long enough to show him my approval.

"Someone's been talking to Kallie a little too much," I laugh. We turn back into the Food Lion parking lot and I take the spot next to

Aidan's Mustang. "She'd probably also say I should scatter their teeth, make it harder to piece together."

This is what she gets for being a forensics psychopath and telling me how to get away with murder all the time.

"Definitely." He nods.

"So you had nothing to do with this? Y'all aren't conspiring against me, right?" I eye him. He's never been a great liar, he's worse at it than I am, so this should be easy if they were conspiring against me.

"I had no idea. I was seriously just going home after work," he says.

I keep my stare suspicious, but either he suddenly got good at the whole lying game or he's telling the truth. And honestly, I think he's telling the truth.

"'Kay." I drop my gaze. "Sorry to cut things short."

"It's all good," he says. "I'm honestly surprised Kal is seeing anyone."

"Seeing anyone?" I scoot back. "Like *seeing* seeing someone, like dating?"

Surely not.

"Yeah," Aidan says, like it's as obvious as the sun shining in the morning. "What else is she doing?"

"Having dinner with a friend?" Dating. No. She can't be dating. Not without telling me first.

"Yeah, but not just a friend, boy —" he says, but I stop him with an upraised palm.

"Nope." I interrupt.

"Bu —" he tries.

"No." I throw my hand up, and he starts smiling.

Aidan giggles and reaches for the door handle. I shake my head. Is this really happening? Kallie's a traitor and I'm dropping Aidan off. What crazy, no good shit is next? So help me, if they announce Tom Holland is no longer playing Spider-Man, I'll lose my mind.

"Guess I'll leave you to plan that murder then." Aidan opens his door and starts to slide out.

"I'll let you know how it goes. You're part of this now. If I go down, you go down," I jest.

"But that means you have to talk to me, like, voluntarily." His brow lifts, and I can see him second-guessing his decision to say it at all.

I can't blame him. For a split second I was about to shove him out and run over his ass for that comment, but something stops me.

"Who says it's voluntary? Kallie put you in this," I remind him. It's true, it's not how I planned tonight.

"Eh." He shrugs and gets out. "Talk to you later, Ty."

Before I can say anything, like "maybe" or "we'll see," the door shuts behind him. I look away, staring into the trees dividing the parking lot from the bank.

What just happened?

AIDAN

"Your workbook assignment is due tomorrow," Mrs. Williams shouts above the shuffling and zipping of book bags and feet.

I slip our much-too-thick math textbook into my sack and sling it over my shoulders. The last thing I want to hear after the last bell of the day rings is that we have homework. At least it's not Coach D's American History. Math and science make sense, history, it's just a bunch of old white dudes making bad decisions the rest of us are forced to deal with and have to memorize.

And speaking of history, it doesn't fade quick enough. I want to talk to Tyler, but all I catch is his backside shooting past the classroom entrance. We have second and fourth together, and per usual, we haven't spoken a word yet. Sure, it's been like this since the beginning of the semester. That's what happens when you choose your courses before your friend starts dating your BFF, and all three of you fight to get as many classes together as possible, then one starts hating you. Brayden shared second and fourth too, but it got awkward when Tyler and Bray started dating and I suddenly fell out of favor with Tyler.

I don't know. I thought today might be different. Maybe he'd acknowledge me as an actual human being again. I mean things went well last night. Sure, we were stalking Kallie, but I swear he wasn't his normal I-hate-you-Aidan self by the time he dropped me off. Yet again, I thought our talk in the park might have helped, that maybe I'd get a friend back, but I was wrong there too.

I shuffle past Mrs. Williams and filter into the hallway. It's my day off, so I'm more than ready to get out of here and home for a nap and maybe a little writing. I head down the stairs.

Oh yeah, my dumb ass texted Tyler this morning to see how the whole Kallie thing went down last night. It's been total silence on the Tyler front though, so I ended up getting the lowdown from Kallie herself between first and second periods. That's basically the only time she and Ty aren't connected at the hip.

We weren't too far off base. She's "testing the waters" with Jeremiah, but she's not sure if she likes him or not yet. She is sure he's into her, but sometimes I think Kallie thinks all the guys are into her. I asked what Tyler said and she huffed and complained about how he was all over the top about it. Something about how she was abandoning him, and she can't have a boyfriend, then backpedaling and saying yeah, sure, she can have a boyfriend, but not without talking to him first. Basically what he said to me last night.

At least he's protective. That's a good thing, right? I mean, as long as he isn't psychopathic or anything, that's good. I think. Maybe? I've known Ty for a while. Sure, he's different, but he's —

"Ah!" I scream as my foot catches something on the bottom stair and I tumble forward. I throw my hands out. They slap glossed tile before my jaw and hip slam the floor in rhythm.

"Whatcha doing on the ground, faggot?" a much too familiar voice calls from behind me.

Before I can turn or catch my breath, Christian lands a kick in my side. The impact knocks me over and instinctively I cradle my body. He kicks again, or maybe it's Sean Addison this time. Pain lightnings through my chest and wires down my arms.

I hate them so much. There are a lot of homophobes in this school — we *are* in the middle of the country — but they're the worst. Always have been.

"Get up, fag," Sean taunts, and to no surprise, a crowd materializes around us. "Get up!"

"Leave me alone," I yell. I start to get back to my feet, but what's the use.

"Bet you're a bottom fag, aren't you? How about I shove my boot up your ass?" Christian drops his booted foot on my butt and shoves me back to the ground. "You'd like that, wouldn't you?"

"For a *straight* boy you know an awful lot about what I like," I bite back. I don't know where it comes from, but God I wish I could reach out, grab those words and stuff them back down my throat.

"What did you say?" Christian yells. "Say it again! I dare you!"

Nope, not happening, never saying that again. Instead, I rub my side and start pushing off the ground.

"Say it again, fag!" he yells.

"Teacher!" someone in the crowd yells, and bodies dart in every direction.

"Come on, Christian!" Sean tugs at the football player's broad shoulders.

Christian locks his angry eyes on me for a little longer.

"You better watch your little beaner fag mouth," he spews, and then, no joke, spits in my face.

I jerk back, but it's no use. I want to say something back, something mean and degrading, but I can't think of anything in the moment. I can never think of anything in the moment. Christian runs off down the hall with Sean. They slow to a walk just as Mr. Cloaninger comes around the corner, and Sean smiles and waves at him. God they disgust me.

I just want to go home.

TYLER

Monday nights at work are usually dead, but damn. This is a whole new level. I guess no one wants barbeque tonight.

"Dream car?" Josh leans against the metal bar lining the fry cook station.

On a good day he wouldn't have time to lean, and even if he did, the owner always chants her, "You've got time to lean, then you've got time to clean," saying. But if we cleaned any more today, it would just be recleaning the same shit we just finished cleaning for, like, the third time.

Oddly though, I'm glad to be here regardless. The alternative is being stuck at church. It's Monday, but it's revival week, so that means service every day this week, and thanks to a little misinformation to my boss I'm scheduled to work most of the week.

"Uh…" Heather purses her lips like it's a super hard question.

I knew my answer the moment he asked. The Aston Martin DBS Superleggera. It's like the Italians fucked heaven and produced a car, because I'm assuming heaven is supposed to make only the most beautiful things.

"A Mustang," Heather sighs, like she's still not sure.

My mouth drops. A Mustang? That's the best you can come up with, Heather? And by the looks on their faces, Josh and Donald are thinking the same thing.

"Okay." Donald stretches the O out. "How about a souped-up Caddy CTS-V or maybe a Lamborghini? A Ventador, maybe."

Josh frowns in this *The Godfather* type of way that says he agrees but that Donald could have done better. "Bugatti. The Veyron. It's *the* fastest production car in the world. I mean, come on. There's no competition, guys."

"But is it?" I steal a lukewarm fry from under the heat light.

I don't know, I don't have a clue. It seems like an awful big claim, but I don't know enough about cars to know for certain. I basically look at the design and if I like the way it looks, then I might check out some of the specs. Maybe.

Like my Aston Martin, it's a three-hundred-thousand-dollar-plus supercar, seven-hundred-some horsepower, and a top speed of 211 mph. But that's literally all I know.

"Uh, yeah." Josh raises his eyebrow.

"I don't know, just asking," I say.

Josh laughs and shakes his head. He knows my auto knowledge is limited. He's the car guy, him and Donald both.

"What about you?" he asks.

"Easy," I tell them. "The Aston Martin DBS Superleggera. I probably butchered that name though."

Heather and Donald chuckle in the corner while he wraps an arm around her. They've been going out for a month, or maybe two now.

"I dunno, I think it's Italian," Josh says. "It's nice though—5.2 liter V12. Seven hundred and fifteen horsepower. I think it's got a zero to sixty in, like, three point four seconds or something."

See, I was close. Seven hundred and fifteen horsepower, and I did know it was a V12, but I had no clue it was a 5.2 liter. Actually, I don't even know what that means.

All I can think of when I hear liters are bottles of Dr. Pepper. And I don't think it's pumping pure Dr. Pepper goodness through its fluid lines, whatever those are called.

"It's gorgeous," I tell them. "Those cur—"

"You ready for break?" Allison dangles around the corner, half in the dining room and half in the kitchen.

"Sure." I spin around. It beats standing back here in the heat, even if we did finally land on a half-decent topic.

"Go ahead," she yells and disappears into the dining room.

"Looks like I'm off." I grin to the others.

"It's just a break, you'll be back," Heather reminds me.

I roll my eyes at her and take a scoop of half-hour-old fries, a few hushpuppies in one of those little red-and-white plaid paper baskets, and head into the dining room.

It's empty. It's a few minutes after eight and there's not a single table with customers. I switchback around the corner and plop my ass down across from Lori, one of the two servers today.

"That it?" Lori asks.

"Huh?" I pull out my phone. There's a slew of texts, Snaps, a few TikTok messages, all from Kallie. Oh, and a Snap from Katie.

"That's what you're eating?" she asks, raising her brow above big emerald eyes.

"Yeah." I nod. "Carbs to the rescue."

"It's not fair," Lori complains. "You eat all that and stay skinny. I look at it and gain five pounds."

"Nah, you don't." I wave a hand and ignore that she just called me skinny. "It just doesn't stick on me."

I unlock my phone and open Kallie's Snap while Lori keeps going.

"Wait until you turn forty, it'll stick then," she says.

Half listening, I nod and bite back a laugh at an image of Kallie, straight-faced, hiding behind her register at Food Lion, with the caption, *I wish this place would burn to the ground.*

"Ah," I mumble, hoping Lori accepts it as I open Kallie's text message.

KALLIE: Hear about Aidan?

My face scrunches up. I hate these types of questions. It could be really good or really bad, or somewhere in between. There's absolutely no telling. And even more so, why do I care?

TYLER: No.

I snatch up a hushpuppy and dip it in some vinegar, fully expecting to have a minute or two before she responds, but the little bubbles start popping up at the bottom of my screen. Could be she's on break, her manager let her off early, or she just doesn't give a fuck.

KALLIE: ::crying emoji:: ::crying emoji:: Christian beat him up after school.

What? That prick. No one deserves that, but I know Christian. He's one of West's star football players, with no personality beyond being an asshat.

TYLER: Serious? He ok?

I'm not stupid, I know why he did it no matter what he says, if they even try to punish him. It's because Aidan's gay. I've been at the receiving end of Christian and Sean's antics on more than one occasion. I can't stand them.

Christian's one of those *straight* jocks that makes life miserable, at least when he's not trying to get the gay guys to blow him. I'm not proud to admit I indulged him a few times my freshman year. I thought it was great then. I got to experiment a little even if he was always a douche about it, and hell, it was with arguably one of the hottest guys in the school, but looking back it was one of my worst high school decisions.

"You okay?" I'd almost forgotten Lori was sitting at the same table with me.

"Huh?" I look up, re-centering myself, and point at my phone.

"Oh yeah. Just stupid people."

The little bubbles stop moving and another message pops up.

KALLIE: He says he's good. But fuck those guys.

Exactly!

TYLER: Yeah! Fuck them!

TYLER: They get in trouble?

I hope they did. Not like anyone will do anything about it. No one cares when it's a gay boy getting beat up by the school's most important students.

KALLIE: Don't know... Don't think so. ::crying emoji:: ::mad emoji::

That makes sense. I hate it for Aidan. Being on the receiving end of their shit sucks. Christian and Sean are relentless.

TYLER: Figures. ::eye roll emoji::

One of these days they're going to get what they deserve. At least that's what I tell myself every time I hear their names come up. Which is a lot at West.

KALLIE: What we doing for your b-day?

Talk about switching topics. I'm still trying to gather exactly how I feel about Aidan getting harassed. It bugs me, that's for sure, but maybe there's still this little part that's like *oh well*, but maybe I feel a little bad about thinking that too. Maybe. A little.

As for what I'm doing for my birthday, probably nothing. It's this Friday. I'm turning seventeen, but I'll be stuck at church for this damn revival I don't even want to be at. Isn't three times a week enough already?

TYLER: Church ::eye roll emoji:: ::crying emoji:: ::crying emoji::

KALLIE: Church?

TYLER: Revival. You know my dad.

KALLIE: Ah... How about after?

After? That could work. A few hours have to be better than nothing at all.

TYLER: Sure. Taco Bell?

KALLIE: Taco Bell? For your birthday?

She has a point. It's not birthday good, but this is Lenoir we're talking about and we don't have all day. The real question is where are we going to manage to make it after church on a Friday night? It's not like Lenoir is buzzing with life after eight o'clock.

TYLER: Got a better idea?

KALLIE: Taco Bell.

TYLER: You going to ditch me again?

I let a broad smile crease my cheeks as I type it out. She knows I'm not letting it go anytime soon, or ever. While the text message bubbles flicker at the bottom of my screen, what Christian did to Aidan hits me again.

Why are some people so determined to make our lives miserable? What did we do to deserve being treated like shit? What did *Aidan* ever do to them? I mean, I at least have a reason to not like Aidan. They don't.

KALLIE: OMG Ty! I'm not going to ditch you. Promise! Not too fond of Jeremiah anyway.

I wasn't expecting that. Ever since Sunday it had been Jeremiah this, Jeremiah that. How cute he is, how he opened the door for her and how he likes creepy horror murder shit too. It's Kallie, and that last one mattering shouldn't seem weird for her, but it still just hit odd when she said it.

TYLER: Oh... Sorry? Okay. Taco Bell, Friday after church.

KALLIE: Eh. It's whatever, and yep.

I check my watch. Only a minute left on break and I still haven't finished half my "meal".

TYLER: TTYL. Break's over.

I put my phone down and devour what's left in my little paper bowl. I can't seem to get the image of Aidan getting the shit beat out of him out of my head, and I don't like it. Why the hell? It's so fucked up.

I hope he's okay, I really hope he is. Hell, it could have just as easily been me. I left class just a minute before he did, I think. I might have even passed Christian on my way out.

It's time to go back to hell, aka the kitchen, so I fold up my empty paper bowl and eye my phone for a second. Maybe I should say something. I unlock it and open the super short text thread I have with Aidan.

TYLER: Heard about what happened at school. Hope you're okay.

AIDAN

Monday, May 20

There are times I wonder if writing messed up horror stuff makes me a bad person. I sit here and put my poor character through hell. Kit is literally fighting against this bloodthirsty cult that decapitates most of their enemies and sends the rest into an arena constructed from the remains of an old city to fight to their own bloody death to be "saved". It's sort of effed up when you really think about it.

But that doesn't stop me. I'm just going to move past it. That's what Brayden would always say, because I've said it a lot. Just move past it.

My cursor is stuck in place though. I know where I want this to go, but my focus isn't exactly great today. Too much shit I don't want to think about on top of everything the past few months. The cursor just blinks and blinks and blinks.

Come on, Aidan, you can do this.

My fingers hover over the keys. I clench my hands into fists, then stretch my fingers out like it's going to help jumpstart the creative part of my mind. I haven't gotten to the part about the cult yet. I mean, Kit's living with them already, but he doesn't know it's a cult exactly yet. He just thinks they're this group that's survived any way they could, even if they are a bit odd.

What if— My phone dings and the thought vanishes. Dammit. I lift my phone and there's a text from Kallie. Thanks a lot, Kal.

KALLIE: How ya doing?

Not amazing, and your timing could use some improvement.

She's been worried about me all day. Someone obviously told her about what happened after school. She's checked up on me twice—no, make that three times—today.

AIDAN: I'm good.

I do the finger scrunching thing again and refocus on the computer screen. What was I saying? Something about—

My phone dings again. I'm going to kill her.

KALLIE: You're not lying, are you?

I'm not sure whether to be irritated she doubts me or glad she gets me. I roll my eyes and type back.

AIDAN: No. Just trying write.

At least it's the truth, mostly. God, except for the missing *to* in my text between *trying* and *write*. I throw my head back. Really? But I'm not correcting it.

I am doing okay though. Yeah, today sort of sucked, but I can deal with the likes of Christian and Sean. Plus, I'd really like to just not think about it.

KALLIE: Okay. Here if you need me.

KALLIE: When you asking Ty on another date?

Woah! Date? *Another?*

AIDAN: A date? WTF?

KALLIE: Yeah. ::shrug emoji::

AIDAN: Uh… No.

KALLIE: Why TF not?

My head falls back and I blink in confusion. What do you mean *Why TF not?* I can think of a lot of reasons.

AIDAN: 1 he hates me. 2 we're barely friends. 3 uh no. Did I mention he hates me?

I love her, I do, but wow. Even if some small part of me was like *maybe*, it's still a big no. He really does hate me, even if it doesn't make any sense. And it'd be weird anyway. He was Brayden's boy. It just seems like it would be wrong.

KALLIE: Technicalities.

Technicalities my effing foot. No. I've got one for that.

AIDAN: Better question. When you ditching Ty next?

KALLIE: And you call yourself my friend.

AIDAN: ::laughing emoji:: You know I ::yellow heart:: you.

KALLIE: Sure. ::laughing emoji:: ::yellow heart:: Neither of you letting me live that down.

It's about pointless to continue writing now. I'm too distracted, so I close out my story and flip the laptop screen down. I lean against my chair and watch the ceiling tiles blur together as I spin around.

AIDAN: NEVER!!! ::laughing emoji:: ::laughing emoji::

Even if, in some weird alternate dimension, I did like Ty, it wouldn't work. He despises me. I think the only reason he talked to me at the park was because he was hurting, and he even has the hardest time admitting it, he always has. Brayden used to talk about how it frustrated him. Tyler would be down about something, but he'd refuse to talk about it. He'd just hold it all in and refuse to say anything. I don't know if I could deal with that. Oh yeah, and there's that again. He was Brayden's boyfriend. And Brayden was, is, always will be my best friend. It seems like I might be wrong to like my best friend's boyfriend, right? I know he's… You know, but it still seems wrong.

My phone dings. I pick it up, fully expecting another text from Kallie unable to get over the imaginary idea she has of the two of us. But a confused frown crosses my brow instead.

Tyler?

TYLER: Heard about what happened at school. Hope you're okay.

My eyes freeze on the words, stuck to the text. He's seriously asking if I'm okay? Did something happen? Did someone threaten him? Kallie?

Kallie! *I know you put him up to this.* Instead of replying, I open up my thread with her and start typing.

AIDAN: Ty just texted me asking if I'm okay.

KALLIE: He did?!?! ::surprise face emoji::

No. You're not getting out of this that easy.

AIDAN: You threatened him didn't you?

The little bubbles flicker at the bottom of my screen. This one's taking a little longer.

KALLIE: Uh no! Offended. ::crying emoji:: Just told him what those asshats did to you. Must have been worried.

Worried? Ty? About me? I throw my head back and let out a laugh. No. Not Tyler. Not about me. If anything, he's happy about it. Actually, he's probably hoping I'm down and depressed about it so he can revel in the fact. That's why he texted. That's it.

AIDAN: Sure. ::eye roll emoji:: You're just trying to set us up.

KALLIE: You want me to? You're replying right?! ::shrug emoji::

AIDAN: HELL NO!

KALLIE: HELL NO to me setting you two up or replying? ::big smile emoji::

Oh my God! The craziest part is this is what I like about Kallie. She's never deterred from a mission, and she refuses to hide it. She's just her—pure, real, crazy-ass, amazing bitch Kallie.

AIDAN: Both!

Okay, that's probably a lie. I'm about ninety-five percent sure I'm going to respond. It's a flaw. I absolutely hate it, like hate-hate it, when I text or Snap someone and they leave me on read. It's a passionate hate-type situation. The way I see it, I took the time out of my day to say something to you, I at least deserve an "OK" or a little smiley emoji or something. Anything less is so rude.

KALLIE: Right. Let me know how it goes.

Oh my! Maybe sometimes it isn't the best when someone knows you so well. But I guess there's no use holding off. I switch over to Tyler's thread. I read it again.

TYLER: Heard about what happened at school. Hope you're okay.

Why am I like this?

AIDAN: I'm good. They're just dicks.

The moment I hit send another text comes through from Kallie and I swear my eyes do a full one eighty.

KALLIE: You texted him didn't you?

I purse my lips and huff over a smile I can't really hold back. How does she do this?

AIDAN: Yes. Shut up. ::laughing emoji:: You know I can't not reply to anyone.

KALLIE: Knew it! ::laughing emoji::

AIDAN: ::eye roll emoji::

TYLER

Thursday, May 23

You'd think after a year working at a barbeque joint I'd be used to smelling like grease and hushpuppies when I get off. Nope. I'm still not, and I hope I never do.

It's all I can smell. It's everywhere on me, and if it wasn't for my car's roof being down and the cool night wind blowing ferociously around me, my entire car would smell of it.

I turn down my music as I pull off Collettsville Road and into my driveway. I take a deep breath. I'm about to attempt the impossible, but who knows, maybe, just maybe, it'll go better than I expect. Not likely though.

I did sort of already tell Kallie that I might be able to hang out earlier tomorrow for my birthday than originally. I just have to convince Dad to let me skip the last night of revival. So basically, the impossible.

I tried begging my boss to schedule me for a short shift tomorrow right after school, but she wasn't having that. Something about not purposefully going against what my dad wants, even if it's my birthday. They're friends from way back. I shouldn't have told them why I wanted to work extra.

The living room window is lit up, so they must still be awake. I brake to a stop next to the gravel sidewalk leading to the back deck and exhale a deep breath. I've got this. It's going to work. Or it's going to die a death of fire and brimstone. That's more likely.

Walking up the stairs, my mind lands fully in home territory. This is a really bad idea. Dad's not going to go for it. But what if he does? Maybe he's in a let's-give-Tyler-this-one-little-thing mood. I shrug and slip inside through the back door.

Criminal Minds is playing on the TV. It's basically the only thing Mom watches, sort of like Kallie. I stop and ground myself before walking into the living room. Everyone's here. Mom looks up from her tablet as I walk in. She's watched the show enough times to have them memorized anyway.

"Hey, honey." She smiles. "How was work?"

"It was okay." I try my best not to be stiff. I really want this to work.

I spy Melinda at the other end of the couch, her eyes lost in her phone. I didn't even have a phone at thirteen, let alone spend every waking hour on it. But she accepts me, unlike everyone else in the room. I roll my eyes and find my target sitting on the recliner at the other end of the room. Dad.

"You missed a good service tonight." He nods at me. "We had three people come forward during the invitation."

"That's great." I try my best to sound supportive, but so far it's already not looking good. He's on one of his church highs right now, which means the idea of me not going tomorrow is losing points real quick. But you lose one hundred percent of the battles you don't fight, right? "Uh… About church. It's my birthday tomorrow-"

"That's right! Hitting seventeen!" Dad interrupts me, smiling from ear to ear. "And how great is it? You'll get to thank God for another year of life *at* church!"

"About that." I bite at my lip. This is not going in the direction I hoped at all, and I haven't even gotten my question out yet. I pause, changing my mind like ten times. I should just say *forget it* and go upstairs, but no, I have to at least try. "Kallie wants to take me out tomorrow for my birthday… Can I miss the service tomorrow?"

"You can go after church," he says. I look to my mom, hoping she'll be my advocate, but she smiles weakly at me. Thanks for nothing.

"But she wants to go eat and then go to Bo's," I tell him. She did mention Bo's the other day, but it was more like, we *could* do it, not something she was super determined to do.

"You'll have time." Yet again he finds a way.

"Okay." I purse my lips and turn to walk up the stairs. *No!* I've had enough of this. I'm tired of giving in and keeping my mouth shut. It's my birthday! I'm not asking for much. Jesus isn't going to miss me that much if I skip one service, and I'm pretty sure He wouldn't approve of half the stuff they preach anyway. I turn around and face him. "It's just one service. And it's not even a normal one. It can't hurt to miss one night."

"But it could be the one service you need," he tells me, and it's everything I can do not to roll my eyes. I know exactly what he's saying even if he doesn't come right out and state it. "And we go to church whenever the doors are open. That's what God wants, and we're to give our best all the time."

"Seriously?" I huff. "Just this once! Please!"

"No, Tyler." Dad shakes his head and straightens in his recliner. "Going to church is the least we can do, and it should be an honor to give that time to God. We never know when God is going to speak to us."

"Just say it." I raise my voice but manage at the last possible second to keep it from being a yell. "I know you're dying to. So just say it. You're hoping God speaks to me and tells me I should be ashamed of being a faggot and need to turn from my evil ways."

"You know it isn't right. We taught you better. It's your choice to make the right decision." He starts to stand up.

"The only decision I made was to be who God made me, even if you hate it," I yell. I'm not standing for this shit anymore. I'm done with it. Dad wouldn't know God if the Almighty came down and sat right beside him in the flesh. All he knows is this hateful vision. And I'm tired of being under it.

"Don't blame this on God. He didn't make you like that." Dad steps forward.

I glance at Mom again, but she won't look at me. I wish she'd just look at me, acknowledge me, say something. I know she's not going to contradict him, and I know she agrees with him, but still. Something.

"Oh my God! I can't even." I twist around and start up the stairs.

"We're not done here." Dad raises his voice to reach me.

"Yes! We are!" I yell and slam my bedroom door behind me and send the lock home.

I fall against my door, clench my eyes shut and ball up my fists. I'm normal. I'm exactly how I'm supposed to be. Who I am is perfectly okay, and I couldn't change it if I tried. Hell, I have tried. I tried so fucking hard. He doesn't know how horrified I was when I was younger and started to like boys. All my life I'd been taught gays went straight to hell, like it was some express track, and you couldn't be a Christian and gay at the same time, and I believed it.

I did some hard searching back then. Finding anything I could to explain why I am the way I am, and how it could possibly be wrong. It didn't take long to see that the words used in the Bible didn't mean exactly in their original context as people want to act like they do now to justify their hatred. It was about temple prostitution, and men exerting sexual domination over others, not loving and consensual relationships. There's a big difference.

But it still took me a long time to see through the fear and misinterpretations. But I finally did it, and I'm not regressing back into that now.

I gather myself and make it to my bed. I need to talk to someone, aka Kallie. I pull out my phone and dial her number. It rings and rings and rings.

"Come on, Kal, answer the damn phone!" I beg the screen, but after a few more rings it goes to voicemail. I try again, but it ends the same. "Dammit."

My eyes dart around my room. My body is shaking. I hate this so much. Why can't I have one day? Just one freaking day. I guess the silver lining is that at least Dad didn't threaten sending me back to camp. I'm assuming he knows that shit doesn't work now, but if he gets desperate enough he might try it again.

Aidan's name pops into my head. No. I'll just wait for Kallie to get off work and call her then. Or maybe I could call Rhys. No, we've not talked lately, and that's my fault, as always. Maybe Katie? God, no, I don't know her that well. You know what, I'll be good until then. I can do that. I really can.

But... I don't know.

I might be able to get Aidan on the phone now. Hell. Why not? I just need to talk to someone, and Aidan is someone. I don't have to be all friendsy to just talk and get my mind off all this, right?

I find Aidan's contact and hit Call. What the hell am I doing? No. Bad call. I go to end it, but he picks up.

"Hello?" It comes over the line as a question.

Dammit.

"Hey," I say like someone carrying loads of guilt they're about to admit.

"Everything okay?" Aidan asks.

"Of course, why?" It's such a stupid thing to ask, but I'm in defense mode. That's really the first thing anyone would ask.

"I mean, you *are* calling me…" He pauses a second.

"Can't argue with that." I smack my lips and sprawl out on my mattress. "Doesn't mean something's wrong though."

That's exactly why I'm calling. Why the hell am I so defensive?

"Uh… Okay. So what's up?" he asks.

It's so obvious he isn't buying it. And his voice sounds nervous as hell.

"Okay, you're right. I couldn't get a hold of Kallie, so…" I groan.

"Huh?" Aidan asks. "Oh yeah, she works until nine."

"Apparently. Was really hoping I'd get her on break. Either way, my dad is getting on my last nerve!" I tell him. I just want to scream it, but I keep it calm…mostly. "My birthday's tomorrow, but he's determined I have to be at church. I swear he thinks the world will end and hell is going to swallow me whole if, God forbid, my feet don't enter the building tomorrow. But Kallie and I were going to go out, and I really don't want to go to church on my birthday and have someone tell me I'm this horrible person again."

"Okay, first, why would you be at church on a Friday?" Aidan sounds confused, and I get it. Like, same!

"It's revival this week, so it's church, like, literally every night except Saturday." I roll my eyes and prop up on my side. I'm honestly surprised they're not having it Saturday too. "It's ridiculous. As if three times a week isn't enough."

I'm just waiting for Dad to come knocking on my door, but I guess he gave up. *Please have given up.*

"Don't want to knock it, but that does seem a bit like overkill. And it *is* your birthday. That only happens once a year," Aidan says. "You not doing anything with your family?"

"We are," I tell him. "Saturday night. It's just like if Christmas falls on a church day, even flipping Wednesday, they'll postpone it too."

"Woah." Aidan sighs over the telephone. "Can you and Kal not just go after?"

"I mean, yeah, we can. That's sort of what we're planning, but I don't want to go to church on my birthday!" I repeat. I'm beginning to sound like a bad rap song repeating the same thing over and over again, but to hell with it. I don't care. "What gets me most is how Dad's so determined I'm this horrible person *just* because I asked to not go this one time. Like, really?"

I didn't plan on acting like a total little bitch downstairs, but still. It's not that hard to treat me like a normal person and stop acting like I'm some Satanist simply because God made me gay. It's not like I don't believe in God. I do. Just not the way they do.

"Sorry," Aidan apologizes.

"Not your fault," I say. I don't even know why I'm talking to him about this. Why *did* I call him? Oh, right. Kallie's sorry ass is at work. "Sorry to drop this on you. I shouldn't have called."

"No!" he yelps. "It's okay. I don't mind, swear it."

I don't say anything for a moment as I get my heartbeat back to normal, and Aidan laughs with all the nervous energy of a squirrel.

It's just all so much sometimes. There are moments it feels like every time Dad looks at me he's wondering how hot hell is going to be, and how my skin is going to char up. The crazy part is I know he's scared.

I know he does it because he really believes it and he cares about me. But it's like he doesn't get how to channel that without me being messed up and sinful and less than. He doesn't understand how I feel, and what I know about myself. He just doesn't.

"You've got it easy, Aidan. Your mom gets it," I tell him.

"She does. Of course, Dad hasn't been around since, you know, *forever*, so I don't know if he'd be okay with it or not." His voice trails off a little. "Who cares though, right? Fuck him for leaving."

Damn. Now part of me feels guilty for bringing it up. Aidan doesn't even know his dad. From what I understand, his dad ditched his mom in high school when she got pregnant with him.

"Sorry, I wasn't thinking about that," I say.

He laughs quietly. "It's okay. Not your problem."

"I just wish my parents were good with it, you know?" I tell him. His mom is so cool about it all. I'd give so much for that. I'm not going to let it hold me back, but I still wish they'd get it. Hell, I even got the talk when I came out. It should have been a time when they realized my struggle and supported me. Instead they sent me off to hate camp. It gives me chills thinking about it. And it hurts.

"Yeah, but you've got a lot of people. We've got your back," he reminds me, and I know he's right. It's just hard to see when one of the main people I'd like to have behind me isn't. "Kallie, Katie, Bryce. Most of the non-assholes at school. Obviously me. I mean, I *am* gay. It's sort of a requirement."

"Truth," I laugh. It's nice to smile, but my smile breaks when I think about how I've treated him the past year. I did have good reason though. I don't need to think about that right now. "It's just… I don't know."

"That's okay," Aidan says.

"I got to go," I tell him. The fact that I even called in the first place is starting to eat at me. Still, I do what any half-decent person would to end the call. "Thanks for listening."

"No prob!" Aidan says. "Talk to you later."

"Bye," and I hang up.

AIDAN

Thursday, May 23

"Bye," I say as the call ends. My phone slides from my grip and plops on my bed. Genji flinches and stares at me wide-eyed and then decides all is okay and cuddles up next to me again.

Did that just happen? No. What just happened?

I scoop up my phone and check the call log. I couldn't have imagined it all. Not in that clarity. There's no way. I scan the log and there it is. *Tyler Gentry*, it was actually him. I'm stuck somewhere between shock and total disbelief. I might have been second choice to Kallie, but he did voluntarily call me.

It sucks he has to deal with all that though. The non-acceptance, the snide remarks. All I deal with is outside the house. Mamá's great. She wasn't surprised when I came out. Nah, she literally told me she was glad I finally figured it out, as if she'd been waiting or something. She said she loved me regardless, and then asked what I wanted for dinner. She's been amazing from day one. My abuelos were a bit of a harder sell, but it only took them a week or so to come around. I think it was more the shock that got them up front.

But Tyler? No. He deals with it every day. Every. Single. Day.

I can't imagine. And I tend to forget there are still people who do. I mean I know there are still assholes out there. Christian's a prime example, but the world's pretty accepting now, compared to what I hear of the past. Even here in this backwoods North Carolina county in the foothills that's overwhelmingly not happy with us gays, they're still mostly friendly, at least to our faces.

It's bad enough he has to deal with it at all, but now, for his birthday? Wait. His birthday?

An idea slips in through a crevice in the back of my mind, that place where monumentally stupid ideas form, but you can't seem to shake them—at least, I can't. I should ask if he wants to go to the movies this weekend. He's going to say no, and I'll end up regretting that I asked, but whatever.

"What's playing?" I glance at Genji. "What should we see, Genj?"

He meows at me like the crazy person I am.

I nod. "Something scary? Sounds good."

I scroll through the *Now Playing* list at our tiny little cinema. Nope. Nothing there. Maybe Hickory? It's the closest we have to a decent-sized city, about forty minutes away. There's something. *Brightburn.* It's supposed to be like a dark horror take on if someone like Superman was a bad guy. It looks cool at least, and I know Ty likes a good scary movie.

"How about that?" I show Genji the movie poster depicting a black silhouette of a kid in his cape against a menacing red background. He doesn't look. "Yep, that'll work."

I check the show times and settle on an early afternoon showing. Hopefully that won't get in the way of lunch. I open the sparse text thread I have with Tyler and let my fingers type out my stupidity.

"Maybe this isn't such a great idea, Genj," I huff. "But it's not as if I'm trying to take him on a date. It's just a movie for his birthday. We were friends after all, maybe we are again? Right?"

But it seems so much scarier than that. Fuck it. Just do it.

AIDAN: Want to go to a movie with me for your b-day Saturday? Know you hate busy theaters, but ::shrug emoji::

Damn. He said his family is taking him out Saturday. Yep, this was pointless. No, hold up. Didn't he say that was in the evening? But what about work? I bet he works Saturday afternoon… So, I double text him.

AIDAN: You probably work though. Sorry.

The little bubbles jump at the bottom of my screen.

TYLER: Nah, I'm off Saturday. What movie?

My eyes glue to the screen. What? Really? He didn't just ignore me or say no? I don't waste any time responding.

AIDAN: Brightburn. Superhero horror movie. You like horror, right?

AIDAN: You'll finally be old enough to see an R-rated movie without your parents too!

What am I doing? Also, another double text. *Dammit, A.*

TYLER: I LOVE HORROR! Let's do it!

AIDAN: Afternoon? Figure it out later?

TYLER: Should work.

I'm honestly surprised, and I'm just going to assume *should work* means *afternoon*. I so didn't think he'd actually go for it.

AIDAN: Awesome. Well, night.

TYLER: Night.

I already have the showtime ready, 2:15 p.m. Of course, it's not set in stone. But we're going. Tyler is going to the movies with me. Cool! That wouldn't have happened two months ago. It wouldn't even have been a thought. I need to call Kallie. She's going to freak over this.

It's just after nine, so she should be off by now. I dial her up on FaceTime and wait for her to answer.

"A, what's up?" She flashes those dark gray eyes at me. "Didn't we just talk?"

"Not the point," I tell her. "You'll never guess what just happened."

"Is this a test?" she asks. Light from a streetlamp glows over her pale face, briefly illuminating her eyes.

"I'm taking Ty to the movies Saturday for his birthday!" I grin.

"Wait, like, date taking him to the movies," she glances at her screen for a moment in confusion and then finds the road again, "or, like, we're just friends seeing a movie together?"

I roll over, almost crushing Genji in the process.

"Sorry, bud!" I apologize, then focus at my screen again. "No. Like friends going to the movies type of deal. That's it!"

"Uh-huh…" She nods a little too slowly. I know what she's thinking, so I just stare. "Does *he* know you're taking him on a date?"

"No!" I say and immediately realize how it sounds. "I mean… You know what I mean. It's not a date! Stop it! I'm just trying to be a friend because he's finally letting me."

"That's sweet," though I can hear the condescension. She doesn't have to believe me. It's the truth even if she doesn't get it.

"God!" I groan and roll my eyes at her. "Why do I tell you anything?"

"Because you love me." She bobs her head.

"Just don't tell Ty I told you, okay?" I ask.

"We'll see." She purses her lips. "Nah. I gotcha."

TYLER

"Am I the only one who thinks this is stupid?" I lean in next to Aidan so everyone in the line doesn't hear me.

There's a line at each register because some idiot decided the concession stand registers should be used for both ticketing and concessions on a Saturday afternoon. I mean, how is that a good idea? It just takes longer to do everything, not just get my damn popcorn.

"Me." Aidan raises his hand next to his face like it might be dangerous to do so.

"Exactly, it's just," I gasp, "like, really?"

"We can get our drinks at the same time at least." Aidan shrugs.

He's been stiff since the moment I met him in the parking lot. It's funny, actually. I think I intimidate him. Probably something about how I hated him. Not saying I don't still, but I'm trying.

"And popcorn, don't forget the popcorn," I remind him.

Did you even go to the theater if you don't get an oversized bag of super buttery popcorn?

"You've mentioned that a few times. I got it." Aidan nods, chewing on his lip. "You and Kallie have fun after church last night?"

"Yeah." It would have been better if we'd had more time, but courtesy of Christopher Gentry, that didn't happen. "Went to Taco Bell the second church let out. I literally ran out the door. Okay, I didn't run, but I got out quick. We just hung out for a while then went to the arcade at Bo's."

Part of that hanging out involved Kallie talking me through what

I'm not supposed to do today. I mean, it was my birthday evening, and I'm getting coached on basic etiquette. And the number one rule was to be nice, as if I'm incapable.

I'm trying, and if I can say it myself, I think I'm doing good so far. There was also something about not letting my face speak for me.

"I schooled her in eight-ball," I tell him.

"Eight-ball?" Aidan seems confused.

"Yeah." I squint. Who doesn't know what eight-ball is? "Like, pool, billiards."

"Oh! You could have just said pool. No one knows it as eight-ball." He acts like it's obvious.

Excuse me?

"Uh, no. Everyone knows it's called eight-ball." I'm pretty sure they do, but I make it a joke. The family of five—no, six—in front of us walks off, and the stick of a cashier for our line calls us forward. "*Finally*. Oh, and don't forget—"

"Popcorn, I got it." Aidan grins at me but shakes his head at the same time. I giggle a little as he steps up to the counter. "Two for *Brightburn*, please. And a *large* popcorn, large Dr. Pepper, and a…"

Aidan looks at me expectantly.

I was just joking. I didn't mean for him to actually do it. "I can get my drink and the popcorn. I didn't mean for you—"

"It's your birthday." He tilts his head and grins. "What do you want?"

"Uh… Dr. Pepper," I say, but I feel like maybe I should have chosen something different instead of getting the same thing he did. I don't know why, maybe I should have asked for Sprite.

"And another large Dr. Pepper," Aidan says and pays the man before I can change my mind.

As the tickets print, I scan the crowd. There's every variation of person here. It's almost like our high school.

In the middle of the lobby is a group of teens probably around our age, but they're way more annoying. They're the type that scream and yell like no one else is around, with the girls hanging all over the guys. Beyond them is a little trio, looks like a mom, a dad, and their daughter. They seem like the well-off types — you know, the ones who hold their noses up a little too high in their name-brand everything. Next to them is another trio, but older and with a son, maybe grandparents taking their grandson to a movie. Closer is a couple I can only describe as rednecks, but maybe meth heads is more appropriate. Innocent until proven guilty though, right?

"Ready?" Aidan grabs my attention. He has our tickets in hand and passes my drink over. They might cost a fortune in here, but damn, they mean large when they say large. "Our movie's about to start, we need to go."

"Then let's go." I follow him toward the ticket stub person. What are they even called? The ticket tearer-upper, the stub taker, the ripper. Ooh, the ripper. It should be that.

The ripper is this short black girl with wavy brown hair pulled up into a ponytail. Aidan hands her our tickets and she rips them in two and hands him back the stubs. Yep, the ripper.

"Theater four to your right." She nods to our right, her left, and Aidan practically races off.

I catch up and he hands me my stub before he opens the door to theater four and holds it for me. I slip by and pocket the stub. It's dark, just like it should be. It just better be quiet too, or I might have to go haywire on someone.

Nothing bugs me more in a theater, especially for a horror movie, than obnoxious people. You know the type, the ones that narrate or laugh to cover how scared they are. Stay home, people. Just stay home.

"How about there." I point to a row almost midway up the stacked seating.

"Sure," he agrees and slips in after me and we settle in. "Hope this is good. The concept is cool. Like evil Superman or something, right?"

"Sort of. I think it's more like how Superman would have turned out in real life because people are assholes." I bounce my shoulders like it's nothing unusual to say. People are.

"Gotcha." Aidan purses his lips, then laughs. "Truth. I did hear it's sort of gory too."

"Yeah, Deago saw it this week." He's in our history class at West. I don't really talk to him much—well, I don't really talk to anyone except Kallie—but we both like horror stuff, so he told me about it. "Said it was good. Something about an eye scene. Not sure what he meant though."

"An eye scene?" Aidan gives me a confused look, and I shrug back. I don't know what he meant. "A little vague."

"You don't want it spoiled, do you?" I throw myself back in mock disgust and laugh when he catches it.

"Course not," he says way over the top. "Just better be good."

"Same," I say as the curtain widens and the lights dim away.

I lean back and recline my seat. Then it hits me. The last time I was here, the last time I went to a movie, was with Brayden. It was the weekend after Valentine's Day, and we went to see *Happy Death Day 2U*. I swallow a lump in my throat. I can almost feel how his hand felt in mine that day.

No. You're not doing this to yourself. Stop it.

"You okay?" Aidan nudges my shoulder.

"Huh? Yeah." I slide my hand between the armrest and my thigh and grip my fists just out of view. I am okay. I have to be. "Why?"

"You got all tense and quiet," he tells me. "I asked if you were ready, but I don't think you heard me."

He did?

"It's okay, it was a stupid question." Aidan bites his lip and looks down nervously.

"Nah. It's good. I just got distracted," I say.

"Okay," he says, and the first preview trailer starts up. "Well, here we go."

"Yeah, here we go." I try to repeat it with his enthusiasm, but all I can think about is how Brayden isn't here.

AIDAN

Saturday, May 25

"Thanks for the movie." Tyler waves one more time before slipping into his car.

"Bye." I slouch into my seat.

Woah! That actually wasn't one big clusterfuck after another like I expected it to be. If I didn't know him better, I'd think maybe he doesn't hate me. I mean, he also unblocked me on Insta, Facebook and SnapChat yesterday. I glance up at my car's cloth ceiling and pooch my lips out in thought. Maybe he doesn't…anymore.

Tyler drives off and I turn the ignition. The engine roars to life and Pantera's "Walk" blares to life halfway through one of the choruses. I take a deep breath.

Not only did it not go bad, the movie was actually good. Not Marvel-quality good, but cool. It even startled me a few times, and oh, that eye scene. Dayum! I had to look away, like that's not even cool.

After the movie we stood out by Ty's car for…God, what, like thirty minutes, talking about it. I think he liked it more than I did, then again, he always was higher strung, a lot like Brayden, so maybe it was just that. And neither of us expected that ending. Like, not in the slightest, and honestly, I loved that part! Real deal to the max.

But my biggest surprise is that this whole venture wasn't the total epic failure I was expecting it to be. Nope. It was like old times, back when we all hung out together, as a group. And the longer we talked the more I wanted him to stay. I'm not sure what it is, but part of me feels like having him around is getting a small piece of Brayden back.

It's like there's something left of him that I can talk to.

I know it probably sounds stupid, but I swear it feels like it.

I just have to get past this nervous itch around him. There's something about him hating me for so long that has me worried about every little thing I say. It's like I'm anxious the wrong word might set him back to ignoring me, but I can't be like that. He's obviously trying, and today was a good show of that. Of course, I did bring him to a movie and get him a drink and popcorn, and the boy loves popcorn, so that might have played a role too.

Either way it's progress. I'm just not going to tempt fate too much. You know, take it slow and hope he'll keep being a friend.

TYLER

Today's been harder. It's better, but I've been…I don't know, down I guess?

I just keep thinking about Brayden, wondering what we would have done over the weekend. Maybe a Star Trek movie marathon, dinner in Hickory, maybe a late-night picnic at the park. And I keep thinking how that'll never happen again.

It's not like he dumped me and I'm waiting for him to call back and apologize. No. He's gone, it's permanent. I can't beg him back or stalk him just to get a quick glance. He's gone.

I sniffle in a quick breath before my feet hit the landing and slip into the cafeteria. Kallie's slouched against one of the glossy rock columns next to the lunch line as usual. I smile, hiding the overwhelming emptiness burrowing in my chest.

"You okay?" She sees right through my tough guy act.

I keep walking, faking a smile as we get in line.

"Uh, yeah," I lie. Like I'm going to say, "No, I'm hurting, I miss Brayden," right here in the middle of all these people? No. Hell, there's, like, a ninety percent chance I wouldn't even if no one else was around.

"You're lying," she points out the obvious.

"Can we not?" I pick up a tray and slap it against the buffet line harder than I intend to. I avoid looking up and meeting the inevitable questioning glares, and immediately work on loading my tray with what the menu today claims is Salisbury steak.

"Sorry," Kallie apologizes.

We drone through the line in silence. It's so loud in here. There are too many people, so many hot-blooded, hormonal bodies pushing and shoving and talking and complaining. I just want some quiet, some goddamn peace and quiet. I stop at our usual table and let go of my tray. It falls with a smack and gravy splatters on the table.

"Dammit!" I huff.

Kallie sits and wipes it up before I get a chance to do anything other than take a hard breath in.

"Ty. Come on, what is it?" she leans in and whispers.

I close my eyes to level myself, but instead I see Brayden's pale brown eyes darkened by night. It's the same way I usually see him in my dreams. It's the last night we spent on a blanket at the park before peering through his telescope to see Breegge, just moments before he kissed me and wrapped me in his arms.

"I just miss him." I dismiss it.

"I know," she whispers, and her eyes drop to the table for a moment in this almost reverential type of way. "Wanna talk about it?"

A grunt leaves my lips and the stupid little bitch boy part of me wants to say yes, but I know it won't help anything.

"Nah, I got it," I tell her. "Have you decided when you're taking the SAT?"

"I thought we decided on the last one in June?" She eyes me down.

We talked about it over the weekend, along with her usual asking if I'd talked to Aidan any, namely after he took me to the movies. I thought she said she wasn't sure yet but that we might do June, because we *are* taking it at the same time. That much is certain.

"What? I thought you weren't sure," I say.

"No, I said I have to check with my parents," she reminds me, and it clicks. She did say that. What is wrong with me?

"What do you have to get with your parents on?" Aidan sets his tray next to Kallie's, and suddenly Bryce is straddling the chair next to me.

What the hell? What do they think they're doing?

"Wha…" I start, but then it hits me. *What am I doing? He's not so bad. He took you to the movies this weekend, asshole.* I did have fun, I actually enjoyed it, and I'd be a total asshole to be mean right now. "Uh, hey."

"Hey." Aidan's eyes narrow and his lips thin out to match the amused sound in his voice.

"SAT," Kallie tells him.

"We were just talking about when to take it," I tell him.

"Ah." Aidan sighs.

"Same." Bryce literally raises his hand as if it wasn't enough simply to say it, like I couldn't locate his voice right next to me. "When you looking to take it?"

"Last week of June," Kallie tells him.

"Think I chose the second session in July…" Bryce's voice trails off and his eyes run toward the ceiling.

"You did. I'm so glad I'm done with that," Aidan says, and pauses to spoon a mouthful of mashed potatoes. I don't know how anyone stands eating this school's mashed potatoes, they're basically liquid. It makes my stomach churn just to watch. "Longest test of my life!"

"Isn't life just one big test?" I ask, trying to sound all philosophical. It seemed cool in my head, but now I'm just hoping no one gives a fuck, because I'm not sure where to take that line of thought.

"Uh…" Aidan grins at me crookedly and laughs.

"You're not that bright, Ty, just stop," Kallie drops a smackdown on both my mental prowess and pride.

"Damn." Aidan covers his mouth to keep his food from spewing and leans over his tray, coughing. "He's not all that dumb."

"A little above average," Bryce chimes in. I could about punch him. He's the one at this table I know least, and I'd have no remorse. *Don't test me, Bryce.*

"He's better than that," Aidan tells them and smiles at me.

Thank you, at least someone's not a total asshole. I know it's all in fun, and it's not like I'm worried about it. My aspirations right now are simply to get out of high school and go to college somewhere at least two hours away so I can justify not living at home.

Beyond that, I don't have a clue.

"Don't give him hope, A." My *best friend* pats his shoulder.

"Some best friend." I give her the middle finger, and the table bursts into laughter. "I hate y'all."

"It's okay, we still love you." Kallie sticks out her tongue playfully.

"I'm genuinely scared to know what it would be like to be hated by y'all," I joke.

"It would suck so bad," Kallie tells me and then switches subjects. "I wonder if the SAT will have any questions about your comet?"

My brow instinctively squishes up with the way she called it my comet. I mean, if anything it's Brayden's comet. He's the one who was obsessed with it, not me. I just want… Hmm… Maybe I am a little obsessed, but that's okay, right? Yeah, that's okay.

"I doubt it," I say and turn to Aidan. He took the SAT last year. I know Breegge wasn't a thing then, but maybe he'd know if it talked about stuff like that. "Did it have any specific questions like that when you took it?"

"Uh…" Aidan thinks about it for a moment. "I don't think so. Most of the science was more general. Not really about specific events."

"Good." She nods. "When is it going to be visible again though? I keep forgetting, it's taking forever."

"Patience, fool," I tell her. "It's literally taken it thousands of years since it formed to get here, and it'll be another 19,000 years before it comes back around."

"But it could take longer," Aidan chimes in. "Didn't Brayden say they won't know for sure when it'll be back until it slingshots around the sun?"

"Yeah." I nod. Until that happens it's hard to pinpoint.

"That's all nice and shit, but *when* will we be able to see it?" Kallie throws her hands out. I guess we weren't answering her question quick enough.

"Mid-July," I tell her, then clarify. "Uh, I think they say, like, July 12 or something."

"So they don't know?" Bryce squints.

"Well it's a best calculation right now," Aidan says and glances at me. I'm not sure if he's looking for affirmation or what, so I give it.

"Yeah." I nod. "I think they'll know better once Breegge's closer."

"Ah… And what was its actual name? Isn't it some weird long-ass thing?" Bryce asks.

"Yeah, it's technically the Breeggemann-Holt-Turner Comet, or C/2018E2," I tell them.

I didn't realize before Brayden came around that they had weird scientific designations at all. Even Halley's Comet was technically 1P/Halley and Hale-Bopp was C/1995 O1. Each piece means something. All I remember is that the letter for Breegge stands for it being a non-periodic comet, and the number is the year it was discovered. And by non-periodic, I think that means the comet either doesn't orbit the sun, which Breegge does, or they take longer than two hundred years to orbit.

"Nerd," Bryce comments.

"Excuse me." Kallie perks up. "Coming from the comic book dude?"

"No offense." Bryce smiles and puts a hand up.

"I'm a nerd." I own it.

"We all are," Aidan jumps in.

"Woah." Kallie leans back. "Speak for yourselves."

AIDAN

"See you in fourth." I throw up a peace sign as Ty and Kallie split off at the top of the staircase.

"See ya," Tyler shouts over the crowd. I think Kallie said bye, but I'm not sure. I turn and take off for the English wing with Bryce at my side.

"That went better than expected." Bryce says exactly what I was thinking with exactly the surprise I expect.

It was a gamble. One I almost didn't take, and if I'd been asked to state the odds, I would have given it about a ten percent chance of not going down in flames. I know he's been nicer, and in some odd way, he doesn't seem to outwardly hate me anymore, but for such a long time he did. And I just can't believe a weekend of hanging out with him made all that go away.

"I know, right?" I shake my head. "I thought he was going—"

Something hard and blunt jabs into my side, and I stumble into Bryce. I cover my waist instinctively. Of course.

"Watch where you're going, fag." Christian shoots me the bird, walking backward a few steps, making the most of the scene he created. I clench my jaw and look away. He's either really fucking insecure or he just really likes attention, or maybe it's both. I don't know.

"Come on, A." Bryce tugs at me and I let myself be pulled away.

"I really hate that guy," I tell him, and I don't hate people. "What was I saying?"

"Lunch. Tyler." Bryce bobs his head back and forth.

"Yeah, right." I try to let it go, but it eats at my mind. How hard is it not to be a douche? Even Tyler's doing a good job. Take a lesson, Christian. "I thought Ty was going to tell me to leave there for a moment."

I laugh when Bryce does, even if I have to force it a little. It's crazy how things can go from great to ugh so quick just because of one too-pretty-for-his-own-good asshole. But I shake it off as we make the turn into Mr. Hagan's class.

Focus, Aidan.

Tyler. Lunch. Like Bryce said. Yeah, Tyler was actually nice. He has been the last week. The movie date—not like a *date-date* of course—went well. And he texted some and even Snapped a few times. And apparently he still plays *Overwatch.* He said we could team up again like we used to soon. I can't wait for that.

"What was your plan, had he told you bug off?" Bryce asks.

I take my chair and start unloading my notebook and pen.

"Don't know." I shrug, smiling because I really don't know. I was just hoping for the best. I didn't plan any further.

"Oh." Bryce looks surprised. "Okay."

I giggle. It was a bad plan. It worked, but it was a bad plan.

The bell rings and Mr. Hagan starts up, something about our final project being due Monday, and something else about our exam. I should probably listen. Maybe that'll go good too.

TYLER

Friday, May 31

Sweat pours down my back and forehead. The kitchen at work is like an oven, with all of us packed in tight behind serving lines, fryer vats, heating elements, and only two window air conditioners to cool the entire space.

I have it best at the drive-thru window. At least I get a little air and the chance to walk outside to take the next car's order, because unlike McDonald's we don't have a cool intercom setup, so we go outside to get the rest of the cars in line. Everyone else is stuck at their station on the busiest night of the week.

"I need more fries and pups, please," Heather yells across the kitchen, asking Josh to drop a basket of each into the scorching hot oil. She looks at me. "That was a lot."

"Yeah, a lot," I agree. I search the serving line, trying to find anything they're low on to give me an excuse to go to the backroom. I want to stand in the big walk-in fridge and cool down, plus my phone buzzed a few times in my pocket. Napkins. They're only about half empty, but hell, it's an excuse. "I'm going to get y'all some napkins. Be right back."

Before Heather or Alicia can protest I shoot off, past the massive dishwashing sinks, into the backroom, and disappear inside the fridge. My body shivers against the initial onslaught of cold on my sweaty skin, but it feels so good.

I just breathe for a second, letting the cold slither down my throat and coat my neck, before I slip my phone out. I've got a few messages, but one is from Kallie so it's obviously first.

KALLIE: Would you kill me if I invited Aidan to movie night next week, or maybe tomorrow?

Why even ask? Just because we're friendly doesn't mean he's invading our most sacred evening.

TYLER: ::skull emoji:: Without hesitation.

I hit send. I'm trying to pull up a text from Katie, but another comes in from Kallie.

KALLIE: ::middle finger emoji:: Come on!

TYLER: No.

KALLIE: It'll be fun.

TYLER: What'll be fun is him NOT coming. OUR movie night.

KALLIE: Fine! Asshole. ::eye roll emoji::

"Window!" Heather's little voice carries through the thick freezer door. It's how we say a car just pulled up and no one's at the window to take the order. My bad.

The bubbles light up at the bottom of my screen again though, so I give it a second and another text comes through.

KALLIE: What about Wilson's Creek tomorrow? You, me, Aidan. Maybe Bryce and Katie too.

I huff and my breath crystalizes in the air around me. She's really determined, but I can't say no to that without being a real asshole.

"God why?" I groan.

TYLER: Whatever. Gotta go.

AIDAN

"Did you see the second *Happy Death Day?*" Bryce points at the new release movie rack.

"Yeah." I nod. "Remember? The four of us went."

We're bored. There isn't a ton to do around here, so naturally we end up scouting the movie aisle at Walmart. At least we're not congregating with our other classmates in the parking lot, acting like total idiots in their big jacked-up trucks and blaring country music.

I'm betting the Walmart employees probably would prefer we stay out of the Nerf gun and sports aisle though. We might have had an impromptu Nerf fight, but eh. The only other thing to do is Bo's, the local bowling alley and arcade. I mean, there is a skating rink out in Collettsville and I think there's one somewhere else too, but my balance isn't what I'd call great.

"Oh look! There's another Nic Cage movie," Bryce laughs. "When are they going to realize—"

"Woah." I stop him from committing blasphemy. Cage can be…different, but he's an awesome actor, thank you very much. I don't care what anyone thinks, Cage is awesome! I mean *National Treasure*, that's all you have to say, but what about *Face/Off, Joe, The Frozen Ground, Rage, The Rock,* and hell, *Gone in 60 Seconds*. The man won an Oscar, an Academy Award, a Felix, and a Golden Globe Award. "The man is a legend. Watch your dirty mouth."

Bryce covers his mouth and laughs. "You and your Cage obsession. I don't get it. No, actually, *no one* gets it."

"Eff off," I snicker.

I find the movie he's talking about. It's something called *Between Worlds*. I've never heard of it, but I'll probably watch it someday, just not today. Bryce would end up going home if I picked it out for tonight, but there's nothing wrong with teasing him a little. I'd be a horrible friend if I didn't, so I pick up the title. "We should get it. Watch it tonight."

"Excuse me?" Bryce eyes me wildly, like I just had a concussion or something. "You'll be watching that alone, in your room, so no one else has to suffer. Your mom won't even stay for that."

"Actually…" I raise my hand with my pointer finger extended, and then pull it back and to my mouth after I've had time to think it through. Maybe not. "Nope, you're right."

"You think?" He shakes his head.

"But—" My phone saves me from digging a deeper grave. It's Kallie with a FaceTime call. I debate whether to accept it in the middle of Walmart. I mean, it's Kallie, so there's a fifty-fifty chance of her saying something that'll make me look insane or horrible. I show the screen to Bryce before accepting. "Hey, Kal!"

"You really have to stop calling me a cow." Kallie looks at me deadpan.

I roll my eyes. She knows what I called her. The story goes that when she was, like, three or something, her mamá called her Kal too, but Kallie thought she was calling her a cow. I'm guessing she was just learning what a cow was and I mean, yeah, the two do sound a lot alike. So at random she'll swear that's what I'm calling her, especially in public around people.

"I didn't call you cow." I shake my head. "What do you want?"

"You have plans tomorrow?" she asks.

"I'm planning to write," I tell her.

"So no? You don't have plans?" she asks again.

"I *just* said I'm planning to write," I try again.

"So you're free then?" The smirk on Kallie's face is huge now. Guess I won't be writing tomorrow.

"What is it you want to do?" I can't hide the grin.

Bryce picks up a movie and waves it in front of my face. It's *Overlord*. I think it's a WW2 zombie flick or something. He points at it, as if I couldn't see him waving in front of me, and mouths, *how about this one?* I nod, I've been wanting to see it anyway.

"I was thinking of having some friends go to Wilson's Creek in the afternoon," Kallie says. "You know, take snacks and drinks, go swimming, hang out. I was going to invite you, Bryce, and Katie."

"I'm in!" Bryce jumps behind me, and his face comes into view for Kallie.

"See, Bryce is coming!" Kallie rallies with his support.

"I don't know, I need to write. I've been slacking." I really have. It's not like I have a deadline, I just want to finish, and between my school writing project that has a deadline, hanging out with Bryce, and my other homework, I don't have a lot of time to write.

"Really, A? You want to sit at home and write over hanging out with *me? With me?*" she guilts me, with a major put-on pouty face.

"I could go, but…" I shrug. What can I say, I'm not a big crowd person even if it is friends, and I do want to write.

"Ty's coming," she says, like it's some big reveal. "I forgot to mention that. He's coming too."

"So?" I shrug again, hiding the twitch in my lip.

I guess I could make the time to go. But it has nothing to do with Tyler. Maybe I should spend more time with them. It's no secret I'll be going off to college in a few months anyway. I should probably spend what time I have left with them.

"So…" Her eyes widen. She stares into my soul.

"Whatever," I give in. "Just because you insist."

"Or because a certain person's going to be there," Kallie suggests.

"Oh…" Bryce coos and looks at me suggestively.

"Eff off," I tell him, "and *no*, it's because I want to."

TYLER

Saturday, June 1

It looks like this pale boy's getting a sunburn today.

It's clear skies, the temperature is in the mid-eighties, and courtesy of my mother's genes, it doesn't matter how much sunscreen I put on, it's burn baby burn. Having the top down doesn't help, but that's what a convertible is for, so too bad.

I top Kallie's driveway and brake to a stop at the staircase leading to her house, where she and Aidan are waiting.

"Y'all ready for a swim?" I wave.

"Hell yes!" Aidan hoots and stashes in the trunk a duffle bag and two coolers full of snacks and drinks, I hope. I'm not taking any chances. I stocked another cooler with Dr. Peppers before I left the house.

"I get to play DJ," Kallie shouts the moment her butt hits the passenger seat. Aidan jumps over the side of the car and into the back seat.

"Please no!" Aidan begs.

"I'm with A on this." I grin, pulling us away from the house and onto the tiny country road toward the park to pick up Bryce and Katie. Apparently—and Aidan just informed me of this an hour ago via text—Bryce has a bit of a thing for Katie. Which finally connects a few dots, especially why Kallie would invite Katie in the first place. I guess Kallie already knew, but she still denies playing matchmaker.

"Come on," Kallie whines. "I have shotgun, it's my right."

"Majority rule. Plus, when did shotgun get that right?" Aidan throws his hands up in confusion. He leans forward, pressing against his seatbelt. "You heard the new I Prevail album?"

"Doesn't matter," Kallie grumbles.

"Nah. Any good?" I don't bother hiding my amusement. Usually I'm the one stuck listening to music I don't care for with Kallie, so this is a nice turn of events. Maybe having a little backup sometimes is good.

"It's awesome! I'm surprised you haven't heard it yet, that's your type of music, right?" Aidan asks. "Give me the aux cord and I'll get it going."

Kallie rolls her eyes but reluctantly hands the cord back. I'm surprised she isn't holding it hostage, it's something she'd do—has done, now that I think about it. I can't express how glad I am not having to listen to fifties music. Aidan's right though. I Prevail is one of my bands. I knew they had a new album out months ago, but it came out the same week everything fell apart. I didn't much feel like enjoying anything then.

"Yeah," I agree as an electric guitar brazenly rips through my speakers, and the singer screams *Let's fucking burn this down* on our scenic drive through the country. "Already hooked."

Kallie rolls her eyes. "*God*, I'd rather listen to your emo rap shit than this."

I glance at Aidan through the rearview mirror and he smiles back.

"Poor Kallie," he coos from the back, his voice barely cresting the wind whooshing into the car and the heavy beat of the drums.

"You're going to think *poor Kallie* when I drown you both in the creek." She glares at me. "That's if we make it there alive."

"Huh?" I take my eye off the road just long enough to give her the side-eye.

"You know why." She makes it sound obvious. And I do know

why. No one likes my driving. "Why did we let you drive again?"

"I don't know how to get up there," Aidan says.

I'd think after the number of times he's been up to Wilson's Creek he'd remember the route, but I guess some of us just don't pay attention.

"And for some reason I put the pleasure of riding in a convertible, driven by the reaper, above my own safety. God help us." Kallie looks to the sky with hands together in mock prayer.

"Oh, fuck off," I tell them and pull into the Old Ruritan Park. Bryce's and Katie's cars are parked near the entrance with the two of them propped against the tail end of Bryce's tiny Nissan. "May I remind you both I have the safest driving record of any of you so far."

"Safest driving record?" Bryce asks.

I guess I did yell it. It's the only way to be heard in a convertible.

"Yeah, they're complaining about my driving." I shrug.

"Oh God, I forgot about that." Bryce's face crinkles up. "Maybe I'll drive separate."

"Get in the fucking car!" I roll my eyes.

"Let me get our things," Bryce laughs.

Katie slips around the back of my car and taps the trunk. "Can I put my stuff back here?"

"Yeah." I pop the trunk. She's much too nice for this group.

"Hey, Katie!" Kallie twists in her seat and pops over the headrest to smile at her.

"Kallie!" Katie does her trademark high-pitched excited scream and wiggle.

I turn and look at Kallie, asking what the hell is going on without saying a word. She shrugs as Katie comes around my side of the car. I get out and pull my seat forward to let Katie slip in the back seat with Aidan.

"So, what's with your driving? I don't think I've ridden with you before," Katie asks, trying her best, and failing, to hide a nervous itch.

I shake my head as Bryce drops a bag and another cooler in the trunk and jumps in next to Katie. I'm sure he likes that he gets to be crammed against her the whole ride up.

"Everyone complains when I drive, because—" I try.

"It's terrifying." Kallie does an over-the-top, wide-eyed look of horror.

"So terrifying," Aidan echoes. I'd so slap him right now if only I could reach him.

"It's not terrifying," I tell her and drop my seat back in place. "I'm just a little aggressive."

"Aggressive? A little?" Kallie pooches her lips and pops them open with a literal popping noise. She twists in her seat to face Katie and Bryce. "More like insane. The boy literally can't make a smooth turn or brake softly. It's all abrupt, and he goes way too fast."

"Y'all are free to get out at any time," I tell them. "In the meantime, buckle up."

I put the car in reverse, and very intentionally cram the accelerator to the floor. The car lurches, and screams greet my ears as I slam the brakes.

"Oh, I'm sorry," I mock them.

With Katie unduly horrified and the rest wanting to kill me, I put it in drive and take us on the main road and up the mountain. There's not much anywhere in Collettsville. The farther we go, the more country and natural it becomes. The sporadic houses and driveways transition into the ever-larger evergreens and maples. Mailboxes give way to field grass and random roadside flower patches.

A few miles past what everyone calls the visitor center, which is basically this little fishing gear store with a few coolers for drinks and beer, I pull to the edge of the road and park. This is the only place so far that hasn't been crowded with cars.

"It's so hot." Aidan pushes at Kallie's seat.

"I'm moving, I'm moving, damn," she crows and gets out of the car, letting Aidan fold her seat forward and jump out behind her.

"Damn, it *is* hot," I say.

"You did wear sunscreen, right?" Kallie asks.

"Yeah. Great timing, by the way," I tell her.

"Oh, shut up," Kallie dismisses me. "Did you bring more?"

"No." I involuntarily skew my lip. She got me there.

"I have some if you need it," Katie pipes up, pulling out a can of 80 SPF. Perfect. She's a pale girl too, the difference is she's prepared. It never crossed my mind to bring more.

Kallie points at her and pooches her lips into this surprised smirk. "At least someone's prepared."

"Always." Katie smiles. She stuffs the can back in her bag and steps aside to let Bryce and Aidan grab a cooler each.

I push a button and wait for the cloth top to stretch back over my car and lock it down before joining everyone to transport the last cooler and my own bag of goodies. A towel to dry off with later, another to sit on, some Andes Mints which in hindsight probably weren't the best idea and are probably liquid by now, and a fresh set of clothes.

"Come on," Aidan urges. "I bet the water feels great!"

We form a mob and cross the tiny gravel road, making our way down an outcropping of rocks between a grouping of trees. It opens up to a semi-calm segment of the wide creek bed where we deposit our bags and coolers.

"Not bad," Bryce says. "And it's all ours."

"We could skinny dip!" Aidan grins.

"What?" The word jumps from my throat.

"Huh?" Katie and Kallie echo in unison.

"JK." Aidan throws his hands up. "There's no way in hell I'm skinny dipping with any of you around."

"Good." I swallow back an imaginary lump. This was about to be a much different swimming trip than I'd envisioned. I'm not ready for that trip, not now, and I don't think ever.

"Well, let's swim!" Kallie pulls off her shirt and shorts to reveal a simple black one-piece bathing suit, and the rest of us follow.

I lift my t-shirt over my head. The sun hits my skin and I can feel the burn starting. A few feet to my right Aidan loses his shirt and my eyes lock on his tan stomach. I freeze up for a second, but I'm quick to save myself. I shake my head as if the sight might be flung from my head. *What's wrong with you, Tyler?*

AIDAN

Saturday, June 1

A wall of water slaps me in the face. I didn't get my hands up quick enough.

"Someone's slow today," Kallie teases, crouched over the water ready to dish out another wave.

"At least I don't have to stand in the shallow water," I dish it right back and send a wave her way. She shakes the water from her face and laughs behind her evil eye.

In my defense, I hadn't expected a wave to come flying in like that. We'd been lying around lazily the past hour, moving barely enough to fight the current, talking about everything and nothing. Most of it I'd already heard, like Bryce's obsession with Melissa Benoist, aka the actress who plays Supergirl, not something I'd talk a ton about if I were trying to win over Katie, and he is whether he admits it or not. Katie is planning to run for Beta Club president next year, but she doesn't think she'll get it; Tyler finally got those concert tickets to see his favorite band, nothing,nowhere., at the end of the year and he's making Kallie go with him; Kallie is trying to find a way to fake her own death so she doesn't have to go. Oh, and much too much talk about what goes on up here late at night when no one's around—the "fucky fucking", as Kallie put it.

"You're not calling my Kallie short, are you?" Tyler eyes me.

"I mean… Yeah." A laugh slips out as I say it.

"She prefers miniature." Tyler sticks out his tongue at me, and my mouth morphs into a wide O as Kallie's eyes lock onto Tyler.

"Ex-cuse me?" Kallie separates the syllables and puts her hands on her hips, even though they're underwater.

Tyler blows her a mock kiss, and a deep blush overtakes her cheeks, but it's not the sweet nervous type of blush, not even close. If she were a cartoon, the smoke would be rolling.

"Miniature." I let the word roll off my tongue like a fancy Italian wine. "I like it."

She glares at me with the eyes of Charon himself, and I shoot her back a wide grin. "I mean, it's sort of true."

"I hate you all," Kallie huffs, but a sly grin of her own betrays her.

"Hey, I didn't say anything," Bryce says.

"You're Bryce." She leers at him.

She doesn't hate him, at least she's never told me she hates him, but he can be a bit much sometimes, and well, she's never been overly fond of him. I give Bryce the it's-just-Kallie look and he grunts and goes back to bugging Katie.

"You ready for lunch?" he asks her, as if she's the only one in the water. I mean, I'd like something to eat too.

"Sure." She twitches her head in this cute little nervous way and starts off after Bryce to the shore.

"Do we get to eat too?" I call after Bryce. "Or is it just a couples thing?"

"Come on!" He twists around, eyes wide open in this glare that says shut-the-eff-up.

Kallie and Tyler snicker.

"Yeah. It's obvious he likes her," Tyler whispers next to me, sloshing toward the rocky shoreline. "You think she's caught on?"

"I'd hope. I mean, he's not exactly stealthy," I tell him.

"She hasn't," Kallie says curtly.

"Got to be kidding me." I shake my head in dismay. Bryce isn't what I'd call smooth. I mean, I'm not either, but I'm not that bad. How couldn't Katie pick up on it?

"They're on the same level," she says, nodding her head and frowning. "It's sort of sad and cute."

"Cute?" Tyler jerks his head to the side and stares at Kallie. "Cute? You think they're cute?"

"I think all types of things are cute," she defends.

"But you just said they're cute. You hate people," Tyler repeats.

"I thought couples made you sick or something," I question, smiling at Ty.

"Uh, yeah. I'm, like, semi-allergic to people." She raises her brow like it's obvious. "Except Ty, he's not quite human. And you're all right, A."

"Ah." I sigh, not sure what to make of that.

"At least you're *more* human," Tyler tells me, or more whines. I think he's enjoying the tag teaming though.

I'm not sure if I should take that as a compliment or not.

At the edge of the water Kallie crawls out, slipping with each step until she gets her footing on the smooth rock bed. I'm next.

"So I am or I'm not human?" I ask, using another slab of rock to my right to help lift my waterlogged body from the creek and onto mostly dry land. I step out of the way to allow Tyler space to climb up.

"Closer than Ty, but—"

"Oh fuck," Tyler blurts, and I look quick enough to see his arms flailing and him falling backward.

I don't think, I just reach. My fingers wrap around his slippery flailing wrist and stop him from tumbling into the water. I pull hard, a little too hard, and he stumbles forward. His chest flattens against me, and for a brief moment I'm staring into his eyes, skin against skin. In this split second I discover the slim golden rings encapsulating his pupils before the deep forest green I'm accustomed to takes over, and I feel the heat of his breath against my lips, and I'm all too aware of how fast my heart is beating. That's when I realize I can't breathe, and I can't move, and all I want to do is wrap my arms around him.

He pulls back and yanks his wrist away, and all at once it feels so wrong to look him in the eyes, like it's too much to take in. Like he's judging me for the mere look.

"Uh," Tyler mutters. "Thanks."

"Yeah." I refuse to look back up. Instead, I inventory the rocks at my feet and Kallie's feet until I finally get the nerve to even look at her. She's smiling so big, that all-knowing, sarcastic Kallie smirk, so I switch to the left where Tyler is standing, but I still can't look at him. My eyes catch his chest, but damn, no, not there, his shoulder, no. God. This is so stupid. "You're welcome."

I turn, trying my hardest not to come off weird, but something has me totally riled and it's eating at my nerves. I keep walking toward our little temporary picnic site where Bryce and Katie are already sitting, all eyes on me, or us, or maybe none of us. But instead of them, all I can see are those golden rings flashing in my mind, and I have to keep swallowing back this nervous lump in my throat that doesn't exist.

"Good reflexes, man," Bryce yells, pulling me further out of my stupor.

I nod and grunt in reply. I can't think of anything to say. There is nothing to say. It was a stupid move. I should have just let him fall and saved myself from this.

Bryce has already opened the cooler by the time we get to our little circle between two jagged rock formations. I pick out a can of soda and pop the top, waiting to see where Kallie and Tyler are going to sit. That's where I'm not sitting. Tyler grabs a can, a candy bar—I think it's a Twix—and one of those little meat and cheese packets, before dropping next to Bryce. I grab the spot opposite Katie.

"Y'all ready for exams?" Katie asks. It's not what I'd call exciting talk, but it's better than letting Kallie direct the convo. I know exactly where she'd take it with the way she keeps grinning at me.

"No! I've got math, biology, *and* a damn Creative Writing exam." Bryce blurts before anyone can gather their thoughts, his glare set sternly on me for that last one. "Thanks for that one, by the way."

"You'll get through." I shrug. He's been on my back the entire semester about it. For some reason he didn't think we'd have a final. I still can't figure out where he got that idea.

"I've got English III, Honors Biology, and a forensics exam. I think we're just watching a movie in Art during exam period," Kallie says.

"Yeah—" I start, but Bryce has to say something.

"Like *we* should be doing in Creative Writing." He eyes me again.

I ignore him. "I've got stupid people biology, history, Creative Writing, and math."

"Stupid people biology?" Tyler winces, and honestly it catches me off guard. I thought for sure he'd act like I didn't exist after that little moment at the edge of the creek. Okay, it wasn't a moment. Note to self, don't ever refer to it as a *moment* again.

"Yeah. You know." I say. "Just regular bio, not that honors stuff you and Kallie are taking."

"I still don't know how I got into that. Like, I'm not that great at science. I think I've got maybe an eighty average right now." He smiles at me.

I still can't figure out why I couldn't get into Honors Biology. I'm actually half decent in science, like, I actually enjoy it, sort of, but no, I got stuck in regular bio. The only reason Ty even cares about science is because of Brayden. Okay, maybe that's a little mean.

"Passing, that's all that matters, right?" I say, but I don't really mean it. I've worked hard for my grades. I'm no straight A student, but it took work to keep my grades high enough to get the athletic scholarship that's paying for my college at Charlotte in August to play soccer.

"Eh." Tyler shrugs and nods at me. "I've got history, Honors Bio, and math. I think we're just shitting around on the computers in drafting class."

I'm not sure if Tyler has already forgotten about our little run-in a second ago, or if I just happen to be the only one whose skin it got under, but he seems to be normal Ty. I grab a Butterfinger from the closest cooler and start into it. I have to calm my nerves. I'm being stupid.

Bryce says something about us all going to Bo's tonight for a little bowling, but Kallie has work at three, and Tyler has work at two.

"What about you, A?" Bryce asks.

I delay a second. It's not that I don't want to go, it's just that I was hoping to write tonight. I've already put it off today. But what type of lame nerd, especially a senior who's about to graduate in a week, stays home on a Saturday night when his friends want to go out?

"I'm game." I nod.

"Speaking of games." Tyler throws both his pointer fingers up in this I've-had-an-epiphany gesture, and those eyes catch me again, but there's something reserved, maybe nervous in them. Or I could be reading into it a little. I don't know. "You still play *Overwatch* much?"

I fight back the urge to swallow, and nod.

"Every once in a while."

"You want to play with Jacob and me sometime this week?" he asks, biting at his lip.

My eyes switch between him and Kallie, who's looking at me hopefully. Do I say yes, because I really do want to… I mean, it's been a while since I've played with people I know. Or do I say no because I'm too chicken shit? I hate these moments!

"That'd be great!" I lift my shoulders like it's no big deal, but the truth is I'm nervous as hell about it and excited. Maybe our little snafu didn't freak him out. "I don't play a ton though, so I sort of suck."

"Just means I'll get to take all the gold medals." He grins.

TYLER

"Can you bring me a tub of coleslaw?" Heather doesn't bother to look up from her station where she's wiping stray pieces of barbeque from the serving line.

"Sure, be right back." I slip by the fountain drink station and squeeze behind Misty, who's filling up what I'm certain she hopes is the last pitcher of sweet iced tea for the night. "About empty out there?"

"Almost. Got one more table." She flips the nozzle to the off position and starts for the dining room but pauses to check her watch. "They've got fifteen minutes to leave before I don't care about my tip anymore."

I grin as she disappears into the dining room. We close at nine, and thank the genies I get off at nine too. That's why my goal is to make this coleslaw errand my last for the night. I'll just have to clean my station and I should be good.

A chill runs down my back when I open the walk-in fridge door and step in. Add to that I'm wearing shorts, and my legs break out in millions of little goose bumps.

I crouch next to the metal shelves stacked high with miniature metal pans full of beans, barbeque, soup, and of course the massive plastic tubs of coleslaw. They're super heavy, so I fix a good grip on each side and slide it off the shelf, bracing for the weight. Gravity pulls it down a few inches before it settles under my grip.

I escape the fridge and start back toward the front of the kitchen, screaming, "Coleslaw coming through," the entire way. We're required to yell it. It's the equivalent of screaming get the fuck out of my way, or police sirens on the street. The sea literally parts.

Back at the serving line I drop the tub on the table between the serving line and the fry cook's station full of hot grease, fries, and pups to catch my breath. I wonder which character Aidan plays now. He's supposed to join Jacob and me tonight on the PlayStation. I keep thinking he was usually DPS back when we used to play, a damage character, one of the let's-go-in-and-shoot-'em-up, guns blazing types, but maybe he played tank. Pharah? No, Reaper. Okay, maybe it was Pharah.

"You putting that away any time soon?" Josh asks, staring at me with his head crooked to the side.

"Uh, yeah," I blurt. I lift the tub and nod toward the small portable fridge door. "Could you maybe get that?"

Josh steps to the side and opens the door for me, and as I'm walking forward it hits me. He does plays Reaper. I remember—

The tub catches the edge of the fridge, but my feet keep moving, and before I can do anything to stop my momentum, I'm careening southward. I grasp for the tub, but as my ass hits the hard laminate floor my whole arm, from fingertip to shoulder, plunges into the tub. It's so cold! And wet!

"Oh fu—" I catch the word before it slips, both from the pain shooting up my ass and the frigid chill biting at my senses. But it's done. There's nothing I can do. I just sit on the ground, face lowered for a second, taking in what I did with my arm still shoulder-deep in coleslaw. I groan and pull out. It slips out with this nasty suction noise as I free myself. My arm is covered in gritty pieces of thinly diced cabbage, carrots, and sticky, liquidy mayonnaise.

"Woah!" Josh chuckles, and when I turn to see everyone's reaction the only person not laughing is Alicia, but it's clear she's barely holding it in. Josh and Chris are doubled over holding their chests coughing, they're laughing so hard.

"Yeah, yeah, yeah." I shake my head at them.

"Guess I'm goin' to need another tub," Heather laughs. "You want to try again?"

What I want to say is, "Not really," but instead I shrug as she hands me the mop and I get back to my feet. Nine o'clock isn't looking too good right now. I get to mopping and a few minutes past nine, with the last bit of my mess cleaned up, my arm finally dry after washing it, and without incident this time, I bring up another tub.

"Alicia, can I go?" I ask, but it's more than a request. I'm all but pleading before I do anything else stupid.

"Get out of here," she laughs.

I shake my head, but I'm laughing too. It's good having a boss who can laugh at your stupid mistakes, God knows I make enough while I'm here. Suffice it to say they keep bandages close by on the mornings I work because it's my job to dice the onions and carrots.

"Thanks." I jog into the dining room and punch out, and then jog back through the kitchen and yell a quick bye as I fly out the back door and lock myself in my car.

As usual there's a text from Kallie. I'd actually be worried if there wasn't. It seems she's bored and wants to play Ball Pong on the phone, but that was an hour ago. I text her back and tell her maybe later as I start up the car. I have to get home. I'm ready to play some *Overwatch*.

We were supposed to play yesterday. I mean, we could have, but I canceled. It was supposed to be me, Aidan, and Jacob, but Jacob ended up having to work for some reason and the thought of being stuck gaming with just Aidan was a little overwhelming. I don't really know why, but it just felt that way, so I lied and told him I had a headache and we'd have to try tomorrow, aka today. I almost used the *I got called into work* excuse, but that's a no-go since we're closed on Sundays.

But tonight Jacob said he'd be up to play, and it worked for Aidan too, so now I just have to make it home in like ten minutes. It's a fifteen-minute drive, but I've made it quicker.

AIDAN
Monday, June 3

"Such a flawed creation." Tyler's avatar, Moira, simultaneously belittles me and sprays me with her healing biotic fluid. She's one of those characters that you love to hate. Or maybe that's just me.

"Thanks." I throw the word out as quick as I can, my fingers moving fast over my controller sending volleys of shotgun blasts toward the other team's Doomfist.

"No prob! I gotcha!" Tyler's voice shouts over my headset.

I lean forward, legs crisscrossed tight against myself in my chair. I maneuver Reaper behind the corner of a gated wall in King's Row. Reaper is my avatar, sort of like a more human take on the mythical reaper, except with two massive shotguns instead of a scythe.

"I've got him!" Tyler says, and I flank as he runs by shooting his purple aura, literally pulling the life out of Doomfist and absorbing it into his own body. It's actually sort of gruesome if you think about it.

"Jacob, D.Va's taking damage," I tell him. She—or he, not really sure with a gamer tag like EatLead_04—is ahead of me near the point but taking fire and their health is taking some serious blows.

"Got it," Jacob sounds off, and Mercy sails overhead waving her Caduceus Staff at the massive mech suit. A stream of healing flows between the two avatars. She's like an artificial angel, robotic wings and halo to top it all off.

I'd heard of Jacob before, but I'd never actually talked to him until tonight. So far he seems like a nice guy. He's competitive, that's for sure, but when you're a Mercy main you have to be. She's hard to play.

You literally have to switch your weapon, and my mind just doesn't work like that. I think I like Jacob though. Tyler and him for sure put on a good support team combining Mercy and Moira, so I'll give him that.

I go in guns blazing, shells popping, but I come up short when the opposing team's Mei, the devil herself wrapped in an innocent little snow globe, freezes my ass and Ana snipes me from atop a phone booth.

"Dammit!" I blurt, as I'm thrown into spectating mode for the five seconds it takes to respawn. It feels like minutes having to watch helplessly as my team gets decimated. We're not doing great.

"Ah come on, A," Tyler moans. I swallow back the disgust of my own failure, and how I strangely like the sound of Ty's voice on the line. I shake my head and refuse to think about it. "I just healed you! Jacob, can you resurrect him?"

"Mercy on call," Jacob mimics Mercy's voice line, and I see him swoop in. The word *Reviving* lights up in this angelic gold font in the middle of my screen, but just before my character is raised from the dead I hear Mercy exclaim "Ah!" and my character respawns back at the spawning bay.

"We're about to be destroyed, boys," Tyler calls over the chat.

"Sorry," Jacob apologizes. "I tried. Their Mei's good."

"All good," I assure him, running back to the fight as quick as Reaper can move, which isn't fast at all.

The computer announces, "Thirty seconds remaining," and my blood starts to boil. We have to win our last round of the night. Have to! I vape my character forward—at least that's what we call it when Reaper dematerializes and then rematerializes in another location—landing yards away from the point and blasting away their Junkrat from behind.

"I've got this," Tyler yells. His avatar ults. Massive rays of intermingled purple and yellow blast from his hands, and the enemy starts dropping or running.

"Get 'em!" I yell, pushing forward, still trying to knock their Junkrat out of the fight.

Then all our hope for victory is dashed when Sombra's little Latin voice comes over the line with, "Initiating the hack," and Tyler's ultimate goes dead.

"What the?" Tyler gasps, as their team regroups and literally mows him down. I try to step in, but Doomfist pounds me into the wall and the time winds down before the rest of our team can make it to the point.

"Defeated" flashes across the screen in doomy red.

"Agh!" I moan, nearly in time with Jacob, wherever he is. "We were so close!" I say, watching the *Play of the Game* showcase the other team's Mei taking me and Ty out earlier.

"We didn't make it past the first point," Jacob corrects me. "There's another whole point to take. I wouldn't call that good."

"Yeah, we sucked," Tyler agrees.

"Okay, yeah." I drop my shoulders as if they can see me.

While we were playing, this stupid idea popped in my head, and come to think of it, maybe I was distracted. Hope I didn't eff the match for them.

So, I was thinking, I'm graduating at the end of this week, and I have an extra graduation ticket. There aren't a lot of people for me to invite. My family around here is basically mi madre, mamá Isabella and papa Diego, tía Sofía and tío Gabriel, and Pilar, mi prima, and they're all coming, but I thought maybe, just maybe, I could ask Ty if he wanted to come too. It's probably a stupid idea. I don't think it's common to invite your friend to your high school graduation, but a part of me sort of would like for him to be there, the same part that is going to miss Brayden so much that day.

"Well look at that." Tyler's voice comes over the line smooth and confident. The stats board is on the screen and his avatar is one of the four cards plastered in the center just above his gamer tag, TAGtheBorg, lauding his four gold medals. "Four golds. Top healing. Suck it, Jacob."

"Only took you eight matches to beat me," Jacob sears him.

The medals board comes up and two bronze circles appear on my screen, one above *Objective Time*, and the other above *Eliminations*, meaning I stood my ground on the point the third longest and had the third highest number of kills. God, the rest of our team must have sucked even worse than me then. I only had four kills.

"I got a bronze for elims." It comes out weak.

"Gold," Tyler echoes.

"Of course you did," Jacob riles him, "you're always a DPS Moira."

"Uh, I also had gold healing this time, Jacob, and you were Mercy." I can imagine Tyler cocking his head to the side when he says it in his bedroom, and I laugh.

"What's funny there, Aidan?" Jacob snaps.

"I uh…"

Jacob chuckles, and Tyler's cute laugh—as much as I don't want to think of it like that—joins in. "Just kidding."

"Oh, good," I laugh.

"Well, I'm out, guys," Jacob says.

"Talk to you later," Tyler's voice echoes over the headset at about the same time I speak up.

"Bye."

"Guess I'll see you tomorrow for that history exam." Tyler clicks his tongue, and Jacob goes offline.

"Hope you're more ready than me. I'm so not," I say.

"It'll be easy." His confidence oozes over the headset.

"Speak for yourself. I gave up studying Saturday evening. It's useless," I tell him.

"It's just memorization. It all already happened. It's done, gone." Tyler talks like it's the easiest thing in the world. "You're more a science guy though, if I remember right. About the only science I'm into is astronomy. That shit's cool, plus it's what...uh... It's what Brayden liked."

"Yeah." I let those words run through my mind. *It's what Brayden liked.* With that, I'm done, and all the good feelings that were just here vanish. "I'll see you tomorrow, Ty."

And I log off.

AIDAN
Tuesday, June 4

I gotta piss, and I'm so over this version of *Hamlet*.

It's one of the perks and downfalls of the last week of school, especially in an elective class like Creative Writing. We handed in our final projects yesterday, much to Bryce's dismay. He's determined he's failed, even after I pitched in and helped him tighten it up a little. But now we're stuck watching whatever movies Mr. Hagan chooses, and nothing against Mr. Hagan, but his choices suck.

At this very moment, we're dredging through the adaptation of *Hamlet* with Mel Gibson in the title role. I'd much rather something with Patrick Stewart if I have to watch these Shakespeare movies, or better yet, something that's not about the 1500s to 1600s. Like *Black Panther*, *A Quiet Place*, hell, I'd even go for the new Mary Poppins movie over this.

But it's not my choice, it's not required viewing, and it doesn't count for a grade, so I'm not worried about missing any of it. I stand up, and immediately I get confused gazes from both Bryce and Ty.

"Where you going?" Tyler asks.

He's lying on the floor next to where I just was, texting Kallie, I think. It's almost weird having him stick around with Bryce and me in class today. It's been so long. Of course it's not like we're chatting it up either. We've just been staring at our phones the entire time, with the occasional texted meme coming up.

"Bathroom," I admit.

"Oh," Ty says and goes back to whatever he was doing. Bryce

shakes his head and does the same.

I duck my way up the aisle to Mr. Hagan's desk and ask for the hall pass to go to the bathroom. He hands it to me without question and I escape into the hall.

It always feels weird being outside the classroom *during* class. It's so empty. If you ignore the voices from the rooms you pass it's almost as if you're all alone in this big old building. I'm not, but it's just a thing.

Out in the main corridor I take the corner and slip into the bathroom, and take up temporary residence in the last stall. I'm going to delay going back for as long as I can, so I take out my phone and start scrolling through Instagram. It's a lot of the same. Lots of supercars, bookstagrammers and their aesthetically pleasing book pictures, and of course a few cute Insta boys I'll never meet.

The entire time I'm debating the main question that's been on my mind all day. It's not a hard one. The answer should be no, or maybe it just *is* no, but I'm still tossing it around, and I'm leaning heavily toward yes.

Should I invite Tyler to my graduation Saturday?

This *big* part of me feels like it's a really horrible idea. Maybe it's too soon. There's something about him and me… Dammit. I guess I like him. I think. No. I don't like him. That's just stupid. I mean, the boy spent time hating me. How could I like someone who literally hated me? It's stupid, I shouldn't, but I think I do. But I know he can't feel the same. I don't know. I really want him to be at my graduation, but if I ask, then is it going to be obvious that I'm an idiot? And if he knows I like him, how is he going to react? Will he get all weirded out? He just started being my friend again a few weeks ago, and I don't want to lose that.

Why does this have to be so hard?

Someone walks into the bathroom, and somehow I get my

answer. Just do it. I'm going to ask him to come, and if he gets weirded out, oh well. I'm going to do it.

I zip up and leave the stall. I'm running my soap-covered hands under warm water when the other person in here speaks, and I'm left wishing I'd stayed in the stall a few more minutes.

"Look who it is." Christian's voice grates my ears, and then his too perfect self comes into view in the mirror. "The little beaner fag boy."

Leave it to Christian to slur me twice in one sentence. I roll my eyes and finish washing my hands without so much as acknowledging him. That's what he wants, to be seen, right? He must have a horrible life at home.

"You not hear me, fag?" he asks.

I ignore him, grabbing a paper hand towel and drying my hands. I go to leave, but he blocks the path out and puts his hand on my chest to stop me.

"I'm talking to you." Christian plants his face right in front of me.

"Yeah, I caught that," I say. I want to let him have it, verbally at least. I wouldn't stand a chance in an actual fight. The problem with slinging insults isn't so much that it'd lower me to his level, but for those with little imagination like him, those words just lead to actual fights. So no.

"Where you going?" He pivots in front of me, continuing to block my path.

I sigh and roll my eyes again, this time making certain he sees. "Class."

He frowns. "Class? Boring."

"Uh, we're at school?" I say.

Christian coughs, not like a real cough that you can't control, but a nervous cough, except he doesn't seem nervous. I hear a zipping noise and his hand digs into his own pants. What the actual fuck? I keep my eyes up.

"How about you help me out a little?" Christian nods down like I didn't realize he was exposing himself.

I bite nervously at my bottom lip. I just want to leave. This isn't happening.

"I'm not—"

"Come on, that's what you fags do, right?" Christian shuffles on his feet. "Come on! Suck it, fag!"

"Eff off, man!" I blurt. I don't know if it's the fight-or-flight in me or what, but my voice deepens and it just comes out. I'm not doing this today. Just because I'm gay doesn't mean I want every guy's dick in the school. I'm not that guy, eff your stupid stereotypes. I brush his entitled hand off my shoulder and skirt around him.

"I said suck it, fag!" he tries again.

"This *fag* isn't doing anything for your ass," I throw back. What the hell is his problem?

"Maybe Tyler will then. Has before." Christian's voice is back to its usual smooth annoying way, and I want to punch him right here and now. I don't care if it's true, that's Ty's business, but Christian needs to keep his mouth shut. "That's all you fags are good for. Just a waste of space otherwise."

I'm not doing this. I clench my fist and make a beeline from the bathroom and back to Mr. Hagan's class. There's this part of me that knows I should say something, that I should go to Mr. Hagan or maybe the office, talk to Mrs. Reich, but I can't. In the end the school would just say he didn't actually do anything and just slap him on the hand for being a bigot. I know Mr. Hagan would be on-fire angry about it all, but in the end, it isn't his call. There's no use making a fuss when nothing will come of it except me looking like a whiny bitch.

Instead, I slink back into class like nothing happened and take my seat next to where Bryce and Tyler are lying on the floor, my hands in my lap, taking slow long breaths.

"You okay, man?" Bryce asks, and even in the dark room I can see a tinge of bewilderment in his face. Tyler's attention flicks away from his phone.

What do I say? Nah, I'm freaking out right now. Christian just propositioned me in the bathroom, got a little pushy, and then made a really messed up comment about Tyler and all us gay guys. No.

"I'm good, promise," I lie. But I will be. It just takes a little time for my nerves to settle down. It always does. This isn't anything new.

TYLER

Tuesday, June 4

Like any other Tuesday, when the final school bell rings, I'm up and running for the parking lot, to freedom. What's not like any other Tuesday is that Aidan beat me out the door.

Like, he was up and going before I could get off the ground.

He's usually one of the people behind in the horde trying to escape. Lately he's not been as far back, a few times even right with me. Come to think of it, I bet he used to do that because he knew I'd be an asshole if he tried saying anything to me. Damn, that all is really starting to be a pain in my ass.

That's not the point though. The point is today he was almost the first person out the door. I even stayed with him and Bryce today, which is a first for a long time. I wonder if I freaked him out?

But he did seem off the entire period. It's like he got real anxious, and he wouldn't look my way at all. At first, I thought maybe he was thinking about Saturday when he kept me from falling back into the creek—that brief moment when things got a little weird. It was just weird for him though, not me. But no, it can't be that. He was fine yesterday and today for the most part. It wasn't until fourth period that he seemed off.

I weave through the crowd and make it down the stairs, where double glass doors hail our final escape to the student parking lot as I try to catch up to Aidan. I'm not sure why I'm so excited to get out today, it's not like I'm doing anything special. I get one hour between school and my shift at Hannah's, and then it's balls-to-the-wall studying for my math exam tomorrow. Still, I push through the crowd and breathe in the fresh country air like it's a lifeline the moment I pass the exit.

I'll text him when I get to the car. I need someone who has a clue what they're doing to help me study for this exam tonight. Otherwise my ass is going to be repeating NC Math 3. I actually meant to ask before class let out, but I got wrapped up in Insta world and forgot.

And speak of the devil, there he is. It's hard to miss the Metallica t-shirt. The skewed, hard-edged *M* and *A* give it away every time. I quicken my step, and he veers to the right as he comes up on his Mustang. But he sees me.

I lift my hand and wave. Instead of stopping, he twists back around. It's almost like he didn't see me, but I know he did. The look on his freckled face said he saw me, but he turned like I'm not here, like I didn't just wave, like I'm not walking up this very moment. No, instead he jumps in his car and the engine roars to life. Before I can get there he reverses out of his space and takes off.

"What the hell?" I ask the empty space.

What just happened?

I stand dumbstruck while his Mustang disappears past the gate. What's his problem? Did I say something mean and not realize it during lunch? Am I still doing that? What did we talk about?

He complained about our history exam and mentioned something Grace did at his work. I think Kallie said she was there too. I don't remember what it was though. Kallie mentioned doing something as a group this summer, and Bryce got way too excited about being in *the group*. But that's it.

I can't think of anything that would have caused Aidan to ignore me.

"Why you just standing there like a crazy person?" Kallie startles me. "Really? That scared you?"

"Uh." I shake my head. "Did you see that?"

"See what?" She eyes me like I'm a genuine crazy person.

"Aidan." I nod at the exit gate. "He just left."

"Uh… Yeah." Kallie tilts her head and comes around my other side. "And isn't that what we usually do about now?"

"No… I mean yeah, but, like, I waved at him. You know, like for him to stop, I was…" I'm scattered and the more I say, the larger Kallie's smile gets. "I waved. I know he saw me, and he just ignored me and drove off."

"Hmm," Kallie huffs. "Odd."

"Yeah." I nod.

"What did you need?" She puts her hands on her hips.

"Was going to ask him to help me study for our math exam." I shrug. Guess not now.

"'Study'." She throws up air quotes.

"Stop it." I roll my eyes. "No, like, actually study."

"I can help with that," Kallie says.

"Yeah, but—"

"But what?" She smiles.

"You're not in the class," I remind her.

"But I took it last semester." She makes a good point.

"I know. Just seems rude," I tell her.

"So it's rude to me, and not A?" She gives me those I'm-looking-deep-into-your-soul eyes that I hate so much.

"No," I say. There is no right answer. I take it back to the wave to get the attention off me. "But it's basic human decency to wave back at least, right? Or hell, maybe even see what I needed? Maybe I was in trouble."

"Ah yes, just like you would have three weeks ago. Right." Kallie nods way too emphatically. I grit my teeth between pursed lips and God, do my eyes roll. I see what she's doing.

"Shut up." I fidget on my feet. "It's just odd."

"Well, maybe you should find out why," Kallie suggests with a raised brow.

"That's your area," I remind her. There's no way I'm doing that. I'll fail this damn math exam before I do that.

AIDAN

"He's too boyish." Kallie rolls her eyes.

She only has eyes for guys that are too old for her, always has, which is probably why she and Jeremiah didn't make it past a week. Plus, he isn't a world-famous actor or dead musician from the forties or fifties. It's a thing for her.

"You expect them to cast your darling Tom Hiddleston as Jeffrey Dahmer?" I ask. He's at the top of her list the last time I checked. Next is Benedict Cumberbatch, which I just don't get. Hiddleston is charming, but Cumberbatch?

"No," she says, screwing up her face.

She's been going on about that movie they made about Jeffrey Dahmer as a teen, before he became all crazy and killed like fifteen guys or something. I've heard it's insane, but I haven't seen it yet, which is weird considering Kallie's influence. It's even weirder that *she* hasn't seen it and that I'm just hearing about it from her.

"Ross was perfect for it though." Tyler holds his phone in front of me, hovering it above my lunch tray. "I mean he actually even sort of looks like him."

"Uhm… Is it wrong to say Dahmer was sort of cute?" I wince, waiting for the blowback.

"A little weird." Tyler grins at me. I'm so glad we talked last night.

When I got home from school after being a total asshole and ignoring him in the parking lot, I texted him and told him I was sorry. I debated it a while. Like, maybe he just shrugged it off, or maybe it was okay, but I couldn't deal with it. What happened in the bathroom yesterday was effed up, but it wasn't Ty's fault. And it doesn't matter what Ty's done in the past, I can't let that mess with me. Plus, Christian will say anything to get in your head. Of course, I didn't fill Ty in on what happened either.

"Definitely weird. The man killed seventeen guys between 1978 and 1991. And not only did he kill them, he fucking dismembered them and kept parts of them around his place. He even, like, drilled holes in their skulls and injected their brains with some acid or something to make them 'submissive'," Kallie fills in the details, as if it didn't feel wrong enough already to have said it.

"You know she's going to be a serial killer one day, right?" I tell Tyler, in full earshot of Kallie.

"I know." He nods. "I just hope to find out from the police, instead of being a victim."

"I think we're safe," I tell him, at the same time trying to figure out when it's best to ask him to come to my graduation. I'm going to do it. I've made up my mind.

"Uhm… Guys. I'm right here." Kallie leans over the table and waves her hand between us. "I can hear you."

"Well, you are." Tyler nudges her.

"I'm not going to turn into a serial killer. They're just fascinating." She sits up straighter, a tad more defensive.

"Oh no, you're going to be one," I say one more time.

"Whatever," she says, and I'm not sure whether that should worry or amuse me.

"In her defense, it is sort of interesting. And Ross Lynch is hot, so I do want to see it still," Tyler laughs.

"Fair," I agree, catching my eyes on Tyler's lips for just a second too long. I look away and scratch my head, anything to make it not look like I was looking.

When I texted him last night to apologize, I just told him I was having a rough day, today's exam was stressing me out, which wasn't a total lie, and I wasn't thinking straight. We ended up FaceTiming, something I thought would never happen again, and studied for a solid hour, or maybe it was two. And somehow right now I'm a little bit more confident about this exam, plus there's something about Tyler's eyes and lips that I could look at forever. I'll never tell him that, but yeah.

The bell rings, warning of the imminence of our math exam. I look at Tyler in distress.

"You ready for this?" I ask.

"Nope," he answers dryly.

"Same," I moan.

"Gah, I'm supposed to be the dramatic one." Kallie gets up and leads the way to the trash and then the stairs. She looks at me. "You'll be fine, it's math. It's Tyler who needs to be worried."

"Excuse me, bitch?" Tyler throws his hands up.

"I mean, she's not wrong," I point out, laughing with Kallie.

"Coming from the guy who helped me study last night," he reminds me as we top the stairs and enter the math and science wing.

"I'll let you two fight this one out. Peace!" Kallie about-faces and makes off in the other direction.

"You'll do fine," I tell him.

"Oh, now I'm going to do fine," Tyler laughs.

To be honest, I'm not one hundred percent sure. He's smart, but math isn't his thing, as I found out firsthand last night on FaceTime. I think he'll pass at least. But I still have to ask my question. I don't want it to seem weird, and I only have a few minutes to ask. I was going to do it last night, but it just felt weird. Like it would be tantamount to saying *Hey, I like you*, which if I'm totally honest is sort of what I'm saying, but no, not at all at the same time.

"You'll pass," is what I say instead. "You had a…good grasp on it last night. At least enough."

"That's comforting." He rolls his eyes. "Maybe I'll enlist you for motivational talks next."

We laugh. Mrs. Williams' classroom is in sight, and I'm still being too chicken-shit to ask. This is much harder than I expected. So much harder.

"Maybe you can come to my graduation. I'm sure there will be some motivational speech there." It tumbles out in the same instant my mind is telling me how stupendously stupid I am, but I keep going. The mistake is already made. "It won't be from me, I mean obviously, but still. You should though, I have an extra ticket."

I shrug. You know, like an idiot, like an imbecile who can't keep his mouth shut and then tries to act like it's nothing.

A second or two, or maybe it's thirty, passes as we close the gap before our next exam in silence. Dammit, I weirded him out. He doesn't know what to say. Why the hell do I do this?

"Sure." He smirks but not in a mocking way, like I'd expect. "You don't want to invite family?"

"I am," I assure him. I'm not sure how serious he is yet, and my mind is running a mile a minute. Is he fishing around to find the joke, or how to make it a joke, or just how to get out? Tyler's never been afraid of being blunt, but maybe he's trying not to right now. "Mi madre is coming, of course, and some other family. If you don't come I'll just end up giving it away."

He thinks about it for a moment, then looks at me with this cute grin. "Sure. Why not?"

TYLER

Friday, June 7

"Some of you will be happy with your scores, some, not so much. But," Mrs. Kropf says dryly, putting a finger in the air before leafing through a stack of Scantron sheets and dropping one on Hunter's desk. "It could be worse. I could have not given a curve."

"What d'you want to bet I'm the reason for the curve?" I whisper.

"If your being stupid brings up my grade, I'm not complaining," Kallie bobs.

I roll my eyes. Hell if I can remember which group of mammals lay eggs, or what endosymbiosis is, or which environmental conditions don't affect enzymes. Like, how is that going to matter ten years from now?

My test lands on my desk face down like everyone else's and I flip it over. There's a big handwritten seventy-nine at the bottom and a bunch of Xs all over the paper. I lean to check out Kallie's, but she hides it from me.

"Nosey." She grins.

"What did you get?" I ask.

"Ninety-seven, you?" She's still grinning.

I'm not sure if she's grinning because she got a ninety-seven or if she's grinning because she knows I didn't. But oh well. I lift my test so she can see the score, and she smiles harder.

"Good job…" She bounces her shoulders. "So, how's it feel to be stupid?"

"Ex-cuse me," I emphasis each syllable and give her my best

really-bitch look. "I passed."

A few minutes later we're on our backs at the rear of the room in our own little huddle while most of the class watches *The Blind Side*. I love Sandra Bullock, but we've seen it before, and there are more pressing matters at hand.

At lunch Kallie brought up the "group" summer trip she's been on about for weeks. We threw around some ideas like the beach, too expensive; camping, Aidan shot that one down real quick and I seconded the dismissal, I hate camping; Bryce brought up a NASCAR race and Aidan had to remind him that he doesn't even like NASCAR.

"Guess we're doing Carowinds." Kallie sighs.

She'd really hoped we could pull off a beach trip. To the rest of the group she didn't press it a ton, but for me, well, she'd left a few subtle hints like this one little text last week that said, "WE ARE GOING TO THE BEACH IF IT'S THE LAST THING I DO," literally in all caps, and, "Trying to convince Mom it's worth dropping $4k on that beach house," among others. It's good to see her dealing with loss. I think for her parents, it was part money and part not wanting a week being responsible for five teenagers, four of which aren't their own children.

"Carowinds it is," I repeat, and that's fine with me.

The beach would have been fun, but a day down in Charlotte at a theme park means less time for drama. And to be honest, I can imagine some drama going down during a week at the beach between Bryce and Katie, which could bring on more between the rest of us. I say good call, Mr. and Mrs. Peterson. "It'll be fun. We can drive separately from your parents, take my car maybe, drive with the wind in our faces and the music blaring the entire way. And they have a water park, so we'll still get water slides and all of that."

"I know. I was just hoping for a whole week at the beach," she complains.

"Not sure I could stand being stuck in close quarters with all of you that long," I tell her.

"You love me though." Kallie nudges her shoulder into me and wrinkles her nose.

"I didn't say it had anything to do with you, fool." I grin, pushing her right back.

"Truth." She nods. I can see the gears working overtime in those dark gray eyes of hers, but I'm not about to ask. "You still going to A's graduation?"

It comes out of nowhere. I made the mistake and told her yesterday. I knew she'd find out eventually, and if I wasn't the one to tell her, well I know Kallie, she'd end up making it into something huge and grand. Turns out she did anyway, but I managed it, not in the kill-her-and-dump-the-body way she talks about, but my just-shut-the-fuck-up way.

"Yeah," I say. "We still starting the new *Grace & Frankie* season next week?"

It's a diversion. I'm just hoping it'll work. I knew the moment I told her she wouldn't be able to stop thinking about it, and as a result I thought about it a lot after telling Aidan yes Wednesday night and Thursday morning before I let her in on the news. I got all the expected questions. *Are you in love with Aidan? Did you two hookup and not tell me? Do you at least like him? When is the wedding?*

I shot her down on each one. And wedding? Really?

"Sure," she says, but she's not done, obviously. "I still can't believe you said yes."

"But I love *Grace & Frankie*." I eye her stupidly. I know exactly what she's talking about, but I'm not about to let her know it. "Brianna is the best, she's like you twenty years from now."

"I know." Kallie shrugs it off. It's not the first time, and it won't be the last time, I've compared the two. "You like him, don't you?"

"Her." I play dumb. "Obviously. She's hilarious! What's not to like?"

"You know who I'm talking about, asshole." Kallie's eyes bore into me, lips pursed into this shrewd smirk.

"No. I've told you so many times, Kal, I don't like him like that," I tell her yet again. "We're friends again, that's it."

"You sure?" she asks. "He is hella cute. I mean, mhmm mhmm, that tan and chiseled chin, dreamy brown eyes, adorable freckles. And I know I'm not the only one who saw him shirtless at the creek."

I roll my eyes and stare at the ceiling. She's not wrong. He is cute. Maybe more than that. I don't think I realized how good-looking he was until our trip to Wilson's Creek. I swallow back a lump in my throat that comes out of nowhere and refocus. Just because he's cute doesn't mean I like him like that. I can have cute friends. I can even think my friends are cute, and not *like* like them.

"So?" I rebut. It's weak, like hella weak, to use Kallie's word, but if I said she's wrong I'd be lying.

"You've just seemed a lot more… I don't know, like yourself the last few weeks, and you smile a lot when he's around," she tells me.

Do I? I think she's imagining it. That's it. She's imagining it. It's a fantasy in her head, the same one she's been feeding for the last month. That's all.

"I think you're fantasizing a little much there," I tell her.

"You're trying to tell me you don't think he's cute?" Kallie pops her head back and pooches her lips as if to say, "Tell me I'm wrong."

"I… I mean…" I stutter, trying to find the words that will least support her imagined world. "Yeah, he's cute. But that doesn't mean I like him, for like the hundredth time, by the way. Hell, *you're* super pretty, but I don't want to screw you."

"Somehow that makes me happy and hurts at the same time." Kallie's eyes morph into mock disappointment. "And I didn't say you wanted to get in his pants. But do you?"

"God, Kal!" I throw my head back and it slaps against the thinly carpeted floor with a smack. Damn that hurt! "Ouch!"

"You okay?" Kallie flinches and drops the show.

"I'm good." I sigh, cradling the back of my head in my palm.

"That was so graceful." She winces and pats my head like I'm a five-year-old. "So, do you?"

I'm a guy, sure I've thought about it. Who hasn't thought about boning someone attractive? I've thought about boning a lot of guys, that's totally normal and it doesn't mean I want to marry them. Same goes for Aidan.

"Stop it!" I plead with her.

"Fine!" She crosses her arms over her chest. "But I still think I'm right."

AIDAN

"You okay?"

What? I snap back to reality and search for the voice. A weak smile paints its way onto my face when I find Hailey's excited bright greens staring me down like she found a lost puppy in the woods.

"I'm good," I lie. Being quiet most of the time has its perks. People usually don't ask too many questions.

Today's been difficult, and that's putting it lightly. It's one of those damned if you do and damned if you don't situations. It's graduation day. I should be excited. I should be ready for this line to start moving. But I'm not.

Moving puts me one step closer to facing a hard truth. I should be ready to leave this sweat-smelling auxiliary gym behind, but it reminds me of all the soccer games with him on the field with me. I should be ready to walk across the stage, but that seals the inevitable — it's over, and he's not here to walk it too.

"You seem spaced out." Hailey dips around when I try to look away.

"I'm good," I repeat. "It's just…"

"Oh." Her mouth forms a wide O. "I'm sorry. I wasn't thinking about that."

"It's okay." I force a grin and face the front of the line as the procession music begins and people start moving. Blue gowns sway as my classmates disappear into the gym and the music gets louder. I fight the urge to search the front of the line. A slight smile cracks my lips. He was smarter than me, honors even, so that's where he would have been, not with us stupid ones in the back.

The doors give way to the gymnasium. Every inch of bleacher is packed wall-to-wall, and immediately I search them. It takes a moment, but there they are. Mi madre, mi mamá Isabella and papa Diego, mi tía Sofía and tío Gabriel, Pilar, and I guess it shouldn't surprise me, but Tyler smushed up against Mamá. It's obvious they see me too. Mi madre waves furiously and mi tío Gabriel screams, "Go Aidan!" for all the gym to hear. I grin but I'm burning up inside with only my freckles to disguise the redness building beneath my cheeks.

I wave back at them weakly. I can't believe Tyler actually came. I knew he wouldn't, but there he is.

My foot catches and I stumble forward. Gasps fill the air in the same moment my hands flail outward, begging for support, anything to balance myself. I throw my foot forward, my nose dangerously close to becoming much too intimate with Pat's shoulder blade, but I find my footing and it's over. The gasps turn to *ohs* and I force the best fake smile I can. Damn!

Focus on the line, A.

The seating is alphabetical, unless you're an honors student who sits up front, so Molinas are nearer the back. We cut the corner around the metal chairs covering the gym floor and I follow Pat down our row. Up in the second row there's an empty seat with the graduation cap Brayden would have worn. I can't see it now, but I know it's there. I had to see it during our march practice.

The principal tells everyone to sit, and the next half hour is a blur of speeches and presentations, my classmates getting up and sitting back down, applause and recognition. The athletic scholarship to Charlotte that my coach just handed me sits in my lap. Then it happens.

"At this time we'd like to take a moment to recognize a fallen Warrior," Principal Griffin says, his hands placed firmly on the podium. Behind him on the projection screen is Brayden's graduation portrait, the one in the fake suit. I swallow back the lump in my throat and purse my lips like it'll help hold back my feelings. "In March, Brayden Matthew Cole was taken from us. He was a bright student. His science teachers tell me he loved astronomy, and he talked about being an astronomer one day."

The principal goes on, and I hear some of it, but most is a blur, this mix of sounds and utterances that make no sense. My mind is focused on his empty chair as I stare at the pictures shuffling on the screen. In one he's on the soccer field, sweaty and probably out of breath, kicking the ball around. In the next he's sitting on the floor, bunched up with me and Kallie. I think it was in Mr. Cloaninger's classroom last semester—Environmental Science, I think. They keep changing. In each one he's smiling, like he always did, and I stop trying to hold back the tears. Hailey puts her arm around me and squeezes my shoulder. It's still so hard to believe he's not here, that he's not about to head off to college with me. We should be able to celebrate this day together, and it hurts so much more than I thought it would. It feels like a bandage has been torn off a wound that never healed.

Then a photo materializes into existence with Brayden in the hallway talking to Tyler.

Instinctively I look to the bleachers. Tyler's got his face buried in his hands, and mi madre is cradling him like her own child. What have I done? I wasn't thinking. It's enough that I have to deal with this, but Tyler didn't have to. *Please don't hate me for this.*

I look away and catch the last few words from the principal before he calls for a moment of silence. I guess people are praying. I don't even know what I believe, but I pray too.

God, please let Brayden know I miss him. Tell him it's not fair I have to do this alone, that I have to go to college alone. But tell him I know it's not his fault, and that it isn't Tyler's fault either. Stuff just happens.

The ceremony picks back up like we hadn't just lost my best friend, and an hour later I'm walking out of the gym, diploma in hand, and mostly back to normal. And by mostly, I mean I'm only crying now because everyone else in the room is crying, and no one wants to leave the gym, because reality has finally set in. We'll never go to school here again, and chances are most of us won't see each other again. But I'm still stuck with this huge weight. It's like I'm leaving Brayden here. It's as if I can't take him with me, and it's everything I can do to leave the gym.

I force myself to say my goodbyes to Hailey and a few others and make my way upstairs. It's like fighting the current at the beach as it tries sweeping you back out to sea after an exhausting swim. Finally I find my people, or really they find me. A woman's arms wrap around me before I realize it's Mamá. I start to push her away just as I'm catching on.

"Mi pequeño, all grown up and graduated." She squeezes me tight, loosening her grip only to wipe a tear away from my cheek. "I'm so proud of you."

"Thanks," I say. I hate compliments and junk, but right now isn't the time to be against them.

"¡Felicidades!" It's not just one of them, it's all of them, my abuelos, tíos, and my cousin, all circling around in a big group hug that's borderline suffocating, mixed with a "Congrats!" from Tyler. He's standing a foot or two off like he isn't sure he's allowed to join the circle.

"Gracias!" I say again, but I'm looking at Tyler. He smiles. Thank God he smiled. Maybe he doesn't hate me.

"Let's get some pictures," tía Sofía urges with her phone already out.

The totally amateur photo shoot starts up, and by the end of it there are enough pictures to fill an entire photo album. My abuelita even forced Tyler to get in on the action. It was obvious he didn't think he should, but you just don't tell my sweet little abuelita no.

We start to head out to the parking lot, and mi madre turns to Tyler.

"We're taking Aidan out for dinner and then Bo's with some friends," she says.

Friends? Bo's? I didn't know anything about this. I thought we were just going to eat and then home. But I'll take a night out bowling and gaming. "You'll come too, right?"

"Uh," Tyler hesitates. He looks at me, smiling with his bright white teeth showing, and I can tell he's thinking about it, but he's not sure.

"Kallie will be there," Mamá says, and I look at her crazily. What the hell is going on? "And a few others. Aidan didn't know we were doing this. Kallie thought it would be fun. But she wasn't sure if you could keep it a secret."

She wasn't sure Ty could keep it a secret, from me? I squint. Sneaky. She thinks she's sly. I like it.

"Sure. Yeah, I'll come," Tyler stumbles before gaining traction. He looks at me. "You sure it's okay?"

"Of course," I say.

It's more than okay.

TYLER

Saturday, June 8

I'm up.

I take the floor, careful not to slip on the shiny wooden planks leading up to the bowling lane. My pins settle and the rack lifts away. Ariana Grande's "Break Up with Your Boyfriend" is blaring over the speakers loud enough that it's hard to hear Kallie shouting behind me.

"Can't be worse than the last one! You got this!"

I turn to flip her off, but stop. Like, Aidan's entire family is behind me. I turn around and focus on the ten pins left from the immaculate gutter ball I just threw. *Can't be worse* my ass. I start my run and release the ball. It takes everything in me to resist turning the moment I let go so I don't have to watch my ball miss again.

It barrels down the lane, oddly enough not heading directly for the gutter. Instead it veers to the left and clips the last two pins, knocking them over.

"See? Better!" Kallie says when I turn around and make the walk of shame back.

I don't care how good I do, which is never good, it always feels like a walk of shame from the bowling lane back to my seat. I don't know what it is, but I always feel awkward.

"That brings you to forty," Aidan says, picking his emerald-green ball from the ball thingy. "You're not that far behind."

"Since when did eighty points behind not qualify as far?" I shake my head. I know I'm no good at this game, but damn, I didn't know I sucked this bad.

"If it helps, you're only ten behind me." Kallie shrugs.

"That *is* going to change," I tell her.

Aidan can beat me, even Bryce can beat me, but Kallie, no. She isn't allowed to have that pleasure. I'll have to hear about it every day for the next week if she does.

"Big boy words. Just means you're going to fall so much harder." Kallie sticks out her tongue at me.

I take my seat next to her. Bryce and Katie are sitting on her other side, basically talking to each other like none of us exist. It's cute, even if we are here for Aidan technically. I'm pretty sure he gets it, plus he has Rhys, Kallie, and me, and his family sit across from us, minus his grandpa and aunt who I guess don't bowl.

Now, dinner was a bit awkward. It was fun, but I don't know his family beyond Ms. Molina, who keeps insisting I call her Mariana instead. And I kept getting this weird feeling his grandma and aunt think I'm Aidan's boyfriend with some of the stuff they said.

Like asking how we met, but not asking how he met anyone else at the table, and telling Aidan I was cute while I was sitting right there. The misunderstanding aside, which I'm going to ask him about at some point, the expression on his face when she said it was priceless. It was total shock, and the way he changed the topic without answering, and let's not forget how red his cheeks got.

At the same time, I kept remembering what was missing. Every time I'd look around the table my heart ached. Today was supposed to be Brayden's big day too. He should be sitting here with us now, a graduate. But he's not.

I got a lot of it out in the bleachers when they did that moment of silence for him—I couldn't stop myself from crying, and Aidan's family was nice about it. I had no idea the school would do that, but I guess I should have assumed. I hate crying, like, really hate it, even when other people are too.

Stop thinking about it. Today is a good day. Keep it that way.

As for Bo's, it's whatever Aidan wants to do. It's his day. But I will admit I'm ready for laser tag. I know how royally bad I suck at bowling, it's no secret. Something I'm making abundantly clear right now.

"Go Aidan," Ms. Molina yells, and then his whole family starts to cheer. We're competing against them, but they're too friendly not to cheer. Like, they literally cheer each one of us, even my sorry ass.

Aidan starts up and, with perfect form, sends the ball flying down the bowling lane. It slaps the first pin, front and center, and like a domino effect, they all drop to the wood, and the digital scorecard lights up with this little green dancing martian in the corner holding a big card with an X on it.

"Strike!" Aidan yells, pumps his fist, and does this little dance on the way back.

"Make that one hundred and two points behind." I roll my eyes but keep a smile on.

"I would say you could catch up, but…" Aidan scrunches his nose, and it's actually sort of cute. "Not going to happen."

"Ah! Should have accepted your offer to take it easy on me earlier," I say. The crazy part is I think he would have, but I'd rather win or lose on my own merit any day.

"You should have." He takes the seat next to me while Kallie gets ready for her turn alongside Aidan's Aunt Sofía who, for all her niceness, talks smack to Kallie the entire turn, and I'm here for it.

Two rounds later I finish dead last, and by dead last I mean last among our team and his family, at a whopping fifty-five to Aidan's one hundred and sixty. And I will be hearing about this from Kallie for the next week or month. I can throw it up that she only got half Aidan's and Bryce's scores, who managed to beat even Aidan with a one hundred and sixty-five. My only solace is Rhys's sixty-two and Katie's sixty-eight.

"Laser tag?" Aidan throws his hands up.

"Finally! Something I can destroy you all in," Rhys jumps and pumps his fist.

"Fu—" I catch myself and course correct. "Darn right!"

Kallie, Bryce, and Katie glance at me, but I refuse to acknowledge it. Not today, Satan. Aidan bites his lip, obviously holding in a laugh.

"Let's do it," he says, and we're off, weaving through the Saturday night gaming crowd to the laser tag arena.

Some blonde high school chick, probably from South or Hibriten, gives us the rules while we wait under the massive green, blue, and red sign declaring LASER TAG in all caps above the arena entrance and exit doors. She's obviously given the spiel a hundred times before and sounds like she could kill someone if they asked a question.

"I say it's Aidan, me, and Rhys," Bryce starts naming the teams, barely able to stand still, "against Katie, Kallie, and Tyler."

"Yeah." Aidan nods. "Sure."

"We winning fo' sure." Rhys winks at his team.

"I may suck at bowling, but my laser tag is on point," I remind them. Surely they remember.

"Whatever," Rhys says. "But it's a team sport, and well…"

Kallie steps forward, and my eyes go wide. Oh boy.

"Well…" She eyes him.

"I mean—" he backtracks.

"Bitch, please, you're going to wish you were dead," Kallie sasses him.

"Uh… Okay." Rhys takes a step back.

The circle bursts into laughter, breaking the silence while

everyone watches. I keep forgetting he isn't around Kallie much. She can be scary to the uninitiated.

A group of six guys who look to be around our age or maybe college age come out the exit, all smack talk, and the attendant opens the entrance.

"You're up," she says and shows us inside. Her voice is this super excited toneless droning. "Here's your vests and guns. Remember you have to hit the sensor on the vest to get a point. Have fun."

Nothing about her voice gave any indication she meant it, but who cares. Kallie goes for the blue vest the second she sees the options. She hates red. Always has. Don't know why, but she does. I motion Katie toward a blue vest and slip into mine.

"'Kay," Katie says all chipper.

Okay, I'm going to admit it right now. I'm having a hard time imagining Katie with the laser gun mowing down Bryce, or anyone for that matter, but I'm trying not to pre-judge. Maybe she'll surprise us and some sadistic killer streak will emerge, but then again, maybe I shouldn't hope for that.

On the opposite side of the tiny space Aidan, Bryce, and Rhys don red vests. I swear Aidan glances at me, but maybe it's just in my head. Once we're ready, the fake-happy attendant girl lets us into the arena.

"Spread out and get ready for the clock to start," she says in full monotone and shuts the door behind us.

The darkness is interrupted by purple blacklights and glowing fluorescent greens, reds, and blues lining the walls and every corner. I get Kallie's and Katie's attention and nod to the right.

"Let's go this way," I say, my mind begging *please don't make me lose* as Aidan and his team disappear around the opposite corner.

"Battle commences in fifteen seconds," a domineering male voice proclaims over the loudspeakers, and techno music starts ramping up.

We weave through the labyrinth and up a few inclines until I'm satisfied we're on our own turf.

"Y'all ready?" I stare them down. This is serious stuff.

"Oh yeah." Kallie hunches down.

"Let's fuck 'em up," are not the words I expected to hear from Katie's mouth, but it's exactly what comes out as she attempts a snarl. A moment later her big smile is back and she laughs, "I mean, right?"

Kallie's eyes are as wide as mine.

"Yeah!" I laugh.

"A little over the top?" She shrugs as the announcer voice booms over the loudspeaker again.

"Nah," I say, more worried than anything. Woah.

"Battle commences in five, four, three, two, one," followed by a blaring sound, and lights begin to flash. "May the best team win!"

"We sticking together or splitting up?" Kallie asks, her lips glowing blue under the black light along with the straps on her vest.

"Uh—" I start.

"Split up," Katie interrupts. "We're easier to pick off together."

"That," I say, still perplexed by the Katie I'm seeing. Maybe there's more to her than I give her credit for.

"May the odds be ever in your favor, bitches," Kallie sort of quotes *The Hunger Games* and jogs past me and out of sight.

"I'm off," Katie taps my back and runs off in the other direction.

Now that I'm by myself I slink around the corner and peer over the ledge. I have a decent view from here. I can see a portion of the arena, but it's too compact to get a real good view, just flashes of light and shadows. Here we go, I guess.

I take off down the first ramp, laser gun tucked into my right shoulder, face leaning in to follow the barrel's line of sight. I've played enough *Battlefield* to know how this works, plus my dad's a big gun guy so there's barely a month that goes by when we don't shoot targets in the field behind the house. It's one of the few things we do together that I enjoy these days, and I guess it makes me less gay in his eyes. Whatever.

My sight swings around the next bend and my eyes are assaulted by a flurry of glowing orange and green pillars standing erect in the middle of a larger space. I weave through them, eyes alert for any sign of movement.

"Where you at, A?" I whisper.

Footsteps pad by to the right. I swing my aim toward the sound, but there's a wall between us. My eyes sweep to the left and I peer around one of the orange columns. The flashing from purple back to darkness makes it difficult to focus. I squint. Ahead there's a doorway leading around the column. I lean in and take off. I plant my back against the wall, give it a second, then swing around. It's empty. I scowl and run across the small space to the next tunnel.

Out of nowhere my vest vibrates and a loud zapping noise shouts from my chest. I look down and then swing around.

"Gotcha!" Rhys's bright white teeth shine from an excited smile.

I huff, take aim, and pull the trigger, but he's moving before I can get my shot off. He takes off the way I came and disappears among the bright lights. Instead of following I turn and keep moving. Again, I hear footsteps over the music and slow down. They're getting louder. Whoever it is isn't trying to be stealthy, which means I have a good guess who it is.

I wait along the edge, just around the next open doorway, and sure enough Kallie barges by.

"Hey!" I shout to scare her.

"What the actual fuck!" Her feet come off the ground and she literally throws the laser gun against the wall.

Damn, am I glad I wasn't standing closer. I bend over laughing. I might be easy to scare, but when I do get her, it's so satisfying.

"You just going to run through every room without looking?" I can't keep the grin off my face.

"Maybe," she says. "Damn, you got me good. You been got yet?"

"Once. Rhys," I tell her. "You?"

"A few times." She shrugs hesitantly.

"Define a few," I say, leaning around the corner to check our six. We're still clear.

"Uh…four, maybe five times? Mostly by Bryce. Aidan once." She shrugs.

I smile big and laugh in the back of my throat in that way that's more wheezing than laughing. Even in the dark I can see her evil glare.

"Maybe you should use a little more stealth? You know, sneak a little?" I suggest.

"Sure, whatever." And she's off again.

The sound of one of the laser guns going off blares from the direction Kallie just ran off, and I catch a clearly Kallie, "Fuck." I try not to laugh. I don't want to give away my position, but it's too late. Bryce swings around a fluorescent red pillar and catches sight of me. He pulls the trigger, but I dodge to the left and take off through the next room and up a steep ramp. His feet stomp behind me, matching my pace step for step.

Ahead there's a fork. I take the left path into a thin passage lined with bright blue pads and black netting along the walls. Bryce's footsteps get quieter. I turn and wait; if he keeps coming this way I should see him first. But the sound gets quieter until it's gone.

Take that, Bryce.

Satisfied, I twist around and sprint toward the next block. I take a hard left. My vest slams against something solid, and suddenly I'm staring into another set of eyes as we tumble to the ground, and I land fully on Aidan's chest.

My eyes lock with his, but instead of his dark brown eyes, they look black and silver under the lighting. Woah. I mean, they're nice. Just normal. For a moment he stares right back and part of me doesn't want to look away. There's something mesmerizing in them. Hell, what am I saying? It's just the crazy black light effect. Finally, I realize I'm holding my breath and I haven't moved yet.

"Oh," I grumble. I slide off him, grunting as I get to my feet. "Sorry. I didn't see you."

He's still on the floor smiling. He shakes his head, and I put out my hand and help him up.

"You know, if you wanted to be on top of me so bad, all you had to do was ask." He smiles jokingly. "You don't have to make it look like an accident."

"What? No… I, uh… I wasn't—" I stumble on my own stupid words.

He gut-laughs, his vest even jumping on his chest. "I'm kidding."

Then my vest buzzes and the zing of Aidan's laser gun goes off. Seriously? That's low.

"What the?" I laugh, but he's sprinting down the next corridor before I can get the words out. "You ain't gettin' away that easy."

I take off after him.

TYLER

"Dude, I watched it." Kent drops into the pew in front of me, the one closest to the pulpit.

Dad isn't about to let us be Back-Row Baptists. It's one of the many misfortunes of your dad being a deacon.

"Watched what?" I purse my lips. I've recommended so many shows. "There are literally thousands of movies, Kent."

I check my phone. I have places to be, but I try not to dart out of the building the moment the sermon ends. Dad gets pissy about it.

"*The Matrix*." He rolls his sky-blue eyes, as if it's so obvious, and props his arm atop the back of the pew.

"I didn't understand that one." Mom shrugs sitting next to me.

Neither of us is the type to get up and socialize outside our own little group after church, or really anywhere. For me it's because ninety percent of the people in this building, whether they'll admit it to my face or not, are judging the fuck out of me the moment they lay eyes on me. It's like instinct, they can't just see a normal person.

Mom. Well, Mom just isn't social. She hates looking people in the eye, so she doesn't. It works for me. Sure, she does whatever Dad says, but she's cool most of the time. She did make us watch *The Matrix* with a cuss filter so we didn't hear all the horrible *wordy turds*—her word, not mine—a good Christian should never hear or utter. Maybe I'm wrong, but I still think that's more because she just listens to Dad.

"You don't understand half the movies you watch." I side-eye her, and grin massively to make sure she knows I'm kidding. She's sarcastic as hell most the time, second only to Kallie, and honestly hilarious, so she can't complain.

Kent eyes me with concern, but I wave him off. After all the years growing up in the same church, I swear he still doesn't realize how not boring Mom is, and how little I care what people here think of me.

"What'd you think?" I ask.

It was one of the classic movies I told him he needed to watch months ago. Chances are he snuck it on and watched it on Netflix or something late at night. I don't think his parents would approve of it.

"It was awesome! Over the top, but it was cool. The way he bent back in slo-mo and dodged those bullets. I mean, woah!" Kent's mouth is moving fast, but it usually does. "And the gun fights. They were insane! And when Neo stopped the bullets. That was so intense."

"It's meant to be over the top," I tell him. "It literally takes place inside a computer."

He considers it and nods.

Kent belongs to one of those families that never stops multiplying. He's sixteen and has two sisters and three brothers. And insanely enough his mom is pregnant *again*. Out of six siblings, he's the only cool one. His sisters are either insane or too goody-goody, and his brothers are the big macho types that took in every ounce of garbage chauvinistic male-gender-role shit telling them what a man is "supposed to be" and "not supposed to be".

There are times I swear Kent was adopted, even if physically he is a carbon copy of his two older brothers, pale I've-never-seen-the-sun skin and all. Either that, or he has some invisible shield against stupid indoctrination, because he isn't like them at all. Actually, he's, like, the only person in this church that still actively talks to me—other than my mom, of course—and I don't feel like he's making himself do it.

"And that's even crazier. I mean, what if all of this was not real?"

He gestures generally around himself. And I have to admit, I've thought about it before but always stop short of looking for a real answer. "What if by knowing it wasn't real, we could bend the rules and do the crazy stuff they do?"

"It'd be insane," I say. "I would so download Aikido and Jujitsu, and do all sorts of Spider-Man-looking stunts."

"You tried when you were younger," Mom reminds me.

I did.

I was determined I could do the whole bending back and dodging bullets thing Neo does. But instead of bullets it was Kallie shooting nerf darts at me, and now that I think about it, the only reason most of them missed is because she has horrible aim. Probably why she had such a low score at laser tag yesterday.

It's sort of like when we were in our lightsaber fighting stage when *The Force Awakens* came out. Thankfully we live out in the country, so our audience was only family, but they still won't let us live it down.

I wave her off with a little huff. "I got close."

"Not how I remember it." She smiles at me.

I shake my head and check my phone again. *12:33 p.m.* Time to head out. Aidan asked me to come to the park after church for soccer last night after laser tag. I'm not a big sports guy at all, but I used to go.

It's going to be fun. I can endure a little running around and kicking a ball into a net with friends. Yet I'm still wondering why I agreed to it since I don't actually like the game.

"I gotta go, Aidan's expecting me at the park," I tell Kent, and I guess Mom too, technically. I get up, but Kent looks at me oddly.

"Aidan?" Kent squints.

"Yeah, you know him," I say.

"Well, yeah. But I thought…" He drags out the word like I'm supposed to fill in the blank, and when I don't, he glances at Mom uncomfortably and then back at me. "Uh… I thought you two didn't get along."

"Oh." I stop and something in my chest feels a little uneasy.

He's right. We didn't before the world fell apart in March. Maybe we still don't and we're both just sort of out of our own minds right now, I don't know. All I know is it's working right now, and if I'm completely honest with myself, I'm glad. I forgot how much fun he was. "We're good."

I'm not sure what else to say. No one else has brought that up. I push back a lump in my throat and do the same with the thought.

AIDAN

Sunday, June 9

I told myself I wouldn't do it, but my shoulders slump the instant I pull into the parking lot. I've always been the type to get my hopes up too much over the stupidest things. And it doesn't matter how insignificant it is—when whatever it is doesn't happen, it weighs me down like this rock on my chest with gargantuan storm clouds overhead, tempted to pour but just barely holding back.

And of course, Tyler isn't here. Part of me knew last night it was a bad idea asking him to come today. I'm honestly surprised he said yes *period*, but all it meant is I'd put this hope in my head. The same hope that this very moment is pulling me down.

The lot isn't empty though. I come to a stop next to Rhys's patchy little gray Toyota pickup. He and Bryce are propped against the truck bed talking. They wave as I put it in park and force a smile.

"Get a grip, A." I stare through the wire fence and across the empty baseball field. "He's just running late."

I hate how stupid little things get to me so much. I know better. I'm lucky Ty's even being a friend right now, all things considered, and here I am getting too attached already. It's just a stupid soccer game. He doesn't even like sports. I know that. I know he knows that. So the chances weren't even fifty-fifty in the first place. But being the person I am, I'm going to give him some time before I dash it or let it bug me. Okay, it's already bugging me, but that's my fault.

I take a deep breath and exit the car.

"Hey, man," Rhys greets.

"Looks like it's just us," Bryce comments. I force a half-smile, wishing he'd have kept that to himself.

Remember, he could just be late.

"Maybe," I say. "I'll text Ty and see if he's still coming."

I take my phone out and type a quick message, my lips pursed like it'll somehow help get the reply I'm hoping for.

AIDAN: Still coming?

I let my hand drop to my side so I don't stare at the screen in anticipation.

"You got the ball?" I ask Rhys.

"Obviously." He leans over the truck bed and produces a white-and-black checkered soccer ball, complete with months' worth of scuff marks and grass stains.

"Good," I say, but nothing else comes to mind. I suck at carrying conversations, *period*, and right now I don't have the motivation to attempt thinking up something interesting, so it gets quiet for a moment.

"Either of you going to comic con next month?" Bryce pipes up.

"Where's it at? Charlotte?" Rhys asks, rotating enough to get one of his thick arms up on the edge of his truck.

I hold back the urge to check my phone. It'll vibrate when I get a text. But it hasn't done that yet, which is causing my nerves to itch, and I want to check anyway.

"Nah. It's the Hickory one," Bryce says.

"There's one in Hickory?" Rhys looks surprised.

"Yeah, it's twice a year." Bryce looks at Rhys like he's missing a few bolts. "They've been having it at the convention center for years."

"Oh." Rhys nods as if it's still new information. "Cool. Uh. Maybe then. I'm not cosplaying though. Don't even ask. That's just weird."

"Weird?" I ask and check my phone while he explains. Nothing.

"Yeah. We're not little kids. That's what kids do. Plus, I don't want to see a grown-ass man running around in spandex." Rhys shakes his head in disgust.

"Okay, he has a point on that last one." Bryce tilts his head.

"Nah." I grin big. "I'm all for the guys in spandex—"

"Obviously." Rhys rolls his eyes in amusement.

"—and if it's so weird, why did you dress up as Pennywise on Halloween?" I stare him down, eyebrows raised and lips pursed as if to say, "Gotcha."

"Uh… Well, first I knew it'd freak you out." Rhys stutters at first, but he's right. It did freak me out. I hate clowns, and Pennywise is at the top. "But you guys know Jayla made me."

"She made you?" My eyes convey how much crap I detect. Loads.

I give in to the urge to check my phone again. More nothing, except it's been thirteen minutes since he was supposed to be here. I'm about to just give up.

"Yeah." Rhys shrugs.

"So who's the bitch now?" Bryce asks.

I don't say anything, but I hate it when they say shit like that. It's the same sort of stupid thing people say when people like me do something they don't think is *manly* enough. It gets under my skin.

"Shut up, man." Rhys's voice goes an octave deeper.

"You know what, let's just go," I say. I'm tired of waiting, and the longer we do, the more stressed I'm getting. I don't care who you are. Just be on time.

"Huh?" Bryce looks confused. "We not waiting on Tyler? He said he was coming."

"Like, today? He told you that today?" I tilt my head.

"Nah," Bryce laughs. "Last night at Bo's."

"But he's obviously not here, and he was supposed to be here fifteen minutes ago. And he's not replying to my texts, so…" I throw my palms up. "Let's just go. He isn't coming."

I hate myself for how doom and gloom that came out, so to gloss over it I steal the soccer ball from Rhys and dart to the walking path.

"What the…?" Rhys is taken by surprise.

"Come on," I yell back a little more upbeat.

"You okay?" Bryce lingers a moment before catching up.

"I'm great." I bounce my shoulders for added effect. It sounds like I'm anything but okay. But I am okay. It's nothing. I'm just being stupid, and they need to leave it at that.

"So it's one-on-one today," Rhys comments as we reach the closed concession stand.

"Yep," I say dryly. I shake my head, trying to shake out the stress built up under my nerves and give them a more enthusiastic tenor. "You and Bryce can go first. I'll play the winner."

"Actually, I think two-on-two's going to work." Bryce taps my shoulder and motions for me to look behind me.

"What?" And I turn around.

Well look who the hell decided to show up twenty minutes late. Tyler's convertible sweeps down the main entrance and swerves into the spot next to my car. A rush of excitement surges through my veins and I adjust my footing. I don't know why, I just do.

He made it.

"Damn, A." Bryce pulls my attention away. "So, you and Tyler, huh?"

"What? Me and… No! Why would you —" The words fly without my mind taking part in their selection.

"He meant the teams, man." Rhys grins from ear to ear. "Think you got it right, Bryce."

"Obviously." Bryce winks at me.

A car door shuts, and I turn in time to see Tyler starting up the path as he yells to us, "Sorry I'm late."

"All good," Bryce yells back. "Aidan's glad you made it."

"Shut up, Bryce," I whisper out of the corner of my mouth and jab my elbow into his side.

"Huh?" Tyler calls back.

I think I might be sweating, and it's all Bryce's fault. I'm going to kill him. I'm going to bludgeon his face with the soccer ball and drop his body in the creek by the picnic tables. Kallie's influence.

"Aid—" Bryce starts up again, but I scream over him.

"He was just saying *we're* glad you made it." I don't care that Tyler's basically standing in front of us already. All that matters is drowning out Bryce's stupid ass.

"Oh, sure." Tyler catches up and we start toward the open field again. "Sorry for being late. I try not to leave church too quick. Dad pitches a massive fit when I do."

"That sucks," I say. "It's okay though. You ready for some soccer?"

He gives me this look that says, "Not really," but also says, "Why not?"

"How long since you played?"

Rhys grabs the ball from me and kicks it around between his feet.

"I don't even know, it's been forever." Tyler waves his hands around.

Bryce looks at me with this frown. "Looks like you're losing today. No offense, Ty, but…" He shrugs without finishing the thought.

"Sorry, A," Tyler laughs, and I find myself laughing too.

"Yeah, sorry, not sorry," Rhys laughs.

Bryce looks at me like I'm an idiot. I cough and divert my eyes. *Get off my case, Bryce!*

"I asked Kallie to come, but she gave me a big *hell no*," I tell Tyler.

I did ask, and she did say *hell no*. Of course, she also asked how I got Tyler to come, and I just shrugged. She was there when I asked at Bo's, so she knows just as much as I do.

"Definitely not happening. She hates sports. Like, really hates," Tyler says. "That's all I heard when we had PE freshman year. How stupid and useless it is."

We make it to the edge of the baseball field, in the outfield, and stop.

"Guess I'm with you." Tyler grins at me, and for a moment I swear there's a twinkle in those green eyes.

"Duh." I play it off. On one hand I want to kill Bryce and on the other I want to thank him. Oh, the conflict. "Let's do this."

The first round goes pretty quick. It takes no time to realize Tyler is no pro at dribbling and couldn't fake a move if he tried. It's endearing to a point, but after Bryce and Rhys's fourth goal in less than two minutes I had to accept Bryce was right. No matter how hard I tried to outmaneuver them, they had the advantage. Namely, Tyler wasn't on their team. Unfortunately, my heart won't let me hog the ball even if passing it is begging to lose.

"Ready for round two?" Rhys smiles, planting his cleats in the ground and leaning forward, ready to get started.

"Sure." Tyler bounces his shoulders and looks at me apologetically. "Sorry. I suck at this."

"All good. They're not easy to beat." It's sort of the truth. Rhys is fast, but he isn't particularly great at soccer, he's more a football, as in American football, player. Bryce is good but—and I say this humbly because I'm not amazing—I'd put him a tiny half notch below me. Put them together against just me, aka Tyler and me, and I'm no match.

"Let's go," Bryce says, and the second game begins.

Bryce passes the ball to Rhys and he's about to make a goal when the voice I hate most in this world shouts across the field.

"Hey look, it's the fags!" Christian screams. "All four of them."

I stop in my tracks. I'm only supposed to see them at school, dammit.

Why are they here? Neither of them went to Collettsville. Why don't they go to the Valmead or Hudson Park and bother someone else? That's when I notice Ana Randall, and it starts to make a little more sense. She's Christian's girl of the semester and she did go to Collettsville. So I'm putting the blame on her. Sean's girl, Gayle Colley, is hanging on his shoulder, giggling like the cheerleader she is.

"What do you want?" Rhys steps forward.

He's the only one of us that holds any cred with Christian and Sean. They have to deal with him. He's on the varsity football team. He's one of Sean's two main running backs, or maybe it was wide receiver, or tight end. I don't know, I just hear him talk about it all the time.

"Hey, Rhys. Hanging with the faggots again?" Sean laughs. He thinks he's so funny. It's sickening. "Don't let them get to you. We don't need you eyeing us in the locker room during football season."

"Man, stop being stupid," Rhys tells them. He looks back at us and huffs.

"Have fun at your orgy tonight." Christian grabs Sean from behind and fakes dry humping to the thunderous laughter of his crew.

My mind flashes to my bizarre encounter with Christian in the bathroom during exam week. I can see him with his hand on my shoulder begging me to get on my knees like some animal. I want to scream at him, expose him for what he is to his girl, but I can't speak, and would she even believe me?

"Fuck off, man." Rhys speaks up instead and throws his arms up.

"Whatever," Christian yells back, wrapping his arm around his girl. "I'd say come watch what real guys do, but you might get too excited for the wrong reason."

"Just go," Rhys tries again and turns back to us shaking his head. "They some real stupid motherfuckers."

It works this time. They saunter off, high and proud on their own egos.

"Pricks," I mutter.

"Tell me about it," Tyler nods. "Especially Christian."

"Uh-huh," I agree, but suddenly I can't get what Christian said about Ty in the bathroom out of my head. Stop. Think about anything else. Just not that.

"Let's just get back to the game," Bryce suggests.

And we do, but it isn't the same. None of us have the same drive, the same excitement after the goon squad made their presence known. Part of me wishes I'd have said something, that I'd spoken up. But it wouldn't have done any good. The last person Christian's going to listen to is a fag. It would have just dragged it out more. Thank God for Rhys, at least he has some cred with the douche.

Think happy thoughts, A. Only a few more months. Just a few more and I'll be in Charlotte and I might never have to see them again.

TYLER

The food court is bustling with activity and it's a Tuesday afternoon. Don't these people have jobs or something? It's not like it's just teenagers.

We're at the mall in Hickory. Mom, Melinda, and me. My sister insisted on shopping, and I have nothing better to do, so it seemed like an okay idea.

I come for the people watching. It's usually interesting, even if it's not as crazy here as the Walmart in Lenoir. It's two totally different worlds. Mall traffic is a few steps up on the classy ladder. It's more pant suits, lightweight flowery summer button-ups, faded jeans, graphic tees, and full mouths of teeth, as opposed to tank-top undershirts, tobacco-stained jeans, unbuttoned faded plaid button-ups, and exposed beer bellies.

"Can I ride the merry-go-round?" Melinda asks again.

She's thirteen, I think I grew out of liking the merry-go-round by the time I hit ten, but whatever. I don't see the joy in. I was also the pathetic kid that cried on the merry-go-round when I was, like, seven or something.

It's a bad memory. Who gets scared sitting on a fake horse going up and down all slow in circles? It's not like it was carrying me away and trying to kidnap me.

"Maybe later," Mom says, which I'm pretty certain is code for, *"No, I don't want to spend six bucks for you to ride in circles right now."* Instead she says, "Finish up your food and we can start shopping."

Melinda wolfs down another waffle fry. If I keep Melinda waiting, she'll complain, so I shove a mouthful of rice down my throat. We each chose a different restaurant from the food court. It's a thing, almost a rule when we come to the mall. Melinda got Chick-fil-A, I chose this Japanese place called Sarku, and Mom chose the Mandarin Express over this Philly cheesesteak place.

"So where we going?" I ask, still chomping on a piece of chicken and broccoli.

"American Eagle, rue21, Hollister, Aéropostale." Melinda shrugs, which I think means maybe more.

"We have to at least go to Spencer's and Hot Topic," I tell Mom, then look at Melinda. "They've got some good t-shirts."

"Isn't that the store with the special area in back?" Mom asks.

"Special area?" I look at her like I don't have a clue what she's talking about. I do. I just want to hear her say sex toys or dildo or something, just because it'd be funny.

"Yeah, with uh…the stuff for married people," she says.

Well, damn, that took the fun out of it.

"I think." I act like it doesn't matter even though I know it matters way too much to them. Dad says the store is evil and I think he's even called it a porn store before.

"Your dad would have a fit." Mom closes her Styrofoam takeout box and gets up. "So no."

My first thought is *just don't tell him*, but it's futile. I hold back every instinct I have to roll my eyes and nod, like *of course, can't do that*.

"Okay." I get up and follow Mom and my sister to the trash, and then start into the collection of outlet stores.

My phone dings.

AIDAN: Just realized this character in my book is a lot like you. Weird.

I squint at the screen. Weird, as in I'm weird, or weird as in the coincidence? I go with the former just for laughs.

TYLER: I'm weird?

Not a second later the little blue bubble at the bottom of the screen pops up and another message comes through.

AIDAN: No. ::laughing emoji:: Weird he reminds me of you.

TYLER: So he's hot? Genius?

I can't help myself. I'm none of those things. I'm not saying I'm ugly, I'd give myself a six on a ten-point scale. Now, smart. Who am I kidding?

The bubbles jump again and I imagine Aidan typing frantically on the other end. The thought makes me laugh.

"Who you talking to?" Melinda's tiny little voice asks. I'm used to it, but the pitch of her voice has yet to catch up to her age.

"Just Aidan," I say. My phone dings, but my sister isn't done.

"You like him, don't you?" Melinda grins. She has the cutest smile, but right now I want to wipe it right off.

"No," I blurt and immediately look for Mom's reaction. *Not now, Melinda.* Hell, never. But Mom doesn't seem phased.

"Sure," Melinda keeps going. "You keep talking about him."

"No, I don't." I comb my fingers through my hair nervously.

"Yeah, you do." She smiles too big and shakes her head.

"We're just friends," I tell her. "That's all."

"Right," Melinda tries again.

Mom laughs at me, which is so not what I'm expecting.

"Defensive, are we?" Mom pats my shoulder.

What is going on?

Whatever. Instead of digging a deeper hole since Melinda won't accept a no, even though I'm telling the truth, I check Aidan's last message.

AIDAN: Little stuck on yourself? He's this ragged bum with hardly any teeth and a missing eye.

Oh, that's dirty, A.

TYLER: Have all my teeth for the record, and both eyes. ::shrug emoji::

AIDAN: ::crying laughing emoji:: ::crying laughing emoji:: ::crying laughing emoji:: ::crying laughing emoji:: ::crying laughing emoji::

"So he's your boyfriend?" Melinda gives me the cheesiest, knowing grin she's got.

"No!" I roll my eyes.

And not in front of Mom!

AIDAN

I drop my phone by my laptop after sending Ty a buttload of laughing emojis.

"What the hell am I doing?" I ask my computer, or maybe it's the story I have pulled up.

Why would I tell Tyler this character makes me think of him in the first place? Really?

It doesn't matter that the way I envision Kit is like Tyler's standing right in front of me. It doesn't matter. Not one bit.

Plus, that's not how Kit started out. He was literally Ansel Elgort, the cutie who played Gus in *The Fault in Our Stars*, when I started. He looked nothing like Tyler. Yeah, there were similarities. Or not. I mean, Ansel's hair is really brown like Ty's, and his chin line is similar, but that's about it. To be honest, Tyler is way better looking.

The problem is he's basically all I've been able to think about the past week. Inviting him to Bo's and my graduation didn't help. That moment he came running around the corner and knocked me to the floor keeps running through my head like one of those adorable moments in a movie. My life isn't a movie. There isn't a happily ever after already planned and set in stone.

But the way his eyes froze on mine. For a second it felt like he didn't want to look away. The way his weight bore down on me and his arm brushed against me. The closeness of his face. Hell, I could even feel his breath on my cheek. And God, the way he stuttered when I joked that he meant to do it was priceless.

I just wish it meant something, you know? That it *was* like in the movies. That just maybe he feels the same when he looks at me, but I know better. He probably barely sees me as a friend.

Okay. I really have to stop thinking about it. It's just going to bring me down. It's stupid to get attached to a boy who won't like me back. All Tyler will ever see in me is a friend, if I can even manage to keep that. But can I do that? Can I keep him as a friend when I feel like this?

I stare at my computer screen, at the blinking cursor waiting for me to type out the next chapter. It's the part where the cult has this creepy festival, but I can't seem to think about it right now. No, what I have to do is stop talking to Tyler. If I don't I'm just going to look stupid, so effing stupid. I'm just getting my hopes up, the one thing I do without effort, I swear, and it's just going to end. I know it. I already know it and it sucks.

But I've gotten so far with him. It was only months ago he hated me with every fiber of his being. Now though, now he'll even smile and laugh with me. And God, that laugh. Why does it have to be this hopeless, and why do I have to be this stupid?

And how would I even go about cutting him off? I mean without looking like an asshole. I literally made it my goal to get him talking to me, and I had good motives, it wasn't for this. But now I'm just going to ignore him or something? I never intended to like him, not like this. I just wanted to be his friend again. I just wanted to share my grief over Brayden with someone who actually *knew* Brayden. But of course, I go and catch feelings for him.

This sucks so bad.

TYLER

"I can't believe I fought Jesse to get off for this," Kallie complains. I think Jesse's her boss. "It's stupid."

"Eh." I shrug.

It is. The Transformer movies have always been comical and over the top, but the comedy in *Bumblebee* is just piss-poor and sort of childish. "Why were you scheduled anyway? You always have Thursday nights off."

Kallie rolls to her side, done with the movie, and gives me the I-know-right-it's-so-obvious look.

"Exactly! Something about school being out for the summer, and being able to work mornings and afternoons, some junk like that. And something about having to change the schedule up," she rambles. "He should have at least said something first. I have stuff to do, you know."

"You do?" I squint.

"Uh, yeah." Kallie widens her eyes.

"Like?" I ask.

Her mouth draws open and hangs, and this crackly wheezing noise comes out while she thinks of the *stuff* she has to do.

"Movie night." She points at the TV like it's so important. "Paint… Make TikToks?" I swear she just asked me that one. "Go swimming, sunbathe, maybe a little exercise."

I force a super fake cough and lock eyes with her. About half of those even make remote sense for her.

"Kal, you don't exercise. You're just that lucky bitch who doesn't gain weight," I remind her. "And sunbathe? Not that important unless you want cancer."

"Uh…" The wheels turn in her head. But they're grinding to a halt.

"And you barely tan," I remind her. "So nah."

"Rude." Kallie rolls her eyes and purses her lips in that way that makes most people think she's actually mad. Come to think of it, most people think she's mad most of the time. It's just her. "I tan better than you."

She stuffs another handful of buttery popcorn in her mouth and huffs. The smile on my face could barely get any bigger. I love my Kallie so much. She's like the craziest, bitchiest, funniest, meanest but nicest, and coolest person I know.

"So basically, you don't have a good reason?" I prod.

"Look, fool, do you want our movie nights or what?" She snaps her head around and her lips tighten, holding back the urge to laugh.

I'm trying so hard. The impulse is caught in my throat like this itch that needs a scratching. I try. But I can't do it. It bursts out. My head bounces on the pillow and my body shakes with laughter.

"This movie sucks though," I tell her once we calm down a bit, between stuttered giggles.

"Tell me about it," she says. "You know what else sucks?"

"Stop right there." I put my hand up. I'm about ninety-five percent sure I know where that's going, and it's not PG.

"No. Ugh! Is your mind always that dirty?" Kallie scoots back like I've got cooties.

"Well." I wiggle my shoulders and bite at my lip. "Sort of."

"Yeah," she agrees. "And no, for the record, I wasn't going to say how you like to suck—"

"But you just did," I say over her, rolling my eyes.

"—I was *going* to say it's going to suck when Aidan goes off to college in August."

Ah. That.

Three months ago no one, not even Kallie or Brayden, could have convinced me I'd be anything but thrilled to see him ship off to some other city where I'd rarely, if ever, have to see him. But now, I think I might actually miss him.

But not that much.

I mean it's sort of like how I'd miss any old friend, but not like a Kallie-friend. Kallie's like my straight-wife, my BFF, is and always will be my best friend no matter what type, and I don't even want to think about not seeing her at some point.

"I guess." I stuff my head against my pillow.

The colors from the TV bounce along the ceiling, and the shadows play among the bedpost and canopy. I hadn't given much thought to him leaving, and suddenly I don't really like the idea anymore.

Other than some cringeworthy line from John Cena and explosions from the movie playing in the background, silence takes over for a minute. My eyes trace the line the canopy makes from the bottom left bedpost to where it drapes down in the center. I don't like how this is making me feel. And it's stupid. I shouldn't care. I mean I should, but not this much.

"He's cute, isn't he?" Kallie says out of the blue.

"Huh? Who? Cena?" I look at the TV, but there's no Cena. Instead, there's this shirtless dude on the screen who looks to be about our age. So not Kallie's type. "Him? Definitely not your usual. More like mine."

"What? No." She sees who I'm talking about and shakes her head. "Not him. I was talking about Aidan."

"Uh…" Suddenly I don't know what to say. There's this voice screaming *yes* inside my head, and another screaming even louder that it's a trap. "I mean, uh. He's not ugly."

"Well, duh. I mean in terms of your type of guys." She prefaces whatever she's going to say with this serious look on her face. "He's cute, right?"

"He's—" I start.

"Just admit it, you think he's cute. Come on," she prods.

"I mean…yeah." It's sort of like tripping with that crate of coleslaw at work and dipping my arm into it. I know I just got into a big mess, but it was going to happen anyway. It's all about damage control.

"I knew it!" Kallie twists her whole body to face me and digs her gaze into me. "You two have been talking a lot lately."

"*A lot* is a strong way to put it." I put a hand up to calm her. "*More* is more like it."

"Well from absolutely fucking nothing to every day, right? That's a lot," Kallie insists, and I can't really deny it.

I squirm. I know where this is going, but I play stupid. Which in itself is stupid. "So, like, where are you going with this?"

"You like him," she blurts. And the crazy part is I know she's been wanting to say that for days by the way she grabs me by the shoulder and shakes me.

"Calm yourself down before you have a stroke." My eyes widen and I take a deep breath. "I don't like him, not like that. We're just friends. That's all."

"Uh-huh. That's why you two talk all the time now, right?" Kallie says.

"I talk to you all the time, but I don't want to fuck you." I phrase it as bluntly as I can.

"Ugh, bad image." Kallie's body shivers and she acts like she's about to throw up. "And I've seen the way you look at him, and how he looks at you. You smile a helluva lot more when he's around."

"Woah, what? The way he looks at me?" I stop her.

"Isn't it obvious?" She stares me down like I'm stupid, and maybe I am, because I don't know what she's talking about.

"What's obvious?" I ask again.

"He's into you." Kallie crinkles her nose and giggles. "Like *so* into you."

"No, he's not." I literally brush at the air like it'll make the ludicrous idea fly away and leave Kallie's mind.

"Yeah, he is. And you like him too." She throws her palm in front of my face to keep me from speaking. "Don't say you don't. I know you way better than you think. The way you two carried on last night at Taco Bell about that stupid game and some character named Myra and Reap-something. I mean, you two were majorly nerding out together. You might as well have jumped across the table and started making out right there."

"Uck, no. Like *so* no!" I gag. "I don't like him. I swear."

It's the truth. I don't. And just because we found some common ground not to hate the fuck out of each other, it doesn't mean I want him.

Oh, and Myra? Like really? I can't let that stand, even if she is just trying to get to me. "And it's Moira, thank you very much. Get it right, bitch."

"Touchy." Kallie throws both hands up in surrender. "I'm right, and you know it though. You two would make a cute couple."

"Stop it!" I tell her, because now I'm thinking about it, and I don't want to think about it.

I'm not ready for that. I'm just not. Like, it'd be wrong too. You don't just get over your dead boyfriend in a few months and start seeing another guy, especially his best friend! I know some day I have to deal with that, but it's too soon.

"You know Brayden would approve, right? He'd be more than okay with it." I swear she read my mind, and honestly hearing her say it sends me over the edge.

"What the hell, Kal? This isn't about him," I lie. "He's gone. Dead. And we obviously all know why. I don't need any more dead friends."

"Ty… Ty, it's okay," Kallie whispers, placing a hand on my shoulder. But it's not patronizing like everyone else. I still don't want to hear it though.

I'm breathing hard. It's not like I haven't thought about Brayden lately, but I haven't thought of him every minute of every day like I used to. And I know that's not bad, but it feels bad, and why? I've been focused on Aidan. I clench my fists.

"That wasn't your fault," Kallie keeps going, her eyes never leaving mine, even though I'm having a hard time seeing with the tears starting to build up. "It wasn't. You've got to see that. And there is nothing wrong with you liking Aidan or anyone else. Brayden would just want you to be happy. That's all. I think he'd tell you himself that's all he ever wanted. For you to be happy. The last thing he'd want is for you to sit here and worry and feel like you have to hold on to him."

She brushes a tear from my cheek and scoots over so she can envelop me in her arms. I sniffle so I don't cry, but that doesn't keep me from soaking her pillow. We lie in silence for a few minutes as I let her words sink in.

There's this deep, ingrained part of me that says it's wrong to let go, that it would be an injustice to think of someone else like I did him. It's the same part that runs through my head most nights telling me I found and lost the only person I'll ever really love, and I'm just going to be lonely the rest of my life. But that's how it's supposed to be, because Brayden was the one. And it was my fault. Right?

I close my eyes. Maybe Kallie's right.

I hate it, there's little worse than having to admit she's right, but maybe she is. Maybe Brayden wouldn't want me holding on like this and holding myself back. Hell, he despised how I hated Aidan. It's where a lot of our fights started. A tiny laugh bubbles up between my lips when I think about it. It seems silly now. I wish I could even argue with him, but I can't. And maybe, just maybe, I shouldn't let that hold me down.

"Maybe," I mumble. It's barely a whisper.

"What? I didn't catch that." Kallie leans back and looks at me crazily.

"Maybe," I say a little louder.

"I'm sorry, Ty. You're mumbling, can you say it a little louder?" She keeps it up, and I start to giggle.

"You're right, bitch," I say loud enough for her to hear, but not loud enough for her parents to catch it down the hallway.

Kallie snickers and breathes in a big gulp of air in victory. "Of course."

"But I didn't say I liked him." I point at her. If I don't make it clear she'll take it however she wants. "But maybe Brayden would be okay with it. He always did complain when I wouldn't talk to A anyway."

Kallie pulls me into a big hug.

"There is no maybe, only is," she tries.

I cringe at her sad attempt to use the great words of Yoda.

"Don't ever do that again." I shudder.

"Yeah, I won't," she agrees.

AIDAN
Saturday, June 15

"We should do this more often," I suggest.

Per Mamá's requirement I'm sitting on my bed while Tyler slouches over my computer chair. It doesn't matter that we're just friends. She keeps coming to check on us and making sure the door is still open.

"Maybe," Tyler says. "Kallie might get jealous."

"Why would she get jealous?" I ask.

"We have a movie night every Thursday," he says like it explains everything.

He pats his lap and Genji jumps up and plops onto Ty as the credits for *Tag* stream up the television screen. Traitor. Normally I'd have suggested a horror flick, but the way I see it, horror is for cuddling, and the last thing I wanted was to make the wrong impression tonight. So comedy it was.

"But why would she be jealous if we started one?" I ask.

The crazy part is how bold it is for me to even propose it. I mean, this is the first time Tyler has been over *and* in my room *and* with only me here—ever. He came over a few times with Brayden in the past, but that's it. Even back then I tried to keep people away from my house. It's not the nicest, and when you compare it to the cabin Ty lives in, well, simply put there are leaks in the roof, most of the doors creak loudly, and the carpet is from the seventies, I think.

He shrugs. "'Cause it's Kallie?"

"Ah." He has a point.

"Plus, you're not going to want me over for a movie date every week." Tyler spins in my chair, which Genji is having no part of. He jumps to the floor and then up on the bed with me. *Good Genj.*

First off, he just called it a date. I'm doing everything in my power not to blush right now, but dammit if my cheeks aren't heating up. Thank God for freckles to help cover it. Of course, he didn't mean it like a date-date, but still. Second, why wouldn't I want him over every week? Or did I catch his inflection wrong? Did he mean…surely I couldn't think he'd *actually* want to come over every week. I decide to go with him doubting *I'd* want him to come over that much.

"Really? I think it'd be great. I'm not the one who hated a certain person for forever." It's a low blow, but I say it anyway.

"Oh, that hurt." Tyler stops spinning in his chair and looks at me with puppy dog eyes and clutches his chest. "Like, dayum."

"Uh, well, the truth hurts, right?" I stare him down, trying not to let him see how bad I feel for saying it.

"Yeah, yeah, whatever." He rolls his eyes, but his tone changes into something *almost* apologetic. "Sorry."

"It is what it is." I bounce my shoulders. "Let's play a video game."

It's a major change of subject, but I don't want to sit here and dwell on the past and get all bogged down in apologies or explanations. I want tonight to be fun, I want him to *want* to come back.

"Good idea." Ty sits up. "Whatcha got?"

"*Over…* Nah, that's online. How about *The Division*?" I suggest.

"Also online only." Tyler grins.

"Uh…" I think about it as I slide off the bed and go to my TV stand, where all my movies and games are packed beneath. "I think the only split screen game I've got is *Grand Turismo*. So, racing. Don't think I want to race though."

I sift through the game cases. *Overwatch, Grand Turismo, Alien:*

Isolation, Fallout, Skyrim, and the list goes on, but other than *Turismo,* everything is either fully online or single player.

"Not looking good," I tell Ty.

"There are so few split screen games," Tyler complains. "My uncle says there used to be a ton back when online multiplayer wasn't a big thing. He's still a big gamer."

"That's not helping right now," I say.

"True." Tyler leans back.

I have to think of something. Sure it's—I check my phone—9:22 p.m., but I'm not ready for him to leave, and I can't make it seem that way. Maybe we can take turns playing Alien and see who can get the furthest. That game freaks me out, but maybe. I'm about to suggest it when Tyler speaks up.

"You still write?" He swivels the chair in a full three-sixty with his legs crossed.

"Yeah," I say, and it comes out nervous. I love writing, I do, but talking about it, that's nerve-shivering.

"What are you working on?" And there it is, that dreaded question, right out of Tyler's mouth.

I swallow and take a seat on the edge of my bed.

"It's just a horror story. It's nothing great." I squint and look away.

"Ooh, horror? I love horror." Tyler sits more erect, and his green eyes brighten. I can't help but smile. "What's it about?"

"It's not that great."

"You already said that," he reminds me.

"You don't want to hear about it," I tell him.

"What? Yeah, I do," he prompts.

"It's stupid," I say.

Is it? Oh my God, have I been writing it all this time only now to realize my story is crap? Of course not. No. I'm overreacting.

"Stop!" Tyler draws it out and rolls his eyes. "He always said you were negative about your stories."

And by *he*, I'm pretty sure he means Brayden. He used to fuss at me for putting them down, but they just never sound that great. I'll come up with an idea, like *The Bleeding*, and it seems so cool in my head and when I talk about it to myself and when I write it down, but the moment I open my mouth to tell another human being about it, the veil of awesomeness is ripped away.

"But maybe they do suck," I tell him.

"Brayden didn't think so," Tyler says. "He used to tell me about them. Well, I mean some, not everything. He didn't want to spoil anything for when you published it."

For when I published it? I bite back the urge to tear up. I sit a little straighter and grunt, one of those happy types.

"It's called *The Bleeding*," I decide to tell him.

It still feels stupid the more I speak, but I go on anyway.

"It's about this guy, Kit—he's the one I said reminded me of you— who lives after this event happens that decimates most of the population. You know, post-apocalyptic." Tyler seems to be following. "He's all alone at the beginning, but he gets taken in by these people who he doesn't realize are a cult. Like, a bad cult. I guess all cults are bad though, right? Whatever, they're, like, super crazy religious."

"Ooh." Tyler's lips form into an O. I can't tell if it's fascination with the idea or how much I'm rambling.

"So, he eventually realizes he's sort of stuck, and there's this dude he falls for, and then The Bleeding happens." I shrug. "That's it. Well, I mean, that's not it, but that's all I can tell you. Don't want to give it away. Actually, hell. I think I already did."

Did I give away too much? The whole cult part was supposed to be a reveal. I think. I mean, sort of. But maybe not. I groan and shake my head.

"Uh… You did?" he asks.

"Yeah. I shouldn't have told you it was a cult. At least, I don't think so." I squint my right eye, and my cheek raises with it. "I don't know. I've never actually tried summarizing it for anyone except Brayden, and I just told him all of it."

"Not even Bryce or Rhys?" Tyler looks at me with surprise, his eyes widening, that deep green jumping out at me.

"Nah." I think about it. Nope. Not even Mamá. I want her to be as surprised as everyone else, plus it's a bit gory.

"So just Brayden, and…" he bites at his lower lip, and it's so sexy, I have to hide my clenched fist next to my leg, "…and me?"

"Don't get too excited. Brayden knew the entire story, beginning to end, everything," I tell him. I'm surprised I told him as much as I did. "You got…more than others."

"Can I read some of it?" Tyler leans forward with this eager look in his eyes.

I think he actually genuinely wants to read some. He's one hundred percent certifiably crazy if he thinks I'm actually going to let him, but I think he really wants to. And honestly, that's horrifying and cool.

A high-pitched laugh escapes my lips before I can speak. "Not going to happen."

"Come on." Tyler slouches and flashes me puppy dog eyes. And let me tell you, they're damn near melting my heart. If the thought of letting him read my baby wasn't so absolutely terrifying, those eyes alone would be enough to just hand it right over.

"Noooo." There's no way it's happening. "I'd be so embarrassed. You don't even understand. It's nerve-racking. I know it's going to sound stupid."

"Oh my God, A. Stop being like that," Tyler says. "Confidence. Get some!"

Yeah, that's not a topic I want to get on right now. Confidence is a thing for other people. Guys who grew up straight, and white, and had their dad stick around past their effing birth.

"You know what?" I divert. "We should go to the park and watch the comet soon…for Brayden."

It was the first thing that came to mind to get the focus off me and my writing. It's not a bad idea. I, for one, would love to spend a little time stargazing with Ty. Okay, well maybe it is a bad idea. I am supposed to be working on not feeling for him. Stargazing with Ty is sort of on the opposite list, the one for the hopeless idiot who's begging to get his heart broken. But I said it, and if I take it back now, I'm going to look stupid. And I mean, I did tell Ty he should keep up with the comet for Brayden anyway. I am, and why can't we do that together, just this once?

"Why not now?" Tyler jumps to his feet.

"Uh… I… Uh…" I stumble over my uncertainty.

"I… Uh…" Tyler mocks, but there's that signature Ty smile.

I look away coyly and nibble at my lip before I realize what I'm doing. God I hope he didn't see that. My arms go stiff, and I focus on Tyler again so he doesn't think I'm being weird, or at least, for the love of God, I hope he doesn't.

"Sure," I blurt before I can really think about it.

What am I doing?

TYLER

Saturday, June 15

I'm not sure why I said now.

There's a mechanical whir as the convertible top retracts, revealing a mostly clear night sky. The sound of cicadas chirping and other insects echo around us.

"Clear skies." Aidan reclines his seat until he's lying horizontal.

"Then what's that?" I do the same but point at a shadowy formation of clouds obscuring the sky.

"Eh, that's not bad. That's, what, two percent of the sky?" Aidan reasons.

Yeah, but it's two percent we can't see.

I let myself relax and focus on the stars. There are so many. Millions, no billions, or maybe even an infinity's worth. It's a sight I never get used to. Which is sort of crazy when you think about it. It's literally just black with countless little specks all over it like dandruff, but there's something uniquely beautiful and awe-inspiring about it.

"I wish it was this clear at my place," Aidan says.

"Sure it is," I say. "Gamewell isn't exactly the big city."

"Yeah." He turns his head to look at me and rolls those deep-brown eyes. Something about the way the light reflects in them makes me shift in my seat. "I swear it's not as clear at home though. Swear it."

"Maybe. You can see everything out here. Everything," I repeat.

"Well, not everything. Pluto, the sun, Breegge's Comet, Proxima b, China," Aidan starts to list the obvious things.

"Shut the fuck up," I laugh. He laughs too. "You know what I mean."

"Yeah." He nods, and I lose his gaze to the sky. "It's nice though."

A few minutes pass and we simply stare at the stars. It's crazy when you think about it. Each dot is a massive ball of flame and gas set lightyears away, hanging in empty space, consuming itself. And some of them, maybe all, I don't know, have planets like our solar system. It's all the stuff Brayden would talk about when we'd do this sort of thing.

"I think I found Jupiter." Aidan tilts his head to the side and squints. "Ninety-five percent certain it's right there."

He's pointing, but I ask, "Where?" anyway.

"There. Right there." He's got his arm extended to my left and his index finger aiming, I think, just above the tree line. There's a lot of sky up there he could be pointing at. "See? Look along my arm."

I raise up a bit and scoot over to get a better view. I settle with my cheek less than an inch from his elbow.

"There," he says again, and his elbow slaps my cheek. "Sorry!"

"I'm looking, you don't have to assault me," I joke.

"You haven't seen assault," he laughs. "But sorry. Didn't mean to. Do you see it though? It's to the right of Serpens, left of Scorpius, near the moon."

I follow his finger toward the sky. It surprises me that I actually know what he's talking about. The constellations Scorpius and Serpens.

"That's more helpful." I find them right where I expect them to be. It's one of the things Brayden embedded in my brain. It's easier to find a speck in the sky if you know the arrangement of the other specks.

"See? It's the bright tannish dot below the moon," he says.

I keep scanning, jumping from one speck to the next and the moon between the two constellations. I should be able to spot it easier, but this has always taken me a bit.

There it is! In a way it's just like any other speck in the sky, but it's a little brighter, and like Aidan said, it has a glow to it.

"Found it," I grin.

"Looks like it might disappear behind the moon soon," Aidan points out.

"I don't know, maybe." I feel like I should know the answer to that, like Brayden talked about it enough, I should be able to rattle it off and know all the answers to space and life itself. But I don't.

I let my eyes drift among the stars and I make a find just over the tree tops in the direction of my old elementary school. Saturn. I think. If I'm right, Saturn is supposed to appear light tan too. And it's not blinking or anything, so I think I'm right. I get my phone out to check before saying anything stupid.

"What are you doing?" Aidan asks.

"None of your business." I look at him like he's crazy.

"Oookay," he laughs.

"I'm right!" I about yell. It is Saturn.

"Right about…" Aidan lets the question fade off.

I point at Saturn. "There. That's Saturn."

"Nice." Aidan squints and leans closer to follow my arm like he made me do.

"See it there? Like ten feet from Jupiter," I say before I realize how stupid a statement it is.

"Ten feet from Jupiter, huh? So Saturn's just chillin' next to ol' Jup." Aidan looks at me, flashing a cute wide grin, but he twitches away when I look.

"You know what I mean." By ten feet I mean how it looks in the sky. Still stupid. "Okay, like, it's a lot farther away from Jupiter than Jupiter is from the moon. Better?"

"Uh, not really, but sure." Aidan shrugs.

"Oh my God." I groan for effect.

How else do I explain it? It hits me. Do exactly what Aidan did. Find a constellation. I map it out in my head and find what I'm looking for. "Okay, to the left of Sagittarius and below Scutum."

"Now we're on to something." He smiles and repositions himself to get a better vantage.

In the corner of my vision I can see his lips purse while he looks for Saturn. There is something adorable in the way he squints, searching for the tiny speck.

"Got it!" he exclaims, falling back into his seat, but not before his lip grazes my arm.

I yank my arm back, trying to ignore the chill that just flew up my skin and down my spine. I glance at him to see if he's looking at me, if there's anything knowing in his eyes. But he's gazing at the stars, maybe at Saturn or Jupiter, or maybe Sagittarius. Hell, he could be looking at a blank space between them all for all I know.

It doesn't help my nerves any though. He glances at me and then back at the sky, I think. Or maybe it was just a twitch of the eye. But shockingly I don't want to look away. I linger a second longer on his side profile. The glow of the moon is just enough to see the freckles spotting his cheeks, that hard V-line that marks his chin and how it curves into ample lips and an adorable button nose.

He is cute.

AIDAN

"I have to admit something." I blow out a nervous breath.

"Oooh! Let me guess." Kallie shakes. She literally does the whole butt wiggle thing like my cat when he's about to pounce on something.

"Uh, sure." It's not that hard to guess. Honestly, I think she knows I like Tyler already.

I pace in front of the metal bench where Kallie's sitting outside work. We're on break. I know she's going to be excited—it was mostly her idea for me to talk to him anyway—I'm just nervous to actually admit it.

"You're gay!" she shouts.

"What? No. I mean, yeah." I trip over my words and shake my head. "Old news."

"'Kaaaay," Kallie taunts. "So… Uh… Okay, I give up."

"You didn't even try," I laugh.

"Just tell me," she says.

"So, you know how I've been talking to Ty more lately?" I make circles in the air with my hand.

"Yeah." The smirk on her face transforms into this slowly growing grin. This is exactly how I envisioned her response. She smacks her lips and the smile highlights the dimples in her cheeks. "Do go on."

"Yeah, well, uh…" I throw my head back and grunt. Okay, this isn't anywhere near as hard as it was to come out, but if we're talking a scale of one to ten—ten being coming out, and one being talking about all the great music from Metallica and Five Finger Death

Punch—then it's probably somewhere around a six. For reference, I'd put giving class presentations at a seven, so it's not that bad.

"Oh my God, A, spit it out!" Kallie throws her head back and whines.

"I like him," I blurt. "I really do."

"I knew it!" Kallie jumps up and grabs me by the shoulders and starts bouncing. I think she wants me to bounce with her, but it's not happening. I didn't even say his name, but she knows. "I knew it!"

"Well it *is* your fault," I tell her.

She bobs her head and smiles in that way that screams I-know-and-I'm-so-fucking-proud-of-myself. "So, like, really like him? Like, like-like him?"

"Yes! Like-like him." I roll my eyes. "But I shouldn't."

At that, Kallie lets go of my shoulders and steps back. She stares at me like I've lost my mind.

"What do you mean, you shouldn't?" she asks.

I kick at the concrete and clear my throat. This is the part I wasn't looking forward to, and the problem is I need her to understand. Or do I? Oh my God, did I subconsciously tell her so she'd convince me I'm wrong about this? Surely I'm not that stupid.

"It's a bad idea," I tell her. "Really bad. He doesn't like me. He isn't *going* to like me. Ever. You know how he hated me. Yeah, we're friends now, but that doesn't mean anything. I'm just Aidan to him, and it's going to get me hurt. You know?"

"No. I don't know." Kallie bops her head toward me, all the humor in her voice gone. "That's—"

"I'm already so anxious when I'm around him," I interrupt her. She isn't getting it. "I know he doesn't like me, but I keep thinking about him, but I know he isn't thinking about me. And if I say something to him about it, things are just going to get awkward and go back to him hating me, and everything's going to go downhill. I need to just stop texting him so much, and maybe I won't think about him. But I don't want to be mean and just stop talking to him. And I—"

"Shut up, A." Kallie shushes me with her pointer finger pressed against my lips.

"But—" I try around her finger.

"No." She shakes her head and drops her finger. "First off, that last part isn't going to work for you. I know you too well to believe that."

"Thanks for the support," I huff. She's got me there. Chances are I'd say I'm not going to text him for at least two days and I'd end up texting him within the hour, or I'd say I'm not going to reply to his text for two hours minimum but I'd end up replying in less than a minute. It's a curse.

"You're welcome." She smirks. "But all of that's bullshit. You can't run around dodging love—"

"*Like*, not love," I point out, but she ignores me.

"—just because it scares you or you don't think Ty feels the same yet. Did that stop me from talking to Luka?"

"You talking about the German foreign exchange guy your freshman year? The senior?" I ask. Surely that can't be who she meant to bring up. If I remember correctly, and I'm about certain I do, he flat out rejected her in the school hallway. I was there.

"Yeah," she says.

"Uh, I don't remember that going so well. Didn't he ask why a short little freshy was asking him out with, like, everyone watching?" I ask, squinting ferociously.

"Not the point." Kallie shakes her head like it really isn't. "You—"

"I think it's—" I try to interrupt, but she's obviously not going to let me.

Kallie puts a finger up right in front of my lips without actually touching me this time. Wow.

"It doesn't matter. Bad analogy. Is that even an analogy? You know what, who cares." She stops herself from rambling, but I'm already cracking another smile. "The point is if you like Ty you shouldn't hold back. You're both great guys. Yeah, he can be a stubborn little ass sometimes—maybe a lot, actually—but still. I know you like him. I can see it every time we talk about him, and when you talk to him. You invited him to your graduation, for fuck's sake. How much more obvious can it get?"

"Eh." My head teeters back. Yeah, okay. She has a point there.

"I think he knows," Kallie says.

"Really? Has he said something?" I come a step closer, shock setting in.

"No, but he doesn't really have to." Kallie grins. "Sort of like you."

"So you think he likes me?" I ask, trying but one hundred percent failing not to get my hopes up.

"I mean, yeah. He'd be stupid not to," Kallie says.

"Sounds more like you just think he should." I drag out the last few words so she knows I don't quite believe her.

"Look, you just need to man up, gay up, whatever the hell you guys do, and tell him you like him, because his stubborn ass isn't going to make the first move." She pauses a moment. "Don't let him get away. Don't!"

My heart and mind are at war. My heart is rooting for every word Kallie says, cheering it through my veins and fighting to overthrow any reason and logic, like a losing battle up in my brain.

"Even if you are full of bullshit, you're such a wise-sounding little Buddha." I stick out my tongue, fully and completely unsure what I'm going to do next.

"Did you just call me fat *and* short?" Kallie's eyes go wide and her mouth drops.

"No, no, no! Not fat, *wise*." I put a hand up. I didn't think of it that way. However, I assure her, "Short though. Yeah."

"You know I hate you, right?" Kallie gives me the evil eye.

"You just hate you love me so much," I counter.

"Eh… Do I?" She squints. Then her eyes go super excited. "Oh my! If you two get married, you'd be my brother-in-law."

I sigh and run a hand through my hair. Like, where does she come up with this shit?

"Not how that works."

TYLER
Thursday, June 20

It's been weeks since I've posted on TikTok. And I know this dance has been way overdone, but here I go. I tap the Post button and my rendition of The Renegade flashes onto my wall.

Since Brayden died I haven't posted anything. And it felt good to finally make a new video. Like, I wish Brayden was still here and that he could have done it with me, like he did on a bunch of other dances, but it was great to just do it anyway.

I mean, that's why I do it, for me. It's definitely not for my followers, there aren't enough for that to matter.

I've got something like two hundred followers, which isn't amazing or anything, okay it's not even close to amazing, but that's not the point. The point is that it's not like a ton of people are following me and begging for content, so it's okay. It would be cool to go viral though, even just once. But I highly doubt this is going to be the one.

Oh look, a like.

I open my inbox and there's my first like in ages. When I see the username, I laugh. Sandman_Slayer6, aka Aidan Molina. The little red flag pops up at the bottom of the screen and I see Aidan made a comment too.

Shake that booty! Go Ty!

Oh, I'm going to rag him for that. I check the time. *10:23 p.m.* It's not too late. Let's bug my first commenter in months.

I pull up his last text and FaceTime him. All at once what I'm doing hits me. I mean, what *am* I doing? I would have nev—

"Uh, hey." Aidan's face appears on my phone, a pillow behind his head, and his bare shoulders showing. Oops. Maybe it is a little too late. He's in bed already. And he's visibly confused. I grin and act like I didn't just make a mistake.

"Hey." I try to remember why I called. "How you doing?" TikTok! My video. He was the first to like it, that's right.

"I'm good." He nods and squints. "You?"

He's confused, like really confused. But I think he's trying to act like he's not with the way he strings out "you".

"You liked my TikTok. Well, actually you were the first to like it." I minimize his face on my phone and check it again.

"Where'd you go?" Aidan asks. I forgot that pauses my side of the video.

"Just a sec," I say and check my likes again. Still just Aidan. I go back to FaceTime and his freckles come back to life. "Yeah, you were the first and only like so far. *And* the first comment."

"Cool." Aidan acts like it's nothing and yawns. I guess it isn't anything really.

"*Shake that booty?* Really?" I laugh. "That's what you got from it?"

"Well, I mean you were basically just shaking your ass." Aidan smiles and shrugs. "I'm just rooting you on!"

"So you're saying you like my ass." I side-eye him, knowing it'll get under his skin. He's always been the type to get too nervous too quick.

"Uh… No. I—" Aidan tries, but I'm not done having fun.

"So you don't like it? Too flat?" I give him my best pooched pouty lip.

"No," Aidan blurts, sitting up on his bed. "I didn't—"

"So it's juicy?" I make it obvious I'm joking this time before he has a heart attack.

"Eff you, Ty." He smiles and gives me the middle finger with his free hand.

"I had to," I apologize. But I can't stop. "So, you stalking me or something?"

"Stalking?" Aidan questions. Poor A. "Why would you think that?"

"I don't know, you *were* the first to like and comment," I tell him. It's true. "And it hadn't been up but maybe half a minute."

"My phone tells me when you post," he says.

"Ah," I sigh. Isn't that nice. I only pay attention if my phone notifies me when one of the hot guys I follow posts. "So stalker."

"Ugh." Aidan rolls his eyes. His video stops.

"Where'd you go?" I ask.

"Hold up," he shushes me, and a second later his face comes back. "Shouldn't you be happy with me supposedly being a quote-unquote stalker, seeing how I'm *still* your only like. Just saying."

"Oh, that hurts." I clutch my heart dramatically, which earns me a laugh. "Speaking of which, how the hell do these other guys go viral? Like nothing I post gets more than thirty likes."

"Good content?" Aidan says dryly, but a massive grin slips out pretty quick.

"Fuck you," I say.

"Oh, poor little Ty. Nah. Just kidding." He laughs, and it's cute. Almost harmonious, little but not insignificant all at the same time. "Most of the big ones I watch rarely wear a shirt. So, there's always that."

I look at him like he's a lunatic.

"What?" he asks.

"You're saying I should take my shirt off for likes?" I ask.

"I mean, it works for others," Aidan says with less confidence.

"So, get half-naked for likes," I reword. I mean, it's not like I'd be stripping for anyone, but I'm not certain I have that level of confidence.

Aidan shrugs. I laugh. It's like he's just done, and that's the best he's got.

"Not sure I'm confident enough to do that," I tell him. I maybe could—dance shirtless, that is. I mean, it's not a big deal, but then again, maybe it is. I'd be putting myself on display. What do they call that again? Thirst traps. Yeah. I don't know.

"Why not?" he asks.

"I don't know. I'm not the best-looking guy," I tell him.

"Oh my God." Aidan rolls his eyes. "Give me a break, Ty. You're a good-looking guy."

I feel like I should take that as a compliment, but he says it in this weary sort of way that almost sounds annoyed.

"Oh, you think so?" Instead of contradicting him, I go with it. The look on his face is priceless.

"I… Uh…" he struggles. He's blushing, even beyond the freckles.

I wrinkle my nose and giggle. "Just kidding. I might do it. I mean, more likes just for that? It'd be easy. Maybe."

"Yeah, sure." Aidan yawns.

"Well, I gotta go," I tell him. I think I woke him anyway. "Talk to you later."

"Okay, bye." He throws up a peace sign and his face disappears.

I don't think I can do it. I lift my shirt and glimpse myself in my phone camera. Eh. Nah. What the hell does A see that I don't? He's probably just trying to be nice so I'm not an asshole. God, I used to be an asshole.

AIDAN

Saturday, June 22

He's late. He usually is, I guess, but he's not responding to my texts. I check my phone again, but it's still just my last text.

AIDAN: On your way?

I stare at the screen, hoping maybe he'll start typing and ease the tension in my neck from all the anxiety I've let build up. I don't know why I do this to myself. I know he doesn't like me. But I want to talk to him. How stupid is that? And I'm totally letting it get under my skin.

See, what happened is we decided yesterday we'd go back to the park tonight for Brayden. At least that's how my stupid ass pitched it before saying we could go to Cook Out or something first. I feel sort of selfish, like I'm using Brayden to be around Tyler. Oh God, am I? No, please don't let that be true. I mean, we're going to see Brayden's comet, just like I said we should a while back. It's for Brayden, right? But it's not really like that either, is it? I roll my eyes. Breegge isn't visible yet, and I don't have a telescope to see it, so it's more just staring at the sky. So yeah, I guess it's more an excuse to see him. Why am I like this?

I have to stop thinking about it. I check my phone again, nothing. Genji is cuddled up on my pillow. He likes to steal it when I'm not sleeping. Actually he tries to steal it while I'm sleeping too.

"I'm just going to write, Genj," I tell him. He stares back and meows. I'll take that as agreement.

I swivel around and find my words still on the computer screen. I scroll to the end. *If you're going to make me wait, Ty, I'm going to write and not think about it.* Exactly, I'm just not going to think about it.

I scan the last few paragraphs. It's the part where Kit confronts Jaxon over rumors of the upcoming festival. Jaxon gets real shady with him on the details and tries to convince Kit he's just being paranoid. It's not like they actually bleed people out or sacrifice newcomers who don't convert. And he sort of convinces him, but Ben's been around a few years, and he's certain they're not rumors. He says he's witnessed it.

Don't do it, A. Don't do it. I blow out a long slow breath and close my eyes. *Just don't.*

But I do. It's like autopilot while my hand picks up my phone and I check my texts again. More nothing. *Oh my God, just stop, A!*

Write. Just write.

Okay, so the next scene is…

I swap over to my timeline and find my place. I can't write without an outline. It's annoying, but it's just how my brain works. I find my place in the document.

Okay. It's two days out from the festival, and Kit's snooping around the ritual grounds where he isn't supposed to be. I put my fingers on the keyboard and let the words flow, and by flow I mean stutter and stop and start again, and then stare at the screen a minute wondering if Tyler is dead or just decided to ignore me, then shake it off and write again.

Ding!

My eyes fly to my phone and land on a new text notification. Tyler. The tension in my wrists, arms, and body melts away. I roll my eyes at how easily manipulated I am by my own stupid feelings and then pick up the phone.

TYLER: Almost there. Sry. Bad signal.

I sigh. It's true. Signal royally sucks out in Collettsville where he lives. And he's always late anyway. I've got to stop stressing. It's stupid. Plus, I have no freaking reason to stress in the first place. Hell, I shouldn't even be waiting on him. This shouldn't mean so much to me.

AIDAN: All good. See you soon. Don't text and drive.

I sound like a total mom, but I don't want him getting hurt. All I can think about is Brayden. That's how they say it happened. I close my eyes and will the image to the back of my mind, replacing it with Tyler and my book. Ty's green eyes do the trick, and that smooth quirky laughter puts a grin back on my face. But it's mixed with goofing off in the Walmart sports aisle with Bray. *Stop it. Stop!*

Wonder how close *almost there* is? *No, don't do that either, Aidan. Just write.*

I refocus on my screen and send Kit slinking behind buildings, between crates, and weaving through trees scoping out the ritual grounds, trying to deduce whether all the doomsday hearsay has any truth to it.

Does he mean, like, ten minutes? Five? Maybe only a minute out? What the hell is *almost here*?

Genji meows and kneads my leg with his paws.

"I know, Genj, me too." I pat his head and rub under his chin, which he adores. I'm impatient too. "Why are we like this?"

He meows back, and I nod. *You keep me sane, buddy.* "Yep. Same. Don't have a clue. But it sucks!"

Write Aidan. Write!

My phone dings again, and I about drop the effing thing trying to pick it up too quickly.

TYLER: I'm here.

A stupid cheesy grin broadens my lips, and I do this cheesy happy dance in my chair. Why am I so stupid? I don't want to sound too eager, and I *was* just writing, sort of, so I send him a quick message.

TYLER: *Scene?*

AIDAN: Come in. Finishing up a scene.

TYLER: Scene?

AIDAN: My book.

TYLER: K.

A few seconds later I hear Mamá opening the door and telling Tyler hey, and then her mouth doesn't stop and I tune it out. He'll manage his way back here eventually, but that should give me time to get to a good stopping point, plus the last thing I need to do is go rushing out to save him.

I try not to think about it as I send Kit around a corner and his foot catches on a sack of food—potatoes, maybe, I'll decide later—and he trips and falls to the floor. He's scared someone may have heard, so he starts to run off.

"I'm here!" Tyler throws my bedroom door open.

I jump and a bunch of random letters jumble up the screen.

"Dammit, Ty." I put a hand over my mouth when I notice Mamá is standing behind him, and I give her a big smile that says, "I'm sorry."

"Language." She frowns. Usually she doesn't say anything about it unless it's a big one or other people are around. And of course, other people are around.

"Sorry," I say and shoot Tyler a silly grin. "Give me a second, I'm about done."

"Still writing," he says more than asks.

"Yeah." I type out a few more lines. But it still isn't a good stopping place. I want to stop though, just leave it mid-action, let it hang there so I can get out of here with Ty, but no.

"He does this to you too?" Mamá asks, presumably talking to Ty. "Zones out to his own little world. Acts like no one else is around."

I don't turn. I hear her loud and clear. If I didn't zone out, I'd never get any writing done around here.

"So I should learn to expect it?" Tyler asks her.

At that, I almost do turn around. Learn to expect it? What's the supposed to mean? Why would you be here that often? Unless… *No. Stop it, A. You're reading into it too much. Like, way too much.*

"Yeah," she says.

"I'm right here," I mutter, trying and largely failing to type at the same time.

Mamá leaves and Tyler comes up next to my chair smiling and laughing.

"Your mom's something," he says.

"Hands off mi madre." I eye him down.

"No! Oh God no, that's not what I meant." He flashes me his middle finger, and I laugh. I quickly refocus. This just needs to take long enough for me not to look too eager, like this is more important. "She's funny."

"That wears off pretty quick," I joke. She is funny. I love her to death, I mean, she's mi madre. "I saw your new TikTok."

I swing around to face him but remember I'm writing and I'm just distracting myself. But that doesn't change anything. He did another video last night. I don't know the name of the dance. All I know for certain is he shook his ass and I might have watched that part on repeat a few times. I mean, why not?

"You like it? I mean, I know you *liked* it, but did you really like it?" he asks.

I shake my head in faux disappointment.

"No. I hated it," I say as deadpan as I can master.

"Huh?" He physically moves back a step.

"That was too easy!" I stick out my tongue and laugh. "Yeah, I liked it!"

"Oh good," he says, but he isn't done. "You should do one with me sometime. It'd be great!"

"Uh, first, hell no. And two, hell no again. And three, I can't dance," I tell him. Is he insane?

He throws his head back all theatrical-like. "Oh my God. You're so dramatic."

"You're distracting me again." I swing back around to my screen. "The more you distract me the longer this is going to take."

I'm giggling the entire time, mainly to make sure he knows I'm not irritated. Last thing I want is for him to think I'm mad and leave. Plus, it's not like I'm actually getting any writing done. I *want* to leave.

"Okaaaay, I'll just sit over here." Ty drops his ass on my bed. Genji jumps up next to him and starts purring and rubbing up all over him, and I attempt to go back to writing.

At this rate, poor Kit is never getting off the damn floor. I think how best to phrase the next sentence for a solid half minute before finally picking him up and letting him make it around the—

"So what you writing?" Tyler interrupts.

I type the last few words in my head. Kit sees something that I don't tell the reader, and I end the chapter in spite of the interruption. Okay, it might or might not be the end of the chapter, but for now it is.

"My book," I say, like it's obvious. I mean it is, isn't it?

"I know that, fool, but, like, what's happening?" he asks. "Actually, no, can I just read some?"

I swing around and give him bug eyes. Read some? Has he lost his ever-loving effing mind?

"Please?" He wiggles on my bed, and this raunchy part of my brain really likes the idea of him wiggling on my bed. A fantasy of him twisting and writhing on top of me on my bed blares in my mind. I swallow back a lump in my throat and force the image away. I don't want to, but if I don't stop it, it's going to be pretty obvious something's going through my head that shouldn't be down low.

"Uh… I… But we're already late," I stutter.

"Late? Really? Cook Out's open until midnight or some shit like that, and the park doesn't close, and the stars have been up there for, like, billions of years and haven't left yet." Tyler absolutely ruins my excuse. "I know you don't let people read your stuff, but I bet it's really good. And I'm not *people*, I'm Ty."

Why do you even want to read it? And no, it probably sucks.

"I mean… I don't—" I try, but he looks at me with those effing cute puppy dog eyes and a pouty lip, and oh my God, I can't say no. I can't do it. "Okay."

"Sweet!" He jumps off the bed and wraps his arm around the head of my chair, leaning in to see the screen.

What? No. I didn't mean it. I was tricked. I throw my arm over the screen, shielding it from his view.

"I mean…" This is too much. I can't let him read this. Not now, maybe not ever. It's so bad right now. "It's really bad."

"Can't be that bad." He shrugs and gives me a smile that, again, I can't say no to.

I want to tell him how devious he is, but then I'd have some explaining to do. I'd have to tell him why his sad puppy dog eyes can even do that to me, and that's a real no-go.

"Just a little!" I point at him to make it extra clear.

"Okay." He nods.

It's one hundred percent weird to me how excited he appears to be about this. I didn't think he liked to read that much.

I scroll through my manuscript until I find a piece I've edited a little, something that doesn't seem too crazy but not too boring at the same time. It's a part near the beginning where this dude gets his hand sawed off for stealing. It's a bit intense, but Ty likes the bloody stuff. I get up and let him sit at the computer to read, and immediately I can see his eyes scanning the words.

"Jaxon ties Aaron's hand down and places the blade against his wri—" Tyler starts reading my words, my words! *Out loud!*

"Oh no you don't! Stop! Right now," I jump in, my skin crawling from the sound of the very words I wrote. "Stop!"

"He starts to saw. The skin parts, and blood—"

I try to cover my ears, but it does no good. He just reads louder, so I chant like a three-year-old, "La la la, stop! Stop! Ugh!"

"—spurts between torn ribbons of flesh as the blade carves—"

I grab my pillow and slap him upside the head, and finally the room is silent.

"What the fuck?" He looks at me, surprise plastered across his face, but he's smiling. He covers his mouth and looks toward my bedroom door when the last word comes out. "Hope she didn't hear that."

"Don't worry about it." I can't help but grin.

"But seriously? WTF?" Tyler grins.

"I hate hearing people read my stuff," I groan. I swear he already knows this. "Like, utterly hate."

Tyler stares me down for a moment, then suddenly his eyes flash back to the screen. "I want to look away, but I can't—"

I slap him again with the pillow. He stops, looks at me, and grins.

"So that's how it is," he giggles, and before I can react he runs to my bed, and swipes my other pillow.

"It's on!" I say, and the swinging begins.

TYLER

Saturday, June 22

The cloth top on my car whirrs back, revealing a perfectly clear sky, and Aidan lays his seat as far back as it'll go. We couldn't have picked a better night.

"You really like the title?" Aidan asks.

"Yeah," I say.

It's cool. I mean, who wouldn't want to read a book called *The Bleeding*?

"It's simple but all ominous and scary at the same time. And I'm guessing there's a lot of blood in it." It was definitely bloody. "I mean, just what I read was gory."

"Yeah. A lot, a whole lot." Aidan nods, his freckles barely visible in the moonlight. He takes his eyes off the sky and glances at me questioningly. "So…you didn't hate what you read?"

"Hate?" I scoot back like it's this crazy unheard-of type of question. No. I didn't hate it. I liked it. "Really? It was good. At least what you let me read. The rest could be crap for all I know."

I curl my lips and look away. I hope I didn't just take that last one too far. I swear I'm joking. I hope he gets it.

"It's probably all crap—" He pulls his eyes away just as I open my mouth. I'm not having any of that negative shit right now.

"Stop that," I urge.

"Stop what?" Aidan squints like he doesn't understand.

"The self-deprecating 'oh my writing sucks' shit," I tell him. "Be proud of what you're doing. It's good. I was just kidding."

To that he shrugs and finds something else to look at. It's silent for a little, and I'm not really sure what to say.

We had a good time at Cook Out. There are two sweet teas in huge Styrofoam cups between us to prove it. Over Cajun fries, chicken strips, and hot dogs I milked out everything I could about *The Bleeding*. It really is interesting stuff. It's this whole society, a cult, after the shit hits the fan.

They're insane, total religious wackos that make my family look liberal as hell, and they're making his main character's life total hell.

I could never be that creative. The most imaginative thing I can do is put together a model, and that's iffy. I haven't done one in years. It's one of those perishable skills I probably lost since Dad pushed it down my throat after I came out with all the war planes and hot rods that I didn't give a shit about. It was one of many *manly* things he tried to use to rid me of my homosexual disease or make sure I didn't turn out too feminine. Can't have that.

Aidan though. He has genuine talent. Like, I swear he could make something of it if he stopped putting himself down so much.

"You remember when Brayden first found out about Breegge?" Aidan breaks the silence.

I think about it, and I sigh. We'd been dating for, like, two weeks when he saw the news on space.com. He was always the excitable type, but news of a comet almost as bright as Hale-Bopp that might come closer to Earth than Halley's Comet got him going. He was such a nerd.

"Yeah. He was *so* excited," I say. "That's all he talked about for at least a week or two."

"All you got was two weeks?" Aidan looks at me with this amused curiosity. "It never stopped for me."

"Well, obviously not. It was just the most intense the first two weeks," I clarify.

"True," he sighs. "I wish I had a telescope so we could see it now."

I saw it a few times through Brayden's telescope back in January and February, but it was so far away then. I bet it's awesome to see now.

"That would be cool," I say.

I pause a second, debating whether I should say the words that pop into my head, but I figure why not.

"I didn't care about the damn comet when he started talking about it. It actually bugged me at first. Like, I didn't give a hell about stars and comets and planets and all that stuff. I know that's weird coming from me. You know, 'cause I love Star Trek and shit, but that's different. That's all aliens and battles. I don't know, I just didn't care about it," I tell him. And God, it sounds horrible the more I talk. "It's weird to hear myself say that now. It's like being with him gave me this appreciation for it all. I don't know, it's just weird."

"I guess that's what happens when you really love someone," Aidan says softly, his gaze flicking off to the right and then back up to the sky. "We adapt. Is that a bad thing?"

"I don't know," I say. I really did change though, and I didn't even think about it. It's not like I woke up one morning and thought, *he likes astronomy so I will too*, it just happened, and it's not like it was fake either. I still like it. I really do.

It gets quiet again.

I survey the sky, eyes lazily moving from one glimmering speck to the next, tracing the constellations together. First Aquila, then Scutum and Serpens. I spot Jupiter again, then Scorpius and Libra. Each and every star is so clear tonight with the moon yet to make its appearance over the treed hilltops.

"Let's take a walk," I break the silence. I don't wait for an answer before I start raising my seat.

"Huh?" Aidan twitches.

I think I startled him. I restrain a laugh as I pull the handle and get out.

"Let's take a walk," I repeat. "It'll be fun. Get a little exercise in."

"Fun? You call exercise fun?" Aidan questions, but he's getting out anyway.

"You play soccer, A," I remind him. "You literally run around a field for, like, eighty minutes or some bull like that, kicking a ball nonstop. That's exercise and 'fun'." I throw up some air quotes just to drive the point home. I at least admit what sports are: a man-made attempt to make me exercise willfully, the main reason I'm not a fan.

"Eh," he sighs as I catch up around the front of the car.

We start down the path. It feels too good out to be holed up inside somewhere, even a top-down car, and not enjoy the chirping of the katydids, the cool summer breeze against my arms and ruffling through my hair, gazing at untold trillions of stars overhead, and strolling the perpetually fault-lined walkway.

"You should have gotten a convertible," I tell Aidan a minute later, looking back at my unintentionally two-toned Sebring and sighing. "Would be so much cooler to come out in a Mustang than my rust bucket."

"I wish," Aidan says. "I'd never put the top up."

"Winter is cold, my friend," I remind him.

"Bitch." Aidan knocks his shoulder against mine.

"The baddest bitch," I tell him.

"Who can't stand a little cold?" He refuses to let me have it, complete with mocking pouty face.

I roll my eyes, making certain he sees. I mean, he's right.

"Even the baddest bitches have their limits, and mine is freezing temps. Forgive me, but I'd rather not die of pneumonia." I shrug and skip across a crack in the walkway like it's a mile-wide canyon. Aidan does the same, but there's something cute about it.

"Name that constellation," Aidan says randomly and thrusts his arm toward the sky and points.

I follow his spindly pointer finger.

"Do you even know where you pointed?" I ask. He barely had time to look, let alone choose a constellation.

"I know where I'm pointing," he giggles.

I bounce my shoulders and trace his finger toward the sky. It could be any of them, but I think I've got it. Cygnus is in the general area, but maybe he's pointing to Lyra. I think for a split second.

"Cygnus," I answer.

"Good," he approves. "And above it?"

"Lyra," I say.

"Exactly." Aidan puts his hand down.

"Did you just go with Cygnus because I said it first?" I squint.

"Maybe," Aidan laughs.

I roll my eyes and laugh with him. "I did at least get the constellation right, right?"

Aidan takes a second to look at the sky and nods. "Yeah. You got it."

I can't help but think he's a little crazy, but in a good way.

"Do you know the brightest star in the Lyra constellation?" I ask. If we're quizzing, I might as well take it up a notch with one more fact I owe to Brayden.

Aidan furrows his brow. He chews at his lip and I have to look away.

"I don't think so," he says after a few seconds.

"You don't? What?" I almost stop moving.

"Nope." Aidan shrugs.

"That's fair I guess." I nod, but then I remember how much he loves sci-fi stuff and I still can't believe I know it and he doesn't. "But I thought you loved sci-fi stuff."

"You're confusing sci-fi with science, my friend. But yes, and no," Aidan corrects me.

Ah, yeah. That's true.

He pauses like there's some horrible truth he's about to admit. "Brayden loved all of it. But me? I guess it's a little of both. All that Star Trek stuff—you know, like warp speed and phasers—is just too much for me. It's too far out there. I can't suspend my disbelief. Science though, yeah. Bray was more astronomy than anything. I like the stuff down here more. Like biology and anatomy, or physics. Don't get me wrong, I remember a lot of the outer space stuff he told me, but that was more Brayden."

It hits me that just because I absorbed every bit of it, or most of it, not everyone did, and that's okay. I couldn't tell you what half the soccer terminology Brayden used to rattle off meant, or Aidan for that matter, but I still supported him. I guess it's no different.

And the way Aidan is looking down at the sidewalk right now says he's feeling bad about it.

"I'm sorry. I didn't mean it to sound like that." I cough away my nerves.

"It's o—," he gives me this cute sideways grin right as he trips.

I jerk forward and I'm about to grab him, arms out and reaching, when he catches his footing. I yank my arms back, locking them at my side like a rigid mannequin in one of those awkward "walking" poses.

"You okay?" I ask, the heat rising in my cheeks. I don't even know why.

"I'm good." Aidan smiles back and giggles. "Just a clumsy bitch."

"I'm supposed to be the clumsy one." I immediately run my mouth as quick as possible because I swear it sounds like I just talked about us as a thing, but that's not what I meant. "You play sports, you can't be clumsy."

Did it even sound like that, or am I overthinking it?

I lock eyes with him for a brief second, and my chest pounds at the way the lamp light reflects in his eyes. All at once I want to scoop him up and kiss him so bad. What the hell? No!

I sling my gaze ahead and get a few paces in front of him. Just keep walking.

TYLER

If there's anything worse than being forced to go to church, it's family reunions, and the annual Gentry family reunion has to top the list. We're in some warehouse-looking "events" space that's more fit for storing tractor supplies than hosting any occasion where food is present.

The room is filled with the people I actively avoid on the daily, the same people who gave me *the speech* when I came out or incessantly harp that it's just a phase. Psyche Aunt Tilda, it's a long-ass phase.

But that's why I have a phone. Avoidance is key, and it's easyish since Mom is even more antisocial than me. Dad, on the other hand, makes it his goal to speak to every single body in the building, while Melinda makes laps around the plastic dining tables with two of our cousins.

I have the group chat up, the one Kallie started yesterday with Aidan. It was her idea, and I admit it feels safer talking to him in a group after Saturday night. It was so awkward, and we barely talked on the way home. I was horrified the entire drive he'd read my mind, that he knew what went through my head when we locked eyes, but that's stupid.

AIDAN: GoldenEye.

I do a double take. There is no way I read that right. But there it is. That can't be left to stand. I type a reply and hit send, and at the same instant a message from Kallie jumps in the thread.

TYLER: What?! Tell me your kidding.

KALLIE: ::mind blown emoji:: How?

Don't get me wrong. *GoldenEye* was a good Bond movie, but the best? That's pushing it—a lot.

AIDAN: Pierce Brosnan as Bond, and Sean Bean as the bad dude! Yes please!!

I roll my eyes, and for a minute almost forget I'm at this god-awful reunion. On the bright side, being the only gay family member means at least part of the family just doesn't want to come around me. Like, it literally makes them awkward, and they just don't. I'll take that as a small victory.

TYLER: You and your old stuff. Any of Craig's movies beat it hands down!

"Who you talking to?" Mom leans over my shoulder, probably spying on my conversation. It's not like I'm sexting, so whatever.

"Kallie and Aidan," I tell her. "A thinks *GoldenEye* was the best Bond movie."

She wrinkles her brow, and it's evident she doesn't have a clue which it is. I doubt she can tell one Bond movie from the other anyway.

"The one with Pierce Brosnan, you know, your guy in *Dante's Peak*." I give her a reference I know she'll get. It's one of her favorite natural disaster movies.

"Oh," she sighs, then leers mischievously. "Sean Connery, mhmm. He's still the most handsome Bond."

"Ugh." I poke out my tongue and gag. "Old!"

"He was something when he was younger," Mom tells me.

"Hard pass." I shiver.

AIDAN: But Sean Bean! That voice!

TYLER: Don't care. You probably agree with my mom. She likes Sean Connery.

I say it mostly in jest. He does like old stuff, not sure what his guy type is though. Maybe it's old too, just like his old rock music I can't deal with.

KALLIE: Oooh! ::red heart:: Young Sean Connery.

I roll my eyes. Should have known she'd be on board.

TYLER: No!!!!!! ::eye roll emoji:: Skyfall, that is it. THE best. End convo.

"Why don't you go talk to your cousin," Mom interrupts and nods toward David.

He's sitting two rows over, elbows planted on a rather bland green plastic tablecloth with the most redneck division of the family. My granddad, my cousin Randall, and Dad's two brothers, Liam and Shane.

"Pass," I blurt. "Why don't you go talk to Aunt Tilda?"

Mom smirks at me and shakes her head. She's just like me, or maybe I'm like her.

As for David, I have about as much in common with him as Sean Addison at school. He's this hypermasculine, broad-shouldered hunter who has my dad's mentality that he's going to marry some girl who isn't capable of being more than a housewife—and he's trapped in a body that's about three inches too short for his attitude. I wouldn't know what to say to him, and I don't want to.

Some old lady I know I've seen before, whose name I don't know, distracts Mom and saves me from further suggestions. I go back to my phone.

KALLIE: Yes!!!

AIDAN: SO LONG!!!!!!!!!!!!!!!!!!!!!!!!! ::puke emoji::

What the hell? I thought he liked *Skyfall*. Didn't I watch it with him before Brayden and I were a thing?

TYLER: Thought you liked Skyfall?

AIDAN: I do. ::shrug emoji:: Hahaha ::laughing emoji:: ::laughing _emoji::_

TYLER: I hate you. ::laughing emoji::

I see how it is, just trying to get a reaction. I'll take it. At least things aren't awkward. Either that or he's playing it off well.

I was so worried I'd freaked him out, like somehow, telepathically, he knew I'd wanted to kiss him in the park. I don't want to. It was a weird moment. Just a moment, just a millisecond when we locked eyes after he about fell that I had this urge to wrap my arms around him and kiss him. I can't even explain why. The idea makes me want to vomit now.

The crazy thing is how he got so weird after that. I mean, there is no way he knew what I was thinking. So, like, what the hell?

"Honey." Mom taps my shoulder.

"Huh?" I'm in the process of sending a slew of middle finger emojis. When I look up the old lady who was talking to Mom is smiling at me. I take a second glance at my phone and hit send.

"Do you know who I am?" the lady asks me in this super expectant tone through a long Southern drawl. It's like she's begging me to get it wrong.

I'm not playing this game. Like, I don't want to be a bitch, but I don't know you.

"Not really," I admit.

"I'm your great-aunt Vickie," she tells me.

I crack an unsure smile and glance at Mom, silently asking why she's making me go through this. It takes everything in me not to say, "So that's why I don't know you."

"Aunt Vickie's married to your dad's Uncle Frank," Mom fills in the gaps, while Great-Aunt Vickie nods and her arms shake, or maybe her arms have been shaking the entire time.

I smile and grin like I care, but I'd rather be texting, and not here, and not talking to whoever Aunt Vickie is.

"I hear you're going to be a senior. I remember my senior year. I was the class of 1973. That's back before your school was built." She stops and does this old lady giggle with her eyes half shut, and I try to feign interest. "It was Gamewell-Collettsville High School when I was there."

She goes on and on about how it's where the current Gamewell Middle School is and a bunch of other useless factoids about the seventies I'm not in the least bit interested in. Maybe Aidan or Kallie would be, but not me.

I zone in and out and catch something about my great-uncle Frank, who I also barely know, wearing a Tar-Heel blue suit at their wedding with bell bottom pants, and the Beatles breaking up the same year, and how she thought that meant her marriage was doomed. All I take away from it is my great-uncle Frank and great-aunt Vickie didn't adhere to the same level of fundamentalism my family did—does. Being a Beatles fan back then would have been like Satanism or something.

"You have a girlfriend? You're such a cutie. I bet you steal all the young ladies' hearts," she adds.

It's the third time tonight someone's asked me the dreaded question. The only difference is that Uncle Shane and my granddad both know better. They just think it's their sworn duty to berate me with that same timeless question every time they see me. Great-Aunt Vickie doesn't have a clue, so I can forgive her.

But I'm done saying no for the day. Already hit my quota. I'm full and over it.

My instinct is to say something like, "Well, see, Aunt Vickie, I'm a raging homosexual, so a girl is the last thing getting in my pants," but I decide to save Mom the embarrassment. I start to fill her in just as my dad is walking up.

"No." I shrug and decide to go with something a little less abrasive. "No boyfriends."

"Boyfriends?" Her face wrinkles up a few more folds, and what tiny bit of progressiveness I thought might be there vanishes. How shocking.

"I'm gay?" Somehow it came out more as a question than a statement. It's so uncomfortable, but it's even more uncomfortable to lie.

Mom gives me this nervous grin, and I can feel the look in my dad's eyes before I hear him correct me.

"He just hasn't found the right girl yet," Dad butts in.

I stare at him blankly. Really? That again?

Dad continues, "I'm just waiting for a pretty one to show up at church so he can marry a good godly girl." Dad elbows me like I'm supposed to smile and go along. I don't. "But I'm sure he's got his eye on a few at school too."

"No," I insist, standing up. "I don't. I obviously don't and won't. Like, why would I?"

"He's just being a teenager." Dad shrugs me off and tries to laugh with my great-aunt Vickie, but she isn't laughing. She actually seems a bit concerned.

"Just stop." I roll my eyes.

Mom puts her hand on my shoulder and urges me to sit down. I do and take a few breaths.

"He'll find *someone* when he's ready," Mom says, and there's something different in her voice, something aggravated.

She's eyeing Dad with this annoyed frown. What just happened? I shake my head as Great-Aunt Vickie runs off, and Dad does that I'm-going-to-laugh-because-I'm-uncomfortable thing and leaves me with

Mom. Yeah, I'm getting a talking-to tonight. Yay me.

I don't bother reading the last five unread texts in the group chat before sending my own.

TYLER: I HATE FAMILY REUNIONS.

AIDAN

There was a text from Tyler waiting for me when I clocked out tonight. He wants to play *Overwatch,* so naturally I sped home. I step in the door and Genji slithers between my feet and I have to catch the wall to keep from falling.

"Genj!" I admonish him, mean look and all, as if he cares. "You've got to stop doing that."

"How was work?" Mi madre calls from the kitchen as I'm trying to escape down the hall.

"Good," I toss back without stopping.

"Whatcha doing?" she yells a little louder.

"Going to play games with Ty and Jacob." I grab the doorknob and pull it open as she yells again. I roll my eyes. What now?

"Wait a minute there," she calls after me.

Footsteps pad down the hall. She's got her hair up in a black ponytail, and she's still wearing her uniform with the Fatz Café logo stamped on the left breast pocket. "I need to talk to you."

Need to? Was there ever a time those words were spoken when it was a good thing? I groan quiet enough that hopefully she doesn't hear from the other end of the hall. Hurry up! Let's get whatever this is over with. Ty's waiting.

"So… Well." She reaches me and stops, sighing.

What did I do? I run the last few days through my head, and nothing worse than leaving a few dishes in the sink or leaving my unfolded laundry in the corner of my room comes to mind. Unless she's thinking about the sidewalk I was supposed to weed. I did forget that.

"If it's about the sidewalk, I'm sorry," I apologize. "I'll get it tomorrow."

"Sidewalk?" She squints.

Dammit. Guess she hadn't noticed yet, and now I *have* to do it tomorrow.

"Don't know what you're talking about." Mamá waves it off. "Tyler. He's been over a few times lately. Which is great. It is. He's a good kid. Cute." She nudges me and smirks. *Oh no.* "Just want you to be safe."

What the hell is that supposed to mean?

"Uh, okay…" The corners of my lips turn down in uncertainty. I'm so confused right now, but I don't have time for this.

My phone buzzes in my pocket.

"You are being safe, right?" she tries again, but this time it's a question.

"What are you talking about?" I've got a game to get to, so I need *this* little game to wrap up.

Mom shifts uncomfortably and twists at the waist. "You're using protection, right?"

"Mamá!" I put up a hand for a full stop of that thought. "Can we not? Ugh, no."

"You're not?" Her eyes go wide. "Mi amor, tienes que tener cuidado." She stops and shakes her head nervously. Sometimes when she gets riled up she starts speaking real fast in Spanish. But she knows I don't understand most of it. "You have to be careful. You don't—"

"That's not what I mean. I… We're not… We're not like *that!* Ugh." I shudder my shoulders and grunt, and Genji darts past me into my room. I want to dart in after him so bad. This is not the conversation I want to be having right now.

"Just promise me you'll be careful though," Mamá begs me.

"Of course," I say. "But we're not…doing that. He's just a friend."

Mamá grins and shakes her head. "Okay, just be careful."

"Oh my God!" I roll my eyes. "Bye!"

I can't even. I wave and shut the door behind me. My whole body shivers, like it can somehow wash that conversation out of my mind. Oh my God!

Just think about the game. That's it, the game. I rush over to my TV and power on my system, then I strip down to my underpants and slip into some comfy basketball shorts and an oversized graphic tee with the Metallica M covering the front. At the same time I check my phone.

TYLER: Home yet?

It's weird how excited I get when I see his name pop up on my phone. Like, I know I shouldn't be, because that's a bad thing, but I can't seem to help it.

AIDAN: Logging on now.

Part of me wants to tell him what mi madre just did in the hallway, make him have to deal with it just like me, but that's begging to make this game awkward. Instead, I pick up the controller and crawl into bed while *Overwatch* loads up. A few minutes later, my headphones are alive with activity and we're grouped up, with the Horizon Lunar Colony map loading.

I choose Reaper as always, and Tyler groans.

"Again?" he asks.

"Yeah," I say, unperturbed. I'm a one-hit wonder, but I do Reaper right, or at least okay. I think.

Tyler locks in Sym, and Jacob takes Mercy.

"I'll be watching over you," Jacob does his best Mercy impersonation. It's not that great. I can tell he's going for a feminine voice, but that's about it.

"Should we be worried, Ty?" I ask. Jacob's great with Mercy, but I figured out recently that Ty loves giving him a hard time about it.

"Don't know. Just hope someone else picks a healer," Tyler jokes back.

The countdown reaches zero and none of the other three randoms we're playing with chose a healer.

"We're screwed," I say.

"Come on," Jacob says. "When have I let you down before?"

"Uh, well, there was that—" Tyler starts.

"Shut up, Ty," Jacob laughs as the game begins.

We chat tons of game strategy through the match. It's a tense one. The other team's Doomfist is an absolute beast, and their Reaper is making me look like a total noob. But I'm still having a blast. Every time Tyler says something I tune in harder, wanting to hear every last cadence. It's insane, but there's something about it, the way he'll talk really fast the more excited he gets, and that little staccato laugh.

VICTORY glows across the screen and Tyler's Play of the Game pops up with Symmetra's turrets doing all the work.

"Play of the game!" I yell. "Go Ty!"

"Damn boi, you really did set up the car wash," Jacob chimes in.

People call Symmetra's laser turrets the car wash when someone lines them up along an archway or someplace like that and they virtually block access. They're annoying as hell if you're on the opposite team.

"What can I say?" Tyler says.

The leaderboard comes up and naturally Ty's up there. I'm surprised to see my Reaper next to the other team's. As if I did something right this time.

"Nice, A," Tyler congratulates me. "Thirty-two percent team

elims. Not bad."

"I thought I did worse." I shrug as if they can see. Genji scoots closer and wraps his little paws around my forearm. I nuzzle my nose in his side and he meows.

"Nah, it's just like your writing. You're doing good," Ty says. I blush. "Oh yeah! Jacob, did I tell you Aidan writes? Like, fiction stuff."

"Like, books?" Jacob asks.

"Yeah," Tyler says. "And it's horror!"

"They suck," I try to take over the conversation, but Tyler isn't having it.

"Horror?" Jacob sounds interested.

"Yeah!" Tyler blurts. "And don't listen to A, they're great. Well, it's great. You've only got one so far, right?"

"Well, sort of. I'm not actually done with it," I correct him.

"He let me read some. It's going to be so good," he tells Jacob.

Part of me wants to crawl under a rock and never be heard from again, but the other part is sort of reveling in the fact that Tyler's bragging about me to a friend. I mean, bragging about my book.

"Cool!" Jacob says. "At the coffee shop I go to down here sometimes, there's this older bald writer dude that comes around and writes all the time. Think he writes horror too actually. Haven't read them. Maybe I can read some of yours."

"No!" I yell into the mic. "I mean, it's not ready. It's not done yet."

"I thought you said you read it, Ty," Jacob asks.

"I read, like, a paragraph. That's all he'll let me see," Tyler explains, and I just try to focus on the sound of his voice instead of what he's actually saying. That part is soothing. "He gets real anxious about his writing. Doesn't have enough confidence in it. But he *should!*"

"Eh," I grunt. Maybe someday.

TYLER

Saturday, June 29

The park is empty.

Bugs chirp away in the trees — cicadas, I think — and the last rays of sunlight are creeping away, giving way to a serene black, diamond-lit blanket.

A few clouds spot the sky, but it's not bad. The humidity and temperature, on the other hand, are an issue. I don't like to freeze, but I don't like to sweat either, and there's absolutely no wind. Which is why I'm sitting in my car with the A/C blaring waiting for Aidan to pull up. He texted about fifteen minutes ago that he'd just finished his shift, so he should be here any minute.

KALLIE: Still waiting on your man to show up?

I smack my lips and roll my eyes. That girl.

TYLER: Waiting on A. Not my man.

KALLIE: ::eye roll emoji:: Tell that to your face.

TYLER: ::middle finger emoji::

In my rearview mirror I see the blare of headlights pass and settle on the chain-link fence cordoning off the main baseball field. A car pulls up next to me and I turn to find Aidan smiling. I smile back. *Curse you, Kallie.*

TYLER: TTYL.

I pocket my phone and get out.

"How was work?" I ask as he's shutting his door. "Sorry you had to work with Kal."

"Eh, I'll get by." He smirks. "Those really are the best days though.

It's *boring* when she's not around."

"I know, right?" I throw my hands up and nod toward the walking path. "How 'bout we walk again?"

"Sure." Aidan shrugs.

I lead the way and he catches up, coming around on my right.

"What did you do all day?" Aidan asks.

"I worked this morn—" I start.

"Ah, I knew that, sorry." He shakes his head like it's this big thing.

"It's okay," I tell him. "But yeah, other than work, I played some *Apex* and *Overwatch* with Jacob. I tried making a TikTok, but I didn't like it."

"What about?" Aidan asks.

"It was another dance video," I say.

I tried so hard, but something just didn't look right. Not yet at least. I still can't place a finger on it. "Have you seen the Obsessed dance?"

"Maybe." He squints. I feel like he means *no* but doesn't want to admit it.

"It's a dance. I couldn't get my phone to cooperate and the lighting was off," I tell him. "I'll get it eventually."

"Of course. And I'll fight Kallie for the first like." Aidan nudges me.

"You're playing a dangerous game there," I tell him. She takes being the first like very seriously. "Some dude happened to beat her to it recently, and I *might* have complained for a week that she didn't love me enough. So she's sort of on her game there."

"I wouldn't happen to be 'some dude', would I?" Aidan asks.

"Maybe," I tell him. He is most definitely *some dude*.

"Ah," Aidan laughs. "Yeah, she complained to me too."

I bob my head back and forth. That's definitely Kallie.

"Oh! Kallie scared me good tonight." Aidan throws his hands up and smirks at me.

"Do tell," I say.

It's refreshing to hear when Kallie scares someone other than me. I'm an easy target. I've told her this, but I think it just makes it more pleasing.

We make the bend around the second baseball field with the tennis courts off to the left. The lighting is better here since all of the streetlamps are actually working.

"I was coming back in from helping this lady with her groceries and when I came around the corner, she was just there. Like right in my face." He shakes his head and sighs.

"You scream?" I hope so bad he did. How great would that be? Making Aidan scream in the middle of Food Lion.

"No! Thank the genies, no."

"Hold up, that's *my* phrase." I act offended.

"You don't have it copyrighted or anything." Aidan grins. "Thank the genies. Thank the genies. Thank the effing genies."

"How rude," I scoff, which sends him into a fit of laughter. I join in.

The path splits ahead. The left leads down a shortcut back to the parking lot, and to the right passes the playground and picnic tables by the river. I keep to the right, glimpsing at the back of Aidan's pants when he gets a step ahead of me. I yank my gaze away so I don't stare.

"You should be flattered. It's not every day you say something worth repeating." He cocks one eyebrow up high.

"Fuck you," I stress between a hard smile. The picnic benches are off to our right so I start toward one. "How about we stargaze a little?"

"Isn't that the entire reason we're here?" Aidan asks.

"Yeah, just thought, you know, we could sit here. You know,

instead of the car," I ramble.

"I'm just being difficult." Aidan jogs past me toward the table.

I take off after him. He's quick. All that soccer gives him an advantage, but I catch up. I throw my hand out to slow him down, shoving my arm against his stomach.

"Cheater," he yells, as I twist around and my ass hits the rough wooden bench and he skids to a halt next to me, like right next to me.

I glance between us, and his breath brushes my face. I swear I can feel the tension inside the tiny inch that separates our thighs. For a second, I fight back the urge to close the gap, but I catch myself. *Don't be stupid.*

AIDAN
Saturday, June 29

"Who you calling a cheater?" Tyler eyes me with this grin I can't take my eyes from.

"You," I laugh.

I catch my breath, but it's hard because it's not just the sprint to the bench that's got me out of breath, it's how close we're sitting, and how bad I want to slide over and lie my head on his shoulder.

But that's the last thing he'd want.

"You're the one who started running without warning," Tyler points out. "That's cheating."

"Maybe," I admit.

"We should do this every Saturday," Tyler says out of nowhere. What? Did he seriously just say that? "You know. Come stargaze for Brayden. At least until Breegge's close."

"I'm game." I bounce in place. No. What? I'm not game. What am I thinking?

It's bad enough I can't stop looking at him, but now I agree to coming to the park and stargazing every Saturday night *for Brayden*? It's a great idea in theory, but there are some major problems. But it's for Brayden. Or at least it really should be for Brayden. Okay, maybe there's just one major problem.

I'm falling for him. Okay, scratch that, I've *fallen* for him. This was all supposed to be about Brayden. Remembering him and carrying out his dream, but here I am losing my shit over Tyler, over my BFF's boyfriend. But he's not anymore. God, why does this all suddenly feel so wrong?

Even out of breath he has the cutest voice, and right now I sort of hate him for it. How am I supposed to not want him when he talks like that?

Night has fully cloaked the sky in stars and infinities, and most of the clouds are gone too. It's beautiful. I trace a few stars together in my head. I think it's Virgo, but I could be wrong.

"He knew all of the constellations," I interrupt the silence. I have to get my mind back on track. We're here for Brayden, nothing else. And suddenly, my heart hangs a little lower. How could I be so bad a friend?

"Yeah, like, all of them," Tyler agrees. "Even the minor ones. I remember him naming them. There was this one called Canes Venatici. I'm probably butchering its name. I think it's there between Ursula Major and uh… That one."

"Uh, it's *Ursa* Major, not Ursula." I take my eyes from the sky and look at him crazily. "It's not the sea witch from *The Little Mermaid*."

I giggle and he nudges my shoulder and laughs with me.

"Right." He puts his palm over his face and sighs. "That was bad."

"And 'that one'? I *so* know which one you're talking about," I tell him. I don't have a clue. How could I with that description?

"Bitch." Tyler nudges me again, and the space between us just got smaller. "Like I was saying. Canes Venatici, or whatever, it's only got two main stars, so it's small. But he still knew it."

"Still a constellation," I say. My mind goes back to before things got complicated and before all the pain, back *before* Tyler was my BFF's boyfriend and Brayden was here. "You remember the beginning of our sophomore year, when we all joined the Art Club to go to Biltmore just to get of class?"

I need to remember Brayden. I need to think about him, but I also want to remind Tyler how we used to be, all of us together.

"Yeah." Tyler does this half-grunt and laughs. "They let anybody join. And we missed it our freshman year."

"Yeah, as long as you fundraise for them," I remind him. We had to sell discount coupons to the bowling alley and local restaurants to cover some of the trip expenses.

"I hated fundraising," Tyler says. "Nothing like trying to sell some random piece of paper with some pathetic discounts to a total stranger."

One hundred percent agree. I hate the stranger part as much as he does, maybe more.

"You remember waking up at Biltmore on the bus with Cheetos stuck up your nose?" I ask. It was mostly Brayden's idea, but I did happen to be the one delicately placing the Cheetos.

"Yeah, 'cause I nearly suffocated!" Tyler eyes me accusingly.

"Dramatic." I roll my eyes.

A light breeze picks up and sends a chill over my damp forehead.

"That's all I smelled *all day long*," Tyler stresses. "Get off the bus, Cheetos. Walk into Biltmore, what did I smell? Not flowers, Cheetos. Lunch, Cheetos. On the bus back home, Cheetos."

"But we did eat Cheetos on the way back home," I remind him.

Tyler grins and his gaze drifts back to the stars. I linger a moment on his dimly lit profile. His hair is a little extra wavy tonight, and it hangs just above his eye. His nose slopes gradually into this perfectly cute point above small parted lips. I swallow back some nerves as my mind imagines kissing him.

That's a no-no thought. It's so off limits. Like, it's the worst idea ever. He'd lose his shit probably, and it'd be a guarantee we wouldn't be talking again.

Tyler wiggles around a little, like he's trying to get comfortable, and suddenly I'm much too aware our thighs are touching. Maybe it's more accurate to say smushed together. I swallow back a whole new set of nerves and shift my gaze away, anywhere but on him.

"What about when you had to save me from that spider in Mrs. Zimmerman's class?" Tyler says without taking his eyes off the sky.

"Which time?" I laugh. I can think of a few times. Her classroom obviously had a spider issue. "You talking about during our Earth Science lab?"

"Yeah." Tyler's eyes get big.

"Okay, but there were at least two, if not three times I had to protect your ass from a tiny little spider in lab," I remind him.

"Details," Tyler says. "We didn't talk much last year though, did we?"

I think about it before answering. How blunt should I be?

"I mean, you sort of hated me. I think, at least," I tell him.

Tyler looks at the ground under his feet and doesn't say anything for a moment.

"I'm sorry, I shouldn't have—" I start.

"No. I'm sorry," Tyler interrupts and the words take me by surprise. "I was a douche. You didn't deserve that. I was being stupid."

"It's okay," I say. It's one of those things you say when you don't know what else to say and when what you want to say would sound sort of mean and you don't want to be that person. "We're making memories now."

I immediately want to take it back. Oh my God, why would I say it like that? I should have just screamed *I like you.* I clench my fists in my lap and do my best to keep a straight face.

"I guess we are." Tyler smiles, his dark green eyes locking on mine.

Everything around us slows. The clouds stop moving. The bugs whirring around the nearest streetlamp hover motionless in the air. The gentle churning of the river beyond the tree line stretches out. And Tyler's lips move in slow motion.

I lean in, like some fool, like a machine with no regard for the consequences, with no understanding of the stupidity of what I'm doing. I inch closer in those slowed seconds, my heartbeat thumping faster and faster, and then what I'm doing hits me like a brick wall. I jerk back and sling my gaze in the opposite direction.

"Uh…" Tyler leans away.

"It feels great out here doesn't it? A little humid but not bad." The rambling begins. "Are we all still going to Kallie's for the Fourth of July? When is that anyway?"

"When's the Fourth of July?" Tyler looks at me oddly and pushes out a strained cough.

"Yeah," I ask, not knowing what else to say. I just need him to say something. Anything to put distance between us and what I just tried to pull.

"It's on the fourth of July…" He grins and starts to laugh. "You know, like it says. Fourth of July."

"Oh yeah, right!" I get up, closing and opening my fist, trying to hold back the jitters crawling up my spine. What the hell was I thinking? I force a laugh. I can't sit still right now.

"And of course. I always go, it's like a rule," he tells me.

"I think I need to go…" I say. I have to get out of here.

Tyler stops laughing. "Uh, okay."

"I told Mamá I'd be back by eleven tonight." I pause, trying to think up an excuse to the questions I expect to hear but that don't actually come. Why the hell would I need to be back home by eleven on a Saturday night? "She wants to watch *Bridesmaids* again."

Bridesmaids? That's what I use?

"Okay." He sounds confused. "Sure, yeah."

"I just need to get home. Mamá doesn't like it if I'm late," I lie.

TYLER

Saturday, June 29

I wave at Aidan as his car speeds out of the parking lot, and I shrink into my seat, clutching my chest. Was he about to kiss me? The crazy part, the insane part, is that there was a second when I wanted him to.

My mind is a blur of thoughts. He's so cute—no, he's actually sort of hot. But no, it's too early. I need to just enjoy the summer. I don't need the stress or the worry. I don't need someone wanting to always be doing something or making plans. I don't need anyone expecting me around all the time. Plans suck anyway.

But I already want to see him again. Like he just left, and I want him to come back. This is so fucking stupid. I don't need a boyfriend or a hookup or anything. I had a boyfriend, and I remember how that turned out. I killed him.

AIDAN

It's been two days, two very long days, since I saw Ty at the park. I freaked him out. I know it. He wouldn't text back yesterday, and he didn't come to the park for soccer either. It wasn't until this morning that he finally responded to my *"You okay?"* text from last night. Even that was a very short and to the point, *"Yeah."*

I so effed up, and it's making work way more difficult. I know my job is easy, but every time someone stops me in the aisle, I tense up thinking maybe it's Tyler coming to say he hates me again, and I'm immediately trying to figure out what I should say. Should I lie and say I wasn't trying to kiss him, that he's just imagining it? Or should I say that yeah, of course I was trying to kiss him, I like him. But it's always some rando instead. Oh, and Kallie keeps side-eyeing me. She's on to me. She knows something is up, but so far I've avoided telling her what *it* is.

And when he didn't say anything back to my latest text, I sent him another, asking if I'm riding with him up the mountain to Kallie's Fourth of July fireworks or if he's riding with me. Because, you know, it's always a great idea to double text a guy who obviously doesn't want to talk. I didn't last a minute before sending it either. At this point I'm about certain I'm riding with me and he's riding with him up the mountain.

That was all three hours ago, before I clocked in. I've checked my phone religiously ever since, peeking at it in my pocket any time management isn't looking. And besides a few Insta and TikTok notifications, it's blank.

"What's up with you?" Kallie asks as I hand over the last bag to this elderly lady in a floral-patterned shirt and skirt.

"Up with me? Huh?" I say it too quickly to be believable.

"Yeah, what's up?" she repeats.

"Nothing. I'm good," I say, but she's not buying it. Those dark eyebrows are raised, and her gray-green eyes have this strange ability to see through every charade. "Promise."

"No—" Kallie starts, but a tall, handsome college-age boy with skin about the same shade as mine, minus the freckles, and bright green eyes drops a sixteen-pack of Coors on the belt. "Oh, hey… How are you today?"

I roll my eyes. At least the focus is off me for the moment. She starts checking him out, and my phone buzzes in my pocket. I do a quick check of my surroundings. All is clear, so I peek my phone just far enough out of my pocket to glance at the screen. My heart does a jump when Tyler's name lights up inside a green box. I check again for my manager, Jesse. He's nowhere to be seen, so I slip out my phone and open the message. I'm sure college boy here won't mind.

TYLER: ::shrug emoji::

Nausea rolls through my stomach and my mind is ablaze with how to respond. He doesn't know if I'm riding with him or he's riding with me? Or is he saying he doesn't want to ride together? Or is he just saying he doesn't know now? Or is it he doesn't care? And just an emoji, really?

Maybe I shouldn't even respond. No, I shouldn't. *Leave him on read, Aidan. Leave him waiting for a response.* But what if that's too much, too obvious that it got to me? I should probably wait a little before replying at least.

AIDAN: OK.

I type it out and hit send before I can communicate with my hands to stop their stupidity. Argh! Looks like I'm riding alone.

TYLER

It takes under a minute for the reply to come back.

AIDAN: OK.

The tiny little part of me that wanted him to kiss me wants to reply back. It wants to say yes, you can ride with me. But the bigger part, the part that's been raging and screaming in my head since I got in my car Saturday night, says no, don't reply. And no, you're not letting him ride with you all the way up the mountain to Boone. You're not voluntarily going to be stuck in a car for almost an hour with him.

It's not like I deserve happiness anyway.

I stare down at the message another second, then swipe it from my screen and open Instagram instead. I just can't deal with this, so I don't. Instead, I swipe down my Insta feed, trying to focus on all the hotties I follow. What better way not to think about Aidan than focusing on a bunch of other chiseled jawlines, perfect six-packs, and brand-name underwear I couldn't care less about?

It doesn't work though. No matter who's on my screen I see Aidan. The way he leaned in. The way his eyes began to close the closer he got. I want it to stop. I need it to stop. Why can't I just hate him again? Hate him!

It can't happen. It's too soon, too quick. To let these…these feelings take over would be disaster. I'm not ready for it. I know what I told Kallie, but it's too soon. I was crazy to even think it. It'd be like cheating on Brayden, like forgetting we were ever something more than friends. He's my comet, was my once-in-a-lifetime, and I can't let go of that. But something in my chest won't let go of Aidan, and that's the problem. If I let him in, I'm going to hurt him. I know I will, because I can't do this.

I have to stop talking to him. I have to cut him off. But I can't just drop him. I have to see him Thursday at Kallie's, and the only way not to see him is not to go, and Kallie would kill me if I didn't show up. Why does this have to be happening now?

My phone buzzes, and a text from Aidan pops up at the top of the screen.

AIDAN: See you there I guess.

I throw my head back and sigh. God, this is going to suck. I want to text him back, but instead I fire one off to Kallie.

TYLER: Can't wait for the fireworks!

AIDAN

Monday, July 1

"Hold up, A!" Kallie yells from the exit doors.

I've been in my head all day, and to be honest I was hoping I could avoid this with her, so the moment my shift ended I darted. Guess it didn't work though.

I stop dead in the middle of the parking lot to let her catch up. I know what she's going to ask. She tried a few times while we were on the clock, but I kept shutting it down.

"Before you say anything, I know something's up. Spill it, bitch," she says right on cue.

I start walking and give her a long huff before saying anything. "I'm just ready to get home and write."

That last part is an outright lie. I tried writing last night. I thought it'd help get my head out of this funk, but apparently I can't when I'm stressed like this.

"Liar," Kallie says.

We stop at the tail end of my Mustang, and I fight the urge to just leave.

"Huh?" I ask.

"Don't huh me," she says. "You know what I mean. Something's up."

"I'm good." I fidget under each syllable.

"No, you're not." Kallie purses her lips and does the hip thing.

"I'm good. Promise," I lie again. I think I'm up to nine, maybe ten for the night.

I crack my neck like that's an absolutely normal thing I do and not a nervous tick. How the hell is it that I could stay in the closet until eighth grade without anyone questioning it but can't hold this back for three hours?

"You're a sucky liar, A. Spill it. Now," Kallie demands. The crazy part is it still manages to come out caring. I don't know how she does it.

"It's… Uh… It's stupid. Don't worry about it," I try again.

"Uh, well, now I'm really going to worry about it." She widens her eyes and shakes her head. "Something's bugging you, A. Let's hear it. I'm not leaving until you tell me."

"Then I'll just leave?" I say it like a question.

"Nope." Kallie grabs my arm. "Not letting go until you tell me. And I'll know if you're lying."

I don't know whether to hate or love her sometimes. Love her, obviously. But I could really go for hating her sometimes. And this? It all seems so stupid when I think about saying it out loud, so ridiculous. Boy falls for another boy. Other boy doesn't give a damn about said boy. Now boy is feeling stupid for falling for said boy and did something stupid.

"It's Ty," I tell her.

"What did he do? Do I need to kill him?" Kallie squints deviously. I think she's kidding on that last part. I think.

"No!" I yelp. A grin actually finds its way onto my lips. "No. It's just me."

"Thought you said it was Ty." Kallie looks confused.

"I did, but it's me too. Mostly me actually." I roll my eyes.

"Ah." The light bulb goes off. Although I'm about certain the light bulb went off in the store hours ago when she saw me checking my phone over and over again. She's just playing the part so I don't feel dumb. "Go on."

I drop my ass against my bumper and sigh. Here we go, I guess.

"It's just that… I don't know." I pause, and Kallie puts a hand on my shoulder and scoots next to me. "I like him. I really like him."

"I know," Kallie says softly.

"But he doesn't like me." I drop my eyes to the concrete and trace the thick white lines outlining the parking spot.

"How do you know that? Did he tell you he doesn't?" Kallie asks.

"No. I just know." I huff. "And to make it worse, I almost kissed him Saturday night when we were at the park. Like, I almost did it. I leaned in and everything. I thought maybe he didn't notice, but I'm certain he did now. He wouldn't talk to me yesterday. He's only texted me, like, once today, and it was a damn emoji."

"Oh. I see."

"I effed up, Kal. *I so effed up*," I say again with frustration. "I knew better. Why did I even start talking to him? I knew he hated me. I should have just left it alone."

"Because you're a good guy, Aidan. You wanted to be a friend. You wanted to help him get through this shit," Kallie reminds me.

My mind goes back to that night in the park when I found him crying. It was the first time in months I'd spoken to him, and he still hated me back then. She's right though. That's all I'd wanted — to help him. Just like I'd want someone to help me. I hadn't meant to fall for him. I swear it.

"Well, I'm shitty at it, because now I like him and it's all screwed up," I tell her.

"No, it's not," she says.

"Yeah it is, because he was talking to me. It was great. We were friends again, and I don't know, it was just great. But now I've scared him off," I tell her and shake my head violently like it'll make the past few months disappear. "He probably hates me again."

"He doesn't hate you," Kallie tells me.

"You sure about that? Did he tell *you* that?" I ask as matter-of-factly as I can.

"No, but I know Ty. He's never been great with how he feels. Even with Brayden it took him some time. And right now it's even worse. You know he blames himself, right?" Kallie asks.

"Yeah," I mutter. But he shouldn't. "I mean, I know, but it wasn't his fault."

"It wasn't, but he's convinced himself it is. I have to tell him it's not all the time. He tends to pull back when he starts to feel anything. He just sort of shuts down." Kallie frowns. "He always has, really."

I can tell it bothers her to see him like this. And I knew he hadn't dealt well with it, but I honestly thought he was more past it than this.

"But he doesn't like me anyway." I shake my head and swallow back the saliva gathering at the back of my throat. I can't really tell if it's more to remind myself or to make it hit home somewhere in Kallie's head.

"You sure about that?" She smiles.

"Yeah," I tell her. I try not to read into her smile. She knows him well, but I'm not stupid. "There's no way. I just have to stop trying."

"Well, I'm going to talk to him—"

"No!" I blurt. "He'll know I talked to you about it, and that'll just make things even more awkward if he ever does talk to me again."

"It's okay. I'm not going to call him and be like, 'Hey, so A wants to bone you.'" Kallie sticks out her tongue.

"So help me God, you say that, I'll disown you." I smile at her.

"There's my Aidan." She grins, and I roll my eyes, but I can't stop smiling.

"Shut up," I say.

"Just don't give up. I think you have a shot. I'm rooting for you." Kallie shrugs and looks off into the parking lot, past a few beaten up cars and an out of place Jaguar SUV. "I think you two would be great for each other."

Now I'm blushing and one hundred percent positive the streetlamp next to Kallie's Kia is showing off the shades of red brilliantly.

"Stop." I pooch my lips nervously and look away.

Kallie laughs at me.

"I'll have a talk with Tyler. I won't tell him we talked, and I won't be weird or obvious. I have my ways." She smirks deviously.

I look at her and smile. "Yes, you do."

TYLER

I wake up to the sound of "Mr. Sandman" by the Chordettes. It means Kallie is calling. She stole my phone back in tenth grade and set the ringtone herself. It's from, like, the fifties or something. She threatened to kill me if I ever changed it.

I grapple aimlessly for my phone, prying my eyes open in the process, and oh…she's FaceTiming.

"Ugh!" I groan at the same time as accepting the call.

"Morning!" Kallie yells.

"Quiet down, fool!" I complain.

"It's past ten," she says.

"What do you want? I was sleeping," I tell her. "Why are *you* up?"

"I'm up at the old place." Kallie moves her head so I can see the exposed wooden beams running along the ceiling and down the walls. It's an old cabin, sort of like my house but older. We have so many memories up there. Mostly playing with horse figurines, Hot Wheels cars, and running and screaming around the huge rolling hill the house sits on. "It's weird coming up here for the Fourth and you not being here."

"I haven't spent the night up there in years," I remind her. Since my dad can't accept I'm gay and that I have no inclination toward anything sexual with a girl, he stopped letting me spend the night when we hit eighth grade.

"Still. You used to come up the whole week. Okay, maybe not the whole week. You know, when you didn't cry and make your parents come pick you up." She smirks.

"I was a kid, thank you very much," I remind her.

"Once a bitch, always a bitch," Kallie says. She starts down the stairs and ends up outside. I can see the lake at the bottom of the property behind her flowing brown waves. "Did you ever manage to stay a full week?"

"I don't know," I tell her. It's too early to remember every time I ever went up there.

"Probably not," she exaggerates. "I can't wait for you to get up here though. We're going to roast marshmallows—"

"Which only you'll eat," I interrupt. I hate marshmallows. Like, ew, disgusting.

"—tell stories, watch fireworks out on big blankets. All of us! You, me, I'm assuming Bryce and Katie, and of course Aidan."

"Uh-huh," I grunt. There's something in the way she says it that gets my brain grinding into gear, but I let it go.

"Oh yeah, are you two riding up together?" Kallie asks, and she looks away at something, then back at the camera.

"Not sure yet," I grunt. Psyche. I'm completely sure we're not.

"Not sure?" she prods.

"Yeah," I say, pausing long enough to decide if I should fill her in a little. "I haven't really talked to him the last few days. He tried… Well, I mean, I *think* he tried to kiss me the other day at the park. He didn't. But he was about to."

The more I say it the more I wonder if I was imagining most of it. I mean, he didn't actually kiss me. And he didn't fully close his eyes, and that's what usually happens when you move in for a kiss, unless you're a psycho. He barely even leaned forward, actually. But he did, right? Yes, of course he did. Otherwise it wouldn't have been so weird after, and he wouldn't have suddenly needed to leave like he did.

"You two aren't talking, like, at all? How does that make sense?" Kallie asks. "You should have finished the job and kissed him yourself."

"Excuse me? No," I blurt. "The last thing I need right now is to catch feelings, I don't—"

"Too late for that," Kallie talks over me, but I ignore it.

"—need anyone holding me down, expecting to do shit, planning stuff all the time—"

"So you don't need me?" Kallie gives me a cursed glare.

"I didn't say that." I sit up defensively.

"Sounds like it." She isn't backing down. Ugh.

"No, I just don't need, like, you know." I shrug, not even wanting to say "a boyfriend".

"Oh, that." Kallie rolls her eyes, and it's just as overexaggerated as I've come to expect. "You're a stupid bitch sometimes."

"Uh, thanks?" I squint. I don't really know how to answer that, but I'm not backing down either.

"You like him. And don't tell me I'm wrong. I know I'm right. I can see it in your eyes every time you talk about him. Hell, I can see it now," she tells me.

"But that doesn't mean he needs to be my…you know," I say, not even trying to deny she's right.

"Again, stupid bitch. Text him. Tell him you two are riding up together," Kallie demands, and the look on her face is final. "Even if it's just as friends. You can do friends, right? You don't like him."

"What? No," I fight back.

"You can't just do friends, or no to riding up together?"

"Ah!" I growl. There is no reasoning with her when she gets like this.

"You know I'm right!" she says. "Do it. Text him. I expect you two to be in the same damn car when you get here."

I groan and huff. She's right. I want to. I still think it's a bad idea, even if I do want to, but who says I have to actually talk to the boy. Just ride up the mountain with him, that's it.

"Okay. Whatever," I give in. "But *just* friends."

"For now." Kallie beams in victory and my screen goes blank.

AIDAN
Wednesday, July 3

"You heard from Ty yet?" Kallie asks.

What's the use of even answering that question?

It's the first time since Kallie clocked in an hour ago that we've been able to talk. I've been here since eleven a.m., and the moment it hit noon, the store's been packed with bodies loading up on supersized packages of hot dogs and buns, beef and chili, and a surprising amount of beer.

"No," I say dryly.

"Seriously?" She eyes me while scanning a bag of chips.

"Yeah," I say. I mean, what did she expect? "I told you he wouldn't."

She called yesterday and filled me in on her little talk with Ty. I'm not going to lie, I got real excited. It's like I just knew he was going to text me that moment, and everything was going to be great and nothing was going to be awkward. But no. It didn't happen. He never texted. Actually, he hasn't texted since Monday, and well, it's Wednesday and we're all going up to Boone for fireworks tomorrow. *Tomorrow!*

"He promised he would," she says, her voice high-pitched. She fakes a smile at the woman in glasses she's ringing up to compensate as she scans yet another pack of beer. I'm not even keeping count anymore.

"Well, he didn't." I give her an I-told-you-so look.

Honestly, it's bugging me a lot more than it ought to. I knew this was going to happen. I've known it since the day I started having effing feelings for the idiot. I mean, it's my fault. Why did I even talk to him in the park back then anyway? I should have let him go on hating me all by his damn self. It's not worth the stress.

"But he promised me, and Ty keeps his promises," Kallie tells me as if it affects me somehow. "He's going to text you."

"I'll give him until tomorrow morning. If he doesn't by then I'm just going to ignore him after that," I tell her. I hate ultimatums, but hell, it's how I feel right now. Maybe she'll tell him that, and it'll do something. It's a stupid shot in the dark, but whatever. "I should ignore him anyway."

"Don't be like that, A," Kallie groans, and then switches back to customer service mode. I swear her whole voice changes and she becomes this completely separate person. It's almost schizophrenic. I'd even think she liked people if I didn't know her. "Ma'am, your total is eighty-four dollars and twenty-seven cents."

I wait for her to take the lady's money as I put the last bag in the cart, then she waltzes off. I answer Kallie as this balding guy in a Cowboys jersey steps up.

"I'm being like that." I give her a blank stare. "Not sure how showing up tomorrow and seeing him is going to go though. With him not talking to me and all. Maybe I just shouldn't."

"That's a big *no*. You're coming. Period." Kallie side-eyes me again. "It's not up for debate."

"He better text me then," I tell her. "Or at least not act like an ass tomorrow."

"Well, I'll beat his," she leans toward me and whispers, "ass if he doesn't."

"Good luck," I tell her.

The last thing I'm doing is holding out hope for that. Chances are

I'll end up driving there on my own and standing around awkwardly, avoiding him at all costs so I don't have to face how stupid of a situation I put myself in. But I am going regardless. Tomorrow isn't just about me, it's about Kallie and freedom and all that stuff. But she'll probably have to deal with us not talking.

Yay me.

TYLER

"See you Friday." I wave to Heather and Donald and start up my car.

It was a busy shift at the barbeque joint, and I reek of hushpuppies and grease again. And again, I'm heading across the street for Taco Bell with Kallie. I pull across the street and park. Yeah, Taco Bell is literally straight across the road.

Kallie's sitting in her little black Kia waiting for me when I park. Her hand's waving in the air behind her tinted windows, and she's looking at me like I did something wrong.

"Took you long enough," Kallie complains the moment she gets out.

"I worked until nine. I can't help that your boss is cooler and let you off early," I tell her.

We walk in and order.

"He's not that cool, believe me," Kallie tells me, not even a crack of a joke on her face. Guess not then. "I had to wait over here, like, half an hour."

"Poor little ol' Kallie," I fake whine.

My name is called, which means our food is ready, and we find a seat in the corner.

"Why haven't you texted him yet?" It comes out of nowhere.

"What?" I lean back, leaving my poor cheesy gordita crunch lying open and defenseless on the table.

"Aidan. You haven't text him yet," she says, leaning over the table. "I asked him if you two were riding up together or not, and he didn't know. Which can only mean you haven't texted him."

She glares at me. It was only a matter of time.

I had every intention of doing it when she called yesterday and basically guilt-tripped me into it, but then I got to thinking, and it's really such a bad idea. I was just hoping I could avoid this convo until after the Fourth of July shindig tomorrow.

"Oh, that," I sigh. "Yeah, no. I didn't."

"And *why?*" Kallie really stresses the why.

"I don't know. I just haven't." It's sort of a lie but not entirely. I mean, at first it was just like *maybe, maybe not,* but then it really became a *hell no* later in the day yesterday.

"Well, 'just haven't' turn it the hell around and text him," Kallie mocks me, and part of me is amazed at how she incorporated that. Like, it did and didn't make any sense at the same time.

"I don't—" I try.

"No, no." She puts a finger up to stop me. "You told me you were going to. You lying to me now? That what this is?"

Damn, Kallie. You're really taking this junk seriously. I'd almost think it was you who liked him.

"I just… You know… I…" I stutter all over myself. The last thing I want to do is admit I might, just might, have lied to her. I mean, it wasn't intentional. At the time I really meant it, even if it was through coercion, I did. My mind just changed before I could get myself to do it.

"Stop. Just stop." Kallie sighs, then smacks her lips the way she does when she's irritated, which means she's not playing around anymore. "You told me you'd text him and agree to come up with him. You know you like him—"

I open my mouth to speak, but she shushes me again.

"—so don't deny it. You're just being a scared little bitch. Yeah, I said it. Deal with it." She doesn't pull any punches. It actually hurts, it hits like a hammer in my chest. She means it. But I think what hurts most is I know she's right. I am scared. I am. "I want you to hear me here. You know I love you, so this is because I love you. Aidan likes you a lot, and he's a great guy. I know it's taken you a while to see that, but I know you know it."

She stops and lets it sink in. And yeah, she's right. I know he is. And maybe that's part of the problem. Maybe he's too good. I mean, I'm not a horrible person, but I'm not the best. I've done things I'm not proud of, and maybe he deserves someone better, maybe he deserves someone who isn't scared to death of letting their guard down.

I'm looking down, so it catches me off guard when her hands grip me.

"Text him," she says.

"I will," I whisper.

"No, I mean like now. Like right now." I catch her smirking.

"I can do it late—"

"No! Now. I want to see you do it."

I laugh, I actually laugh. It's such a Kallie move. I pick up my phone from the table next to my still untouched gordita. Why not? What's the worst that can happen?

"Okay." I open our text thread. The last message is from him on Monday. I read it again.

AIDAN: See you there I guess.

I suck in my lip nervously and push out a breath through tightly pursed lips.

"Come on," Kallie prods me, but her voice is different, more concerned than anything.

I type a quick concise message, no apology, none of that crap, just a quick question. But I let my finger hover over the Send button for a moment. I don't—

"Oh come on!" Kallie reaches over and slaps the Send button.

"What the?" My eyes dart up to her and then back down at the text I—she—just sent to Aidan.

TYLER: Still want to ride up to Kal's together?

"There we go," she says. "Now you're not a total bitch. Just a little bit of a bitch."

I give her my middle digit and smile, even if I'm horrified inside right now. I'm glad I did it—well, she did it. If I'm honest with myself I wanted to before, but I just couldn't bring myself to do it. But that doesn't change how scared I am inside.

"You're the bitch," I remind her, and she smiles like it's the greatest compliment a girl could ask for.

My phone buzzes, and Kallie's eyes light up.

"Yeah, yeah. It's him," I tell her. I'm excited that he replied and I wish he didn't at the same time.

AIDAN: Yeah.

It's not much, I think he's trying to play it cool, which I sort of admire.

TYLER: Riding with me?

The little bubbles pop up at the bottom of the screen.

AIDAN: Hell no. I'm driving.

At least he still has his sense of humor.

"What'd he say?" Kallie leans over the table to spy.

"He's driving," I tell her.

"Duh. No one's insane enough to ride with you up the mountain," she says.

"I hate you both."

AIDAN
Thursday, July 4

Okay, sure, Ty is talking to me again, but I'm still nervous. I mean it took Kallie getting involved for him to text me, and in a way that sort of feels cheap, like maybe I should have told her no. But I didn't, and honestly I don't think I could have made myself.

I steer down Setzer's Creek Road, winding down a hill encased in trees and field grass, my hands glued to the steering wheel. What if he's all quiet once I pick him up? What if he doesn't talk the entire trip up the mountain? Oh God, what if he doesn't even show up?

No. You're doing it again. Just be in the moment. He'll be there, and sure, it might be awkward, but it'll be all right. Just like Kallie said, it'll be all right.

I take a right onto the Collettsville Road, loop around this big open field, and the red tin roof of his family's log cabin comes into view to the left. I'm not going there. Ty's dad has a thing about him being picked up by other gay guys, even if they aren't dating, and he knows I'm gay. So instead, at Ty's driveway I take a right up the hill to Peterson Circle. It's where all of Kallie's family live. It's her, her parents, her grandparents, and I think like half her aunts, uncles, and cousins. Tyler is supposed to meet me at Kallie's house even though she isn't around.

I crest the hill, but there's nobody here. At the stairs leading up to Kallie's place I pull to the side and put it in park. I twist around, searching. I scan the swing on the other end of Kallie's house. No. Behind her grandparents' where their cars usually sit, their back patio.

No. Down by the old sandpit under the big oak tree farther down the drive. No.

I check my phone. *4:01 p.m.* Okay, I'm technically a minute late, so where is he?

AIDAN: I'm here. Where are you?

I stare at my phone, waiting for a response. No little bubbles. Nothing. I give it a little more time. More nothing. What did I say? He's not coming. It was all—

"Aidan!" Tyler slaps my window, and I about jump into the passenger seat.

"Damn you, Ty! You're going to break my window," I yell, clinging to the center console and cloth edge of my bucket seat.

He's grinning from ear to ear, bent over laughing. He puts his hand up, like I'm supposed to wait or something, then finally gets his composure enough to stand and make his way to the other side and gets in.

"I'm not going to break your window." Tyler smiles. "That was good though."

I put it in drive and start onto the main road.

"If you're trying to kill me before we get there, sure." I roll my eyes, still trying to get my breathing back to normal. He scared the hell out of me.

"You'll make it," Tyler says. He scoots around in his seat like he's uncomfortable; I think he just did the whole I'm-a-little-nervous-so-I'm-going-swallow-'cause-that-helps thing but with his butt.

It doesn't help for the record, but at the moment it makes me feel better, because unless I'm wrong, I'm not the only one who's got a bit of pent-up stress. So I'll take it.

"Or not. Maybe my heart is weak, and we just don't know it. Maybe one of these times it'll just give out and you'll be left there staring at my cold dead corpse," I suggest and immediately realize I shouldn't speak when I'm nervous.

"That got dark." He sighs, and I catch him pooching his lips from the corner of my eye. "So, uh, let's not do that?"

"Are you asking?" I glance at him and scoff sarcastically.

"I…well," he tries.

"Just kidding!" I roll my eyes and give him a smile.

"I knew that." He shrugs. As if.

"Right," I mock.

"I did. So, we going to listen to some real music since you won't let me drive?" Tyler switches the topic and insults me, and all within the first five minutes of our drive.

I don't even respond. Instead I unlock my phone, which is already hooked up to the car via Bluetooth, and hand it to him. He can do the rest. It just means my eardrums will have to recover from whatever hip-hop crap he puts on.

We hit the highway and our trek up the mountain really begins. It's one of those gorgeous scenic drives. It's the old rolling Blue Ridge Mountain range. It goes on for eternity like some sea of green. And with a sky barely dotted by clouds, it's going to be especially beautiful, even if it is almost ninety outside.

"So, what have you been up to?" I ask since he hasn't said too much since turning on the music, which has actually been a half-decent mix of some rock I can stand, like In This Moment and Shinedown. He's definitely compromising.

"Mainly video games and avoiding the house when I can," he says. "You?"

I haven't really done much, at least nothing worthy of his attention. I wrote, watched a bunch of TikToks—mainly Ty's—and stressed over how today was going to turn out.

"Just writing," is what I go with.

I want to make this trip easy, so I'm not taking any chances.

TYLER

Thursday, July 4

My marshmallow is on fire. Like, it's in flames.

"Shake it," Kallie laughs.

I do and after a few good shakes, it's out and charred. And charred is okay because I don't care how well done it is. I'm not eating it either way. I hate marshmallows. I think it's the consistency that gets to me. I just can't. However, being the only one in the group that doesn't like them means I have a stick for roasting too.

"Want it?" I aim the end of my stick at Kallie.

She looks at me like I'm doing something wrong, then nods subtly past me, and I immediately know what she's thinking. I mean, it can't hurt. It's stupid and I don't want to, but it can't hurt. I swing the puffy burnt ball over the fire and in front of the boy sitting to my right.

"You want it? I can't." I squirm on the halved log I'm sharing with Aidan, which was Kallie's doing. She's to my left on her own log with her blonde-headed cousin. Tammy, I think; I should know, it's not the first time I've met her, but I'm horrible with names. Across from us is Grace and Rhys, and then Bryce and Katie. The whole gang, plus one.

"Sure," Aidan says, smiling. He takes it and even peels off the nasty gooey leftovers. I look away. I can't watch. It's disgusting. "You don't like marshmallows?"

"Ew. They're nasty," I tell him.

"Even on s'mores?" he asks.

"Nope." I shake my head.

"It's depressing, isn't it?" Kallie laments.

She made me try them again last year, because supposedly your taste buds change every seven years, she says. Don't know if that's true, but she was determined. What I can say for sure is that my lack of appreciation for them hasn't changed one bit.

"I know, right?" Aidan says.

I roll my eyes and put another of the little puffy white rounds on my stick…for Aidan, I guess. I'll probably end up with a few more before it gets dark enough for fireworks.

"Are you two dating or something?" Bryce asks, still chomping down on a marshmallow.

"Uh, what?" My mouth is empty, but it suddenly feels like there's a cotton ball stuck in it.

"No!" Aidan does one better.

"Why would you say that?" I ask, glancing at Aidan and giggling in that way that unfortunately says I'm-nervous-as-fuck-right-now. But he does the same thing, so at least it's not just me.

"I…I just thought I'd ask," Bryce stutters. "You two have hung out a lot…uh…lately. And you rode together."

"Yeah, well I hang out with you a lot too," Aidan throws back at him. "Tyler's too young for me anyway."

Without thinking I sling my head around to face him.

"Huh?" I ask before my mind has time to compute how not to react. "I'm only like a year, year and a half younger than you."

"He likes older guys," Kallie says. "Smart."

"What can I say?" Aidan glances at me for a moment, then looks away.

"I hear you," Grace says. "Mhmm. Ryan Reynolds or Christian Bale."

"Chris Evans," Katie continues. "Oh, and Jensen off *Supernatural*."

"Yes! And don't forget some Tom Hardy," Kallie finishes it off.

"Okay, you are talking a little older than I am." Aidan calms them down with a raised hand.

"Oh my God." Rhys puts his face in his hands. "This is not the conversation I want to be having."

Laughter bubbles up around the fire, but my head is still trying to wrap itself around me being too young for Aidan. Have I been misreading him? Or was I imagining it all?

Oh God, now I'm questioning everything.

"You're more a Tom Holland and TikTok boy type of guy," Kallie teases him.

"I won't deny that," Aidan grins, glancing at me again.

"Ooh, Tom Holland. Now he's hot," I dive in.

"How's the college stuff going?" Rhys glares at Aidan.

I giggle a little. He deals with a lot being friends with two gays and our BFFs. I'll give him that.

"It's going. Supposed to get my dorm assignment this week, and orientation is in, like, two weeks," Aidan tells him.

"Cool. Where are you going?" Tammy asks.

She's a lot like Kallie, except a little heavyset, with dyed blonde hair, much-too-thick makeup, and a personality between Kallie's and Grace's. Actually, come to think of it, she's not that much like Kallie.

"UNC Charlotte." Aidan nods, and I can see the excitement in his eyes.

"What's your major?" Tammy keeps going.

"Nursing. Hopefully." He shrugs.

"Hopefully?" She tilts her head.

"Got to do pre-nursing first, then I can apply to get into the nursing program after that," he tells her.

"Oh wow. I didn't know it was that complicated," she says.

"Yeah, but he's going to do great," Kallie tells her. "And he's going to play soccer for them too! So get ready to watch them kick some ass this year!"

"Stop!" Aidan waves her off.

"Oh, y'all are going to wipe the floor with some of those other teams," I tell him.

He rolls his nut-brown eyes at me and shakes his head.

Our conversation continues all over the place. There's a quick sad note that we all try to glaze over about Aidan leaving us all for Charlotte. Rhys is hoping to buy a cheap car before school starts again because he can't wait to confuse everyone with his country music blaring through the school parking lot. Grace is thinking about joining the swim team at Hibriten.

An hour passes and the sun makes its final bow for the night, letting the stars and clouds take over the shift. The family cannon booms, announcing the show is about to begin.

"That thing scares me *every* time," Aidan laughs.

The three of us sprawl out on our backs atop a thick *Toy Story* comforter. It's the one with a huge Buzz Lightyear covering it that I brought up a few years ago on one of the weekends I was supposed to stay the night and ended up leaving.

"Every. Damn. Time." I cup my face in both hands.

It's so loud, not quite ear-shattering loud, but loud. And it's homemade. Her family made it years ago, and they fire it off all day every hour before the firework show each year. I can't remember if this was one of those myths or not, but I think Kallie said her dad and uncles stuff it with old underwear as the projectile. I've never watched, so I don't really know.

"Bunch of pussies." Kallie shakes her head. "You know it's coming."

"Yeah, but, like, I don't at the same time," I say. "You know?"

"Exactly." Aidan props himself up on one shoulder so he can see Kallie and me at the same time. "I know it's coming. But I don't know exactly when, so it still gets me."

"It would still get you even if I told you before it went off, A," she giggles.

She's right. It would. I think I'd fare a little better, but Aidan? Nope.

"She's got a point," I back her up.

"You both suck, you know that, right?" He grins and lies on his back.

"But we're the best." Kallie puffs her chest.

"Uh, somehow yes," Aidan groans.

The crazy part is that includes me. I mean, he didn't explicitly exclude me, so it does, right? It's stupid, but it sort of makes me really happy. I stare up into the sky and trace the stars, building my own constellations out of any stars I damn well want to. I'll call it…Aidan. That's so stupid. Ugh.

"We should be able to see Breegge in, like, a week." It's random, but it's what comes to mind.

"Yeah. They're saying July fourteenth now," Aidan says. "I can't wait."

I don't think I've ever seen a comet with the naked eye before. It's not a super common thing, like shooting stars or seeing Jupiter cross the sky. And this is a special one, so I'm not missing it.

I was thinking it was the twelfth, but maybe it isn't. "Sweet—"

"Oh! I about forgot. My parents want to take us to Carowinds at the end of the month," Kallie interrupts.

"And by us, you mean…?" I ask. Her and me? Her, me, and Aidan? Or the whole lot of us here today?

"You, Aidan, and me." She bobs her head like she's tapping each of us on the head.

"I'm sure they *want* to take us all." Aidan grins.

"Well, I might have begged." Kallie wrings her shoulders. "Don't tell the others. I couldn't get Dad to agree to more people than just us."

"Promise. Do you know when?" Aidan asks, and I swear he glances at me.

"I think it was, like, the twenty-second or so." Kallie squirms. "I'll find out."

"I just need a week's notice," I tell her.

"Same." Aidan nods. "Hopefully James won't mind us both being off again in the same month."

"James will have to deal with it," Kallie answers back.

I'm about to ask who the hell James is, but someone off in the field starts yelling that the fireworks are beginning, so I shut up.

"Here we go." Kallie wiggles excitedly.

"Bring it!" I shout, which gets a laugh out of Aidan.

A high-pitched squeal announces the first rocket, followed by an ear-popping boom and a brilliant burst of red and green. Then another and another. All colors, shapes, and sizes. All the crazy noises you can imagine, and all the *oohs* and *ahs* you'd expect. It's better than any local city's fireworks show, all courtesy of a bunch of good ol' country boys who love to play with fire.

Out of the corner of my eye, I can see the round tip of Aidan's nose light up with each burst. I know it's stupid, but I want to look, I want to see his reaction to each explosion. Something in me wants to know if he smiles when they burst into thousands of little glimmering sparkles, or if he flinches at the booms.

I tilt my head and look as a purple explosion brightens the sky above us and casts a flickering lavender glow on his face. He glances at me. My mouth opens in shock and I throw my gaze back to the sky. I want to close my eyes, clench them shut, and never open them again. But I can't appear that guilty. Even if I am.

Instead I cough away the nerves when the next firework screams into the sky, leaving a trail of sparks and smoke climbing the stars. It feels like he's still looking at me, but I'm not about to check.

It's just my nerves, that's all. That's all it is.

AIDAN

Monday, July 15

Our student orientation guide is this way-too-peppy redhead chick in black skinny jeans and a forest-green t-shirt with *CHARLOTTE* stamped in big bold white letters across the front over *NINER NATION* in gold. I think her name is Tara, but she's rattled off so much information about every building we pass I'm not so sure now.

"Is that where you'll be spending your time?" Mom points at the building where we just turned around, the one Tara called Fretwell.

"I don't know." I shrug.

"She said they did science in there, right?" Mom asks.

"Oh." It hits me why Mom thinks I'm going to be stuck in that particular building my entire college career. "No, *political* science, it's a little different."

"Oh." Mom nods.

The campus feels massive, like it never ends. Every square foot is filled with another three- or four-story building, some mammoth statue, or decorative red brick paths next to perfectly manicured lawns. I snap a picture in the middle of an open field of this huge statue of this dude hammering a stake into some rock and text it to Tyler. I think this dude is a miner—our mascot is Norm the Miner, after all— but I'm not one hundred percent certain.

Things with Ty have been good since the Fourth. He's talking again, and I'm being careful not to do anything stupid. The only problem has been work. Our schedules have sucked. If I'm not at work, he is at work, and if I am at work, he isn't. We've only been able to hang out a few times, like last Saturday night at the park when we finally got to see the comet without a telescope for the first time. It was so small, but it was there, and it was magnificent.

"To your left is where the Belk Tower used to stand," Tara calls back from the front of the line. "It was this huge cigarette-looking monstrosity before they tore it down. And just ahead is Atkins Library."

"Are you paying attention?" Mom asks.

"Yeah," I say and pocket my phone.

We're supposed to visit my residence hall after the tour and class registration. That's the part that sort of scares me about all of this. I knew I was coming here. I've known this is going to be home for a while, but something about getting ready to see the building I'll be living in for months is making it all settle in the closer it gets.

It means I'll be two hours away from home, away from Mamá and mi abuelos. But it also means I'll be away from Tyler. And maybe that's not a bad thing. Maybe that's actually best. Maybe that's just another reason I shouldn't let myself get attached.

TYLER

I keep forgetting how many comic posters Aidan has in his room. There's a bunch.

One whole wall is lined with them. There's this cool one of Venom with his long tongue curled all over the poster, a few Spider-Man renditions, a Thor and Captain America, a Groot, and one of Black Widow and Hawkeye.

The next wall is darker. It starts off with one of Batman holding a dead Robin, a Harley Quinn and Joker, then one of Flash next to an unusually big painting of this magician lady that honestly reminds of Symmetra from *Overwatch*. I think the character is Zatara though. She's Aidan's favorite DC superhero. He's such a nerd.

It's our usual Saturday evening to go to the park, but Aidan had to work a little later, and I was bored, so I came to his house a little early. Which means I'm walking around his room by myself while he's in the bathroom showering and changing out of his work clothes.

Breegge's been visible for days now, and she just keeps getting bigger and brighter and more amazing. I still think it's sort of crazy that we can just look up, and there she is. Like, it's become more real now, there's literally this giant ball of frozen gas, rock, and dust hurtling by us at hundreds of thousands of kilometers per hour.

And I won't tell A this, but I'm glad he's sticking around to watch it with me. I know Kallie would, but it's not the same, and she doesn't quite see what's cool about it either. She just sort of looks at it and says something like, "Okay, that's cool," and then she's bored.

The door creaks open and Aidan walks in wearing nothing but a pair of khaki shorts and his tan boat shoes. I glance at his taut stomach and look away as quickly as I can. Got to stop that.

"You ready?" Aidan asks, as if he's even ready.

"Been ready the last twenty minutes," I remind him. "You do realize you're a nerd, right?"

"Huh?" He furrows his brow.

I point at the walls. "These. Nerd."

"Oh yeah. Of course. You knew that," he laughs.

"I just wanted to remind you," I tell him. "And Groot? Really? That's pushing it. Plus, if we're nerding out, where's Star Trek?"

"You need to shut up before I kick you out." Aidan grins and finally slips on a gray t-shirt. I shake my head when I see what's plastered on the front of it. *I PAUSED MY GAME TO BE HERE.*

"Oh my God," I laugh.

"Suck it!" He sticks out his tongue. "Let's go."

I follow him down the hall and through the living room, say goodbye to his mom, and head out to my car. It's too warm tonight to enjoy the top being down, so I keep it up as we drive for some food before the park.

"Did you know today is the fiftieth anniversary of the first moon landing?" Aidan asks. He's scrolling through his phone, so I'm not sure if he already knew or if he just happened to see it.

"Nope," I say. "Was that Apollo 11?"

It's one of the side effects of knowing Brayden for any bit of time. It wasn't just comets and stars he was fascinated with. Of course the first moon landing had come up once or twice…or more.

"Yeah. Apparently NASA celebrated today by meeting the president in the Oval Office and talked about getting us back on the moon by 2024." Aidan sounds excited about that.

It is a cool idea. The thought of people walking up there on the moon we see every night. It almost seems too cool to be possible, but it is, it's been done.

"Awesome! Seems like a long way away though," I say.

"Eh, it's not that bad," Aidan says at the same time my phone starts ringing on its little platform just below my center dash. It's Kallie. She's FaceTiming again. This is at least the third time today.

"You know I have to answer this." I smirk at him, flashing the phone at him.

"Yeah." He grins back, and before I have a chance, he accepts the call for me. It's probably safer that way anyway.

Kallie's face comes on the screen. It looks like she's ready for bed and it's not even nine o'clock. She's wearing this pair of black pajama bottoms and a draping gray t-shirt, and she's got no makeup on.

"Hey bitch," she says.

"Hey," I say back and then aim the phone at A so she knows he's listening.

"A!" she screams. "So that's why you left work in such a hurry."

Aidan rolls his eyes and throws her a quick middle finger, which she smiles at gleefully.

"Ha ha," Aidan says, sarcastic as fuck. "What do you want?"

"So angry." Kallie does this eye fluttering thing like she's surprised by the response. "I have deets on our Carowinds trip."

"Finally!" I say. I've been waiting to hear what the plan was for days. "Spill it!"

"The weather is supposed to be nice, but Mom said they're calling for a little rain maybe in the evening, so just be prepared for that," Kallie says. "But I did get them to let us drive separately."

"Thank the genies!" I exhale. That was my main request. Her parents are fine and all, but I don't want to listen to crappy music all the way down to Charlotte. Not for two whole hours.

"You're welcome." Kallie sneers. "I told them we'd take your car, and either Aidan or I would drive, as long as it wasn't you."

"Ooh, burn." Aidan frowns at me.

"Not nice." I pout, pulling us into the Cook Out drive-thru so we can get something quick before the park.

"Oh my God, A. I just realized you're letting Ty drive." Kallie throws her hands over her face.

"Living on the edge," Aidan says.

I roll my eyes.

"Praying for you." Kallie does a mock Hail Mary. "So yeah, just make sure to get lots of snacks and drinks so we can gorge ourselves all the way down and back. I'm talking diabetic coma levels here."

"Got it. I'll have a bag full of Reese's and Nutty Buddies." Aidan does this little happy head dance.

"I'll bring a bunch of Doritos, a humongous bag of Skittles—rainbow of course. And let's see…" I pooch my lips in thought as we move up a space in line. One more and I'll be ordering. "Maybe some Kit Kats?"

"Yes! Kit Kats." Aidan nods.

"'Kay, and I'll get the drinks. So, what? Dr. Pepper and Cheerwine?" Kallie suggests.

"What else would we drink?" Aidan asks.

"Exactly," I agree. "I guess you have a big cooler or something, Kallie?"

"Oh…" Kallie looks away from the camera. "No, I thought you did. You know that one we used at Wilson's Creek?"

"Well, yeah, but it's not big enough for all that shit," I tell her.

"I have a few. I can bring them too," Aidan promises.

I smile at him. That's what I'm talking about. Problem solver.

"Perfect. Sounds like a plan," Kallie says.

"Oh, and I'm spending the night with you tomorrow still, right?" I ask.

This one took some convincing on my parents' side. Dad still doesn't get why it's not a bad idea for me to spend the night with Kallie. I swear he's convinced himself that every time I go up there I'm trying to "get some," and staying overnight apparently crosses the line for him. I begged Mom though, and she finally got him to change his mind.

"Yeah, that's still a go here," Kallie confirms.

The car ahead of us pulls up and I start toward the ordering speaker.

"Sounds great!" I tell her. "Gotta go, we're about to order."

A I D A N

Monday, July 22

It's been cloudy all day, but at least it's not too hot. It's basically the perfect conditions for being stuck in line for the Intimidator.

"God! I wish this line would move," Kallie complains.

"Same!" I nod. There's no need to say anything. This is what we've been doing since before noon when we got here. It's what you do at Carowinds. Wait, and wait some more.

"Maybe we should ride the drop tower next, the line looked a lot shorter," Tyler suggests.

"That's because people aren't stupid enough to ride it." I glare at him, and then switch quickly to a grin.

"Calling me stupid, eh?" He looks serious, but a smile breaks the hard lines for a moment before going all serious again.

"Yeah." Kallie steps in to save me, which is so her. "I'm not getting on that thing. I want to keep my legs and my lunch."

"Your stomach isn't that weak, you can deal with it," Tyler tells her.

"But I'm not going to." Kallie shakes her head.

The lines moves again. The coaster must have stopped at the station and unloaded.

"How many more rounds until you think it'll be us?" I ask.

"I don't know, there's a lot of people," Tyler says.

The line stops again, and I still can't see inside the building housing the Dale Earnhardt-themed rollercoaster. Yeah, we're that far.

"We *might*, just might get on before the park closes." Kallie rolls her eyes.

"We better," I complain. I might be quiet most of the time, but oh my, I'd be so mad if it took that long. "I hear this one's good."

"It can't be better than that bee one," Tyler says.

Bee one?

"Bee one?" Kallie takes the words out of my head.

"Yeah, the…" Tyler struggles. He grunts and throws his head back in frustration.

"You mean the Fury?" I ask.

He bounces his shoulders. "Maybe."

Kallie and I laugh. I'm pretty sure it's the Fury, that's the only one I know that had anything to do with a bee—a hornet, actually. Supposedly it's the highest drop on the East Coast and one of the fastest, maybe *the* fastest. And damn, was it exciting. Like, literally stuck-to-the-seat exciting.

"It was so fast!" I say. "Absolutely insane."

Half an hour later I'm unbuckling myself and stumbling off the Intimidator. It was all right, but not worth standing in line that long and having my shins beat to death the entire ride.

"What did you think?" Tyler asks.

"Eh, it was okay." I shrug as we take the stairs down to the walking paths and merge into the crowd.

"I swear it felt like I was coming out of the seat a few times." Tyler shivers. "Not a fan of that."

"Yes! So not a fan!" Kallie goes wide-eyed.

"Can't say I had that problem," I laugh.

We start off in no particular direction, weaving between families and kids, and more kids. I don't think we've seen Kallie's parents but once the entire time we've been here. We took off on our own the second we arrived. But the sky was a little clearer then, and now the clouds are dark and heavy, heavier even than when we got on the Intimidator. They're practically teasing us.

"It looks like rain, guys." I purse my lips. The weather forecast didn't call for rain until later, and it better not be until later.

"I'm going to choke the weatherman if we have to leave early," Tyler claims.

"He might like that though." Kallie sighs.

"I mean…" I purse my lips and smirk, just to make it uncomfortable.

"Okay, let's just stop right there." Tyler fake gags and acts like he's going to vomit.

"So dramatic," I laugh.

"Hey, let's grab a drink and some funnel cakes." Kallie pulls us to the side and up to one of the little concession stands. We each get a drink and one funnel cake to split between the three of us, and Kallie pays with her parents' money.

We settle down on a bench next to the food stand and watch people go by. We see every shape and color, every manner of dress you can imagine, but mostly summer appropriate. There are shorts, short shorts, a surprising number of people in full-length pants, and I even see one woman in a skirt, which really surprises me. Hats of all kinds litter the crowd, along with a few hijabs, and every graphic tee imaginable, plus a few polos.

"What's your favorite ride?" Tyler asks me.

"Definitely the Copperhead," Kallie speaks up.

"Uh, I didn't ask you," he tells her, like it's so obvious, and she just smiles back. Tyler rolls his eyes before returning to me.

"I don't know." I shrug and inhale another piece of sugary white funnel cake. I'm going to be in sugar overload by the time I slip into bed tonight. "Maybe the Vortex or the Nighthawk."

"The Vortex?" Tyler gives me his best surprised look. "You mean the ball buster?"

He sort of has a point. It's this stand-up rollercoaster with a bike seat-type thing supporting you and a big harness over your shoulders to keep you upright while your feet dangle. If you don't adjust the seat right, downstairs gets a beating.

"I mean, well, if you don't set your seat up right, maybe," I argue.

"No, it's always a ball buster," he corrects me. He sort of has a point, but it's not that bad.

"Just think how it does me," Kallie complains.

"No. No. Don't need that image, fuck no." Tyler closes his eyes and throws his hand between us.

"Such a pussy." Kallie shoves him. "I'm not going into detail."

"Thank you," I chime in, and Tyler gives me a silly grin.

"The Nighthawk is—" Tyler stops.

"It's wha—" I do the same. Something wet splashes my nose, and then another and another.

"Hell, it's starting to rain." Kallie jumps up and cradles the funnel cake under her chest like a newborn baby and starts to walk off.

"Obviously." I get up and chase after her.

"It's not supposed to be bad, right? Just, like, a sprinkle?" Tyler asks.

"That's what they said yesterday, but it was supposed to be later too," Kallie says, like the weatherman ever gives an exact forecast.

I grab for the last piece of the funnel cake and break it in two before Kallie can gobble the whole thing down in an attempt to save it. I hand a piece to Tyler and stuff the other in my mouth.

"It's not bad," I comment, looking around the crowd of people. No one really seems to care about it that much. "Let's just find another ride."

"'Kay," Kallie says, and we start off again.

We pass through Camp Snoopy and a slew of kiddie rides, and the rain dies down for the most part.

"How about the Afterburner?" I suggest, pointing at a sign just ahead.

"You mean the Afterburn," Kallie corrects me.

I check the sign again. Well then, guess there isn't an "er" on the end. It sounds more awkward without the "er" though.

"Whatever, that one." I shake my head.

We start up the hill, but Mother Nature has other plans. It's like the clouds all at once lose their will to hold back the tears in their fluffy gray folds. The rain crashes down. I'm soaked within seconds and trying to figure out what to do.

"What the hell?" Tyler shouts.

"Let's find cover," Kallie yells and takes off.

Tyler and I glance at each other and then take off after her. We jog through the rain looking for cover, but there are so many people here, and all the shops and gazebos are already crammed to the edge with bodies. We keep running, but I start laughing. It's just absurd. Us, the three of us, running through the middle of this huge park in the rain. And it actually feels good. It's cool against my skin and something about it is just right.

Kallie slows down and we catch up.

"There's nowhere to hide," Kallie complains, and lucky for her she didn't bother with makeup today.

"Fuck it." Tyler throws his hands up and laughs. "This feels awesome!"

"It really does!" I yell over the pounding droplets.

I step back a few and do a stupid little dance in the rain, and let myself glance at Tyler to see if he's watching. He is, which causes me to keep dancing. I spin around stupidly. I don't know how to dance, but I don't care until it hits me that it's not just us in the rain. There are tons of people packed under cover around us, staring, judging me. I stop and clench my fists, wrapping them around my waist with my head down. Why did I do that?

"Hey," Tyler shouts in the softest way he can over the droning torrent.

I look up and his hand is stretched out to me, waiting for me to take it. What is he doing?

"Come on." He smiles, his hand unwavering.

I can't move. There's no way he wants to do what I think he's wanting to do…right? We're in the middle of the park.

But something deep down in my soul overrides the fear in my chest, and I reach for his hand. I let his fingers lace between mine, and he pulls me toward him. His hand is warm compared to the cool drops coating my body, but my fingers still tingle. My body presses against his, and reflexively I pull away.

"Dance with me," he says softly.

"I… uh…" I stutter.

Tyler smiles. It's beautiful and I want to so bad, but I can't dance. He's the dancer.

"It'll be okay," Tyler insists gently.

"Do it, Aidan!" Kallie shoves me forward.

My chest collides with him again, but this time I don't repel back. He wraps me up in his arms and all at once we're dancing in the rain together. We're actually dancing, like some fairy tale, complete with the rain tumbling in slow motion around us, light shimmering off every droplet. I don't ever want him to let go. It's amazing and crazy and funny all in the same instant. I giggle, which gets him giggling too, and he looks away coyly.

"See? This isn't so bad," Tyler says.

He takes my hand, which was doing nothing but hanging at my side, and spins me away dramatically, then reels me back in. In that moment, while I'm spinning and the world moves around me, I see others doing the same thing, not worried about the water, not worried about how they look or what people think, not worried about anything but the person they're dancing with.

It's freeing. It's beautiful. I stop spinning and collapse back into Tyler's embrace.

"Like this," he tells me, placing my hand on his waist. "Just move with me."

He wraps his arm around me again and lays his palm on my lower back, pulling me even closer. I look up and he stares into my eyes, like he's been waiting this entire time to see me. I give him the smallest smile, and we saunter between crowded buildings and goliath roller coasters and spin under the trees and crazy decorations, all with the rain pelting our heads. But I don't notice any of it. All I see is this boy, this beautiful, sweet boy who's looking right back at me, and in the moment that's all that matters.

The longer I look into his eyes, the more I want this moment in time to last forever. God, they're so mesmerizing. I've never given myself the opportunity to stare unabashedly into his eyes like this, and it's worth every second. Not only is there a ring of gold around them, there are tiny little flecks of gold intermingled in the green, like this magical fairy-tale globe.

His hand moves at my waist and for a second I think he's letting go. I can't let this end. I don't want this to stop. I lean in, and I refuse to stop this time. Our lips touch, and an explosion of heat and electricity I've not felt in a long time rushes through my body. It feels like forever, him and me, no rain, no curious eyes, no earth or sky. Just us.

"Guys!"

Tyler jerks back at the sound of Kallie's voice.

"Huh?" I step back, taking my arms back and putting a few steps between us.

"Guys!" She keeps yelling it.

"What?" I ask, suddenly too aware of what just happened, and all the people watching, and the rain pouring over my face.

"That was *so* sweet!" She jumps and sways and claps in the rain like it was the best show in the entire world. And maybe it was.

I look at Tyler, and he won't meet my eyes. No, not this again. Not this. I'm not letting it be this again. I grab his hand and pull him closer. Finally, his beautiful eyes find me. I know what I want to do, but I don't want to scare him.

"You okay?" I ask.

"Yeah." He grins and nods spastically.

I think it's sinking in.

"'Kay." I grin back. "We good?"

"Of course," Tyler laughs.

"Good," I say, relieved, and pull him in for a hug. I give him a little excuse, "It's warmer like this."

I feel him nodding his head against my shoulder, water rolling down our bodies.

"Yeah."

He squeezes me, and I don't think I could want anything more than this.

TYLER

Monday, July 22

The weather is insane.

An hour ago, I was dancing in a total torrential downpour in the middle of a theme park, and now I'm riding shotgun in my own car up I-85 with the top down and clear skies. They still won't let me drive.

And I still can't believe I danced in the rain with Aidan. I don't know what came over me. The crazy part is that I'm glad I did it, and he kissed me. He kissed me. And I'm not totally freaking out about it.

"Can we listen to something that doesn't destroy my ears?" Kallie yells from the back seat.

"What was that?" I yell back. I heard her.

"Can we listen to something else?" she screams over the wind and music.

"You want to listen to 'Feral'?" Aidan yells.

"'Feral'?" Kallie questions.

I squeeze Aidan's hand on the center console. He takes his eyes off the road long enough to smile at me. I think I know what he's talking about, and it's no doubt not what she wants.

"Yeah, Bad Omens," he says.

"Fuck no!" Kallie yells. *"No rock!"*

"That's no fun!" I turn and grin at her. "How may we please the queen?"

"That's better. A compromise. How about some Posty?" Kallie suggests. "'Goodbyes' maybe?"

I can deal with that. But why make it easy for her? She is in the back seat after all. Driver gets to choose, and shotgun is at least second choice, maybe with some veto power.

"What do you think, A?" I shout over the wind crashing through my hair, destroying any style all the rollercoasters hadn't already. It's one of the downfalls of not keeping it short.

"Why not," he says. I start looking for the song on my phone, which is connected to his makeshift Bluetooth transmitter. "But it's 'Feral' after that."

"Whatever." Kallie rolls her eyes. "So… Are we going to talk about it?"

I find the Post Malone and start up "Goodbyes".

It? There really isn't anything to talk about, but it's the way she said it that puts an uncomfortable feeling in my stomach. I push it away. This is good. This is okay. This is what I want. I think. No, it is. Fuck my fears and insecurities. This is good. And that kiss. Damn.

"What's there to talk about?" I twist around and stare at her.

Kallie thrusts her shoulders upward. "I don't know. I mean…you know. You two? Holding hands? That kiss in the rain?"

"Ah, that." I nod and look to Aidan. I think I know what I want to say, but I wonder what he would say.

He glances at me and gives me a nervous smile, then throws his eyes back to the road, where they need to be. They'd be screaming at me if I took my eyes off the road for a second.

"I don't know." I tilt my head and try to get comfortable contorted around in my seat, while not letting go of A's hand. "I mean, we kissed."

"Yeah, but you two… You know, didn't like each other?" She says it like it's a question.

I open my mouth to say something, but I don't know what to say. She's right. I didn't like him, maybe I really didn't like him, but things are different now. I guess I've liked him for a while actually, but I don't know, I just couldn't. God, why is it different now? No. I'm not going to do that.

"Yeah," is what I decide on. "But I guess he's not so bad after all."

"I'm not that bad? Or I'm not bad period?" Aidan asks without looking away from the road.

I squeeze his hand and fight back a sudden nervous tick in my throat. It's harder to talk about and to rationalize than it was to kiss him in the park.

"Not bad period," I say and look down. God, I've been a dick. And why? Because I was jealous. That's all it was. Jealousy. Stupid jealously.

"So that's that?" Kallie asks, eyeing me with wide eyes.

"Yeah, that's that. Right, A?" I shoot him the question.

"That's that." He grins, and I catch him nibbling on his lip.

The taste of his lips rushes through my mind again, and I can feel every sway of his body under the downpour. It brings another smile I can't hold back.

"Okay." Kallie wiggles.

"Okay." I grin back at her.

"Okay," Aidan joins in like it's required. "Now can you get me a Dr. Pepper?"

"Uh, yeah. Hold up." Kallie shakes her head like she thinks there should be more to this but isn't going to push it, which is honestly surprising. She leans over to dig into the cooler anyway.

The music fades and I switch it over to the Bad Omens song Aidan wanted earlier. The speakers blare and Kallie looks up at me with her resting bitch face and rolls her eyes.

"Oh fuck!" she screams as the lid to the cooler flips up, caught in the wind, and flies out the back.

My eyes go wide as it spins in the air and crashes into the pavement. It bounces and twists, jumping like it's playing hopscotch across the interstate. The car behind us jerks to the right, barely missing it.

"Oh God!" I yell, ducking like somehow that'll keep me from being seen.

"Did we kill someone?" Aidan yells. "Please say we didn't kill someone!"

I check again. The lid is finally motionless on the edge of the road, and my heart settles now that there isn't a ten-car pileup behind us.

"Nope," I tell him. "All good. But oh my God, Kal!"

"I'm sorry, I didn't mean to," Kallie yells back. She's still ducked down like I was. "Are they looking? Aidan, speed up! Come on, faster!"

"I'm not speeding up because you just about murdered someone with a damn cooler lid!" he yells back, and something about the way he says it gets me laughing.

"It's not funny!" Kallie screams.

"Yes, it is!" I bend over the seat, pressing against the seatbelt, trying to calm myself down. Aidan starts laughing though, and now there's no hope of stopping.

"Good job, Kal," Aidan laughs.

She rolls her eyes, but by the time I look back she's laughing too.

I mean, we about committed interstate murder by cooler lid.

AIDAN

Tuesday, July 23

I knew it was too good to be true. It's always too good to be true.

I stuff a third box of cereal into an already full plastic shopping bag. It rips, and I have to stop to keep the stress from spilling out of my mouth in front of the customer.

"You okay?" Kallie asks, still ringing them up.

"Yeah, good," I spit out, trying to get myself together and re-bag the cereal without destroying everything this time.

"You sure?" she asks again. "The bags says otherwise."

"I'm good," I say, a little more aggressively than I mean to, trying to make eye contact without making it obvious I'm not okay.

Tyler's ignored me all day. I thought we were okay. Hell, I thought we were better than okay, I thought we were great, that we were, you know, a thing. But it looks like I was wrong. I should have expected it. But I didn't want to think it could happen, not after yesterday.

I texted him this morning before work to say good morning, but he didn't reply. So I texted again asking how his day was going. You know, like couples do, right? He didn't respond. I waited a few hours, and Snapped him a random picture of Kallie behind the register. That was, like, four hours ago and he still hasn't opened it.

My whole body is tense. I feel it in my arms, and my stomach is churning. How does it go from amazing to zero so quick? How can everything be so perfect one moment and the very next I'm literally sick with worry? I know it takes him a lot to feel, and I know he didn't like me a lot before, but I thought once he let me in it would be enough.

Am I not enough?

I pack the last bag and drop it into the customer's cart. I grab my phone and check my SnapChat and texts. Nothing. So I text him again.

AIDAN: I hope I didn't scare you. Sorry about the kiss. Please text me.

Kallie hands the customer their receipt, and the moment they walk off and the coast is clear, she props her ass against the register and stares me down.

"What's up?" Kallie purses her lips. "And if you say nothing, I swear I'll hit you."

I want to come back with something witty, something funny, but my mind isn't working like that right now. It's a turbulent sea of confusion and stress.

Instead, I flinch.

"I swear, I'll hit you. Don't test me," Kallie says.

A tiny grin lifts across my face despite the way my heart weighs me down.

"It's Ty," I tell her.

"What the fu… What did he do?" She quiets down a little.

I scratch my neck and look away. He didn't *do* anything. That's the problem.

"Nothing," I whisper.

"Nothing? Then what's the problem?" She's confused.

"No, I mean, that's the problem," I tell her. "I texted him this morning before work, and he won't respond. I Snapped him a few hours ago and he hasn't even checked it. And I know he's seen the texts."

"Oh." Kallie pops out her lips. "I see."

"Yeah. Has he talked to you?" I ask. I know I shouldn't ask, but I have to know if he's actually ignoring me or if maybe I'm just overreacting to nothing.

"Yeah," she says, stringing it out and giving me a look that says she feels for me. "Want me to say something to him?"

"No. I just texted him again actually," I tell her.

"What did you say?" she asks.

I shift nervously.

"What. Did. You. Say?" Kallie stares me down.

"I apologized for kissing him?" I ask. I literally ask her. What the hell?

"A! Why would you apologize?" She steps forward.

"I don't know. I think I scared him. Maybe it was too much." And maybe it was. I mean, I know he's weird about that stuff.

"No! Yeah, he's stupid sometimes, but you don't need to apologize," Kallie tells me, and her surprise changes to concern. "Give him some space. He's odd with letting people in. But he's absolutely insane to go silent on you! I'm going to have a talk with him."

"No!" I blurt and throw my hand up. That might make it worse.

"No, yes. He's being stupid. You're a great guy, A. And he knows it. He just gets all scared and doesn't think straight. It's just Ty. And don't keep texting him. That'll just make it worse."

I'm not sure what to say. I want him to stop ignoring me. I don't want our dance in the rain yesterday to be our last. I want it to mean something.

"Okay." I nod. "Okay."

TYLER

"Jacob! I need healing, like, yesterday," I yell over my headset.

My avatar, D.Va, isn't doing too well, so technically *I'm* not doing so hot.

"Calm down, I got you," he says as his healing stream hits my Meka suit and my health starts going back up.

"About time," I say.

I'm about to warn him that Sombra appeared to his right when my phone starts blaring with a FaceTime call from Kallie. Can't do that right now, so I ignore it. That's going to get me a slew of texts.

"Dammit, Sombra's on my ass," Jacob complains.

Oops.

"I'm on her." I let a volley of missiles out, but most of them miss. She's a tiny target, and of course, she does her little disappearing act again. "She's gone."

"She's going to be the death of us," Jacob says.

She's been on our tails the entire match, and we've not been doing so well. We're on the attack and we've barely moved the payload past the first point on the Blizzard Park map. And we only have a minute left to make it to the end.

My phone buzzes again and again. I glance at it. Text after text, all from Kallie with nothing but my name, lights up my phone. It's her go-to when I don't answer immediately. I roll my eyes and go back to the match.

"This isn't going to end well," Jacob complains.

"Definitely not," I say, and immediately I'm frozen by Mei's freeze bubble. Not a second later I'm getting hell rained down on me and I'm watching the kill cam. "Dammit. The demon got me again."

"And me," Jacob laments.

Before I can respawn I hear, "Defeat!" echo in the background and the word plasters across the screen. I drop my control and roll my eyes.

"Ugh," I groan.

"That was such a bad match," Jacob says.

The leaderboard cards come up and neither of us are anywhere to be seen. Yeah, bad match. And in perfect sequence, Kallie FaceTimes me again.

"I got to go, Jacob, Kallie's calling, and she won't stop until I answer," I tell him.

"Okay. We'll play later," he says, and I sign off.

At the same time, I accept Kallie's call so she doesn't text me twenty more times.

"God, what took you so long?" she asks. It looks like she's still at work. She's sitting in her car in her Food Lion shirt.

"I was playing *Overwatch* with Jacob, fool!" I tell her.

"So?" She acts confused.

"I was busy," I say.

"Not too busy for me. Never, right?" Kallie does this head twitch thing.

"Obviously." I smile. I can't even be annoyed with her.

"So, why are you ignoring Aidan?" Kallie asks without intro or attempt to soften the question.

"Ignoring? What?" I'm thrown off, not sure what she means.

Oh. Wait. Okay, maybe I can be annoyed by her. And well, I guess I am ignoring him.

He texted me *Good morning!!* when he got up, I guess. I almost replied, but I just couldn't. I couldn't stop thinking about yesterday. About the kiss, the dance. About holding his hand in the car. And I liked it, it felt right, but it hit a nerve, and everything in me started to revolt against what I thought I wanted.

I couldn't do it. I couldn't text him back.

I started shaking just thinking about it, like responding was some kind of huge commitment, and I had to sit down and calm myself. I'm not ready for this. I can't do a relationship, I'll just fuck it up. I know it.

"Uh, yeah. Ignoring him," she spits back.

He texted again a little later asking how I was doing, and I just glazed over it and let it go. I had to avoid it. I couldn't go through all that upset again.

Then he Snapped me, but I haven't opened that yet, and I probably won't. And then not half an hour ago he texts again apologizing for kissing me, and I'm definitely not responding now. Like, he's already being too clingy, and I can't deal with that. It's what I was afraid of.

"So?" I ask. It's not like we're a couple.

"So? He likes you, and you like him too," she tells me. "Don't *even* tell me you don't. 'Cause if you don't, why did you kiss him back yesterday? Why did you hold hands all the way home?"

"I don't know." My whole body twitches and fall back on my bed. I really don't want to have this conversation. "I was stupid?"

"Stupid? No. No. No. No. Don't even go there," Kallie goes off. Yep, she's pissed. "And he's devastated that you're not talking to him, Ty. Devastated."

"Sorry?" I ask. "I'm not ready for this. I just need to be single for a while. Plus, I can already tell he'll be too clingy."

"Seriously? That's a huge load of bullshit, Ty, and you know it," she rails. Her shoulders bounce and she keeps bobbing her head from side to side and pointing at the camera.

"I'm better by myself. Plus, it'd be weird to date Brayden's best friend," I tell her.

"So, you were thinking about dating him? Exactly." Kallie eyes me.

"I… No," I tell her. "I've got to go. Bye, Kallie."

"Don't you hang—" she tries, but I end the call and throw the phone on my pillow.

I'm not doing this. I'm not doing any of this. I can't, and I won't. It's too much. I close and open my fists. It's like every nerve in my body is shooting and I hate it. Just no.

I need to focus on me, and Kallie, and seeing Brayden's dream through. I have to focus on the comet, nothing else. It's the only thing I'm sure of.

AIDAN

Thursday, July 25

AIDAN: Hey. Don't want to bug you, but… I wish you'd text back. I didn't mean to scare you. I'm sorry. Maybe we can play Overwatch?

I hit Send and immediately regret it.

Why can't I just leave it alone? You know, like a smart human being with half a brain. Someone who gets it when someone doesn't want them.

But no. Not me.

I'm the stupid one who just keeps thinking about it, and thinking about it, and thinking about it some more, until my head is heavy and my stomach hurts. I mean, he hasn't answered since Monday. I did sort of okay yesterday and managed to fight the building urge rushing through my entire body to text him, but it was too much today.

I had to. I need answers. I need to know why one day everything is suddenly great. I need to know why he wanted to dance in the rain. Why he held me so close. Why he made me feel like the world was mine. Why he let me kiss him. Why we held hands all the way home. And then why suddenly the next day I'm less than shit to him.

I know what Kallie's told me. The whole, *Tyler's just like that*, and how he doesn't like to be chased, and well, I might have been chasing a little. But was I? I don't know, it still seems stupid to me.

"Aren't you supposed to be leaving for work?" Mamá calls from the living room.

Yeah, I should be up already. I should have been dressed ten minutes ago, but I don't want to lift the covers, because that means I have to face the day again, and frankly I don't want to do that. All I want right now is to stay in bed, curled up with my phone, and wait for Tyler to say something.

"Getting ready," I yell through my closed door and drag the covers away.

It doesn't help that Tyler's been posting stories on SnapChat and he's smiling like everything is okay. Well, Tyler, news flash, everything is most definitely not okay.

I force each leg into a pair of work-approved black slacks and groan into my Food Lion polo. My hair's a mess, so I make the least effort possible to tame it, then start off down the hall.

"You okay?" Mamá asks.

I haven't told her. The last thing I want is her trying to coddle me and act like I'm a big baby, even if I am.

"Yeah," I say and make for the front door. "Gotta go."

"Have fun," she says as I shut the door behind me and my phone buzzes.

I ignore it and flop into my car and start up the engine. I close my eyes and let my head fall back against the headrest. I expel every ounce of oxygen from my lungs, wishing with every ounce I didn't feel like this. How do I feel so low about a boy who doesn't give a damn about me anyway?

I pull my phone out and freeze when I see the screen. Tyler. A lump forms in the back of my throat. I'm stuck between this massive need to know what it says and a dark horrifying pit in my stomach telling me never to open it. I tap the message.

TYLER: You're a good friend. But that's all. All this, it's just too much. I need to be alone for a while.

Too much? What? It's not like I asked to fuck Monday night. That's not me. I just want to be his, that's all.

I throw my phone on the passenger seat. It bounces to the floorboard, but I don't care. The screen could shatter into a trillion pieces and I wouldn't give a fuck.

Tears invade my eyes and any hope of this being temporary, of once again holding his hand or feeling his arms wrap around me, vanishes into nothing, nowhere. Gone like some bad vanishing trick. I grab the wheel and bury my head against it while the waters flow.

What did I do wrong?

TYLER

"Come on!" Katie pouts. "Do it! No one cares."

"Yeah, no one cares," Kallie echoes, but her eyes say she's not one hundred percent sure.

"Uh, no," I tell them. I'm not dancing in the middle of the Valley Hills Mall.

There's got to be hundreds of people in here. It's Thursday night, and I swear half of Hickory and the surrounding cities are here. I might not be shy, but I'm not stupid. And I'm ninety percent certain the security guards or some Karen might not think it's as cool or funny as Kallie and Katie do.

"Why not?" Katie begs. I thought being the shy one would make her get it, but apparently the irony is lost on her.

"I don't want to get kicked out," I tell her. We've been in the mall for less than an hour killing time before we go watch the new live-action *The Lion King*, and they're already on me trying to get me to make a fool of myself. "And I only know, like, one dance anyway."

"Well do that *one* dance." Kallie stares at me like it's totally obvious what I should do.

I throw my head back and sigh.

There are so many people. Couples and families, big groups of overly giggly girls and squads of I'm-too-cool-for-you teenaged guys, old and young, every sort passing around us in the middle of the massive corridor lined with storefronts.

"You're just trying to get me in trouble, aren't you?" I ask.

Neither of them answers, and I roll my eyes. When I look forward again, I see a cute Latino boy holding hands with who I assume is his girlfriend. His hair is just like Aidan's, and he even has dark brown eyes, though they're not the same, and he's missing the freckles.

Who cares though? *God, Ty, really?*

"Okay, I'll do it." I switch course and wipe the image from my mind.

I move to the edge of the big hall next to the entrance to some place called Relaxation Station and suck in a breath, hoping I get a little stupid courage in the process.

Here we go.

AIDAN

Saturday, July 27

It's too humid to be out here.

My brow is wet and all I'm doing is walking. It's not even warm, just sort of nasty, and the sky's not clear. And he's not here.

I knew he wouldn't be, but it is Saturday, so I still made the drive out to the park to stargaze. *It's just for you tonight, Brayden. Ty's not talking to me, so it's just us.*

It feels weird, sort of, to talk to Brayden out here. I want to think he can hear me, like at the cemetery, but I don't know, it just feels weird. But what the hell, he's all I have now. And now I even feel bad for thinking of it like that.

Brayden, why's this all so hard? Has God given you any insight into that yet? First, He takes you from us, from me. I miss you, Bray. I don't say that enough.

And now, just when I thought things were working out, He's taking Tyler from me too. I hope you don't mind that I sort of fell in love with your boyfriend. Yeah, no, I know you don't mind, but still. You wouldn't want him being alone, right? Or am I being selfish?

I kick a tiny ant hill on one of a thousand spider-vein cracks in the walking path. Dirt sprays over the asphalt and loads of tiny little ants flee for cover. Sorry.

I turn my eyes to the sky, and between the clouds Breegge's Comet shines bright. Its tail—or coma, if I remember right—marks a sparkling blue-and-purple trail across the sky. I think Brayden said it was supposed to be, like, two hundred-something kilometers long, so pretty damn long. It's gorgeous, magnificent. But I wish Ty was here to see it with me.

Ahead is our bench. The picnic table where it all started, where I just wanted to be his friend but couldn't seem to hold back everything that had built up since. It's where my first mistake happened. I tried though.

I can see him sitting across the table, crying. I just wanted to be a friend, to help him, because I was hurting too and I knew how it felt. I didn't know this would be the end of it.

I swear I didn't know, Bray. And if you hadn't… You know. If you hadn't died, this wouldn't be happening. I wouldn't feel this way, and he'd still be happy, and you'd be here. And everything would be okay. But nothing is okay. Nothing! No. I can't say that. I'm sorry, Brayden, I know it's not your fault. It can't be. It's not!

Damn, I miss you, Bray. I need you now.

I take a seat on the bench and gaze at the sky, dotted by puffy clouds, and watch the comet. It's crazy something so massive and volatile can be so beautiful, and yet I can't even get the boy I like to talk to me. Maybe that's the most volatile thing. Our minds.

I keep staring, but the longer I do the less I see because of the water welling up in my eyes, carving trenches down my cheeks. I don't want to cry — who does? — but what else can I do?

TYLER

"Where's Aidan?" Jacob asks.

It's good he's down in Kannapolis and can't see me throwing my head back.

"He's not playing today," I say. It's one of those overtly obvious statements, but it's all I care to say.

The Ilios map loading screen comes up, and I talk to fill the gap. I don't want him asking more questions.

"Ilios," I say in my best impression of the female announcer's voice. "I love this map."

"Why?" Jacob asks. "It's like Lucio boop heaven."

"But it's cool," I say.

"Vague," he drills me.

The hero roster comes up and I grab up Moira before anyone else on the team can steal her. I'm planning to wreak some damage orb havoc, and maybe a little healing in there too.

"I don't know. It just is. The point's easier to hold once you get it," I try. It's sort of true, I think.

"But it's hard as hell to get back when you lose it," Jacob counters.

The game begins. Hopefully this goes well. Typically, if our first match goes well, we do at least decently with the rest.

"Why's Aidan not coming?" Jacob pushes.

Why is everyone always like, "Where's Aidan? Why's Aidan not coming? Have you talked to Aidan lately?"

I mean, really? I don't want to think about it.

That's why I kept talking, Jacob. Catch a hint. But now I'm thinking about it, and to be entirely honest I wish Aidan was here, but I also don't need that.

"He's busy," I lie.

I don't need to tell Jacob we're not talking, or more like *I'm* not talking to Aidan. He's definitely been trying to talk to me. The first few days he texted a lot, but it's lightened up. I just need to keep it this way because I can't afford to like anyone right now. I need to focus on myself and Breegge.

"He have to work?" Jacob brings Mercy soaring in from behind and revives our dead Hanzo. He seems as distracted as I am right now.

"I don't know," I snap at him.

Just stop asking, dammit. Why does everyone just want to know about Aidan? It's the same with Kallie, and Katie, Heather and Josh at work, and hell, even my sister keeps asking. Guess it's the one good thing about your parents hating that you're a fag—they don't ask when you stop talking to a boy.

"Sorry," Jacob drags out the word, and that's when I realize how mean it sounded.

"Sorry," I say too. "Didn't mean to snap at you. It's just been a bad week."

"Want to talk about it?" he asks.

I push Moira past the open courtyard and throw a damage orb into the point. It bounces around the enclosed space, sapping the life out of our enemies, just like everything in my life this week. I try to focus on dealing damage and staying alive. I don't want to have this conversation.

"Nah, I'm good," I tell him.

AIDAN

Work's been slow today, and that makes this all so much worse. I want to go home. I don't want to stand here doing nothing at the end of a register, even with Kallie, but at the same time I would just be bored at home.

I can't write, so I'm not going to log onto my computer when I get there and start typing away. I tried the other day, and all I did was stare at the blank screen and fight back the urge to yell *fuck* every five seconds or bust out crying. And I can't stand the thought of playing video games, because that's what *we* did.

Hell, why am I even crying about it? It's not like we'd been going out for months or weeks, or even days. We weren't going out. It was all in my head. All of it. It was nothing more than a fragile fantasy I concocted, an unreachable, stupid idea that I managed to hurt myself with when I was stupid enough to *make a move*.

"Were you up here when that old man wouldn't stop flirting with me?" Kallie asks.

I pull myself back into the here and now, and I give it a second to sink in. Old man flirting with her?

"Uh…no," I say.

"Yeah, he just stared at me the entire time I rang him up." Kallie leans her hip against the register and her hands move every which way. "And he kept giving me this creepy smile."

"But you like older guys," I say. It is creepy, I know how they can be with the girls here. It's messed up.

"Not *that* old. This was, like, grandpa old," she tells me.

"Ah." I nod.

I piddle my fingers around the bagging station, hoping Jesse doesn't come around and make me actually do something. I've only got about ten minutes to go, so I'd rather stand here with Kallie even if I am bored to tears. Not like it's anything new.

It's quiet for a moment, except for the music playing faintly overhead. I think it's one of Shawn Mendes' older songs.

"Bryce is here." Kallie nods toward the entrance by the buggies.

I look and there he is, standing tall and awkward. He texted earlier wanting to hang out when I got off, but I never responded. Now I feel even worse. I should have said something, but I just didn't feel like it.

"Hey, A. We doing anything tonight?" Bryce asks.

"I don't know," I tell him.

"Come on. We can go get Burger King and bug everyone at Walmart." He shrugs. "Fun, right?"

I grunt a tiny excuse of a laugh. It doesn't sound that bad, to be honest, but it means staying out in public. And that requires interacting with people. And that requires maintaining some visage of a halfway functioning person. And I don't have that in me right now.

"Eh, I mean, maybe. I think I just want to go home and watch TV." I lean against the end of the conveyor belt ledge.

"Seriously?" Bryce complains and darts his eyes away to Kallie, then back at me.

"Maybe you should go out, have fun, do something stupid." Kallie steps in on cue.

"Already done that," I whisper under my breath, and then speak up. "TV sounds good."

"Already done that?" Kallie mimics me and does her little hands on hips and pursed lip thing. "For the millionth time, you didn't do anything stupid, A. Tyler's the stupid one, and I can say that because he's my best friend. He can be *so* stupid sometimes. Like, monumentally stupid."

"Nah," is all I give her. I swallow back the empty feeling in my throat, but it just settles atop the nausea in my stomach. "Sorry, Bryce. I can't."

"You sure?" Bryce squints, just enough concern, just enough prodding.

"Yeah." I check my watch. *8:59 p.m.* Time for me get out of here. "I got to clock out. I'll catch you later."

"Okay, see you, man," Bryce says and heads out the door. "See you, Kallie."

I head off as Kallie tells Bryce goodbye. I punch out and make my way back to the front. The store seems so much bigger right now, like every aisle is a mile long, like it's this huge trek across a cold desert to get from one end to the other. At the registers Kallie stops me before I can get out.

"Aidan!"

"Yeah?" I turn around, sighing. I just want to leave.

"You really should go hang out with Bryce. It'd be good for you," she says. "Like, really!"

"You hanging out with Ty after work?" I ask as bluntly as I can manage.

"Uh, yeah," she says quieter.

"Well, at least he's talking to you," I bite. "Hope he doesn't just ghost you all of a sudden."

I'm not standing here and debating with anyone what I should and shouldn't be doing right now. Not doing it. I twist around and fast-walk out the sliding glass doors and collapse in my car. *Breathe, Aidan, breathe.*

I take in a slow breath, then exhale through my nose, letting every atom of air escape my lungs, and then do it again. That deep trembling in my chest starts to well up and the edges of my eyes get moist and my vision blurs.

Fuck him. Fuck him! This is so stupid. He never liked me, and I'm an idiot to have ever thought he did or would. I pound my fist on the steering wheel but stop because it hurts more than I expect. I can't even do that properly. God, what can I do right?

And I snapped at Kallie. Dammit. She didn't deserve that. I squeeze my eyes shut and grit my teeth together. What is wrong with me?

I pull up my text thread with Kallie.

AIDAN: Sorry for jumping on you. ::crying emoji:: ::crying emoji:: Just sucks right now. ::yellow heart::

I don't expect her to text back, she's got another hour before she's off, but the little text bubbles at the bottom start blipping across the screen. Such a daredevil.

KALLIE: It's OK. ::yellow heart:: Tyler's being an ass. ::shrug emoji:: Trying to work on him.

I like the boy, but she loves him probably more than anyone in this world does. And she still calls him out. I pocket my phone and stare out the windshield. It's dark and my view is nothing but trees lining the edge of the parking lot. I don't want to go home, but I don't want to stay here.

I pull my phone back out and groan. I hope Bryce hasn't gone too far. He's going to hate me if he has.

AIDAN

Thursday, August 1

They finally got me out of the house again.

I swear it's been Bryce and Kallie's combined mission since last week, and I haven't made it easy for them. But maybe they're right. Maybe being stuck, and by stuck I mean *choosing* to stay at home, isn't the best thing for me right now.

"What did you get?" Kallie asks.

"Cinnamon Roll Frappe," I tell her as Bryce steps up to the register and orders.

"Does that even have coffee in it?" Kallie asks.

"I don't know." I take my drink from the redheaded Starbucks barista girl.

"No. It uses the cream base, it doesn't actually have coffee in it." The barista completely loses my confidence.

I roll my eyes as Kallie gears up.

"See? Totally pointless. It doesn't even count," Kallie goes on and on. "You need a real drink, like this, a Nitro Cold Brew."

Kallie holds up her drink. I swear it looks like a real thick beer with all that foam on top.

"Nah." I brush it off and look for a table. There isn't a lot of room in here, but luckily the lunch traffic has died down. I steal a high-top table in the corner.

"Uh, yeah. That thing you got isn't going to wake you up in the morning," she tells me.

"I don't get it to wake me up. I get it because it tastes amazing," I say, then I take a sip, and yeah, it's amazing. It's about the only amazing thing in my life lately.

I know it shouldn't bug me. She's only trying to make conversation and make me smile and all that junk, but it's not working. But I promised myself I wasn't going to be a sore little depressed ass and I was going to go out today, one because I need it, and two because they wouldn't stop begging.

"Katie will be here in a few. She's just running a little later than she thought." Bryce puts two drinks down on the table, one presumably Katie's.

"We've got all day," Kallie says, and my eyes dart toward her.

The look on my face must appear a bit more horrified than I meant, because Kallie gives me her calm-the-fuck-down look. I melt into the metal chair and start nursing my coffee-free drink.

Tyler should be here. It's the group. It's supposed to be all of us. But he's not, because I'm here. He's not here because he doesn't want to be around me. So when you get down to it, I kept him from showing up, it's my fault he didn't get to come.

"How's everything coming for Charlotte?" Bryce asks.

At first I don't know what he's talking about, but then it clicks. Charlotte. College. We haven't talked a lot lately. There've been texts and a few calls, but I think I was too focused on Tyler, and then when Tyler stopped talking, I think I sort of stopped talking to anyone unless I was forced to see them in person. It's so stupid. I just stopped.

"It's coming," I say.

"Met your roommates yet?" he asks when I don't elaborate. I guess he wanted a little more detail. But we don't always get what we want, do we?

"Yeah, sort of," I tell him.

Charlotte sent my roommate assignment a few weeks ago, and we exchanged cell phone numbers and SnapChats. My roomie is this guy named Cameron. He's this tall boy from Atlanta who's apparently really into anime on something called Crunchyroll, and I'm thinking he likes rap. We're definitely not going to get along on the music front. "I've only got one. Guy named Cameron. Goes by Cam."

"What's he like?" Kallie asks when I again don't keep going.

"I don't know." I mean, I do, but I just don't want to talk right now.

"You don't know? You don't get to talk to them before you move in?" Kallie leans back like it's horrifying, and it would be if that were the case, I guess.

"No, I do. Uh… He's from Atlanta, likes anime and rap," I tell them.

"Rap?" Bryce pooches his lips out and smiles jokingly at the same time. "You're going to love that."

"Not exactly." I roll my eyes, but a sliver of a grin does slip across my lips somehow. "I told him how much I like rock. Like, real rock music, and he says he can deal with it, so the way I see it is we'll listen to rock when I'm there…or not. I don't know."

"Good luck with that. Hopefully he's not some sociopathic serial killer." Kallie shivers as if she suddenly had a cold chill.

"Really?" I ask. The odds are so slim, and it's college, he's just a roommate. I think it'll be okay. "He seems pretty normal to me. He's sort of cute too."

I throw in that last bit for Kallie. And it gets exactly the reaction I expect. She purses her lips and shakes her head. He is cute though.

"Katie!" Bryce jumps up and throws his arms around her tiny waist. I didn't see her come up, and she's sitting down in the seat between Bryce and me before I have time to register what's happening.

"Hey everyone." Katie lets her eternal grin do its thing.

"Hey," Kallie and I say at the same time.

"What did I miss?" Katie asks.

"Not much, you're not that late," Kallie jumps in before Bryce can say anything.

"Yeah, A was just telling us about his roommate down in Charlotte," Bryce fills her in. "Sounds like a real nutjob."

"Oh no! Is he crazy?" Katie's genuinely concerned.

"No!" I throw up my hands and eye Bryce, who's smiling gleefully behind his thick-rimmed glasses. "He's fine. Bryce is just being Bryce."

"I see." Katie leans toward him and pecks him on the cheek. "Wouldn't have him any other way."

I'm not sure if I want to throw up or run outside and bawl my eyes out. Like, I could do either with no effort. What they have is what I want, and I want it with Tyler. To give him an innocent peck on the cheek. I want to hold his hand anywhere and say stupid little corny shit like that, but I can't because he's an asshole and he's too scared to let me in.

I take a sip from my cup. The cinnamon sweetness coats my throat and sends chills up my neck. It's so good, but it's still not as good as it was when all of this shit wasn't happening.

"When do you leave, A?" Kallie asks. I think she noticed how uncomfortable I am.

"I move into my dorm on August sixteenth," I tell her, sipping more from my drink. "School starts the next week on the nineteenth, but I don't have Friday classes."

"No Friday classes?" Bryce asks. "What?"

"Yeah, it's pretty co—" A cough cuts me off mid-word, but I keep going. "Sorry. It's cool. I'll get Fri… Fridays off."

Something feels weird. I put my hand on my neck. It feels tight and scratchy all of a sudden. I swallow, but it's hard, and suddenly it's difficult to breathe. What the hell is happening? What the hell?

"A, you okay?" Kallie asks, but her voice is distant.

"I…" I try, but I can't breathe. My throat feels so swollen.

"Aidan!" Kallie yells.

I stand up, but my head is spinning, and I start to fall.

"A!" Bryce is up, and I feel hands grab me just before everything goes black.

T Y L E R

Thursday, August 1

What is it about Walmart and seeing every single person you know?

Like, I just want my snacks. I don't want a conversation with the woman who lives down the road from me who apparently knows me but I've never spoken to until today. She was nice and all, but having to feign interest and act like I know you is annoying.

Then there's the snack aisle. It's the one and only place in the store I actually want to be. I need some Reese's Pieces for gaming tonight with Jacob, but there's no way in hell I'm going down the aisle; I walked by and was about to make a run for the Reese's when I saw Christian's swept-back hair and football jacket. It took me less than a second to about-face and detour down the drink aisle. Snacks can wait.

I'm not in the mood for a spat with the likes of Christian in public. I peek around the corner. It's clear. There's no sign of the douche, so I take my chance. I scan the shelves and find my prize.

My phone vibrates.

KALLIE: Something's wrong with Aidan. Taking him to the hospital now.

What? Hospital? Something's wrong? What the hell?

My heart drops three stories and my legs buckle. What does she mean something's wrong with Aidan?

TYLER: What's wrong? Is he okay?

I stare at the screen, waiting for her to say something, anything. There's nothing, but the tension in my muscles builds. Is it bad?

They're taking him to the fucking hospital, Ty, of course it's bad.

TYLER: ???

Finally, the bubbles start moving, and I find myself staring at them more intently than I think I ever have before. *Be all right, Aidan, please be all right.*

KALLIE: Don't know. Couldn't breathe. Passed out. Almost at the hospital.

I push out a long breath through tight lips and ground myself. This is so not good. I throw the bag of Reese's back on the shelf and make for the exit, weaving between everyone in my way until I make it out.

TYLER: OMW.

I jog to my car, then speed out of the parking lot.

Slow down, Ty, don't be stupid. It's not going to help anyone if I get pulled over or skip past a stop sign. But then again, who's it going to help if I don't? He probably hates me right now, and can I blame him? No. I've been horrible to him. I've ignored him. I've acted like he doesn't exist, and why? Because he kissed me? Because he literally made me feel on top of the world? What the hell is my problem?

Turning down Mulberry Street, the hospital comes into view. At the sign declaring EMERGENCY ROOM in big red letters I pull in and swing into a spot. I barely switch off the ignition before my legs sweep me out the door and toward the entrance.

"Ty!" Kallie jumps from her seat as I spill into the waiting area. She pulls me into a hug, and I can tell she's been crying.

"Is he okay?" I ask as she steps back.

Bryce and Katie stand up behind her. All their faces are somber, scared, like they each saw a ghost. My stomach knots up and I brace for the worst.

"He's with the doctors," Kallie says, her mouth barely moving. "I don't know."

"What happened?" I beg her to give me something, anything to assure me he's okay.

"I don't know. He was perfectly fine one minute, and then he got up and was having a hard time breathing, and then he fell and passed out." Kallie steps back and falls into her seat. "It was so scary!"

"Did anyone call his mom?" I ask.

Bryce nods. "I did. She's on her way."

"What do we do?" I ask. I want to do something. I don't want to sit around here and wait. I want to make sure he's okay.

"We wait," Bryce says. I want to snap back that we can't do that, but the way he forced the words out between gritted teeth tells me he's not fond of it either. Aidan is his friend too.

I close my eyes. Just breathe and be patient. I take the gray faux leather seat next to Kallie and lean forward, burying my face in my balled-up fists.

Ten gruesome minutes pass before Ms. Molina jogs in the entrance in her waitress uniform.

"Where is he?" She looks directly at me.

I don't say anything. The words get stuck in my throat when I see her and wonder what she thinks about me. I assume she knows what I did to him. I didn't mean to, I swear it.

"He's with the doctors," Kallie steps in.

"Have they said anything?" Ms. Molina switches her attention to Kallie.

"No," Kallie says.

"You stay here. I'm going to talk to them," his mom tells us and disappears around the corner to talk to the nurses.

"Does he hate me?" I ask Kallie the question that's been weighing on me the entire time I've been sitting here.

I don't want to know, but I *need* to know. It's one of those contradictions. I need to know if he hates me for what I did, but I don't want the feeling I know will come if he hates me.

"No." Kallie gives me a sad half-smile. "He could never hate you, Ty. That's not Aidan. You know that."

"Yeah," I sigh.

A tear starts to form, but I'm quick to stop it. I think it might hurt more that he can't hate me, that he's that amazing of a person, and I let him down.

What if he doesn't make it? What if it's that bad?

My heartbeat quickens against my chest, and the blood pulses through my forehead. I don't know if I could handle that. Would that be my fault too? Did I stress him out too much? Was it me that brought him here?

Stop it, Ty. You're being dramatic.

But what if it's true? What if the last thing he remembers about me is that I was an asshole?

But it's not going to be. He's going to be okay, whatever it is, he's got to be okay.

"They're running some tests," Aidan's mom says when she comes back around the corner. "He's awake, and it looks like an allergic reaction, but he's okay."

"Good," I breathe. Allergies aren't too bad. I mean, they can be, but it's livable. Livable. Exactly, he's okay.

Half an hour later a nurse calls his mom back to talk with the doctors and we're left in the waiting room. Another half hour passes before the same nurse comes to get us. I'm honestly surprised they let all four of us go in.

She walks us down a sterile white hall lined with hospital beds, cordoned off by a thick blue polka dot curtains. Other nurses shuffle around the equipment and past us as we keep moving and pass through a set of thick double doors into a brightly lit hallway.

"We've moved him into a room," the nurse explains.

Kallie and I immediately look at each other, and I'm about certain she's thinking the same thing. I thought it was just allergies.

"Does he have to stay?" Kallie asks.

"Just for a little, for observation," she explains. "It's right here."

She stops at a half-opened door and points for us to go inside. I slide behind Kallie, Bryce, and Katie. I'm still not sure how he'll react to seeing me, so I don't want to be the first one inside.

The hellos start the moment Kallie walks in, and my nerves go into high gear.

I cross the threshold and there he is, lying on a hospital bed in a light blue robe, hooked up to every machine imaginable. But he's smiling, and he keeps smiling when his eyes land on me. I look away, worried I'm going to transform that smile into a scowl and he's going to tell me to leave. But he doesn't.

"Ty?" Aidan gasps. He sounds surprised, not mad but surprised.

"Hey," I whisper, finally looking up to see him. "How you doing?"

"Been better. It's just allergies." He rolls his eyes and grins. "Apparently I'm allergic to cinnamon now."

"Now?" Kallie grunts, but then her eyes light up. "Wait, so you were allergic to that drink?"

Aidan nods and sighs. "Yep."

"But you always get that." Bryce looks confused.

"How is that even a thing?" I ask.

"I don't know. I just am," Aidan laughs.

"The doctor said it's not uncommon. Happens all the time apparently." Ms. Molina pats Aidan's arm.

"But why cinnamon? I love cinnamon." Aidan rolls his eyes again.

He does love cinnamon. I know. But the fact that people can suddenly become allergic to stuff is still processing in my brain.

"Okay, I'm trying to wrap my head around this. You weren't allergic yesterday, but now you are?" I ask.

"I mean, maybe. I think I had some symptoms a few weeks ago but didn't pay attention to them," Aidan explains. "I told the doctor about it and he said it might have started then. Like, I had the same drink, and my throat felt all scratchy, but I just thought it went down wrong."

"Well it definitely went down wrong this time." Kallie gives him a skewed smile.

"You think?" Aidan grins.

He's still grinning. Even sitting in a hospital bed, he's smiling. How does he do it? How is he so optimistic?

"The nurse said you have to stay for observation or something?" Bryce asks.

"Yeah, overnight I think." Aidan looks to his mom for confirmation.

"He's just staying tonight so they can do some more tests and make sure that's it," she tells us.

"Okay." I'm not sure what else to say. Part of me wants to be like, "Hey, A, I'm sorry about ignoring you," but there are too many people in here.

Plus, I'm suddenly not sure it would be a good idea. The entire time I was in the waiting room all I could think about was how bad I wanted to make things right. I've missed him, but maybe it's best I don't tell him that. Maybe it's best I don't get his hopes up and hurt him anymore.

A I D A N

Saturday, August 3

I got home from the hospital yesterday evening, probably around six. It was just late enough that I didn't have to go to work, which I'm perfectly okay with. I don't think Kallie appreciated it though. Something about Grace talking way too much.

I should be focusing on how to avoid another reaction. It's simple, I guess. Avoid cinnamon. But what's cinnamon in? I don't even know except for that frappe. But my mind is elsewhere. It's on Tyler.

I still can't believe he came to see me the moment he found out, and according to Kallie he was there before mi madre. I like to imagine him fishtailing through an intersection and catching air at the crest of Hospital Avenue, which isn't where the hospital is, by the way. I know, it's odd. He even texted yesterday while I was still in the hospital just to check in and see how I was. But that was it. After that, all communications ceased like he'd been issued a restraining order.

And I refuse to text him first now. If he's this determined he doesn't want to talk, then so be it. Or even if he wants to, if he doesn't see the importance of initiating a little, then I'm not going to push it. It doesn't matter how much I want to, I'm not. And I really want to, but if I have to push it, then maybe it's best I don't.

That doesn't mean I'm going to sit idly by though. I start typing out a message to Kallie.

AIDAN: Has Ty said anything? He hasn't spoken to me since the hospital.

I thought she was at work already, but either she's not or she's texting anyway because the little bubbles start jumping. Why am I surprised?

KALLIE: About what?

AIDAN: ...Me? ::shrug emoji::

The bubbles start up again. They bounce at the bottom of the screen and keep bouncing and bouncing. This is looking to be a long one. My chest starts to hurt and I have to remind myself I haven't had any cinnamon, it's just my nerves.

KALLIE: He hasn't. ::sad emoji:: I'll talk to him, but I'm going to be real with you. I think he likes you, but he's too stubborn. You don't deserve to have to wait around like this. You might not want to hear it, but maybe you should think about moving on. ::sad emoji::

My phone slips between my fingers and crashes on my comforter.

Move on? I don't want to move on. I want Ty. I want to get to know him better. I want to stay up late and watch the stars with him. I want to fall asleep in his lap watching movies and fuss about stupid stuff like why Resident Evil is the best game franchise of all time. I want to be with him.

A tear rolls down my cheek and wets my pillow. But maybe she's right. Maybe all I'm doing is hoping for the impossible, for a fantasy that's only in my head. Maybe I'm hurting myself.

TYLER

Thursday, August 8

It's raining hard today. My wipers struggle to clear the droplets as I speed down the highway to my three-to-nine shift.

I woke up this morning with this annoying urge. I don't want to feel like this, but something in me wants to talk to Aidan. Like, it just hit me out of nowhere.

It's all I've wanted to do all afternoon, but I can't.

It's simple. I'm dangerous. People get hurt around me. I'm just not ready. That's it, and I have a comet to see for Brayden. That's all I need to know. It really is that simple, but at the same time it's not.

I haven't been able to shake Aidan's face from my mind since I woke up. Those nut-brown eyes, his soft brown hair, the freckles. That cute little nose. The lips I kissed in the rain.

A horn blares. I yank the steering wheel and get back into my lane. *Careful, Ty, careful.*

I have to talk to someone. I need to talk this out, get it out of my head so I can move on and focus on something else, anything else. And of course Kallie's the only one who I want anywhere near this. I know she's sort of on his side, but she's my BFF and I know she'll understand. She has to.

At the same time, I don't really want her trying to reason with me, trying to convince me I'm wrong. I know she's going to try. But I have to talk to her anyway.

I huff the most pathetic huff and press Kallie's name in Favorites on my phone. It rings.

Pick up, Kallie. No. Don't. Don't pick up. That'd be better, right? But no, maybe I do want to know what she thinks. Maybe. God, I don't know.

It continues ringing, my wipers beating away the rain as it slaps my windshield. Then it stops and her voicemail message comes to life. It's the basic default one in that feminine computer voice. Kallie refuses to make a custom one.

Part of me is relieved. It beeps and I pause a second. What am I going to say? Uh…

"Hey, it's… You know who it is. I uh… I just need to say something out loud." I stop and puff out a deep breath between tight lips. Am I seriously about to admit this? "I miss Aidan, I do, but…I'm scared. It just can't work, and…God I hate this. That's it. That's all. Uh… Don't worry about calling back. I don't want to talk about it. I just had to say it."

I hang up and immediately second-guess my sanity. Why did I do that? I don't feel any better. If anything, I feel like saying it out loud made my feelings more real. And I'm not sure that's a good thing.

AIDAN
Thursday, August 8

"Come on, Kit! Help me out a little here," I yell at my computer and throw my face into my hands, growling.

"You okay in there?" Mamá calls from the living room.

"I'm good," I yell back. But I'm so not good.

I can't focus. This story was coming along so well, like, two weeks ago, and now I can't get more than a sentence down without my mind flying every which way, or not flying at all.

Writing is the one thing I do when I'm stressed, but now it's like even that's off-limits, like I'm not allowed this one little joy. And it's all because I let myself be stupid. And it's not just the kiss. It's everything. It's all the time I've wasted this summer on Tyler. It's the veiled hope I let creep in that he'd fall in love with me somehow. It's catching meaning in every action he took and hoping for more. God, I was stupid.

Because this sucks, this feeling in my chest. It lingers, heavy and dense like a mound of massive rocks or even a car atop my body, but it's empty and hollow at the same time. It's like I'm being crushed by absolute nothingness. And the worst part is I should have known better. I know Tyler, I knew Tyler. I should have known this was the end I was begging for. Brayden's the only guy that could get through those walls and keep him, and apparently it's going to stay that way.

"All right, Kit, come on. Give me something." I exhale, and beg my character to help me out.

I'm so close to the end. Kit's supposed to be surviving *The Bleeding* right now and protecting Ben at the same time, but I'm stuck at an impasse. Nothing I write down feels right. Nothing.

My phone vibrates. It's Kallie FaceTiming.

Maybe talking to Kallie will get my mind moving again. I swipe to answer and her face lights up my screen. She's at work, sitting at the same black metal bench she always sits at on break.

"Hey." I force a grin.

"How you doing?" Kallie asks, and I can already tell she has something she can't wait to say.

"Eh. I can't write worth hell right now, so there's that," I complain.

"Why not?" she asks.

"Really? Why not?" I tilt my head forward and give her the eye.

"Yeah." Kallie purses her lips and shrugs. "Sorry. On that topic though, I just heard from you-know-who."

"Ty?" I groan. I've already decided I don't want to hear this.

"Yeah," she says, as if I could even possibly get it wrong. "So… He left me a voicemail, and it had to do with you."

"Seriously? In a good way?" I ask. I'm no fool, I know she might bend something he said to be nicer than it was.

"Yeah." She looks away like she's thinking about it. "Yeah, I think so. He said he misses you."

"*He* misses *me*? Excuse me? He misses me?" I'm taken aback by it, so I have to repeat it a couple of times. There's part of me the notion excites, but at the same time I don't want to be excited again. That's how you fall harder. That's how it hurts more.

"Yeah, that's what he said." Kallie does this little jiggle with her head that I can never imitate.

"Is that it?" I ask.

"Yeah, but he likes you," Kallie says.

"Likes me? He said that in the message too?" I sit back. I'm about positive he didn't say it.

"Well, he didn't say that verbatim, but that's what he meant," Kallie tells me.

Oh, so now we're going to get my hopes up based on interpretation. Nice.

"Not the same thing," I tell her.

"Yeah, but he admitted he misses you. I mean, yeah, he did say some bullshit about being scared, but it's a step," Kallie reasons. She lets her head lean to the side and her hair flops over her shoulder. "He's just stubborn."

"So what am I supposed to do with this?" I ask her.

"Be patient. I'm not saying wait forever, but maybe give him some time," Kallie suggests. "I know I said you should probably move on, but maybe I was wrong."

"I don't know, Kal. The more I wait the more I build up hope. And the more I hope, the more I see meaning in the most stupid, meaningless things and get myself worked up, and it just hurts," I spill out my heart. "It really hurts. I like him, like a lot, maybe even… You know, more than like him, but he doesn't care enough about me to notice or stay. And I'm leaving for college next week anyway."

Kallie stares at me speechless for a change. I sigh, sort of wishing I could take some of it back. I mean it, I meant it all, but I still hate it.

"I'm sorry, A," she says. "But what if he's the one?"

"What if? I don't know. Is there ever really a 'one'?" I ask her. "Maybe, but if there is and I miss it, that'll be just my luck."

"I don't know either," Kallie sighs. There's a sadness in her eyes. "You're an amazing guy, Aidan, but you're too hard on yourself. I know it sucks right now, but maybe it's for the best and not just bad luck. You're smart and cute, and you have so much to offer. One day you're going to make some guy happier than anything in the world. I know it."

"Thanks, Kal." I hate mushy compliments, but I think she gave me my answer. It isn't the one I wanted, but it's what I'm going to do. "I'm just tired of hoping and getting hurt. So for now, I'm done. I'm just going to focus on me and school. That's it."

TYLER

Somehow Melinda convinced me to go with the family for dinner. I don't usually go after church—I've heard enough preaching by the time Sunday night service is over—and the last thing I need to hear is my dad going on and on about it after, so usually I choose between going home, bugging Kallie, or finding something else to do.

But guess who's busy working tonight. Kallie. And I desperately need something to distract me, so here I am.

"Your stupid ass *would* think that." Melinda rolls her eyes about the comment I just made on American History being a good class.

There are moments I wonder if Kallie and my sister are the same person. They're both so sarcastic and mean. We were talking about her freshman schedule and I was telling her she'd like her history teacher, Randall.

"I'm so glad I don't have classes with you," she says. "Don't want anyone thinking I'm that stupid."

I shoot her my middle digit. Mom's not here yet to gasp, so it's less funny, but still.

"Between you, Mom, and Kallie, it's amazing I'm not a total basket case." I shake my head.

"*They* love you at least." Melinda grins and does the same head shake that Kallie's mastered.

"Haha," I mock laugh and give her two more middle fingers as we step into the long Sunday night line in McDonald's. "*I'd* be the stupid one if I had classes with a freshman."

"Wouldn't be surprised." Melinda keeps rolling as I open the door for her and quickly shut it before she can get through. "Asshole."

My eyes go wide. I know she cusses, but it's still so weird hearing my little sister talk like that, not to mention in the middle of McDonald's.

We stop at the self-order stations. "Figure out what you want," I say.

Melinda starts checking the menu. I don't know why I bother, she knows exactly what she wants. It's always a double cheeseburger with no pickle, add mayo, and an order of fries. So basically give me unhealthy, and then add a little more unhealthy on top, with a side of unhealthy. It's no better than what I get though. I don't know how we keep from getting huge.

While she's checking the menu I scope out the crowd, hoping I don't see anyone from church or anyone Dad knows.

It's a sea of white and gray hair to the registers. It seems they avoid self-checkout like the plague, allowing the more varied hair colors to mingle around the automated stations. When I get to the dining room the raucous of tiny voices make more sense. So many kids, so many parents not paying a bit of attention to them as they run around tables. My distaste for kids jumps up a notch. I'm so glad I can't have kids.

Then my heart jumps into my throat. Aidan.

He's in the front corner by the floor-to-ceiling windows, facing away from me, but there's no mistaking that profile. That freckly tan skin and combed-back hair are unmistakable. He's with Bryce and Rhys. They're laughing about something. He's laughing.

For some reason that makes me happy and sad at the same time. Like, I'm glad he's happy, but I miss him, I actually miss him, and I sort of want him to miss me too.

I want to tell him. I want to walk up right now and tell him I miss him, that I messed up. I clench my fists and start to move my legs, but I lock them in place.

Are you fucking stupid, Ty? No. That's such a bad idea, like monumentally bad. He's better off without you.

"Tyler?" Melinda looks up at me.

"Uh, yeah." I nod vigorously, yanking my attention back to reality.

"You look confused." She eyes me.

Drop it, girl.

I take a deep breath and spot Mom walking in the front door followed by Dad, who immediately wraps her up in his arms and smiles so big. Yeah, I'll never have that, but whatever.

"Y'all order yet?" Dad asks.

"No, Melinda's taking forever." I pin it on her.

"Of course, typical woman," he says, and I immediately regret it.

Not only is he a homophobe, he's bought totally into the women-are-less-than mentality. He'd argue it's just how God planned it and that it doesn't make them unequal. Sounds sort of faulty to me.

I give him my best I'm-bugged-by-what-you-just-said-as-usual look way without saying anything. I'm not getting into why feminism isn't just an anti-Christian liberal political agenda to destroy gender roles with him in the middle of McDonald's. Especially with Aidan somewhere behind me.

"Let's order," I say instead.

I swing around and try to focus on the screen, but my attention is pulled away by this invisible force. Okay, it's pulled away by this stupid but horribly massive need to see if Aidan's still here. I peek around the machine and there he is, standing up, about to leave.

He turns. He sees me. Our eyes lock and I have to swallow back a lump in my throat. I don't know what to do, and it doesn't seem he does either.

The happiness on his face vanishes. It's not quite a frown, but it's something else, something scared, or maybe it's just sad. It sinks into my soul, and every part of me feels disgusting. I can't just stand here, so I wave like an idiot.

He nods, and a tiny half-grin breaks through. Without a word spoken he looks down and rushes the others out the back door. And just like that, he's gone, and it all sinks in.

I might have just seen him for the last time.

AIDAN

Wednesday, August 14

"You okay?" Rhys leans around the front passenger seat.

"Yeah," I lie.

Tyler was the last person I needed to see. I'm supposed to be getting over him, moving on, going on with my normal pathetic life. All that bullshit. But seeing him brought it all back, and I'm having a hard time suffocating it. It begs for life inside me, but I can't let it up for air. I refuse.

"Okay." Rhys drops it. He's never been one to get into all the icky emotional stuff anyway, and right now, I appreciate it.

"It's Tyler, right?" Bryce brings it back up without losing a beat. "I saw him in there."

I huff and stare out the back window of Bryce's cube car. Of course it's about Tyler.

"I don't want to talk about it," I tell him.

The car goes silent.

I wanted to talk to Tyler so badly. In that brief moment our eyes locked, every ounce of me wanted to walk up and just say hey. He looked surprised to see me, probably shocked and disgusted. The last thing he wants in this entire world is to deal with clingy me again.

"Can we turn on some music? Anything? I'll even take your crappy rap, Rhys," I blurt. I just need something to fill the silence.

"Got it," Rhys says and starts flipping through albums on his phone. "Shitty rap it is."

Anything to drown him out of my head.

TYLER

My phone rings away with Kallie's face plastered on the screen. I'm driving down Highway 321 waiting for her to pick up. I have to talk to her. I have to, this is killing me inside.

The entire time I was in McDonald's all I could think about was Aidan. It didn't matter how much Melinda tried to distract me like the awesome sister she is, even if she acts like she hates me. It didn't matter how much Dad went on about the guy he witnessed to in line while we waited for our food, or how much Mom smiled and talked about the murder mystery show she's been watching.

Despite all the distractions my head kept going back to the way he looked at me. Those sad brown eyes. The way he averted his gaze at the end, that almost scared twitch. It's eating me alive. But it's not just that. It's me too.

The longer I think about him, about us, the more scared I am of letting him go.

He's leaving for college. He's running off to the big city where he'll meet so many people. And I don't want him finding someone better than me without having a chance first. But do I even deserve a chance? I mean, it'd be like a second or third chance, 'cause I sure blew the others. I'm terrified, but every second that passes I'm getting more terrified of not trying.

Kallie finally picks up. She's in her car too.

"What's up?" She glances at the camera.

"Aidan," I say without introduction, trying to hide that my eyes are glassy from the tears I just wiped away.

She gives me a concerned smile. It's like she knows, but she isn't going to rub it in. At least not yet — it is Kallie.

"'Kay, so what is it?" Kallie asks.

The light from a streetlamp glows over her face and disappears.

"I saw him at McDonald's." I grimace.

"I see," Kallie sighs. "Did you talk to him?"

"I couldn't. He probably hates me right now. And you said he doesn't want to talk anymore anyway," I tell her.

"No, I said he thinks it's best he moves on because *your* stupid ass won't talk to him," she corrects me.

It stings a little harder this time. It's my fault. It is. Why am I such an asshole? What is it I'm so afraid of?

"Yeah." I push back the guilt.

"You want to talk to him, don't you?" Kallie asks.

"Yeah." I roll my eyes and take a left onto Highway 321. "It's gotta be a bad idea though. He's leaving Friday. Maybe it's best I just don't and let him find someone else down there. He probably will anyway, right?"

"Uh, no. That's a super bad idea." She jumps back. Kallie loses the concerned demeanor and transforms into the Kallie I'm used to who doesn't take shit from anyone. "Yeah, he's hurt, and he thinks you hate him. Does he probably think he's better off not trying? Pretty sure. But that's because he thinks you won't let him. I'm your best friend, Ty, like your *best* best friend, as in ever." She smiles gratuitously. I can't help but laugh, even though I want to cry because I'm such a douche. "But you need to stop letting Brayden get in the way. That's the problem, Ty. It wasn't your fault. You're not to blame. It's not on you. You are Tyler, an amazing, cute, funny, nerdy guy who has horrible taste in music, and Aidan's willing to overlook that. That's huge. I barely overlook that."

I purse my lips in confusion. I'm not sure if I'm supposed to take that as a compliment or a burn, but somehow it's comforting.

"I know this isn't what you want to hear, but it's time to leave Brayden in the past." Her words hit like a train. It feels wrong, but she's right. It's exactly what's been holding me back. I've known it for a while, but I just couldn't face it. I don't want to leave him behind, but I don't want to lose Aidan either. "You can still love him and miss him. You can always love him. You're allowed to do that. It doesn't mean loving someone else now is wrong. It means you're human. You can't stay stuck like that. And Aidan deserves that part of you, well, all of you."

"Yeah." I sit up straight. It comes out barely above a whisper, but it's like a dump truck load of courage just got dropped in my chest. "I'm going to do it. I'm going to talk to him."

This is either going to be the best decision I've ever made or the most epically horrible, but I'm doing it.

TYLER

I keep checking my phone like some obsessed idiot, but all I'm getting are Instagram notifications, texts from Kallie, and a random Twitter, like, from something I posted weeks ago.

I've waited all morning for Aidan to write back. I waited up half the night for nothing, and then when I woke up this morning there was still nothing. So I sent him another text. I read them again just to be sure I wasn't too pathetic.

TYLER: Hey A. Sorry I've been an ass lately. Shouldn't have ignored you.

TYLER: Hope you're doing good.

I didn't want to, like, confess I want to talk to him or anything, just break the ice. I hope it doesn't sound desperate. I don't think so, but still. My mind is on fire with how bad this could all go and why he's not texting back, and it's about to drive me crazy.

Maybe he's totally over it. Maybe Kallie was wrong and he's like, *forget Tyler*. I can't blame him. I was a total ass. I knew he liked me, hell, I kissed him and held his hand and even felt the part for a moment, but something in me was horrified and I ruined it. I'm still scared, but I can see what I tried not to then, and it's eating away at my insides.

God, I need a snack. That should help, if it doesn't make me feel sicker, at least.

I slide off my bed and walk down the stairs with a full view of the living room below. Mom's lounging on the couch engrossed in her tablet while the TV plays *Criminal Minds* in the background. I almost stop at the landing to talk, but she doesn't want to hear my boy problems, so I keep moving and find myself in the kitchen digging through the snack cabinet.

It's not that she doesn't want to hear my problems. She just can't disconnect that I'm a boy talking about boys, and it makes her "sad." At least that's what she told me a year or two ago. She seems better about it now, but I know she still can't get past all of Dad's junk.

I choose a Nutty Buddy bar and head back toward the living room. Maybe it'll be enough just to sit around her, let all that motherly energy do its work.

She's still on her tablet when I drop onto our cushy leather sofa across the room and start unwrapping my snack. I want to tell her I like Aidan, that I know I do now, but how I'm afraid he hates me now, and just ask what I should do. But this barrier, aka religion, stands in the way of the conversation I should be able to have with her. It sucks so much. Like, if there is anyone on this planet I should be able to talk to, it's her.

Hold up. What if I ask her but phrase it as if Melinda was in this situation? You know, like a hypothetical. Maybe that'll make it easier.

"Mom." I decide to go for it.

"Yeah?" She pulls her attention from whatever's on her screen. I always forget how pretty she is. Mom is for sure who I got my eyes from, and our hair is almost identical, minus hers being down to her shoulders and curly.

"So, uh…" I struggle at first. She'll probably catch on to what I'm doing, but maybe, just maybe she'll let it go. "So, if *Melinda* liked a guy, and the guy liked her back, but *she* was stupid and got scared and ignored said guy, and this happened a few times, and then he finally got tired of it, and then *Melinda* realized what she'd missed—"

"This is a long story," Mom laughs, but she's actually listening to my rambling.

I grin nervously.

"Yeah, so if *Melinda* did that," I stress Melinda again, "and she finally realized she liked him too and she'd been stupid, what should she do if he won't text her back?"

"Well, *Melinda*," Mom stresses her name just like I did, "shouldn't be so scared in the first place. Everyone's a little scared. And she's an amazing person, even if she is scared. But she should go talk to this guy in person."

"Really? I— *Sh-She* should?" I almost slip up, but only, like, half the sound comes out before I catch it.

"Really." Mom smiles at me. Her grin is so soft and caring, like she's reading right into my soul. "Go after your boy, Ty."

My eyes go wide. Did she just say that?

I don't know what to do, so I sink deeper into the sofa, and I nibble at my lips. I glance back at Mom, and now she's beaming from ear to ear. I didn't just imagine that. She did say it!

"Aidan's too cute to lose."

AIDAN
Thursday, August 15

Today's been crazy.

It's like everything sank in today, and it just keeps getting crazier. I'm driving to my last shift at Food Lion right now. Well, at least *this* Food Lion with the people I know. I'm transferring down to one near the school in Charlotte next week, so I'll still be at Food Lion, but not this one. I have to say goodbye to Kallie tonight after work, and I'm not sure I'm really ready for that. Hell, I'm not sure I'm ready to move out of my house either.

I've never been away from Mamá for more than a week before, so this is all new. And to make things even more insane, Tyler texted me last night *and* this morning. I can't even with him. Yeah, he was an ass, just like his text said. I've read it at least ten times, telling myself not to respond each time I open it up. And yeah, he shouldn't have ignored me, that was a real asshole move to make again, and I'm done with it.

No, it doesn't matter that I think I love him. I did. I really think I did now, but I can't go back and forth like that. I can't go to Charlotte being torn, thinking there is hope, when all he probably wants is a friend, and I can't just be friends with him. I really don't think I can do it, and I need to focus on school. I can't have him messing with my head even if he doesn't realize it.

The store comes into view and I pull into the turning lane. It's weird thinking this is really the last time I'm going to work here. My mind is everywhere and nowhere in particular today as it jumps back to Tyler.

I can do this. I can be strong and not text him back. I can go off to Charlotte and leave it all behind me. Leave it all where it needs to stay. I'm certain Kallie will keep me filled in on whatever happens back here anyway, so it's not like I'll miss out. I'll just avoid my heart being torn apart.

It's going to be okay. I'm going to be okay. This is going to be a great new chapter for me.

TYLER
Thursday, August 15

Why does Kallie have to be at work right now? Of all the times to be at work, right now doesn't work for me. I need to talk.

I huff, lying in bed, squeezing my pillow to my chest. I know what I need to do, I just don't know how.

And I'm still trying to process that Mom literally told me to go after Aidan. She literally said, "Go after your boy," and I can't really believe it. I mean, she even named him and said he was cute.

Like, what?

If that isn't confirmation that I have to do this, I don't know what is. I have to. If I don't, he's going to get away. He's going to go off to college, find some guy who's not a complete asshole like me, and fall in love, and I'm going to be left here hating myself for the rest of my life.

And finally I know Brayden would want this. He wouldn't be mad or angry. If he's up there looking down right now, I know he'd tell me exactly what Mom did. Is there a part of me still that hates that it means moving on? Yeah. I miss him, but I'm killing myself for no reason if I don't.

I need to talk to Kallie. I need to, but she's still not answering. I break down and send her a text. I think Aidan is at work too today. I keep thinking she said he was going to be there.

TYLER: KALLIE! Is Aidan at work?

If he is, then maybe that's my opportunity. Especially since he can't really get away, and it would sort of look bad if he ignored me.

But maybe that's a bad idea. Would he resent me for forcing him into that type of situation?

My phone dings.

KALLIE: TYLER! Yes.

He's there. He's really there.

TYLER: When does he get off?

KALLIE: 9, I think. Why?

I check the time. *7:48 p.m.* I don't have long. If he gets off I'll have to go to his house, and I don't know if that's a good idea. His mom probably hates me more than my stupid ass hated Aidan for so long. It's still so weird to think I literally hated him, couldn't stand the sight of his face for so long. Now it's all I want to see, and it actually hurts to think I might not see it again.

I start typing back, but I can't seem to get it right. Do I say I want to get back with him, or I just miss him and want to talk to him, or I want to grovel at his feet for forgiveness? What? Like, what the hell do I say? Finally, I settle on the "best" thing to say.

TYLER: Need to talk to him before he leaves.

It takes a minute, but the bubbles start churning and my phone dings again.

KALLIE: Now's your time then. This is his last shift. Leaves tomorrow for Charlotte.

That's what I was afraid of. I can't put it off.

TYLER: OMW. Don't tell him, please.

I lock my phone and dart through the house, yelling bye to Mom on the way out, and jump in my car. I speed up the gravel driveway, knocking up plumes of dust in my wake until my tires hit pavement and I gun it down the country road. Trees speed by, but my thoughts fly quicker.

Is this going to work? What if I get there and he's had enough, like totally had enough? What if he decides I'm too indecisive?

I hang the curb at the top of Setzer's Creek Road and take the hill down a little faster than I should, but I can't let him get away.

What if he leaves before I get there? What if his boss lets him go early since it's his last shift? What if he runs off to college and still won't answer my calls and texts?

I shake my head, pulling onto the highway, and gun it again.

No. This is going to work. I messed up. No, I fucked up. I really fucked up, but I think he'll understand. Aidan knows how I am, and he still wanted to be with me—that has to count for something.

Ten minutes later I'm pulling into the Food Lion parking lot. My eyes search for his Mustang, but I find Kallie's little Kia first. Is he not here? I thought she said he— All good. There it is a few spaces over. I sweep into a spot nearby, just in case he happens to be on his way out, and clench the steering wheel.

"You've got this, Ty. Just go in and tell him you messed up, that you want him back," I tell myself, staring out the window at the rows of cars. "Something like that."

I get out and jog across the parking lot and into the grocery store. Kallie's up front as usual, standing behind her register ringing up a family of four. She doesn't see me at first, and my heart sinks because I don't see Aidan.

Where is he? Shouldn't he be up here?

"Kal." I walk up to the end of her register.

"That didn't take long." Kallie smirks at me, not hiding that knowing glare.

"Where is he?" I ask.

"Just went back to get drinks for the coolers." Kallie rings up a head of cabbage, or maybe it's lettuce, I don't know. "He'll be back."

"Okay." I stand, frozen in place.

I'm horrified. I'm legitimately horrified. What am I going to say? Everything sounds so corny, like something a little kid would say in fifth grade or in a movie. I can't do that.

"What do I say?" I beg her for something better.

"Just tell him how you feel." Kallie glances at me between items. "Your total is sixty-three dollars and twenty-eight cents."

"Huh?" I look at her, and then see the guy in front of the register putting his card in the debit terminal next to his wife. *Oh, gotcha.*

"Thank you," she says, and the family walks away. Luckily, she doesn't have another customer, so she twists around and her attention lands on me. "Just tell him how you feel. Be you. You've got this, Ty."

"I don't know if I—" I freeze. Aidan's standing at the end of the aisle by the register, his hands grasping a buggy filled with bottled drinks. He's staring at me like he just saw a ghost. I bet I look the same. "Hey."

"Hey," he mutters back, and I can see his Adam's apple after a nervous gulp.

"Can we talk?" I ask.

"I, uh—" Aidan starts, but I race past Kallie and stand at the other end of his cart.

"I won't keep you. Promise," I tell him.

He shrugs, and I can't tell if he's glad to see me but nervous or if he wishes I'd leave. But I'm not turning back now. I've come too far.

"I messed up," I blurt loudly. Okay that's too forceful. Calm down. "I really messed up. You're an amazing guy, like *the* most amazing. But I couldn't see that because I was scared."

He looks away, and I can just barely see this tiny grin flinch across his face for the faintest second before it disappears again. That's when I remember I'm in the middle of a grocery store on a Thursday night, and all the people walking by are looking at us.

I take a deep breath. I'm not stopping. They can watch and think whatever they want. I don't care if there's a raging lunatic or a homophobe or a Karen who doesn't like that I'm doing this here, I have to do this now. Not later, now.

"I treated you bad. I ignored you. I led you on. I couldn't accept how I felt. I was stupid. I was *so, so* stupid, Aidan," I beg him to understand. "I'm an idiot. You were there, right in front of me, begging me to see you, but I couldn't, I wouldn't. I was scared. I was scared, and I was stupid. And I'm sorry, Aidan. I'm so sorry."

I pause, hoping he'll say something. He shuffles around the buggy and bites at his lip. But he doesn't speak.

"I like you, A," I finally say. And I'm one hundred percent certain it's the truth. I haven't been this certain of almost anything ever, but I am now. I know. "I don't want you to leave tomorrow without knowing. I want to be yours."

I stop. I surprised myself on that one. But it's true. That's what liking him means.

"And I want you to be mine." I smile at him. "Please."

I wait, wishing he'd look at me, wishing he'd give me something, a sign, anything to let me know what he's thinking. He bunches his brow up and shakes his head and finally looks up at me. I lock on to those gorgeous browns, and fear grips my chest. They're watery, and his mouth trembles.

"I can't." Aidan barely gets the words out. "I just can't."

"What—" I gasp, but he swings around and takes off down the closest aisle, leaving the buggy with me.

I drop forward and grasp the buggy. Part of me wants to fall to the floor and just melt away. He said no. He actually said no. How could he say no?

My whole body shakes. I squeeze my fists tight and close my eyes.

This isn't happening. I'm not going to cry. I'm not doing that.

I turn and find Kallie frowning. Not the I-can't-believe-what-you-just-did type of frown, but the I'm-so-so-so-so-sorry type. But I'm the one who's so sorry. I really screwed it all up.

I cough back the torrent building inside and release the ferocious grip I have on the buggy. I look down the aisle Aidan took. It's empty. He's gone, out of sight, and I'm left standing here just as empty as it is.

I clench my jaw tight and start toward Kallie's register. I'm not staying. I'm not waiting to talk. No, I'm going straight home. I just need to be alone right now.

"I'm sorry, Ty." The words are barely audible as they come out of Kallie's mouth.

I nod.

I don't know what to say, and right now if I open my mouth I don't know if I could hold back the misery and rage inside my chest. It feels like every bit of what makes me *me* was ripped from my chest the instant he said *I can't*, and there's nothing left. I'm just this hollow and void thing.

I walk past Kallie, but before I can make it past her register, she rushes around the bagging station and throws her arms around me. She's crying. She never cries. And now I'm crying too. The wet droplets etch down my cheek like little creeks. I grunt to stifle them. People are watching.

"I got to go," I tell her and push away.

I haven't *just* made a mess of things. I've ruined them.

I put myself out there. I was so sure I could just take it all back, that somehow he'd forgive me. But I can't. I've hurt him too badly.

Everything I did led to this. It's my fault. And I have to live with my mistakes. I have to face my life as it is…without him.

AIDAN
Thursday, August 15

Why did I say that? Why didn't I scream yes a hundred times? No, a million times.

I make it to the end of the aisle, but I can't hold back the tears, so I fishtail around the corner and just let them go. They flow down my face unbidden, and no matter how hard I wipe, more take their place. I try to take a deep breath, anything to calm me, but it's not working.

I throw my eyes to the ceiling and inside my head I scream *yes* a million times.

I can't believe he came here, that he said any of that. It's everything I wanted and hoped, but the truth is, now I'm scared.

Every time I've gotten close to him, he pulled away. Every time I'm left hurting and wondering what I did wrong. And a part of me is horrified that, even though there's something different this time, maybe it'll just end the same way, but I'll be more invested and it'll hurt even more.

But there's something different. I know there is. The way he looked at me, the way he apologized. He's never apologized like that. It's almost like in the past he never saw what he was doing, but now, his eyes, those deep green eyes spoke volumes.

He's afraid.

And finally, I really believe he doesn't want to lose *me*.

"You okay?" A voice catches me off guard, and I immediately cover my face and look away.

"I'm good," I blurt, even though it's beyond evident I'm not.

"You don't look okay," the voice says. I finally look and find a curly-haired brunette, probably in her mid-thirties, in a plain blue top and khaki shorts. I don't know her. I've never seen her before in my life, but here she is, asking if I'm okay.

"I am. I mean, I will be. I just…" I struggle. I'm not telling a stranger that the boy I love just confessed he needs me in front of everyone and basically begged me to be his, but I, in my infinite stupidity, ran away.

I cough to interrupt the tears, and it gives me just enough space to still myself. I suck in a deep breath.

"I know what I have to do," I tell the stranger, which apparently is good, because she smiles.

It's worth the risk. And it scares me to death, but how am I supposed to live if I let fear hold me back at every juncture? Maybe the only things worth having are the things that scare you most.

Please don't be gone, Ty. I wipe my face and puff out a breath to prepare myself. *Don't cry, Aidan. You've got this. Just don't let him go.*

I nod to the stranger, then spin around the corner and jog with purpose back down the aisle. At the end, Kallie is hugging Tyler, and then he lets her go and starts to leave. No! I move quicker. I can't let him get away.

"Ty!" I yell. Any other time I'd have cowered at the thought of yelling in the middle of a store, but right now I don't care. Fire me.

He stops, but he doesn't turn around. He just freezes.

"Yes!" I scream.

I break past the end of the aisle, and as I pass Kallie he turns around. His cheeks are wet, and his eyes are broken above a smile. I did that. A pang of guilt echoes through my chest.

"Yes!" I say again, sliding to halt in front of him. "I want to be yours too."

He rushes forward and wraps his arms around me, and I bury my face in his shoulder. For a moment it's just him and me, just like at Carowinds, no people, no registers, no store, nothing.

Just us.

I lean back enough to look into his eyes.

"Yes," I say again.

"Yes." He bites nervously at his lip.

"Stop biting your lip, or I'm going to kiss you," I giggle, as if I'm not going to anyway.

"Really?" He does it again.

"Oh yeah." And I'm no liar, so I do.

TYLER

It's beautiful up here.

The sky is clear. Millions of stars dot the black cloth of space like a swarm of fireflies dancing around a crescent moon over the mountains as far as I can see. But eclipsing it all is Breegge with its massive bluish tail spraying for miles and miles across the sky.

It's incredible.

"Did you know there's a new Nic Cage movie coming out in October?" Aidan asks. He sounds so excited.

"Nope." I don't know what to say. Who would know?

"Yeah, it's some movie called *Kill Chain*. He's an assassin or something," he tells me. "You do like Cage, right?"

Well, no. I didn't think anyone did.

"Not really…" I raise my shoulders.

"You too?" Aidan rolls his eyes. "First Rhys, then Bryce, and Kallie. Now you?"

"I mean, he's not exact—" Aidan puts his fingers against my lips to stop me.

"Don't even finish that sentence," he says. I didn't know he took Cage that seriously. "Don't."

I throw him a middle finger, and we burst out laughing. I scoop my arms around him and squeeze him a little closer, and nuzzle my nose against his cheek.

"You're such a weird one, you know that, right?" I peck at his cheek.

"Eh." He wiggles his shoulders and kisses me back.

"A weird, beautiful, nerdy sort of hottie," I keep going.

"Oh my God, just stop." He rolls his eyes and lets gravity roll him onto his back.

I keep staring. How could I not?

I think back on all the days I spent with Aidan at the park, gazing up at these same stars, naming the constellations, finding planets, giving him a hard time. I was a different person then. Or at least it feels like it.

He did something to me. Or maybe he just unlocked something inside I didn't know was already there. But whatever it is, it's real.

"Are you still looking at me?" Aidan asks.

"Yeah," I admit.

"Stalker," he giggles.

"I'm your boyfriend. I'm supposed to stalk you," I tell him. Okay, stalking might be a bit far, but he gets the point.

I wrap him up in my arms and follow his gaze to the stars. It's so quiet up here. Even quieter than back in Collettsville at the park. The air is thinner and crisper, which gives me more reason to cuddle up close with Aidan. "He would have loved to have seen this." Aidan sighs, snuggled next to me on our little plush comforter.

I slip my arm under his neck, letting my hand rest on his shoulder.

"He would have," I say. "It looks like you could reach up and touch it almost."

It still feels weird that Brayden isn't here to see this, that he isn't here at all. I think there will always be a spot inside me that belongs to him, a part that misses him. But the rest of me, that belongs to Aidan.

"This is for you, Brayden," I say.

"For Brayden." Aidan looks at me, and I grin back, loving every second I get to look into those brown eyes. "And us."

"And us." I smile even harder. How could I have been so dumb just weeks ago? I almost let him slip away. I almost let *this* slip away.

I kiss him. Not even the moon in the sky, or the stars beyond, or the magnificence of this passing comet can compare. Atop this mountain, even the gentle chirping of crickets and the rustle of the wind seem to fall away, like nothing else exists.

"You know what just hit me?" It's like a wire connects, and suddenly the obvious strikes me as something cool.

"What?" Aidan looks at me oddly. He knows how I am though, so it's okay.

"When school starts back, for me at least, since you already started Tuesday." I'm rambling. It's so not like me, but that's what this boy does to me. "I'm going to be the high school senior dating a college guy."

"Oh my God." Aidan rolls his eyes and squeezes my hand. "That's what hit you? Really?"

"Well, yeah." I shrug like it's obvious.

"Just remember that everyone still thinks I'm younger than you," Aidan points out.

"Not the point. Don't take this from me." I grin back.

Aidan shakes his head and laughs. He tries to scoot closer, as if there's any extra room between us left to gain. After a moment he coughs nervously.

"Thank you," he whispers.

"What for?" I gawk at him.

At first he doesn't answer. He looks down and then back up at the stars as if he's searching for the words to travel from lightyears away and land on his tongue.

"Thank you for not letting me go." Aidan smiles at me. The light from the comet reflects in his eyes, glimmering brightly against their dark depth.

"Never," I tell him.

We've talked about it a lot this past week. I almost did. I almost let him go. I almost betrayed myself and every instinct I had and every feeling in my gut.

It's hard sometimes knowing which feeling to trust, which one is leading you to your best life and which is just fear keeping you from all the beautiful things life has waiting for you. And I almost let that fear keep me from Aidan.

I was so stuck on what happened that I couldn't see what was literally standing in front of me. All I could see was hurt and pain, regret and guilt. And the crazy part—and I know this now—is that I had no reason to feel guilt.

I'm not saying it's easy or that I'm not scared, because I am. Every time I look into Aidan's eyes I see everything I want, but that can be so intimidating. What if I'm not enough? What if I mess up? What if?

And that's the problem. *What if* can be anything, and like everything it's uncertain. What I do know is that *what if* had me chasing a comet millions of miles away, when the comet I was looking for was standing right in front of me.

ABOUT THE AUTHOR

Jordon grew up in a small southern town in the foothills of the Appalachian Mountains just south of Boone, North Carolina. Jordon is an alumni of the University of North Carolina at Charlotte with a B.S. in Political Science he'll never use, and works at the nation's largest privately owned shoe retailer as a full-stack web developer to pay off all that student debt. While not writing, Jordon spends most his time entertaining his cat, Genji, watching Schitt's Creek and Parks and Recreation re-runs, and acting like he's any good at Overwatch. He lives in Kannapolis, NC.

Visit Jordon online at
www.JordonGreene.com

*If you enjoyed this story please
consider reviewing it online and at Goodreads,
and recommending it to family and friends.*